I0590119

The Reflection Game

By Grace Meridan

Chapter Guide

Dedication

For as long as I can remember, I've been fascinated by duality—the tension between light and dark, seen and unseen, who we are and who we might become. Maybe it's because I'm a Gemini, forever drawn to mirrored reflections, opposing identities, and the unseen forces that connect them.

I was captivated by identical twins, obsessed with their invisible tether, their unspoken language. There was something eerie yet beautiful about the idea of having another half—a person who instinctively understood your every thought before you even spoke.

That obsession shaped the stories I consumed. Tim Burton's gothic whimsy, the spellbinding power of *Charmed* and *Buffy the Vampire Slayer*, the haunting melodies of Evanescence. I found beauty in darkness, mystery in the supernatural, and endless fascination in the unknown. My culture, too, was steeped in superstition—whispers of fate, Tarot cards, astrology, the unseen forces shaping our lives.

I didn't just consume these ideas; I lived them.

I searched for meaning in the stars, in the cards, in the things people feared to speak of out loud. And yet, for years, this book—the one I always said I would write—remained unwritten.

I would start, then stop. The ideas were there, the characters whispered, but I could never bring myself to fully commit. Life took over. Priorities shifted. The stories inside me stayed locked away.

Until one day, everything changed.

Loss has a way of rearranging your entire world in an instant.

It can carve out a space so vast, you wonder if you'll ever be whole again.

When my mother passed away, it felt like the ground had been ripped out from beneath me. There was no warning. No way to prepare. No way to comprehend a world where she no longer existed. I kept expecting to hear her voice, to see her number light up on my phone. I kept thinking, *I need to tell her this*, only to remember—she was gone.

The grief was suffocating. It was heavy. And in her absence, something strange happened.

Silence.

A silence so profound, so vast, that I didn't know what to do with it. There was too much space where she used to be, too much air where her presence had once filled the room. But in that void, something began to stir.

A voice. A story. A need to create.

One day, I sat down and wrote an outline. Just an outline. That was all.

And then, suddenly, I couldn't stop.

The twin sisters I had imagined for years finally came to life on the page, their struggles mirroring my own. Themes of identity, deception, love, grief, power—they weren't just plot points. They were the emotions I had been wrestling with in real time.

And for the first time in a long time, I felt whole again.

Through this book, I found solace. I found purpose.

I found her.

My mother was an artist at heart, though she grew up in a time and culture where creativity wasn't seen as a "real" career. There were expectations—practical ones. Security. Stability. And yet, she carried creativity in her soul, and she passed that on to me. I can only imagine how she might have flourished in a world where she could have embraced her artistic passions fully.

This book is for her—for the part of her that always encouraged my imagination, even when she worried about where it might lead.

To my mother, Urszula, in loving memory.

However, no book is written in isolation.

There are moments of doubt, pages that refuse to cooperate, entire chapters that nearly break you. And in those moments, you need people who remind you why you started in the first place.

To my beta readers—you were my mirrors. You saw parts of me in these pages that even I didn't recognize. You believed in this book, and by doing so, you helped me believe in it too.

Thank you: Summer Milan, Kristin Aguilar, Morgan Polli, Joy Lancaster, Marty Scaminaci, Ashmar Mandou, & Nancy O'Brien.

To those who lifted me through grief, who held me up when I couldn't do it myself—your love and presence made this book possible. You reminded me that life, even in its darkest moments, still has light.

Kasia Radzki, Krys Murphree, Mary Schoenecker, Summer Milan, Amy Malave, Mary Day, Alexandra Kutnick, Soozie Cotter-Schaufele, Rainbow Hospice, my Zumba students, Bozena Sykurski, Cathy Harris, Andrzej Mitek, Rafal & Kasia Wrobel, Darek & Kasia Witek, Clare O'Rourke, my Sauce Newsletter team, and so many more—you were part of this journey in ways you may never fully realize.

A special thank you to Laura Joyce, my editor, whose keen eye and unwavering guidance helped shape this book into what it was meant to be. Your expertise and encouragement made all the difference.

And to Gogo Melone, whose artistic vision brought the visual identity of this book to life—your talent is truly unmatched. Thank you for capturing the soul of my story in ways I never could have imagined.

And now, dear reader, it's your turn to step into this world.

I hope this book takes hold of you the way it took hold of me. I hope you fall in love with the characters, admire them, question them, maybe even grow alongside them. I hope you get lost in the twists, feel the weight of their choices, and hold your breath at the edge of every chapter.

And most of all, I hope this story lingers with you—that even after you turn the final page, it stays somewhere inside you, a whisper in the back of your mind, asking...

What if?

As you embark on this journey, remember that embracing both the light and the dark within us leads to true self-discovery (Evanescence).

Welcome to *The Reflection Game*.

Enjoy the ride.

—Grace Meridan

Prologue

I dream of the girls every night, though I can't see their faces. In these dreams, they are shadows stretching toward something just beyond their reach—a fleeting light they can never hold. *I tell myself it's better this way.* Better that they never know my face, my voice, or the darkness clinging to my blood.

I didn't ask for this. I didn't choose to bring them into a world that would scar them before they could speak. But life doesn't care about choice. It forces you to carry what you never wanted, until the weight crushes every part of you that ever felt whole.

They are growing inside me, and with them, so does the shadow of him. It loomed—a weight I could not outrun. He didn't just take my body—he took my future, my freedom, my voice. Now, every kick and flutter in my womb is a reminder of his existence. *How can I look at them without seeing him? Without feeling the rage, the violation, the rot he left in my soul?*

I want to hate them for it, but I can't. They are blameless, innocent—gifts born from a nightmare. And I can't hate them. Not when I know that giving them away is the only way to save them from me, from him, from the jagged ruins of the life I cannot rebuild.

Love is a poor shield against the weight of blood. And that weight—it is heavy, heavier than anything I have ever known.

As they enter this world, they will never know the sound of my laugh or the warmth of my embrace on their worst days. They will never call me anything—not Mom, not Mother. *Nothing.*

But I pray to whatever god still listens that the world will open its arms to them in a way it never did for me. That they will have love, safety, and a life unburdened by the weight of their origins.

And yet, I know that blood leaves a mark, one that no love or distance can erase. His blood flows in them, a cruel tether binding them to something they will never understand, and I hope they never know. *It terrifies me to think they might inherit his darkness. It terrifies me even more to think they might inherit mine.*

I write letters to them in my head every night, trying to say goodbye to daughters I will never truly know. *I tell them they were loved—that in my own twisted, shattered way, I did this because I loved them too much to keep them.* I tell them to be strong, stronger than me, stronger than the man who tore us apart.

And when the dreams end, I wake to silence. A silence so loud it feels like the only thing I'll have left of them when they're gone.

I hope they find each other someday. I hope they see in each other's faces what I can never give them: family. A reflection of who they might have been, if they had been born into a world that wasn't drowning in shadows.

May they live in the light, even if I cannot.

Chapter 1

The King's Calling Card

As Detective Audrey Holliday drove through Pilsen's dimly lit streets, past vibrant murals dulled by the encroaching darkness, her thoughts were unusually scattered. The city hummed with restless energy. Audrey could hear the familiar rhythm of muffled conversations, distant sirens, and impatient honks on this cold Chicago evening. Passing Thalia Hall, its ornate facade illuminated faintly, memories surfaced—Sydney laughing beside her, their drinks spilling as they danced wildly on the balcony to The Midnight Hours, a band whose melancholy vocals Audrey still listened to when she felt her own darkness creeping in. But that was a lifetime ago.

Tonight, that memory felt hollow. It couldn't distract her from the unease that settled at the edges of her mind. She shook it off, gripping the wheel tighter.

Audrey parked in front of Crescent Laundry. She observed that the laundromat's rusted beams and flaking sign were the only things holding it together. It was a husk of a place long abandoned to time and tragedy.

She stepped out of her car, brushing a strand of blonde hair from her face, as the chill wind tugged at her blazer. Her hazel eyes scanned the scene, taking in every detail with practiced ease. Even in her understated work attire, there was something undeniably striking about her. She had a natural beauty that could stop people in their tracks if she chose to wield it.

Eddie was already on the scene, leaning casually against his unmarked car, one hand resting on the hood, as his sharp eyes scanned the perimeter. Despite his towering height, his easy demeanor and the cinnamon dolce latte in his hand gave him a disarming presence.

"Always the first one to soak up the crime scene vibes," Audrey quipped, locking her car door as her heels clicked against the sidewalk.

Eddie deadpanned, "And yet, you're the one who ends up in the highlight reel. Life's unfair."

"Like and subscribe." Audrey mimed a selfie pose, but her smile didn't reach her eyes. Her voice carried equal parts disbelief and anger. Beneath it all, an unsettled feeling twisted in her gut—a tension she hadn't yet placed.

The laundromat's windows, caked in grime, refracted the flickering fluorescent lights inside into dull, fractured beams. Audrey pulled the crime scene tape aside, the worn edges brushing her hands, as she and Eddie stepped into the stillness.

The interior was a tableau of neglect, and the silence was eerie. Rows of rusted washing machines lined the walls, their gaping doors like forgotten mouths. A faint musty odor lingered, mingling with the acrid tang of bleach that failed to mask the unmistakable scent of death. Above the stained floor, a wedding dress hung skewed on the conveyor rail, its once-bright train brushing against the ground, now yellowed. Dusty plastic bags clung to the hangers, and crumpled laundry tags lay scattered like relics.

"The corpse belongs to Anthony McCall. Cause of death: strangulation," Eddie recited, flipping open his notepad. "Condom wrapper nearby, no condom in sight. Ligature marks, not brute force. Whoever did this used leverage. Doesn't take strength, just the right angle. DNA processing's still underway, but nothing obvious under his nails."

He paused, pulling an evidence bag from his jacket pocket. "And voilà—this was stuffed in his coat pocket." A single Tarot card, its colorful artwork partially obscured by plastic. Even through the bag, the detailed imagery was striking—a figure seated on a throne adorned with vines, holding a golden chalice.

Audrey's stomach tightened involuntarily. "King of Cups," she murmured.

Eddie glanced at her, curiosity piqued.

"Friend of yours?"

Audrey shook her head, a faint unease crawling up her spine. "Just something my mom used to mess around with—Polish superstition mixed with a dash of folklore. Said it meant control. Stability." She paused, eyes fixed on the card. "Or greed."

The ritualistic aspect unnerved her in a way she didn't want to admit. It wasn't just that the killer had left a signature; it was the calculated way in which they'd chosen this card. Tarot wasn't just a novelty to her. It was a language of symbols, a reflection of fate and intention. And if this killer was fluent in it, that meant they saw themselves as something more than human.

"Was the card neatly placed or—"

"Haphazard," Eddie interjected, anticipating her thought process. "Like they almost forgot the calling card. They wanted to leave a signature but didn't spend much time getting it perfect."

Audrey crouched near the darkened stain on the floor, her eyes narrowing. "So, either he trusted his killer…or they're meticulous."

And that was what bothered her the most.

The method was chaotic, but the message was clear. Someone wanted to be seen, wanted to be understood—but not yet caught.

It was a game. And if there was one thing Audrey had learned from her father, it was that a game like this always had rules.

Eddie gestured to the dingy surroundings. "Any cameras?"

"None inside," Audrey replied, straightening up. "But the street's got eyes. Let's pull the footage."

Eddie grinned. "Already working on it. Four cameras in the area, but only one catches an angle of the laundromat. Working with you is like having my own Columbo—always with that *one more thing* vibe."

Audrey let a crooked smile tug at her lips as she scanned the room. "And you've perfected being the sarcastic sidekick. Let's see what the cameras tell us."

As they stepped back outside, Eddie leaned against his car and gave her a sideways glance. "By the way, my mom made dumplings last night. Got leftovers in the back if you're hungry."

Audrey shot him a look, her tone dripping with mock disdain. "Chan, we just stepped out of a crime scene. Nothing says 'appetite booster' like the smell of bleach and death."

Eddie chuckled. "Hey, I'm offering fine dining on a detective's salary. That's worth some appreciation."

The morning air carried a biting chill, and Audrey was glad for the warmth as she groggily stepped into the precinct building. Inside, the familiar hum of phones, footsteps, and caffeine-fueled determination greeted her like a broadcast from her second home.

Eddie was waiting by her desk, holding a coffee cup, with a look of amusement on his face.

"Morning, sunshine," he said, setting a second cup down. "Vending machine special, just for you."

Audrey took a sip, grimacing. "Still tastes like burnt sadness."

"It builds character," Eddie countered, plopping into the chair opposite hers.

She ignored his quip, flipping open her notebook. "We've got interviews lined up today. Laundromat owner first."

"Betting he swears he hasn't seen the place in years," Eddie said. "I'll start a pool. Eight minutes before you break him."

"Seven," Audrey countered, a flicker of amusement in her eyes.

The interview room was sterile; its fluorescent lights buzzed faintly above the table. Across from Audrey and Eddie sat Salvatore Marino, a burly man with a receding hairline and a scowl etched into his round face. His gold chain glinted faintly against his open shirt collar, and the faint smell of garlic and cologne wafted from him as he adjusted his too-tight jacket.

Audrey flipped open her notebook, her expression neutral. "Mr. Marino, you've owned the Crescent Laundry property for how long?"

"It's Sal, and about sixteen years," Marino said, leaning back in his chair with a faint creak. "Bought it from some schmuck who was going under. Fixed it up, made it respectable."

"Respectable?" Eddie asked, arching an eyebrow as he sipped his coffee. "The place has been boarded up for years."

"Yeah, and? It's still mine," Marino shot back, his tone sharp. "You know what it's like in this city. People see an empty building, they think it's free real estate. I boarded it up to keep out the crackheads."

Audrey's lips tightened into a thin line. "And in all that time, no unusual activity? No visitors?"

Marino shrugged with exaggerated indifference. "It's Pilsen. You want unusual activity, take a walk around the block. Ain't my job to babysit the place."

Eddie leaned forward slightly, his tone conversational but pointed. "So, no strange sightings? No late-night visitors? No one poking around who might've caught your eye?"

Marino hesitated, a flicker of unease crossing his face. "I ain't sayin' nothin' happened, but…maybe I saw someone. A couple weeks ago."

Audrey tilted her head. "Go on."

Marino scratched at his chin, his demeanor suddenly shifty. "It was late. I was driving by to check on the place. You know, making sure no punks were messing with my property. I see this blonde, tall, got legs for days, walking around like she's lookin' for trouble. Fancy shoes too—those red ones all the actresses wear. What do you call 'em?" He chuckled, the sound low and guttural. "Lah…booty…ins or somethin'. Betcha she was lookin' for a sugar daddy."

Audrey's eyes narrowed slightly, but her tone remained even. "It's Louboutins. And you didn't think to call it in?"

"Why would I? She wasn't breaking any laws," Marino said with a shrug. "Figured she was just lost—or up to somethin' she didn't want me knowin' about."

Eddie quipped, "Classy neighborhood ambassador we've got here."

Marino shot Eddie a look, his scowl deepening. "Hey, don't pin this on me. I don't ask questions. It's bad for business, ya know?"

Audrey shifted gears, her tone cool but cutting. "What about the tenants who used to occupy the building? Anything unusual there?"

Marino waved a dismissive hand, but there was a flicker of irritation. "First guy? Dead. Second one ran off to another state. The third—this guy Kim—was all ambition, no papers. Took him on as a favor, figured the guy could use a break. Helped him get on his feet, even let him slide on rent a couple times. Then he ditches me as soon as he finds a bigger spot downtown. Didn't even clean the place out! Left all that junk you probably saw in there. Class act."

Audrey jotted something in her notebook. "Kim didn't stay in touch? No contact since he moved?"

Marino snorted. "Guy sent me a Christmas card once, like three years ago. That's it. Guess gratitude ain't in his vocabulary."

Eddie leaned in, ginned sideways, sharply. "And you didn't think a guy operating a business without a green card might raise some eyebrows?"

Marino shrugged, his demeanor turning defensive. "Look, I'm no snitch. The guy was good for the neighborhood. Besides, everyone's got their hustle, right? Don't mean I keep tabs on people after they're gone."

Audrey kept her gaze steady. "And you're sure you don't recognize the woman you saw near the building?"

"Nope. Like I said, tall, blonde, real looker. Long legs. Probably some rich guy's side piece or somethin'. Didn't stick around to find out."

Audrey exchanged a glance with Eddie, her expression unreadable. "If anything else comes to mind, you'll let us know?"

"Yeah, yeah," Marino grumbled, his eyes darting to the clock on the wall. "Can I go now, or you got more dumb questions for me?"

Eddie chuckled, leaning back in his chair. "We'll let you know if we need you, Mr. Marino. Don't wander too far."

Marino stood with a grunt, straightening his jacket and muttering under his breath as he shuffled out of the room. Audrey watched him go, her mind already piecing together the scattered details.

"Well, he's a ray of sunshine," Eddie said, breaking the silence. "Think he's hiding something?"

"Probably," Audrey replied, tapping her pen against her notebook. "But whether it's relevant to this case or just his life in general, we'll have to find out."

Eddie gave her a knowing look. "Betcha he's got more skeletons in his closet than the laundromat's got dirty laundry."

Audrey sighed, closing her notebook. "Let's just hope one of them leads us somewhere useful."

The suburban street was quiet, the stillness of winter blanketing the neighborhood. Audrey parked in front of a well-kept, modest home, its snow-dusted porch framed by a wreath adorned with red ribbons and pinecones. The faint glow of holiday lights from neighboring houses cast a soft warmth over the scene, contrasting with the chilly evening air.

Eddie knocked on the door, the sound crisp in the frosty silence. Moments later, Lana McCall opened the door. Her black hair was loosely tied with strands falling around a face which bore the unmistakable exhaustion of grief. She wore a simple cardigan and jeans. The faint aroma of a holiday-scented candle wafted from inside.

"Mrs. McCall?" Audrey asked gently, holding up her badge. "Detectives Holliday and Chan. Thank you for speaking with us."

Lana nodded stiffly, stepping aside to let them in. Inside, the faint smell of cinnamon mingled with the clean scent of freshly vacuumed carpets. The house was cozy, but the clutter on the dining table—piles of papers, a few abandoned toys—hinted at a life recently upended.

An older woman sat in a worn recliner in the corner, her posture straight despite the obvious toll of stress and grief.

"This is Gloria," Lana said, gesturing toward her. "Anthony's mother. She's been helping with the kids."

Gloria's sharp eyes flicked to Audrey and Eddie, her lips pressing into a thin line. "Helping," she scoffed. "Barely keeping up with those two little tornadoes."

Audrey offered a polite nod, her tone measured. "We appreciate you both making the time to speak with us tonight. This won't take long."

Lana motioned toward the dining table, and Audrey and Eddie sat across from her. Gloria remained in the recliner, her gaze sharp and watchful.

Audrey began gently. "Mrs. McCall, we're trying to piece together the last few days of Anthony's life. Did he mention anything unusual? A new acquaintance, perhaps, or someone he was worried about?"

Lana shook her head, her fingers fiddling with the edge of a holiday-themed tablecloth. "Anthony was…distracted lately. But he always said everything was fine. Work was stressful, but that wasn't new."

Eddie leaned back slightly, adopting his signature casual tone. "What about people he interacted with? Did anyone seem off, or maybe too interested in him?"

Lana's hands tightened. "He didn't talk much about work. But no, I don't think so. He barely had time for anything other than us and his job."

Audrey's gaze landed briefly on the scattered envelopes, the bold logos of debt collection agencies standing out starkly in the clutter of papers. She felt a quiet pang of empathy, knowing too well the shame people carried over secrets like these. Leaning forward, she softened her tone, carefully approaching the sensitive subject. "I noticed these. Were there financial issues Anthony might not have shared with you?"

Lana's shoulders sagged, her hands falling to her lap. "I started finding those a few months ago. Anthony said it was a mistake, that he was sorting it out. But...I don't know. He'd been so distant lately."

Gloria interjected from the recliner, her tone sharp. "Distant? More like stubborn. He wouldn't even let me help with the finances. Said he had it under control."

Audrey pressed on. "We also received information about a sighting near the laundromat where Anthony was found. A blonde woman wearing distinctive, red-bottomed shoes was seen in the area. Does that mean anything to you?"

Lana's head snapped up, her eyes narrowing. "Are you saying Anthony was with another woman?" Her voice carried equal parts disbelief and anger.

"Not at all," Audrey said quickly, keeping her tone calm. "We're just trying to identify anyone who might've been in the area that night."

Lana folded her arms across her chest, her voice rising slightly. "Anthony wouldn't do that. He barely had time to breathe between work and home, let alone cheat."

Audrey nodded, her voice steady. "I understand, Mrs. McCall. This might be completely unrelated. We're just following every lead."

Gloria stood abruptly, the chair creaking as she rose. Her voice was firm, with an edge of exasperation. "Okay, that's enough. Can't you see she's been through hell and back? My son is gone, and you're here poking around like it's a game."

Audrey met Gloria's sharp gaze, standing as well. "I understand this is difficult, Mrs. McCall. We're only trying to find answers."

"Answers won't bring him back," Gloria snapped, her voice breaking slightly. "Have a little respect."

Eddie, sensing the tension, stood and offered a disarming smile. "We appreciate your time. If you think of anything, please give us a call." He slid a card across the table.

Audrey and Eddie stepped out into the crisp winter air, the door closing behind them with a finality that felt heavier than usual.

As they walked toward their car, the glow of holiday lights flickered softly around them.

Eddie broke the silence as they reached the car. "Well, Gloria's not exactly the warm and fuzzy type."

Audrey slid into the passenger seat. "Grieving mother. Cut her some slack."

Eddie reached into the back seat. "By the way, those dumplings I offered you yesterday? Still have some left. They've aged like fine wine."

Audrey rolled her eyes. "Great. Nothing says 'post-murder interrogation' like week-old dumplings. I think I'll pass."

Eddie chuckled as he started the car. "You're missing out. My mom could open a restaurant."

"Tell her to drop a menu by the station," Audrey replied dryly, leaning back as the car rolled into the quiet streets.

Audrey stepped through the double doors. The sounds of ringing phones, hurried footsteps, and the occasional outburst of laughter or frustration filled the precinct as she made her way to her desk. Eddie was already there, slouched in her chair, with a file in hand.

"Chan," Audrey said, arching a brow as she set down her bag. "Are you planning to work today, or just sit there and test the chair's lumbar support?"

Eddie spun in the chair once before standing. "Got something you'll like. Or hate. Depends on your mood."

Audrey sighed, slipping off her blazer. "What is it?"

He handed her the file. "A case from a decade ago. Same M.O. Strangulation. And guess what else?"

Audrey's brow furrowed as she flipped open the file. A single Tarot card, eerily similar to the one found at the scene with Anthony, stared back at her from the evidence photo.

"A Tarot card," she murmured, her voice low. "Same style?"

Eddie nodded. "King of Pentacles, fourteen years ago. This one was stuffed in the victim's wallet. Same random placement, same lack of DNA. Victim was a guy in his early thirties, lived alone. No obvious connections to McCall yet, but…"

Audrey's mind raced as she scanned the details. "It's too specific to be a coincidence."

"Exactly," Eddie said, leaning against the edge of her desk. "Got me thinking—maybe it's a serial."

Audrey shook her head slowly, closing the file. "If it is, they've been dormant. Fourteen years is a long time between kills."

Eddie shrugged. "Unless there were more victims we don't know about."

Audrey leaned back, her fingers drumming lightly against the desk. The Tarot card gnawed at her thoughts, stirring something deep in her memory.

"I remember these from high school," she said absently. "Used to think they were the coolest thing. A whole world of mystery and meaning in one little card."

Eddie raised a brow. "Didn't take you for the witchy woo woo type."

Audrey shot him a sideways glance. "There's a lot you don't know about me, Chan."

"Guessing Sydney was your gateway to the occult?"

Audrey allowed a small smile. "Something like that. We used to watch all those witchy movies—*The Craft*, *Death Becomes Her*. Thought we were the coolest goth kids in school."

Eddie chuckled. "Goth Audrey. Now that's a mental image I'm keeping forever."

"Focus," Audrey said, though the smile lingered as she tapped the file. "We need to dig into this. Find out if there's a pattern."

"Already on it," Eddie said, standing upright. "Pulled everything we could from the archives. Might take a while to comb through, but if there's a connection, we'll find it."

Audrey nodded. Her gaze drifted back to the file. The Tarot card stared up at her, its intricate design both mesmerizing and unsettling. Something about it gnawed at her—a detail she couldn't quite place.

"Let's hope we're wrong," she said softly. "Because if this is what it looks like, we've got a hell of a case ahead of us."

Audrey traced the edge of the photograph with her finger, her father's steady voice drifting back clearly. "Details, Audrey. The devil's in the details." She felt a familiar shiver of urgency—mixed with doubt—crawl along her spine. She looked out the darkened window. The city lights flickered like distant eyes—watching, waiting. A killer was out there: confident, meticulous. The thought stirred something within her, equal parts determination and quiet dread. She wouldn't rest until she found them—though tonight, it was harder to silence the whispering fear that, somehow, the killer had already found her first.

Chapter 2

Cracks Beneath the Glass

The soft click of Eve De la Gardie's heels echoed across the polished marble floor as she entered her office building. The reception area buzzed with quiet efficiency—a symphony of tapping keyboards and murmured conversations. The office cat, a sleek black feline with a custom Tiffany's collar, weaved effortlessly through the legs of staff and clients alike.

"Morning, Dr. De la Gardie," the receptionist chirped, handing over a clipboard with the day's meticulously planned agenda. A bouquet of fresh white peonies sat on the counter, their soft petals glowing under the ambient light.

Eve's lips curved into a measured smile. "Morning, Lydia. New flowers already?"

Lydia nodded. "Your weekly delivery. Shall I have them arranged in the usual spot?"

"Yes, thank you," Eve replied, her gaze briefly catching her reflection in the glass partition. Loose waves of golden blonde hair framed her face, and her tailored emerald-green jumpsuit highlighted her striking hazel eyes. She adjusted the delicate gold pendant resting at her collarbone before turning toward her office.

Inside, her sanctuary awaited—a study in curated elegance. The vintage oriental rug offset the clean lines of the Arhaus furniture, while a statement chandelier cast a warm glow over the space. Her framed credentials and a tasteful abstract painting adorned the walls, exuding understated authority.

Eve settled into her chair, crossing her legs, just as the soft knock at the door signaled her next client.

Noah entered, his presence filling the room. Ruggedly handsome with disheveled dark hair and a strong jawline, today he carried himself with a mixture of anger and vulnerability that Eve immediately clocked. His broad shoulders were tense, and the faint shadow under his eyes hinted at restless nights.

"Take a seat, Noah," Eve said, gesturing to the leather armchair opposite her.

He dropped into the chair, leaning forward with his elbows on his knees, his hands clasped tightly. "I didn't know where else to go," he began, his voice taut.

Eve waited, her silence calibrated to encourage him to continue.

"It's over," he said finally, his voice breaking. "Another relationship down the drain. I put everything into it—everything—and she still walked away."

Eve tilted her head, her expression empathetic but measured. "You mentioned before that validation was something you often sought in your relationships. Do you think this breakup feels more painful because of that?"

Noah's jaw clenched, his hands tightening. "It's not just about validation. It's this…cycle. I meet someone, I give everything, and then it's like I suffocate them—or maybe they see through me. I don't know."

"Let's unpack that," Eve said, leaning forward slightly. Her movements were precise yet graceful, her voice low and soothing. "When you say 'see through you,' what do you believe they're seeing?"

Noah hesitated, his voice dropping almost to a whisper. "That I'm enough. That I don't have to earn affection." He paused, eyes holding hers with an intensity that stretched beyond their usual boundary. "That's why I can't stop thinking about you."

Eve felt her pulse quicken, caught momentarily off guard. She'd sensed his growing attachment for weeks, felt the subtle but unmistakable shift in the air between them, but hearing him voice it aloud made it real—dangerously real. She swallowed softly, forcing her expression to remain composed.

"Noah, it's natural to develop feelings during therapy. Transference is a normal part of the process—"

He interrupted gently, but firmly, his voice still low. "This isn't just transference. You understand me. It's like…you can see me. And I think—no, I know—you feel it too."

A silence settled between them, thick and heavy, as Eve wrestled with a professional response. She felt her heart speed up—a rare and unsettling sensation for someone who thrived on control. Noah's admission crossed a boundary she'd always managed effortlessly, a line she'd confidently enforced with countless clients before.

"I appreciate your honesty," she said finally, choosing each word carefully, "but our sessions must remain professional."

Noah leaned back, a flicker of disappointment clouding his expression before he quickly masked it. "I understand," he murmured softly. "I just needed you to know. I couldn't keep it to myself anymore."

Eve watched him closely, a subtle unease coiling in her chest even as she nodded reassuringly. "It's important to acknowledge these feelings, Noah. We can explore why they've emerged. It's part of your healing."

Noah lingered at the door, his gaze briefly meeting hers. "Thanks, Dr. De la Gardie. I... I feel like I can breathe again."

As the session ended, Eve nodded, her expression inscrutable. "That's what we're here for. I'll see you next week."

As Noah stood to leave, his gaze lingered a moment too long, a subtle warmth in his eyes that stirred something deeper in Eve—something she immediately forced down. He was intelligent, good-looking, and fragile in a way that tugged at something primal within her.

The door closed softly behind him. Eve felt a crack in the careful control she'd spent so long perfecting.

Eve's fingers hovered over her keyboard as she jotted down notes from Noah's session. For a moment, her thoughts lingered on his words—raw, unpolished truths that made this session cling to her in a way that few client interactions did. A soft knock interrupted her, and the door burst open before she could respond.

"Eve, my radiant goddess, you will not believe this!" Lilah Holtz swept into the office, sparkling clutch in hand. She was dressed for a charity luncheon downtown—a designer gown in an aggressively chartreuse shade, its sequins reflecting the ambient lighting creating a dazzling effect that shimmered in time with every confident step. "I have exactly three minutes before my Uber driver abandons me," she announced dramatically.

Eve glanced up from her notes, her expression composed. "Lilah. I assume Lydia tried to stop you?"

"She did," Lilah said dramatically, waving the sparkling invitation in her hand, "but I told her it was a matter of life and death. She's very professional, by the way. If she ever gets tired of this gig, send her my way—I could use someone who actually types emails instead of just emojis."

Eve allowed the faintest smile to touch her lips. "I'll pass along the offer."

Lilah flopped onto the sleek leather couch, her clutch landing with a thud beside her. "Anyway, forget that. We have bigger issues—like the Rosewood Gala! Have you seen the guest list? It's like the Met Gala's sad little cousin, but still worth the photo op."

Eve arched a brow. "I'm surprised you're so invested. Didn't you call last year's event 'an overpriced snooze fest with bad lighting'?"

"That was before I realized the photographer they hired was secretly a genius with the lens," Lilah shot back, pulling out her phone and swiping to an image of herself, radiant and glowing. "Look at this. The man could make a trash can look like Grace Kelly."

Eve leaned back in her chair, steepling her fingers. "And how, exactly, do I fit into this elaborate scheme?"

Lilah sat up straight, clutching the invitation like it held the secrets to eternal youth. "You fit in, my darling, because your presence elevates any room you walk into. People whisper, 'Who is she?' They guess royalty, maybe an exiled queen. And let's not forget Leo's whole 'tall, dark, and devastating' thing—he'll make the perfect accessory."

Eve tilted her head slightly. "So, you're suggesting I attend to make you look better by association?"

Lilah gasped, pressing a hand to her chest in mock offense. "I would never! But if that happens as a side effect, who am I to complain?"

Eve allowed herself a rare laugh, low and melodic. "Flattering as always, Lilah."

Lilah glanced at the fresh bouquet of peonies on Eve's desk, her manicured finger tracing the edge of a petal. "Tell me these are from Leo. If not, I'm starting a petition to have him step it up."

"They're not," Eve replied smoothly, "but I'll be sure to pass along your disappointment."

Lilah's phone buzzed, and she rose dramatically, clutch in hand. "Duty calls. But I'll harass you daily until you say yes." She paused, expression softening genuinely for a rare moment. "Seriously, Eve—this gala isn't just about looking good. It's about being seen. Your absence will speak louder than your presence."

Before Eve could respond, Lilah swept out of the office. Moments later, Eve's phone buzzed—this time displaying the gala organizer's number. She exhaled softly, slipping back into character as she answered. "Eve De la Gardie."

"Dr. De la Gardie!" a chipper voice came through the line. "We're so thrilled to have you and Leo on the invite list for this year's gala. I wanted to personally reach out about your involvement. Hosting a table, perhaps?"

Eve leaned back in her chair, her fingers lightly tapping the armrest. "We're still considering our plans for the evening. It's such a busy time of year."

"Oh, of course!" the organizer chirped, with just enough passive-aggressiveness to needle. "We'd love to highlight your contributions in the program. After all, last year's patrons set such a high bar."

"Indeed," Eve said smoothly, her voice a velvet shield. "Though I do hope this year's Chardonnay won't turn into another…incident."

The organizer's laugh was a touch too forced. "Oh, we've ironed out all the kinks!"

"I'm sure you have," Eve replied, her tone sweet but edged with finality. "I'll let you know soon. Have a lovely day."

Eve set down her phone, a faint sigh escaping her lips. The gala, the flowers, the endless web of expectations—it was all part of the dance. She grabbed her coat and bag, her heels clicking against the marble floor as she made her way to the car. By the time she reached her front door, the day was already slipping from her shoulders.

Eve stepped through the front door, the soft glow of warm light spilling out from within. Their home was a curated masterpiece, much like Eve herself—elegantly balanced between sophistication and subtle coziness. A handcrafted dining table stood at the center of the room, its argento pyrite stone surface polished to a gleaming perfection, supported by an antique iron base. It was a piece she had handpicked, its rarity and artistry reflecting her impeccable taste. Yet, true to the spirit of their household, Rory had claimed it as her personal canvas, adorning it with her latest 'masterpiece'—a whimsical centerpiece constructed from shiny stones, feathers, and a smattering of trinkets she'd gathered on their last nature walk.

"Very avant-garde," Eve remarked, brushing a feather delicately back into place. "Aurora, your artistic flair is unparalleled."

Leo was in the kitchen, chopping vegetables with precision, his sleeves rolled up to reveal forearms that Rory often declared were "superhero muscles." The smell of fresh herbs wafted through the air.

Aurora—Rory—was sitting cross-legged on the living room floor, her brown French braid, with a few strands rebelliously escaping, swung as she focused intently on her latest Lego build—The Hogwarts Castle. A triumphant smile broke across her face as she snapped the final piece into place. Despite its 16+ age recommendation, Rory had approached the challenge with the precision of an architect.

"Victory, 6,020 pieces!" Rory declared, raising her hands dramatically. "Take that, Dad!"

Leo laughed, looking up from his cutting board. "Don't get cocky, kid. I let you win."

"Uh-huh," Rory retorted.

Eve set her handbag on the entryway table and hung her coat with practiced smoothness. Her eyes sparkled as she took in the scene—her family, the banter, the comfort of their sanctuary.

"Aurora, you're beating your father at everything these days. Should I be worried about world domination?"

"Maybe," Rory replied with a mischievous grin. "But I'll need more Legos. There's a Hogwarts Icons Collector's Edition! It has Hedwig, the potions bottle, and—"

"And a steep price tag," Eve interjected, raising an eyebrow. "So let's not get ahead of ourselves. One empire at a time, my little mastermind."

Leo glanced over, his eyes lingering on Eve for a moment longer than necessary. "Dinner's almost ready. Salmon with that quinoa salad you like."

"And here I thought you were going to order pizza," Eve teased, arching a brow. "I appreciate the effort, Mr. De la Gardie."

"Anything for my ladies," Leo said smoothly, plating the salmon with a flourish. "But don't expect this every night. I'm a coroner, not a chef."

Leo approached the table, his casual stride belying his quiet intensity. As the county coroner, his work often weighed heavily, though he rarely showed it at home. Tonight, though, he looked lighter, relaxed even, as he carried over plates of grilled salmon, quinoa salad, and roasted asparagus.

"Dinner is served," he said, sliding a plate in front of Eve with an exaggerated flourish. "For my two favorite women."

"Superman strikes again," Eve quipped, settling into her chair. She glanced at Rory's centerpiece and leaned over to adjust a slightly askew feather. "Very avant-garde, Aurora. It complements the table."

Rory beamed, already diving into her plate. "Maybe I'll design tables when I grow up. Or castles. Or both."

Conversation flowed easily. Rory recounted her day at school, including a debate where she argued (successfully) that Nerds Clusters were superior to jellybeans.

"It was a landslide," Rory declared proudly. "Even Mrs. Tanner agreed with me!"

Leo raised a glass of sparkling water. "To Rory, the undefeated queen of debate."

Eve clinked her glass against his. "To Aurora, the queen of everything."

Rory giggled, taking a sip of her juice like a seasoned diplomat. "Mama, you're weird."

"And proud of it," Eve replied.

"Mama," Rory began between bites, "do you think you could beat Dad at chess?"

Eve lifted a brow with amusement, leaning back in her chair. "I don't need to beat your dad at chess. I've already won the bigger game."

Leo shook his head, laughing softly. "Careful, you'll inflate her ego."

"Only because it's true," Eve countered playfully. "Aurora knows better than anyone—this family is a team effort."

Leo's expression turned contemplative, his gaze lingering on Eve as Rory continued to chatter. "Do you ever wonder what she'll be like when she's older?" he asked, low enough that Rory didn't hear.

Eve glanced at her daughter, who was now carefully rearranging her centerpiece. "All the time," she admitted softly. "She's brilliant. She's got your focus. Your heart."

"And your drive," Leo said with a faint smile.

The air between them felt heavier, as though an invisible thread connected their thoughts.

As Rory cleared her plate and began rearranging her Lego castle, Eve lingered at the table, her fingers trailing along the edge of Rory's whimsical centerpiece. The laughter from dinner faded and the house settled into its quiet rhythm.

Later, in her room, she sat at her vanity. The vanity itself was an extension of her duality—one side meticulously arranged with glass jars of cotton swabs and neatly lined tubes of lipstick and the other a riot of palettes, brushes, and stray pins; evidence of hurried mornings and busy days.

On the left stood a striking obelisk of polished obsidian, its surface catching the light in flashes of silvery black. Eve's fingers traced its smooth edges, the cool stone grounding her as her thoughts drifted.

She could still see her father's proud smile the day he had given it to her. The obelisk, wrapped in velvet, had seemed almost too extravagant for a birthday gift, but it wasn't just the object itself—it was the moment. An auction in an opulent hotel ballroom filled with society elites had drawn them there. Eve had been captivated by the obelisk's sleek, enigmatic beauty and the description in the catalog: A 19th-century ceremonial artifact used in ancient spiritual rituals, revered for its connection to inner strength and protection.

At the time, bidding on it had felt frivolous, but her father had noticed her fascination. Later that evening, when he placed it in her hands, his eyes gleamed with a rare warmth.

You have a strength that reminds me of this piece, he had said. *Polished on the outside, but forged from fire.*

The words echoed now, as they often did, grounding her amidst the chaos she kept so artfully concealed. The obelisk wasn't merely a decoration; it was a talisman—a symbol of her identity, of the rare moments when her father's high expectations softened into admiration.

Eve closed her eyes for a moment, letting the memory wash over her before she exhaled deeply, her mind shifting to the present. The day had been demanding, though nothing she couldn't handle. And yet, the session with Noah lingered in her mind. His vulnerability stirred something in her, a flicker of intrigue she buried beneath her practiced professionalism. He was a puzzle—broken, but compelling—and Eve found herself drawn to the challenge of fixing him.

All of it stirred something within her. *It was the same something that had drawn her to others before him. A need to feel needed. A need to wield power, to control chaos with the precision of a scalpel.*

The thought lingered, both thrilling and unnerving.

Rory's earlier question about the future replayed in her mind. What would she be like when she was older? The thought sent a faint shiver through Eve; a mixture of pride and trepidation. Rory had inherited so much of her—her wit, her drive—but Eve couldn't help but wonder if her daughter might also carry pieces of the shadows she worked so hard to keep hidden.

Her focus shifted again, this time to Rory's room across the hall. The faint sound of her daughter's steady breathing brought Eve a moment of stillness. Rory was her grounding force, the one element of her life untouched by the games she played in her mind and her practice. But even that thought carried a weight. Would Rory one day see through her mother's facade? Would she inherit Eve's relentless need for control—or, worse, her ability to compartmentalize the truth until it barely felt real?

As she climbed into bed, Leo stirred beside her. He murmured something unintelligible and reached for her hand. Eve allowed herself a small smile as she laced her fingers with his, the warmth of his touch a temporary balm to her swirling thoughts about Noah. Noah lingered in her thoughts. The way he looked at her—not just for answers, but for something more. It stirred the faintest spark of danger, one she could not afford to fan.

Chapter 3

The Devil in the Details

A voice cut through the usual precinct noise with the force of a foghorn.

"I swear on my dead grandmother's soul, I didn't do nothin' wrong!" a woman bellowed, twisting in the grip of the exasperated officer escorting her.

Eddie leaned casually against Audrey's desk. "Ah, the return of Mercedes Martinez. Didn't she swear off 'all illegal activity' last time?"

Audrey glanced up, recognition flickering across her face. "That vow lasted, what, three weeks?"

The woman—Mercedes—huffed dramatically, her oversized faux-fur coat slipping off one shoulder as she waved her hands. "I am a law-abiding citizen!" she declared. "I pay my taxes— most of the time—and I demand justice!"

The officer holding her cuffs deadpanned, "Mercy, you were lighting up in an alley. Right in front of me."

"Allegedly!" Mercedes shot back. "And besides, it was medicinal!"

Eddie's grin widened. "What's the prescription for? Street enlightenment?"

Mercedes squinted at him. "Don't get smart with me, Chan. I know my rights."

Audrey suppressed a smile, shaking her head as she leaned back in her chair. "Mercedes, you got caught red-handed."

"And I still deserve privacy!" She tossed her hair, leveling them both with a glare. "This city ain't what it used to be."

Eddie folded his arms. "You mean it used to be easier to commit misdemeanors?"

Mercedes sniffed, lifting her chin. "Back in my day, at least you had a little dignity about it."

Audrey exchanged a look with Eddie, who sighed theatrically. "And here I thought you were turning over a new leaf."

"Next time, maybe," she muttered as the officer led her away, still loudly declaring her innocence to anyone who would listen.

Eddie leaned against Audrey's desk and nodded toward the commotion. "You gotta love it. Give it up for the *Chicago City Academy Awards*."

Audrey shook her head as she leaned over the files spread across her desk. "What are the odds she's actually nominated this year?"

"Low, but the entertainment value? Off the charts," Eddie replied, setting a cup of coffee on her desk. "Bet she tries to convince the judge she's innocent because 'leopard print is her spiritual armor.'"

Audrey chuckled softly, finally glancing up. "Spiritual armor. That's a new one."

Eddie let out a hearty laugh. "I've got more where that came from. But what about you? What's with the serious face?"

"Just running scenarios," she said, tapping a pen against the corner of a file. The laughter felt out of place now, clashing with the stark reality staring up at her: Anthony McCall's lifeless eyes and the ominous Tarot card. The gravity of the case pulled her back like a cold hand on her shoulder. "Something's not adding up. Two victims. Same M.O. But no clear connection."

Eddie leaned over the desk, scanning the evidence board. "The pieces are there. We just don't see how they fit yet."

Her father's words echoed in her mind as she stared at the evidence board: *Every piece matters. Even the ones you don't see right away.* The memory came unbidden, dragging her back to a time when she'd first seen those words in action. She'd been twelve when he cracked the city's biggest drug bust. The media frenzy around their house had been surreal—reporters swarming outside, cameras flashing as they chased a soundbite. Audrey had stayed inside, peeking through the curtains with Sydney, both thrilled and a little terrified.

"Your dad's case," Sydney had whispered, her goth eyeliner smudged. "This is metal as hell."

Audrey's phone buzzed, snapping her out of the memory. She read the text message.

Don't forget, dinner for Mom's birthday is tomorrow. 7 p.m. Reservation at RPM Italian.

Audrey groaned, typing back a quick reply. *Got it. Thanks, Dad.*

"Trouble at home?" Eddie asked, arching a brow as he sipped his coffee.

"More like 'Don't disappoint the queen,'" Audrey muttered, her lips twitching into a half-smile. "Mom's birthday dinner tomorrow. Totally slipped my mind."

Eddie leaned back. "Man, your mom sounds tough, but she's got nothing on mine. Missed Lunar New Year once. Year of the

Dragon. She became the dragon. Spent a week calling me 'Disgrace Chan.'"

Audrey snorted. "No way."

"Oh yeah," Eddie said, dramatically putting his hand to his chest. "She made me eat soggy dumplings and watch *The Joy Luck Club* on repeat as punishment. Said it was a metaphor for my failure."

Audrey laughed, shaking her head. "Okay, that's brutal."

"Brutal but effective," Eddie quipped. "And hey, you turned out alright."

"Debatable." Audrey gestured to the evidence board. "Back to work. What do you make of these two victims? Strangulation, Tarot card left behind, no defensive wounds."

Eddie crossed his arms, tilting his head as he examined the board. "Same killer, no doubt. But the Tarot card thing? That's showy. Like they want to leave a signature. Maybe we should call the Obsidian Health Group for profiling."

Audrey raised a brow. "Obsidian Health Group?"

Eddie nodded toward a sticky note pinned to the board. The practice name was scrawled in bold letters.

"They've consulted with us before," Eddie continued. "Mostly the underlings, but one of their psychologists—whatshisname—he's the one the DA loves calling as an expert witness."

"O'Connor?" Audrey guessed, vaguely recalling a high-profile case where the name had come up.

"Yeah, him," Eddie confirmed. "Heard the owner of Obsidian is like a rock star in their world. But she usually assigns the grunt work to her team."

Audrey froze, her pen pausing mid-tap. "Let's hold off for now. I'd rather bring them in with a solid direction."

Eddie nodded. "Fair. But keep them in mind. These Tarot cards have 'mind games' written all over them."

Audrey glanced back at the evidence, her focus sharpening. "If this is a game, I'll figure out how to win it."

Later that evening, Audrey flopped onto her couch, her laptop sitting untouched on the coffee table. The day's cases swirled in her head, refusing to quiet. Deciding a distraction was in order, she dialed Sydney's number, already bracing herself for her best friend's brand of chaotic charm.

Sydney picked up on the second ring. "Audrey. To what do I owe this pleasure? Wait—did you finally crack the case of why my Wi-Fi thinks it's a part-time employee?"

Audrey sheepishly shrugged her shoulders. "Sorry, I leave the impossible cases to God. Plus, don't your fancy Hollywood friends have connections?"

"Funny. Speaking of fancy Hollywood, you'll never guess who I got to work with today," Sydney said, her voice full of excitement.

Audrey leaned back into the cushions. "Let me guess. Some twenty-something hot stud that's blowing up right now?"

Sydney snorted. "Noooo. Remember Serena Vaughn? Queen of Vampire Dreams in *Dark Bloodlines*?"

Audrey's jaw dropped. "We literally stayed up all night bingeing so we could finish before our SATs. You almost cried because you thought her character died in the finale."

Sydney's tone turned conspiratorial. "I may have completely embarrassed myself when I met her. I walked right up, opened my mouth to introduce myself, and instead blurted out, 'You're the reason I dyed my hair black in college.'"

Audrey burst out laughing. "Please tell me she was cool about it."

"Super cool," Sydney admitted. "Her assistant brought me an autographed photo and she wrote, *Keep rocking the black hair.* And before you ask, yes, I'll snag you another autograph."

"Damn, you spoil me," Audrey teased.

"Chill. Witty. Gorgeous, obviously. She doesn't age at all, I think she really might be a vampire. It's almost unfair." Sydney sighed dramatically. "Anyway, I've been up to my eyeballs in prosthetics for this werewolf-versus-vampire crossover. Serena's character from the show is being resurrected, and in the movie she is leading a coven rebellion, and it involves a lot of fake blood and fuzz. You know, the usual."

"Sounds like you're living the dream." Audrey's voice softened, genuine admiration creeping in.

"Eh, dream-adjacent," Sydney said, though her pride was evident. "Now, enough about me. Any interesting cases happening right now? You've been sorta quiet, so I'm assuming so."

Audrey's shoulders slumped down as she settled into the day's discoveries. "It's...complicated. Two victims, similar methods, and now a Tarot card left behind at each scene. It's looking like we might have a pattern."

"A serial killer?" Sydney's voice dropped, suddenly serious. "Shit, Aud. That's not the kind of case you can take lightly."

"Trust me, I know," Audrey replied. "We're pulling in every resource we can. It's just...heavy, you know?"

Sydney's voice softened again, tinged with concern. "You need a break. And I'm not just saying that because I want a partner-in-crime when you get here. When was the last time you did something for yourself?"

Audrey sighed. "I can't even remember."

"Exactly. Which is why, when you visit, we're raiding the costume department, stealing the best non-period vampire dresses, and crashing a party like the badasses we are. Maybe I'll even get something from Serena's stash." Sydney chuckled.

Audrey chuckled. "I don't know if I'll fit into her clothes, but I'll bring the handcuff key in case we get arrested."

Sydney laughed. "Perfect. You're the cop, I'm the alibi. Dynamic duo back at it."

Audrey smiled, the weight on her chest lightening just a fraction. "Thanks, Syd. I needed this."

"That's what I'm here for. Now, promise me you'll take at least one night off before you get on that plane."

"No promises," Audrey said, though her tone was lighter. "But I'll try."

Sydney huffed, clearly unimpressed with the half-hearted commitment. "California's waiting for you, babe. Don't forget your party heels."

"Got it," Audrey replied, a small smile tugging at her lips. "Good luck with the mother vampire."

"Luck's overrated. I'll take red wine for dramatics and a good playlist," Sydney quipped before hanging up.

Audrey stared at her phone. The conversation replaying in her mind. Sydney always had a way of making her feel grounded, even when life felt like it was spiraling.

The morning rush at the coffee shop, Spill the Tea, was in full swing as Audrey pushed open the door, greeted by the chiming of a tiny brass bell overhead. The space was a kaleidoscope of quirky charm: mismatched furniture, a mural of a psychedelic owl covering one wall, and a tip jar on the counter labeled *Funds for my Future*. The clientele was as eclectic as the decor—a mix of tattooed baristas, artsy freelancers hunched over laptops, and a woman in the corner knitting what looked suspiciously like a scarf for her Great Dane sitting beside her. The place always gave her a good laugh.

Audrey stepped up to the counter, inhaling the rich aroma of freshly ground beans. She caught a whiff of something floral and expensive lingering in the air—a perfume that felt oddly familiar, though she couldn't quite place it.

"Morning, Kennedy," she greeted the barista, who was sporting lavender hair and a Nirvana t-shirt.

"Morning, Detective! Back so soon?" Kennedy's white teeth flashed. They were just as bright as her neon-pink eyeliner.

Audrey raised an eyebrow. "What do you mean?"

Kennedy leaned against the espresso machine, squinting playfully. "You're kidding, right? You were literally here, like, half an hour ago. Different coat though. And it was so generous of you to leave that tip."

Audrey stilled. "I wasn't here earlier." It wasn't a question.

Kennedy tilted her head. "Huh. I thought you came back because you forgot something. Either you've got a twin I don't know about, or I'm shrooming." She laughed again, setting a coffee cup down with a flourish.

Audrey's polite smile didn't quite reach her eyes. "What did I—uh, she—order?"

Kennedy scratched her head. "Latte with almond milk. Not your usual jam, but hey, maybe it's a new vibe?"

A sharp flicker of unease settled in Audrey's stomach. *I don't even like almond milk.* "And she paid with a fifty?"

Kennedy nodded, lowering her voice slightly. "Yeah, that was the weird part. You're usually, like…precise. This was like, 'Keep the change, peasant.'"

Audrey blinked. "Fifty-dollar bill? Generous? Yeah, definitely not me. What else did I do? Solve world hunger while I was at it?"

Kennedy shrugged, sliding Audrey's usual drink across the counter. "Well, whoever it was, they've got your look and your swagger. Creepy, right?"

Audrey let out a small laugh, though her mind was already running calculations. "Guess I've got a twin running around who's putting me to shame. First almond milk, now big tips. I can't compete."

Kennedy hesitated, glancing toward the door. "You know… She seemed a little off—nervous, maybe. Like she was in a hurry. Kept checking her phone like she was waiting for something."

Audrey's grip on the cup tightened slightly. "Did she say anything?"

"Not really. Just the order, and she told me to keep the change. But…" Kennedy's brows knitted together. "She hesitated before leaving. Like she was about to say something else, then changed her mind."

Audrey pocketed her change, her mind already spinning. As she turned to the condiment station, her eyes briefly caught the name tag of another barista. *Madison.*

She quirked her lips. Kennedy, Madison, Reagan—it was like Gen Z was trying to rebuild the cabinet one coffee shop at a time.

The thought made her laugh, but as she sprinkled cinnamon into her latte, that floral perfume drifted back through the air. The scent tugged at something in the back of her mind, elusive and taunting.

She shook it off, but the unease didn't leave.

The floral perfume from the coffee shop still lingered faintly in her mind as she stepped out of her car, her thoughts snapping back to Anthony McCall. The consulting firm loomed ahead, its modern glass facade a stark contrast to the chaos surrounding his death.

The elevator doors opened with a quiet chime, depositing Audrey and Eddie into the gleaming modern office of Zimmerman-Croft Consulting. A receptionist glanced up from her desk, her face taut with forced composure.

The energy in the office was subdued but jittery, like a hive that had been rattled. Employees moved in hushed clusters, stealing glances at the detectives as they passed. An HR flyer advertising grief counseling services hung lopsided on a bulletin board.

"They're taking this hard," Eddie murmured, his eyes scanning the scene.

"Wouldn't you, if one of your own was found dead?" Audrey replied, her voice low. She squared her shoulders, bracing herself for what lay inside.

They were directed to a small conference room where David Martinez waited. The man looked worn, his shirt sleeves rolled up to reveal tense forearms, his face shadowed by exhaustion. He offered a firm handshake and gestured for them to sit.

"Thank you for coming. I'm still wrapping my head around all this," David began, his voice heavy with fatigue.

"We're sorry for your loss," Audrey said, her tone professional but warm. "We're hoping you can help us understand Anthony's state of mind leading up to his death."

David exhaled, rubbing the back of his neck. "Tony...he was a good guy, but the last few weeks were rough. He started coming in late, missing deadlines. That wasn't like him."

"Did he say what was going on?" Eddie asked, leaning back in his chair.

David hesitated, his gaze flicking to the door before returning to them. "He mentioned some debts. Gambling, I think. He was never upfront about it, but...I could tell it was bad. He even asked me for money once. I helped him a couple of times, but he kept coming back. I had to cut him off."

Audrey jotted notes, her expression neutral. "Did that strain your relationship?"

David's lips pressed into a thin line. "Yeah, it did. I wanted to help, but...I couldn't be his ATM. I told him he needed to get professional help."

Audrey nodded. "Did he ever mention anyone he was meeting with? Someone helping him manage these debts?"

David shook his head. "Not directly, but he did start talking about some...unconventional advice he was getting. Said it was helping him 'reclaim his power,' whatever that meant."

Eddie raised a brow. "And this advice came from...?

David shrugged. "Beats me."

"Could we take a look at Anthony's workspace?"

David escorted them through the hallway and into a standard office room with gray walls, a modern adjustable desk, three large monitors, and some framed McCall family photos. Audrey's eyes swept the desk, noticing a book sitting near the edge. She picked it up, her fingers brushing the embossed title: *The Psychology of Influence: Power, Control, and Personal Identity.*

Audrey set the book aside, her gaze shifting to a stack of folders nearby. She flipped through them methodically while Eddie distracted David with casual banter. "So, how's the office holding up?"

David snorted softly. "HR's trying, but everyone's on edge. Nobody saw this coming."

As Audrey sifted through the paperwork, her fingers paused over a receipt for a floral arrangement tucked inside one of the folders with instructions to include the message, *Thank you for all that you do. You're truly an inspirational woman.* There was no address.

Eddie clapped a hand on David's shoulder. "Thank you for speaking to us, you've been a big help. If anything else comes to mind, give us a ring. Do you mind if we take the receipt?"

"No, not at all," David said.

As they exited the office, Eddie held up the floral receipt.

"What do you make of this? Sounds like Tony might've been doing a little extracurricular consulting, if you catch my drift."

Audrey grabbed the receipt from his hands and tucked it into her notebook. "It's vague enough to be innocent. Could've been a thank you to a mentor or a coworker."

Eddie had a mischievous glint in his eyes. "Or it could've been for someone who made his 'workday' a little more…stimulating."

Audrey rolled her eyes but couldn't suppress a laugh. "You've been watching too much *90 Day Fiancé.*"

"Hey," Eddie shot back, his voice mock-defensive. "If there's one thing I've learned from that show, it's that the florist knows everything. Want to crack the case? Find the florist."

Audrey shook her head, smiling despite herself. "You're unbelievable."

Eddie shrugged. "Just saying. A guy drowning in debt suddenly finds money for fancy flowers? Either he's got a guilty conscience or he's trying to impress someone."

"Or both," Audrey added, her tone sobering. "And if it was an affair, we'll need to figure out who and why."

Eddie tilted his head, considering. "Think the missus knows?"

"Maybe," Audrey replied. "Or maybe she's the one he was thanking."

Eddie let out a low whistle. "Now that's a twist. Still, a floral receipt? Classic cheater move."

Audrey couldn't help but laugh at his logic. "Remind me never to get flowers from you."

"Noted," Eddie quipped, pretending to jot something down on an imaginary notepad. "*Audrey: Fruit basket only.* Got it."

As they stepped into the elevator, Eddie leaned against the railing, his expression turning more serious. "So, what's the next step?"

Audrey held the receipt between her fingers, turning it over thoughtfully. "Let's track down where these flowers came from. If there's a name attached, it might lead us to whoever was on the receiving end."

"And if it doesn't?" Eddie asked.

Audrey's lips tightened. "Then we keep digging."

The elevator doors slid shut, their descent punctuated only by Eddie's parting remark. "Hope the florist's got a good story. Otherwise, I'm sticking to my reality dating show theories."

The morgue was quieter than usual as Audrey and Eddie arrived, sterile air greeting them like an unspoken challenge. Audrey brushed her side-swept bangs away from her eyes and adjusted her medical mask, glancing at Eddie, who did the same. The masks were standard protocol, but today they felt like a welcome barrier between herself and the grim reality before them.

Leo De la Gardie stood near the examination table, carefully adjusting his gloves. His movements were methodical, and his calm demeanor matched the solemnity of his profession.

"Detectives," Leo greeted, his deep voice steady as he gave a polite nod in their direction, briefly meeting Audrey's gaze. For a fleeting moment, something in his expression faltered—his brow knit slightly, a tiny hesitation interrupting his rhythm. Audrey felt the subtle weight of his gaze and shifted uneasily.

He cleared his throat lightly, quickly recovering his composure as he turned back toward Anthony McCall's lifeless form. The sight was as jarring as the first time Audrey had seen it—pale skin, dark bruising around the neck, and that unsettling, serene expression that often followed violent deaths.

"Thanks for making time," Eddie said, professional yet casual. "We appreciate it."

Leo nodded again, attention fixed deliberately on the body now. "Of course. I've completed the initial autopsy. Cause of death is strangulation, as suspected. No defensive wounds, but I found something unusual—marks on the wrists and ankles, faint but present. Could indicate restraints were used."

Eddie raised an eyebrow. "Like he was tied up?"

"Possibly," Leo said carefully. "Difficult to say definitively. Marks are faint, suggesting restraints might have been loose or brief."

Audrey stepped closer, her eyes intent above the edge of her mask. "Do we have a precise time of death yet?"

Leo consulted his notes briefly. "Given decomposition and environmental factors at the laundromat, I'd estimate approximately two weeks ago, give or take."

"Two weeks?" Audrey exchanged a glance with Eddie. "Marino—the laundromat owner—said he found the body just days ago. Could Anthony have really gone unnoticed that long?"

Leo adjusted his glasses, expression professionally neutral. "It's not unusual in a location with limited traffic. The laundromat's humidity and limited airflow likely slowed decomposition, delaying detection."

Audrey glanced at Anthony's folded clothes nearby. "Anything unusual about the clothing?"

Leo stepped aside, revealing the tray. "Attire was generally undisturbed. No obvious struggle marks, but I did note this tear." He pointed carefully to a small rip along the inner lining near the left shoulder seam. "Appears recent."

"Could someone have grabbed him?" Audrey wondered aloud.

"Possibly," Leo replied evenly. "Though it might be unrelated. Difficult to confirm conclusively."

Leo again glanced at Audrey, and once more, something subtle flickered in his expression—a slight tilt of his head, as if trying to place something familiar. The moment passed as quickly as it arrived, and he turned back to the evidence. "Additionally, fibers were found under the collar—dark red. Possibly from a scarf or similar item. I've sent them to the lab."

Eddie's brow rose slightly. "Red fibers. That echoes our witness description of a woman wearing red-bottomed shoes at the scene."

Leo nodded carefully. "Possibly relevant. I'll expedite the results."

Audrey, still acutely aware of Leo's lingering glance, straightened slightly. "Good. Any connection helps."

As they prepared to leave, Audrey offered Leo a polite nod. "Thank you, Dr. De la Gardie. We appreciate your thoroughness."

Leo met her eyes briefly, nodding politely. The subtle crease between his brows appeared again—a flicker of curiosity or confusion—but he quickly masked it behind a carefully controlled expression. "Of course, Detective. Good luck with the investigation."

Outside, Eddie glanced sideways at Audrey. "You okay? You seem a little distracted."

Audrey exhaled, removing her mask. She hesitated, not quite sure herself why she felt uneasy. "It's probably nothing…" She trailed off, shaking her head lightly. "Never mind."

Eddie let a crooked smile tug at his lips. "Coroners are always a little intense. Occupational hazard."

Audrey smiled faintly, still unsettled. "Yeah, maybe."

"So, what do you make of that? Restraint marks, fibers, a conveniently undisturbed body? It's all a little…tidy, don't you think?"

Audrey stared ahead, her thoughts turning over. "It's tidy, but it's not impossible. Someone planned this. They knew exactly what they were doing."

"I'm betting this is gonna get messier before it gets cleaner."

Audrey sighed. "You're probably right."

Eddie nodded, his brow furrowing. "But if they're that careful, they've got to slip up somewhere. Everyone does."

Audrey stared out at the city lights through her windshield, her grip tightening on the steering wheel. "Let's hope it's soon. Because if they don't, the next move's already theirs."

Chapter 4

Calculated Risks

Today, Eve's schedule was relatively open—a rarity. Her inbox, however, told a different story. She clicked open her practice's shared portal, skimming through patient updates, team notes, and new client inquiries. A flagged message caught her eye, forwarded from Lydia. The subject line read: *Urgent Request—Chicago PD*.

Eve exhaled softly. She had built Obsidian Health Group with the vision of pushing psychology beyond the confines of private practice. Years ago, she had recruited Dr. O'Connor specifically for his experience in forensic consulting—expert testimony, law enforcement partnerships, criminal profiling. It had been a strategic decision. Expanding into that world gave the practice credibility, but Eve had never been directly involved.

Until now.

The faint sound of coughing broke her train of thought. She glanced toward the plush corner of her office where Rory sat, curled up in the oversized armchair, her tablet propped on her knees as she absently flipped through a digital drawing app. Rory wasn't a child anymore, but she still had those moments—like today—where she wanted to be near her mother rather than home alone.

"Mom?" Rory's voice was soft, almost hesitant. "Are you going to have one of those long meetings?"

Eve set her tablet down and smiled at her daughter. "Not too long, sweetheart. Lydia's going to keep you company for a bit."

"Okay," Rory replied, her attention drifting back to her artwork.

Eve called Lydia in and moments later she appeared in the doorway holding her tablet, her smile a practiced mix of professionalism and warmth. "Yes, Dr. De la Gardie?"

"Can you watch Rory for a bit? She's not feeling well today, and I don't want her alone while I'm in a meeting."

Lydia's eyes softened as she glanced at Rory. "Of course. We'll be fine, won't we, Rory?"

She winked at Rory, who returned a shy nod.

Eve stood and placed a hand briefly on Lydia's arm. "Thank you. I know it's not in your job description."

Lydia waved her off. "Babysitting isn't so different from managing client schedules. Besides, Rory's much more agreeable than some of our patients."

The comment earned a soft laugh from Eve as Lydia led Rory to the adjacent lounge with promises of TikTok dance videos and snacks.

As the door clicked shut behind them, Eve lowered herself back into her chair, exhaling softly and resting her fingers against her temple. It wasn't unusual for her practice to receive consultation requests from law enforcement. Her team had gained recognition for profiling suspects, assessing victims, and offering expert testimony in court. Over the years, the firm had carefully balanced clinical practice and criminal consultancy, earning a reputation as a pioneer in this niche.

She leaned back, her gaze trailing to the frosted glass walls of her office. A delicate tension pulled at the corners of her mind. Dr. O'Connor had been the lead psychologist on similar cases in the past, but his caseload was becoming unsustainable. Eve scrolled through his recent updates, noting the sheer volume of his commitments.

Her cursor hovered over Dr. Larkin's profile. Younger, less seasoned, but undeniably meticulous, Larkin had carved a niche for himself in the practice—particularly with complex cases involving trauma and manipulation. His clinical notes were always detailed, his therapeutic strategies innovative yet grounded. Eve's lips twitched in a subtle smile as she recalled his last patient review, where the client described him as 'intense but transformative.' His work involved the kind of sharp precision she valued.

Still, she hesitated. Assigning Larkin to a high-profile murder case would be a significant step. *But isn't this exactly why I hired him?* His potential was palpable, and this could be the challenge that solidified his standing within the practice.

Eve tapped a finger against her desk, turning the matter over in her mind. Dr. O'Connor had been handling law enforcement consulting for years, but he had become too comfortable. Too entitled. He acted as though the expansion of Obsidian into forensic psychology had been his doing, rather than hers. She had built this practice, and she would decide who led its future.

"Lydia," Eve called, her tone smooth yet authoritative. "Call Dr. Larkin in. I want to see if he's ready for a challenge."

Lydia came into the office, and her brows rose slightly in acknowledgment. "Right away." Her heels clicked briskly as she left, her efficiency a reflection of the culture Eve had instilled in her team.

As Eve waited, she opened Larkin's profile once more, glancing over his employment history. A graduate of

Northwestern, his application had stood out not only for his academic pedigree but also for the handwritten letter he'd included—a rarity in the digital age. In it, he had spoken of being inspired by her first book, *The Psychology of Influence,* and how it had shaped his understanding of therapy's transformative potential. *Flattery will only get you so far,* she thought wryly, though she couldn't deny it had intrigued her.

A knock at the door interrupted her musings. Larkin entered, his posture straight and his eyes alight with curiosity.

"Dr. De la Gardie," he greeted, his tone professional but warm.

"Dr. Larkin," she replied, gesturing for him to sit. "I have a matter I'd like you to consider."

He settled into the chair across from her, folding his hands neatly. "I'm all ears."

Eve clasped her hands lightly in front of her, studying him for a moment. The sunlight streaming through the large windows played against the polished surface of the desk, illuminating her composed features.

"Tell me, Jordan," she began, her tone both warm and probing. "Why did you get into psychology? And more importantly, what drove you to join this practice?"

Larkin adjusted his tie, a flicker of nervous energy betraying his otherwise confident demeanor. "Well," he began, his voice steady despite the slight tension. "Psychology has always fascinated me because it bridges science and human connection. In undergrad, I majored in biology, but I realized I was more intrigued by why people acted the way they did than by how their bodies worked. What pushed me toward therapy was...seeing a close friend in college struggle with severe depression. They didn't have the support they needed, and it made me realize I wanted to fill that gap for others."

Eve nodded, her hazel eyes narrowing slightly—not in disapproval but in thought. "And why this practice?" she asked, her voice soft but probing. "You had options."

Larkin exhaled a short laugh, glancing momentarily at the titles lining the bookshelves. "That's easy," he said, his voice steadying. "Your book, *The Psychology of Influence*. It was required reading in my graduate program. It shaped how I see therapy— not just as a tool to heal, but as a way to empower clients to reclaim control over their lives."

Eve tilted her head, a faint smile curling at the corner of her lips. "Which part of the book resonated with you the most?"

Larkin faltered slightly, his enthusiasm dimming just a touch as he searched for the right words. "I think...the chapter about reframing narratives. You wrote about how clients often see themselves as victims of their circumstances, and the therapist's job is to guide them to recognize their agency. That really stuck with me. It's not just about fixing people; it's about helping them realize they were never broken."

Eve leaned back, her gaze steady and appraising. She allowed a moment of silence to stretch between them, letting his words hang in the air.

"Well said," she replied at last, her tone warm. "That chapter is one of my favorites as well. I'm glad it struck a chord with you."

The tension in Larkin's shoulders eased, but his focus remained sharp.

Eve leaned forward slightly, her expression softening but still measured. "The Chicago PD has approached us about a murder case. They're requesting support for profiling and potentially expert testimony. Dr. O'Connor has traditionally led these efforts, but his caseload is overwhelming. I'm considering you for this assignment."

Larkin's brow furrowed slightly, intrigue flickering in his eyes. "You trust me with something this high-profile?"

"I do," Eve said simply. "Your work has been exemplary. You've shown a deep understanding of complex dynamics and a capacity for insight. This case isn't just another client file. It's high-pressure and high-stakes. I'm offering it to you because I believe you're ready."

Larkin straightened, a faint hint of pride coloring his expression. "I'd be honored to take it on."

Eve's lips curved into a faint smile. "Good. Review this tonight." She slid a file across the desk. "I'll need your preliminary thoughts tomorrow morning."

Larkin accepted the file, his grip firm. "Thank you, Dr. De la Gardie. I won't disappoint you."

"I know you won't," Eve replied, her voice steady and confident. As Larkin left, she allowed herself a rare moment of satisfaction. There was a thrill in recognizing potential and guiding it toward its peak. And, as always, a sense of control.

In her office, Eve sat reviewing patient notes. Rory had managed to sneak into her office when Lydia appeared at the door. She carried a glass of water in one hand and a small box of crackers in the other.

"She's a little pale but seems fine," Lydia said softly, setting the items on the corner of Eve's desk. "I think it's just one of those quick bugs. Kids bounce back fast."

Eve glanced at the loveseat in the corner of her office, where Rory sat cross-legged, earbuds in, watching a video on her tablet. Her daughter looked up, meeting her mother's gaze with a small, reassuring smile that mirrored Eve's own composed demeanor.

"Thanks, Lydia," Eve replied, taking a moment to observe Rory. "Let me know if she looks any worse. I'll handle it from there."

Lydia hesitated, then leaned closer. "She asked if she could have some of the lemon ginger tea in the break room. I told her to wait for your okay."

Eve gave a slight chuckle. "Of course she did—always the diplomat." She gestured toward the break room. "Let her have some. Just make sure it's not too hot."

Lydia nodded and headed toward Rory, the two sharing a quick exchange before Rory handed over her mug. The moment was fleeting but warm—a testament to the trust Eve placed in her team.

The relative peace was shattered by the sound of the door slamming open.

"Eve!" O'Connor's voice rang out, sharp and unyielding. Lydia's frantic footsteps followed.

"I tried to stop him," Lydia blurted, appearing in the doorway just as O'Connor stormed in, his face flushed with anger.

Eve rose slowly from her desk, her expression calm but unmistakably firm. "Lydia, it's fine. I'll take it from here."

O'Connor barely registered the exchange. "What the fuck?! You gave the police case to Larkin? Are you kidding me?"

Rory subtly removed her earbuds, watching the scene unfold with quiet curiosity.

Eve's gaze flicked toward Rory briefly before locking onto O'Connor. "I suggest you lower your voice, Pat," she said coolly. "This is a private office, not a courtroom."

O'Connor hesitated but pressed on, though his tone dropped slightly. "I've been handling law enforcement cases for years, Eve. This is what I do. Why on earth would you give it to Larkin?"

"Because I decided it was the best choice for the practice," she replied evenly, her words deliberate. "And unless you've forgotten, that's my call to make."

"Larkin's too green," O'Connor shot back, his frustration palpable. "He doesn't have the experience—"

"Yet," Eve interjected, her voice cutting through his tirade like a knife. "He doesn't have the experience yet. And that's exactly why this opportunity is vital for his growth."

"You're playing with fire," O'Connor warned, his tone simmering.

"And you're letting your ego dictate your judgement," Eve countered smoothly.

"Mom?" Rory's voice broke through the tension.

Eve turned, her expression softening immediately. "It's alright, Rory. Just a work discussion. Go back to your video."

Rory gave her a skeptical look but obliged, putting her earbuds back in with a faint shrug.

Eve turned her attention back to O'Connor. "This is not up for debate. I've made my decision, and I trust Dr. Larkin to handle the case."

O'Connor's shoulders slumped slightly, though defiance still flickered in his eyes. "This is a mistake," he muttered.

"Then let's hope Larkin proves you wrong," Eve replied. "Now, if you're done disrupting my office, you can leave."

The finality in her tone left no room for argument. O'Connor hesitated for a moment, then turned on his heel, muttering under his breath.

As he strode out, he nearly collided with Dr. Larkin, who had been lingering just outside the door.

"Good luck," O'Connor sneered, brushing past him with a shoulder check.

Larkin paused in the doorway, his expression a careful mix of curiosity and concern. "Should I come back later?"

"No, he'll get over it. We all started someplace," Eve said, her voice regaining its calm, commanding edge. "Come in, Dr. Larkin."

As he stepped into the office, Eve gave him a subtle wink—an unspoken message that the chaos was under control.

Rory watched the scene play out from the corner, her eyes narrowing slightly in thought. "So, Mom," she began, drawing out the words dramatically, "does this happen all the time at work? Should I bring popcorn next time?"

Eve, still seated at her desk and thumbing through her notes, didn't look up. "Not unless you plan on sharing. And besides," she added dryly, "this is mild. You should've been here the time when someone's ex sent us a bouquet of black roses."

Rory's eyes widened. "Wait, black roses? Like, Gothic 'I curse your name' roses?"

Eve shrugged. "Something like that. Apparently, therapy was going a little too well, and someone wasn't thrilled about their partner's newfound confidence."

Rory tilted her head, clearly intrigued. "So, therapy drama and workplace fights? This is better than reality TV."

Eve finally looked up, her expression deadpan. "Careful, Rory. One day, you might inherit this circus."

Rory put on her best thoughtful face, tapping her chin. "Hmm… I don't know. I think I'd be a better referee than a therapist. You know, something like, 'Ladies and gentlemen, in the blue corner, we have Dr. O'Connor, the heavyweight champ of passive-aggressive guilt trips!'"

Eve couldn't help but laugh. "And in the red corner," she quipped, "we have my daughter, who's about to lose her TikTok privileges."

Rory gasped in mock horror, clutching her imaginary pearls. "Not TikTok! Anything but that!"

Eve raised an eyebrow. "Keep it up, and you'll be banned from FedEx package duty too."

"Oh no," Rory said, deadpan. "How will I ever recover from such a loss?"

"You'll find a way," Eve said, rolling her eyes but laughing softly. "Now go—before I actually put you to work."

Rory stuck out her tongue before skipping off, her laughter echoing down the hall. Eve leaned back in her chair, shaking her head. Rory had her father's sense of humor, sharp and irreverent, but her quick wit? That was all Eve.

Eve was halfway through her second cup of coffee when her phone buzzed on the desk. Glancing at the screen, she saw Clara's name flash. Her publicist rarely called without good reason, and

Eve's heart skipped in anticipation. She answered on the second ring.

"Clara, good morning," Eve said, her tone even, though curiosity rippled beneath her polished demeanor.

"Eve! Finally, some sunshine in this dreary week. I have news!" Clara's voice was effervescent, the kind of energy that could pull a reluctant optimist out of bed.

Eve smiled faintly. "I take it you're not calling to remind me about a deadline."

"No deadlines—just opportunities," Clara teased. "The publisher loved the response to *The Psychology of Influence*. And by loved, I mean they want a follow-up."

Eve leaned back in her chair, a flicker of surprise crossing her face. "A follow-up?"

"Not just a follow-up, darling—a sequel. The book did phenomenally in both academic circles and mainstream markets. They're convinced the next one could solidify your position as the voice of psychological strategy and empowerment." Clara paused, her voice dropping slightly, becoming more sincere. "Eve, this is huge."

Eve let her words settle. Her first book had been a labor of intellect and vulnerability, each chapter requiring her to strip back layers of academic detachment. It had catapulted her career, but it also came with the constant pressure to prove herself.

"And the theme?" Eve asked, steadying her voice.

"The publisher suggests something along the lines of high-stakes environments—how psychological influence plays out under pressure, in situations where the stakes are life-altering. Think leadership, crisis management, negotiation. It's perfectly aligned with your work, especially with your growing reputation in forensic psychology." Clara's tone was carefully persuasive, like a skilled negotiator laying out terms.

Eve tapped a finger against the edge of her desk, her thoughts spiraling. A second book could cement her legacy, but it would also expose her to greater scrutiny. The idea thrilled and unnerved her in equal measure.

Clara seemed to sense her hesitation. "Eve, I know you don't take these decisions lightly. But you've already proven your depth and range. This is the natural next step. They're offering full creative control too. It's your voice they want."

Eve exhaled slowly. "Full creative control?"

"Complete," Clara confirmed, then added with a playful lilt, "Plus, there's the not-so-small matter of a very generous advance. Enough zeros to make even Leo blink."

Eve let out a measured breath, allowing herself a rare moment of satisfaction. Months ago, she had sent in a book proposal—just a possibility, something she could take or leave. But now, the publisher had responded with certainty. The deal was official.

"I suppose this means they liked the pitch," Eve murmured, leaning back in her chair.

Clara laughed. "They didn't like it, Eve. They loved it. The editorial team said your proposal was one of the sharpest they've read in years."

Eve tapped her fingers lightly on the desk, already considering the implications. This was an opportunity, but also a responsibility.

"I aim to please. So, what do you say? Can I tell them you're onboard?"

Eve let the moment stretch, savoring the quiet power of being wanted. "Yes," she said finally, her tone resolute. "Let's do it."

Clara squealed, uncharacteristically unreserved. "Brilliant! I'll draft the agreement and send it over. And, Eve—this is going to be a masterpiece. You know that, right?"

Eve's smile softened, though her mind was already whirring with ideas. "I appreciate your faith, Clara. Let's make it one."

After hanging up, Eve allowed herself a rare moment of pride. Her career had been meticulously built, brick by brick, and now she stood on the precipice of something even greater.

As she hung up, her phone vibrated again—this time, a text from Lilah:

I hear we're celebrating a book deal tonight. If you say no, I'm showing up at your house with champagne anyway. Your call.

Eve shook her head. Of course Clara had told her. She should have known Lilah would sniff out big news before Eve had a chance to breathe.

She glanced at the clock. There was still time before her next appointment. A moment's hesitation passed before she opened the shared practice portal and composed a quick message to Lydia:

Team, I have exciting news to share. Please join me in the lounge at 11:30 a.m.

When the team gathered, Eve stood at the center, her composed exterior softened by a genuine smile. "I just got off the phone with my publicist," she began, her tone calm but laced with excitement. "The publisher has contracted a follow-up to *The Psychology of Influence*."

The room erupted in applause and cheers. Dr. O'Connor clapped the loudest, his booming laugh cutting through the noise. "Well, if they didn't, they'd be fools," he said, his tone jovial. He seemed to have forgiven her, or at least understood what was best for him. Eve was relieved to see the drama blowing over for now.

Even Lydia, usually composed, grinned ear to ear. "Congratulations, Dr. De la Gardie. This is huge."

Eve raised her hand lightly to quiet the room. "Thank you all. This wouldn't be possible without the work we do here. You are the foundation that makes achievements like this possible. So, take a moment to celebrate yourselves too."

Even Rory perked up, abandoning her tablet entirely.

"That's amazing, Mom!" Rory exclaimed. "Does that mean you're going to be on TV again? Do you get to go to an awards show? Do I get to come with and wear a fancy dress?"

Eve's composed exterior softened as she laughed lightly. "Hold your horses, partner. Let's not get ahead of ourselves. First, I need to write the book."

Eve sat at her desk, the late afternoon light casting long, golden shadows across the room. Her phone vibrated, and she glanced at the screen to see Lilah's name flashing with an accompanying GIF of a glitter bomb explosion—a custom signature of her exuberant friend.

Eve tapped to call Lilah instead, but on the other line there was already an incoming call.

"I was going to call you," Eve said, answering.

"Damn right you were," Lilah shot back. "But I decided to save you the trouble. Now—tell me everything! The deal! The advance! The cover photo shoot—are we talking sultry and mysterious or classic intellectual goddess? Wait—don't tell me—both."

Eve laughed, an easy, genuine sound that surprised even herself. "Lilah, I just signed the contract this morning. Can I take a breath before planning the press tour?"

"No, darling, you cannot. This is a huge deal! You should be screaming from the rooftops—or, since I know you, at least letting yourself feel it for five uninterrupted minutes."

Eve exhaled, a smile tugging at her lips. She wasn't one for dramatics, but there was a thrill in saying it out loud. "Fine. It's official. I'm writing another book."

"YES! That's what I want to hear!" Lilah practically squealed. "Oh. My. God! The literary world has blessed us mere mortals with another masterpiece from Dr. Eve De la Gardie."

Eve shook her head, still smiling. "You're ridiculous."

"And you're brilliant, which is why I am demanding a celebratory dinner. And don't even try to tell me you were thinking of staying home and 'relaxing'—I won't allow it."

Eve sighed, but this time it was playful. "I was thinking something low-key."

"Low-key? After securing a sequel to the book that made you a star? Have you learned nothing from being my best friend?" Lilah gasped, scandalized. "Fine, compromise—I'll cancel the fireworks display, but I'm not budging on the champagne."

"How generous of you," Eve teased.

"Details, darling, details," Lilah gushed. "Do you have any idea what it's like to have a best friend who's not only stunning, brilliant, and intimidatingly perfect, but also a bestselling author? It's like having Beyoncé and Ruth Bader Ginsburg rolled into one. People will literally beg to sit near me at galas now."

Eve let out a rare, genuine laugh. "You're impossible."

"And yet, you love me." Lilah's voice softened. "Seriously, Eve. This is huge. I hope you're letting yourself be happy about it."

A warmth settled in Eve's chest. She had worked tirelessly for this, and now it was real. "I am," she admitted. "It feels…good."

"Good! Now, should I give you time to prepare a witty toast for tonight, or are you just going to wing it like the effortlessly brilliant woman you are?"

Eve twirled her hair. "I'll wing it."

"Ugh, infuriating," Lilah groaned. "See you at eight, gorgeous."

Eve hung up, still smiling as she set her phone down. For once, she wasn't just indulging Lilah—she was actually looking forward to celebrating.

Just as Eve was shutting down her laptop and preparing to leave for the day, Lydia appeared in the doorway holding a sleek, black package tied with a shimmering gold ribbon. "FedEx delivery for you, Doctor."

Eve frowned slightly as she met Lydia at the door. "I wasn't expecting anything."

Curious, Lydia followed her back into the office. Eve set the box on her desk and carefully untied the ribbon. Inside was a gleaming, gold-plated microphone, resting on a plush velvet lining. Something about it felt…excessive. Almost eerie in its grandeur.

A small note card accompanied it, written in Lilah's bold, looping handwriting:

"For my star author: May your words shine as brightly as this microphone. You're welcome. —L"

Eve let out a soft laugh, holding up the microphone for Lydia to see. "She's unbelievable. How does she move this fast?"

Lydia blinked, her eyebrows lifting in amazement. "Did you even tell her this morning? Or was she psychic?"

"I called her an hour ago," Eve replied, still shaking her head. "Somehow, she already had this packed, shipped, and delivered."

"That's insane," Lydia said, crossing her arms with a bemused smile. "It takes me longer to get takeout from three blocks away."

"It's Lilah," Eve said simply, still smiling. "She probably has half the city on retainer for her dramatics."

"Well," Lydia said, gesturing to the microphone, "I'll admit, it's on brand for her. Are you actually keeping it?"

Eve placed the microphone back in its box with a faint chuckle. "Absolutely. Ridiculous or not, it's perfect."

As Eve left her office for the day, the box tucked under her arm, she couldn't help but smile. Lilah's antics bordered on absurdity, but there was a certain warmth in her over-the-top gestures—a reminder of the unique, colorful thread her friend wove into the otherwise calculated tapestry of her life.

Outside, the evening air was crisp, and Eve allowed herself a rare moment to savor the feeling of success—both in her career and in the small, meaningful connections that made it all worthwhile.

Chapter 5

Clues and Cabbage Rolls

The McCall residence had taken on an air of quiet desolation since their first visit. The once-cozy home, adorned with hints of holiday cheer, now felt heavy, its warmth extinguished under the revelations of Anthony's secret life. The clutter on the dining table had grown—a mess of unpaid bills, scattered toys, and crumpled tissues. Lana sat in the same chair as before, her eyes hollow and red-rimmed, her movements sluggish, as though each breath required monumental effort.

Gloria hovered nearby, her stern features softened into something almost maternal as she prepared tea in the adjacent kitchen. The clinking of cups and the faint whistle of the kettle punctuated the strained silence.

Audrey and Eddie exchanged a glance as Lana absently fiddled with the edge of her sweater. Eddie's typically easy-going demeanor shifted slightly—he leaned against the table with deliberate casualness, offering a reassuring smile that didn't quite reach his eyes.

"So, what's new?" Lana asked, her voice hoarse, devoid of energy. "You here to tell me my husband had a second life I didn't know about?"

Audrey softened her tone, careful not to push too hard. "We're piecing things together, but it's clear Anthony was dealing with a lot more than anyone realized. We were hoping you could help us with one last thing."

Lana gave a hollow laugh, shaking her head. "Help you? I can't even help myself." Her gaze dropped to her lap. "I don't know how I'm supposed to dig myself out of this. The debt collectors...the lies. My kids are asking questions I don't know how to answer."

Her voice cracked, and for the first time, Audrey saw the full weight of Lana's grief.

"Was I not enough for him? Wasn't his family enough?"

Gloria re-entered the room, setting down a tray with steaming mugs of tea. "Lana," she began, her voice firm yet unusually gentle, "you'll get through it. We'll get through it."

"But how?" Lana whispered, tears slipping down her cheeks. "Everything I thought I knew about him—it's all gone. How am I supposed to rebuild from this?"

Gloria sat beside her, placing a hand on her shoulder. "He was my son," she said, her voice tight. "But even I don't recognize the man I'm hearing about. The gambling, the lies..." She trailed off, shaking her head. "I can't defend what he did, but I know this much—he wasn't doing it alone."

Audrey leaned forward slightly. "What do you mean?"

Gloria hesitated, glancing at Lana before speaking. "Anthony mentioned someone once—a woman. I don't know who she was, but he said something about her helping him 'fix' things. He didn't say much, but it didn't sit right with me. The way he talked about her...it was like he was in over his head."

"Did he ever mention her name?" Audrey pressed gently.

"No," Gloria replied, her lips tightening. "But if I had to guess, she wasn't helping him. She was using him."

Lana exhaled shakily. "There was this one thing," she said, her voice barely audible. "A receipt. From an expensive restaurant downtown—Mirella's. I thought it was for a business lunch, but when I finally looked at the time stamp...it was for dinner. He never mentioned it."

Audrey nodded, jotting down the name in her notebook. "Do you still have the receipt?"

Lana shook her head. "I threw it out. I didn't think it meant anything at the time."

"It's a lead," Eddie said, his voice lighter, offering a reprieve from the tension. "Maybe he had lousy taste in company and great taste in food."

Audrey shot him a look, but Lana's lips twitched, a ghost of a smile. "He did love Mirella's tiramisu," she muttered.

Gloria straightened, her usual sternness returning slightly. "You find out who this woman is. If she dragged him into this mess...I want to know."

"We'll do our best," Audrey assured her, rising from her chair. "Thank you both for your time."

As they stepped out into the chilly evening air, Eddie zipped up his jacket, letting out a low whistle. "Mirella's, huh? Fancy. Guess our guy had a taste for the high life, even if he couldn't afford it."

Audrey's breath misted in the cold as she glanced at him. "You're surprisingly chipper for someone walking out of a house that heavy."

Eddie shrugged. "It's a defense mechanism. You want me to cry into my scarf instead?"

She rolled her eyes, pulling her coat tighter around her. "Come on, Chan. Let's see what Mirella's has to say about their high-rolling guest."

As they walked toward their car, Audrey glanced back at the house. Lana's silhouette lingered by the window, her hand pressed against the glass, watching them leave. Eddie fell into step beside her, his usual banter giving way to quiet contemplation. Despite the levity he brought to their partnership, Audrey could see the case pressing on him too, adding another layer of tension to the unanswered questions swirling around Anthony McCall's life—and death.

The precinct's conference room was filled with the low hum of detectives settling in, the muted clatter of coffee cups against the table as Audrey connected the call to the precinct's speakerphone.

A robotic voice announced, "You are now connected. The host has joined the call."

Static crackled briefly before a hesitant voice piped through. "Uh—hello? This is Dr. Jordan Larkin from the Obsidian Health Group... I think I'm on?"

Audrey moved toward the speaker. "Detective Audrey Holliday. This is Detective Chan. Thanks for coming."

"You're live, Doc," Eddie said as he leaned back in his chair. "No video, huh? What, afraid we'll judge your office décor?"

A brief silence. Then Larkin cleared his throat. "No, just standard practice for consultations. We keep the focus on the case details."

Audrey cut in smoothly. "Dr. Larkin, thanks for making time. Let's jump in—what do you have for us?"

A shuffle of papers rustled through the speaker, followed by Larkin's voice, now more measured. "Of course. It's an honor to work with you both. I've read about your department's cases... Really impressive work."

His voice trailed off as he realized he was rambling. "Anyway, um, I'll just...get this set up." He finally managed to connect their computers and the screen flickered to life with the opening slide of his presentation.

"Sorry about that," Larkin said, brushing a hand through his slightly disheveled hair. "Dr. O'Connor usually takes the lead on these cases."

Eddie leaned back in his chair, arms crossed. "First big murder case?"

Larkin hesitated, his fingers twitching against the edge of his laptop. "Well…yes, but I've done extensive research on criminal behavior and profiling. I assure you, I'm more than qualified."

Eddie teased. "Relax, Doc. We're just giving you a hard time."

Audrey shot Eddie a warning glance before turning back to Larkin. "We're here to listen, Dr. Larkin. Take your time."

Larkin exhaled, visibly collecting himself as he clicked to the next slide. The screen displayed the two Tarot cards found at the scenes: the King of Pentacles and the King of Cups, their intricate designs illuminated under the harsh light.

Dr. Larkin cleared his throat, his voice steady but lacking the commanding presence of his predecessor, Dr. O'Connor. "What we're seeing here is a killer who's both deliberate and symbolic. Both victims had a King card left at the scene. The King of Pentacles, found fourteen years ago, represents emotional control and manipulation, qualities the killer may identify with or aspire to. The King of Cups, found with Anthony McCall, represents material mastery. Together, these suggest someone who sees themselves as a ruler, an orchestrator of events."

Eddie raised an eyebrow. "So, we're looking for a psychic? Or maybe someone who moonlights at a Renaissance Faire?"

The screen advanced to the next slide, displaying a diagram of the crime scenes. "This is more than ego. The killer is methodical. The placement of the cards suggests intentionality, but the condom wrapper found at Anthony McCall's scene adds a layer of complexity. Combined with post-ejaculate evidence, we're looking at a crime that was intimate—possibly sexual."

Audrey leaned forward. "Do you think Anthony was involved with his killer?"

"It's a possibility," Larkin replied. "This evidence suggests an intimate encounter, either real or staged. If Anthony McCall was having an affair, it might explain the personal nature of the crime. The killer could be someone he knew or trusted and could have used that relationship to manipulate him."

Eddie raised an eyebrow. "So, we're looking for an ex, a fling, or…?"

"Not necessarily," Larkin said. "It's also possible the killer used the encounter to establish dominance. The cards could symbolize power dynamics. Perhaps Anthony was seen as someone to control—or punish."

Audrey tapped her pen against her notebook, her mind racing. "The gap between victims—fourteen years—is unusual. If this is the same killer, why stop for so long?"

"That's the critical question," Larkin said, his tone tightening. "Serial killers don't typically go dormant unless they're forced to. Life events like incarceration, relocation, or illness could explain it. Alternatively, they may not have stopped at all. There could be other victims in different jurisdictions that we haven't connected yet."

Audrey leaned forward. "You're saying there could be a trail of bodies we haven't connected yet?"

"It's possible," Larkin replied. "There's a case from five years ago in New Orleans—a man found with a Tarot card in his hand. The method doesn't entirely match, but the symbolism is strikingly similar. If this is the same person, they could be operating across state lines."

Audrey's mind churned. "We'd need to review unsolved cases in other jurisdictions for anything that matches this profile."

"Great," Eddie said dryly. "Not just a killer—an overachiever."

Audrey's pen hovered over her notebook. "And the cards? You think they tie into that manipulation?"

"Potentially," Larkin replied. "The Kings could represent power dynamics. Maybe Anthony was seen as someone to be controlled—or punished. The choice of cards might reveal how the killer views their relationship to the victim."

Eddie tapped his pen against the table. "Great. We've got a wannabe Riddler on our hands."

Audrey shot him a look. "Focus, Chan."

Larkin clicked to the final slide; the word *escalation* was written in bold red letters. "If this is the same killer, we need to prepare for the possibility of more victims. The pattern suggests they're not finished." The line crackled slightly. "They've already restarted. And killers like this don't stop. They evolve."

Eddie let out a low whistle. "Well, that's uplifting. Is there some kind of counter-spell we can cast? Sorry, too many video games."

"I'll leave the theatrics to you, Detective."

Audrey sat back, mind turning. "Alright, Dr. Larkin. We'll follow up after we review potential cases. If anything else comes to mind, send it over."

"Of course," Larkin replied. "I'll keep analyzing the data. Thanks for your time."

The robotic voice chimed in. "The host has left the call. This meeting has ended."

As the meeting concluded, Audrey closed her notebook, her thoughts tangled in the web of evidence. The mention of the New Orleans case gnawed at her—was it truly connected, or was it a red herring? Larkin's insights were unsettlingly precise, but something about his uncertainty lingered in her mind. Eddie nudged her shoulder as they stepped into the bustling precinct.

"You okay?" he asked, his tone unusually serious.

"Fine," Audrey said quickly, though her expression was tight. "Just trying to make sense of this."

Eddie's grin returned. "Well, if the killer's into cards, let's hope their poker face sucks. We've got this."

Audrey gave him a faint smile, but her mind remained locked on the clues, the cards, and the chilling possibility that their killer was just getting started.

The suburban street was still and dark and there was a creeping chill in the air. Audrey was glad for the golden glow from her parents' windows. She barely had time to knock before the door flew open to reveal her mother standing there, a dish towel slung over her shoulder like a general ready for battle.

"You're late," Helen announced, gripping Audrey's wrist and pulling her inside before she could protest. "Come, come. You must eat. Look at you—thin as a rail. No man wants a woman who looks like a starving artist."

Audrey sighed, unbuttoning her coat. "Hi, Mom. Nice to see you too."

The house smelled like home—like warmth and spice, like the tomato-sweet tang of something simmering for hours. Audrey's stomach betrayed her, tightening with hunger at the unmistakable scent of gołąbki, the stuffed cabbage rolls she had grown up eating. She wasn't sure if she actually loved them, or if they just tasted like childhood, but tonight, she wasn't going to complain.

Helen bustled toward the kitchen, waving a dismissive hand over her shoulder. "I made gołąbki. Real food. Not that American garbage you probably eat."

Jack appeared in the doorway, his calm blue eyes twinkling with a mix of amusement and sympathy. "She's been waiting for this all day," he murmured, squeezing Audrey's shoulder in quiet solidarity.

A moment later, Helen reappeared, pressing a heaping plate into Audrey's hands. "Eat. You look exhausted. And your hair! When was the last time you went to a salon?"

Audrey settled onto the couch, stabbing her fork into the steaming cabbage roll, cutting through the layers of tender meat and rice. "Thanks, Mom."

Helen perched on the arm of Jack's chair, scrutinizing her daughter with the intensity of a detective. "Audrey, you're thirty-something years old. What's the plan? You think you'll just stumble into a husband while solving murders?"

Audrey rolled her eyes. "I'm fine, Mom."

"No, you're not," Helen said, unperturbed. "What about that nice Eddie? He's funny, good-looking, and has a proper job. Why don't you date him?"

Audrey nearly choked. "Mom, Eddie's my partner. That's disgusting."

Helen shrugged. "What's disgusting? I always liked him. He's charming, and he'd put up with you."

Jack coughed to hide a laugh, earning a sharp glare from Helen. "What? She's right. Eddie's a good guy."

Audrey gave them both a flat look. "Can we not do this? Please?"

Helen threw up her hands. "Fine. Be alone forever. But don't say I didn't try."

Jack motioned toward the living room, sensing Audrey's need for a reprieve. "Come on, let's sit."

She followed him gratefully, sinking into the familiar comfort of the couch as Jack took his usual chair. His expression turned thoughtful. "What's going on, kid?"

Audrey exhaled, setting her plate on the coffee table. "It's this case. A killer leaving Tarot cards at the scenes. The first one was fourteen years ago, and now Anthony McCall. We can't figure out the gap—or if there's something we're missing. The psychologist profiling the case mentioned a potential connection to a case in New Orleans, but it's thin."

Jack nodded slowly. "Tarot cards, huh? That's symbolic. They're not just killing—they're making a statement."

"That's what we think," Audrey said. "But what kind of statement? And why now?"

Jack leaned forward, resting his elbows on his knees. "Killers like this don't just quit—they get interrupted."

Audrey frowned. "Interrupted?"

"Locked up. Sick. Forced to run." Jack ticked them off. "Or maybe something messier—family, regret. Life doesn't stop for obsession. Sometimes, it just... pauses it." Helen reappeared, unable to resist inserting herself into the conversation. "Maybe they fell in love," she said, setting down a fresh glass of water in front of Audrey. "Love makes people do stupid things."

Audrey's expression softened. "Thanks, Mom."

Jack chuckled softly. "She's not wrong. But focus on the cards. They're the key. They're not just props—they mean something to this person. Find out what, and you'll understand them."

Helen crossed her arms, tilting her head. "Tarot's all about control, no? People pull a card because they want to see what happens next. They want to believe they have power over fate. The killer"—she gestured vaguely toward Audrey's case file— "they're probably doing the same thing. Showing you they're in charge."

Audrey raised an eyebrow. "That's actually a good point, Mom."

Helen beamed. "Of course it is. I watch *Dateline*." She nodded, satisfied. "I'm just saying. People are unpredictable. When I was younger in Poland, I went to a fortune teller who used Tarot. She read my future. Told me I'd marry someone boring. Look at me now." She pointed at Jack.

Jack gave her a dry look. "Flattered, sweetheart."

Helen ignored him, turning back to Audrey. "But that's not the point. If they're using Tarot cards, they're making a prediction—or proving something. Which means they think they know the outcome."

Audrey narrowed her eyes, the puzzle pieces shifting in her head. "If that's true, then they aren't just leaving a calling card. They're leaving a clue."

Jack's voice was steady. "Then follow it. Sometimes the hardest puzzles have the simplest solutions. Stop looking at the case like it's a single thread. Step back. Look at the whole tapestry. You're not just solving a murder, Audrey. You're reading a story."

Helen patted Audrey's knee. "Listen to your father. He's a smart man."

Audrey nodded, her mind turning over the possibilities. "Thanks, Dad. And you too, Mom."

Helen beamed. "Good. Now, eat more. You can't think on an empty stomach."

As Audrey took another bite, she glanced at her notebook. The florist's receipt was still tucked inside—a lead she had been meaning to chase down.

"Actually," she murmured, thinking out loud, "there is someone we should talk to next."

Jack raised a brow. "The killer?"

"The florist."

By the time she left, she was full, carrying a container of leftovers and feeling the warmth of her parents' peculiar brand of love. Helen fussed over her scarf as she walked to the door.

"Remember, if you don't solve this, it's probably because you're too thin," Helen called after her. "And call Eddie. He's a catch!"

Audrey rolled her eyes but couldn't help smiling. "Goodnight, Mom. Night, Dad."

As she drove back into the city, the scent of gołąbki lingering in her car, Jack's words echoed in her mind. Follow the clue. It was a reminder she needed—and one she wouldn't forget.

The morning sun cast a sleepy golden hue over Petal & Stem, a shop that looked like it had survived at least three different economic downturns and still refused to close. Tucked between a bakery that smelled perpetually of cinnamon and a bookstore whose window boasted a handwritten *Tarot Readings Every Friday* sign, the florist shop exuded an old-world charm—if that old world also had a mild scent of mildew.

The window display was haphazard but somehow inviting: pink lilies, yellow daisies, and half-wilted roses crammed together in a way that suggested more stubborn determination than artistic intention. The doorbell chimed as Audrey and Eddie stepped inside.

"Christ on a cracker, what now?" a raspy voice croaked from behind the counter.

A woman—easily in her seventies—stood perched behind an antique register, her frizzy white hair held back by a pair of reading glasses that were nowhere near her eyes. A knit cardigan sagged off her bony frame, sleeves dotted with bits of crushed petals and what looked suspiciously like cigarette ash. The name tag pinned to her chest read *Marge* in aggressively handwritten black Sharpie.

"You take one of my delivery vans?" she demanded, squinting at Eddie like he was a repeat offender.

"Uh, no, ma'am," Eddie said, holding up his hands in surrender. "We're detectives. Here to ask about an order."

Marge snorted, unimpressed. "Ain't got time for cops unless you're here to arrest my grandson."

As if on cue, the back door creaked open, and a lanky twenty-something in a stained hoodie shuffled in, slurping loudly from an oversized soda. His dirty blond hair peeked out from under a beanie, and his eyes darted between them with the sluggish calculation of someone perpetually skirting responsibility.

"Yo, Grandma, the website's down again—" he started before stopping mid-sip. "Aw, man. What'd I do now?"

Marge waved a dismissive hand at him. "Not you this time, Trevor. They're here about flowers."

"God, finally," Trevor exhaled, looking relieved as he moved toward the counter. "Last time the cops came, Grandma accused me of running a Ponzi scheme."

"You *were* running a Ponzi scheme," Marge grumbled, smacking him lightly on the arm.

Audrey cleared her throat. "We're here about an order placed recently. This receipt"—she pulled out the slightly crumpled slip of paper—"from your shop. We need to know who placed it."

Marge took the paper, peered at it, and immediately handed it off to Trevor. "Yeah, this is his department. Computers and whatnot. I just yell at people and keep the plants alive."

Trevor sighed dramatically but took the receipt and plopped down behind an ancient-looking desktop computer that looked like it had survived Y2K. He cracked his knuckles like he was about to perform open-heart surgery and typed with two fingers.

"Let's see… Okay, yeah, here we go," Trevor muttered. "Ordered online, paid with a pre-paid card."

Audrey leaned in. "What name was the order under?"

Trevor clicked through the details. "Uh…G. Archer. That mean anything to you?"

Audrey and Eddie exchanged a glance. "No," she admitted.

Eddie exhaled sharply through his nose. "Figures. And the delivery address?"

Trevor hesitated. "So, uh, funny thing about that—whoever placed the order paid for pickup. No actual address."

Audrey felt her stomach drop slightly. "Wait—so they didn't even have it delivered? Someone came in and picked it up?"

"Yup," Trevor said, popping the 'p' dramatically. "Means there's no delivery log."

Marge, who had been listening from her perch, cackled. "Looks like your bad guy's got a brain. Hate when that happens."

Audrey fought the urge to groan. "Do you have security cameras? Maybe we can see who came to pick it up."

Trevor winced. "See, that's the other funny thing—cameras have been busted since the last time we got broken into."

Eddie pinched the bridge of his nose. "Lemme guess. No footage. No paper trail."

"Welcome to the joys of running a business on a shoestring budget," Marge drawled.

Audrey exhaled. "Okay, fine. Can you at least tell us what they ordered? Was it anything unique?"

Trevor checked. "Uh, nah. Standard stuff. White lilies, some hydrangeas. Fancy, but nothing weird."

Audrey closed her notebook with a snap. A dead end.

Marge patted her on the arm with an unsettling amount of force. "Tough luck, hon. But hey, at least you didn't have to arrest my grandson. That's a win."

Trevor muttered, "For now."

As they turned to leave, Eddie shook his head. "I swear, if we ever solve this case, it'll be in spite of this city's terrible security footage situation."

Audrey sighed, tucking the receipt back into her pocket. The killer had been careful—careful enough to erase their trail before it even began.

Outside, as the morning chill bit at their skin, she glanced back at the shop one last time. The flowers in the window, bright and unassuming, seemed to mock her.

"Back to square one," she muttered.

"Eh," Eddie said, stretching. "At least we got a new suspect."

A shadow crossed her face. "Who?"

"Marge," he deadpanned. "I think she knows more than she's letting on."

Audrey rolled her eyes but let out a small chuckle as they walked back to the car.

Chapter 6

The Edge of Temptation

The soft hum of classical music played in the background as Eve pressed the phone to her ear, waiting. Two rings in, a familiar voice answered—low, rich, and laced with both wisdom and wry amusement.

"Eve."

She exhaled slowly, already feeling the weight on her shoulders ease. Dr. Bernard Levin had been her therapist since she was twenty-one, back when she was a brilliant but sharp-edged graduate student, too stubborn for her own good. Over the years, he had become more than just a therapist—he was a mentor, a guiding force, a voice of reason when her own failed her.

"Bernard," she greeted, her voice measured but laced with something else—hesitation. "Do you have a few minutes?"

"For you? Always." A pause. "Something's bothering you."

Eve raised an eyebrow. "Impressive. You must be a therapist."

He let out a low chuckle. "I've had some practice. But let's not deflect. What's on your mind?"

She hesitated, drumming her fingers against the desk. "I have a patient. A complicated case."

"Aren't they all?"

"Not like this."

That was enough to shift Bernard's tone. "Go on."

Eve sighed, pinching the bridge of her nose. "It's a male patient. Mid-thirties, highly intelligent but emotionally underdeveloped in certain ways. He's been conditioned to be a giver, someone who prioritizes others' needs over his own. Now, for the first time, he's realizing what he's missing—real connection, validation. And he's…looking at me for it."

Bernard was quiet for a beat. "Transference."

"Clearly," Eve replied, "but it's not that simple."

"It never is." His voice was still even, clinical. "Tell me, what about this case is making you call me instead of relying on your own expertise?"

Eve shifted in her chair. "Because I feel it too."

She hated admitting it, but Bernard didn't react with judgement. If anything, his voice softened. "And what is it you're feeling?"

She hesitated. "Drawn."

The silence that followed wasn't uncomfortable—it was weighted, the kind of space Bernard always allowed for real reflection.

"Eve," he said at last, "you know better than most that transference is not about you. It's about him—what he lacks, what he projects. The more important question is: Why does this one feel different to you?"

She swallowed, shifting slightly. "Because it's not just about him. It's me too."

There. It was out.

Bernard's sigh was quiet but knowing. "You've always been drawn to control, to power. Not in the obvious way—never just for the sake of it. But because when you hold control, you don't have to be vulnerable. You don't have to want."

Eve tensed, but Bernard wasn't done. "This patient of yours... He doesn't challenge your authority. He *wants* you. And desire without resistance? That's dangerous for someone like you."

She clenched her jaw. "I have control over this."

"Do you?"

The way he asked it made something cold trickle down her spine.

Eve sighed, running a hand through her hair. "I don't want to cross a line."

"Then don't."

She let out a sharp laugh. "Easier said than done."

Bernard chuckled, but his voice remained firm. "Eve, I won't sit here and pretend desire is rational. It's not. It's primitive, often inconvenient, and certainly not always ethical. But the difference between indulgence and discipline is awareness. Ask yourself: Is this about him? Or is it about you wanting to be seen?"

The words landed deep, like a weight in her chest.

"I just want to handle this professionally," she murmured.

"Then you already know what to do."

She closed her eyes, inhaling deeply.

"Eve, just because something feels inevitable doesn't mean it's right."

There it was—the truth she didn't want to admit.

She sat in silence, letting the words settle. Bernard gave her space, but when he spoke again, his voice was lighter.

"Let me leave you with this." His tone shifted, dipping into something more academic, something she recognized as his way of grounding her in logic. "Freud believed that transference is inevitable in therapy, but it is also *necessary*. The patient redirects unresolved emotions onto the therapist, but the true test—the *real* work—is whether the therapist holds the boundary. That's where the healing happens."

Eve's fingers curled against the desk.

"And if the therapist fails?"

Bernard exhaled. "Then the patient doesn't just lose trust in you. They lose trust in themselves."

The words stung.

He let the silence stretch before his tone softened. "You've always prided yourself on your discipline, Eve. But discipline isn't about the absence of temptation. It's about what you do when it arrives."

She nodded, even though he couldn't see her. "Right."

"I trust you to make the right choice."

Eve wasn't sure if she did.

She ended the call, staring at her reflection in her office window. She'd sought Bernard's guidance to *reinforce* her control, to reaffirm the professional distance she knew she needed.

Instead, all she felt was exposed.

Noah had unsettled something in her—something deeper than attraction. A need. One she wasn't used to acknowledging, let alone indulging.

But she wasn't going to let it happen.

She would hold the boundary.

She had to.

Her breath was unsteady as she whispered Bernard's words to herself.

"Discipline isn't about the absence of temptation. It's about what you do when it arrives."

And yet…

A part of her wondered what it would feel like to let herself fail.

It was time. The door to Eve's office closed with a soft click as Noah settled into another armchair. Tonight, his movements carried a weight that hadn't been there before—deliberate yet uneasy, like he was teetering on the edge of something he couldn't quite name. His eyes, shadowed with fatigue, flicked toward her briefly before landing on his clasped hands. His foot tapped a nervous, uneven rhythm against the floor.

Eve took in the sight, taking a moment to observe. There was an unpolished charm to him, a handsomeness that felt accidental rather than deliberate. The tension in his shoulders, the way he loosened his tie but left it on, the way his gaze darted but always returned—it all painted a picture of a man trying to maintain control.

She crossed her legs, slow and deliberate, the slit in her skirt shifting just enough to reveal the smooth curve of her thigh. The movement was unhurried, almost lazy, but Noah stilled. He wasn't immune to her. That much was clear.

"Rough week?" she asked, her voice as smooth as silk.

Noah exhaled sharply, running a hand over the back of his neck. The motion tugged his shirt collar slightly, exposing the taut line of his throat. "You could say that," he muttered, his voice tight. "Work's been relentless, but it's more than that. Everything feels…heavy." His voice dropped on the last word, and this time, when his gaze met hers, it lingered.

Eve reached for her notepad, her movements slow, controlled. The act was innocent enough, but as she leaned forward, the neckline of her blouse dipped ever so slightly. A calculated shift. Noah's jaw tensed, his fingers tightening where they rested against his knee.

"What other things?" she asked, her voice lower now, coaxing.

Noah hesitated, his fingers fidgeting against his palm. "Sometimes, it feels like I'm constantly running uphill—like no matter how hard I try, there's always someone expecting more." He clenched his jaw, a flicker of something raw flashing through his expression. "But the truth is, I'm not sure it's them. I think it's me."

Eve tilted her head, watching the way his throat bobbed as he swallowed, the way his fingers curled slightly against his thigh, restless. "What makes you think that?"

He exhaled, shaking his head. "I know I have value, but it's hard to hold onto that when the people you give everything to just…take it for granted. I've always been the one to make sure everyone else is okay. Sophia used to call me her rock," he said with a wry smile. "But when she left, she told me I wasn't ambitious enough. That I wasn't…exciting."

Eve's pen hovered over her notebook, but she barely glanced at it. "Do you think she was right?"

Noah's frown deepened. "No," he said firmly. "I know I'm more than that, but sometimes, it's hard to shake the feeling. She made me doubt myself. I think she wanted someone who fit her fantasy of what a partner should be. And when I didn't match up, she left."

"Doubt is powerful," Eve murmured, leaning forward slightly. "It's the seed of every self-imposed limitation. But let me ask you this, Noah—when you look at yourself, what do you want? What about your fantasy?"

Noah hesitated, his gaze flickering to hers before dropping again. His fingers flexed against the armrest of the chair. "I don't know if I've ever really thought about it. I guess I've always been focused on being the person other people need."

Eve smiled faintly, her voice dipping just enough to make him notice. "And how has that worked out for you?"

He huffed a quiet laugh, shaking his head. "It hasn't. I gave so much of myself to her, to other people…but no one ever seems to give back." His voice dropped, rougher now. "I think…I think I'm lonely."

Her pulse quickened, but she didn't react outwardly. Instead, she let the moment stretch, watching his words settle over him.

"And if someone did give back?" she asked, her voice soft but unyielding. "If someone truly saw you—what would that look like?"

Noah's breath shallowed. His eyes lifted, holding hers, the space between them charged now, humming with something unspoken. "Someone who gets me. Who doesn't need me to be anything other than who I am."

Eve crossed her legs again, just a fraction slower this time, letting the movement drag out. She could feel the weight of his gaze now, the way his throat worked as he swallowed.

"And do you believe you deserve that?" she asked.

Noah blinked, startled by the question. His lips parted, but no words came immediately.

She watched as he struggled with it, the conflict playing out in real time. He shifted slightly, his knee brushing against the edge of her desk. His fingers twitched, flexing, like he wanted to reach out but knew better.

"I...I want to," he admitted, his voice hoarse. "But sometimes it feels like that kind of connection isn't real. Like it's something people say, but it doesn't actually happen."

Eve fell still. Her eyes locked onto his, holding him there, forcing him to feel the heaviness of his own words.

Noah's breathing had slowed, but his body remained tense. He stood up, crossed the space between them, and without fully thinking, he reached up, the backs of his fingers grazing a strand of her hair. He tucked it behind her ear, his touch lingering a moment too long, the warmth of his skin seeping into hers. It was dangerous. It was intoxicating. And she wasn't ready to let it go.

Her mind betrayed her, painting vivid, forbidden images— ones she had no business entertaining. If she gave in, if she leaned in just enough, he would pull her against him, his body solid, warm, and waiting. She could almost feel the ghost of his breath teasing the sensitive skin beneath her ear, the way his lips would brush—soft at first, almost hesitant—before dragging lower, tasting the curve of her neck.

His hands would find their place at her waist, fingers pressing with just enough command to make her stomach tighten, to make her crave more. He'd pull her flush against him, his grip firm, possessive, making her dizzy with the unspoken promise beneath his touch. His voice—low and rough with hunger—would murmur her name like a secret meant only for her, sending shivers cascading down her spine.

She could almost hear it, feel it—the way her pulse would race, the way anticipation would coil hot and tight in her belly, the way his scent—dark, masculine, and undeniably him— would surround her, drown her, make her forget why this was wrong. It would be so easy.

But it wasn't just attraction—it was something darker, more visceral, something that made her breath hitch and her thighs clench with restless anticipation.

His gaze held hers. A silent challenge. The air between them felt charged, thick, like the moment before a storm, crackling with an energy that begged for release.

The way he looked at her—like she was the only thing in the room, the only thing that had ever mattered—made her lips part involuntarily, a slow inhale betraying the tightness in her chest. Her fingers twitched at her sides, resisting the urge to reach out, to close the space between them, to let herself get lost in the fire that was already threatening to consume her.

Noah swallowed hard, his own breath uneven as if he could feel the shift in the air, the unspoken gravity pulling them closer. "You're not like anyone I've ever met," he murmured, his voice low, rough, charged.

Although her body and mind betrayed her, she knew if she didn't stop this now, she wouldn't stop at all. Her nails bit into the fabric of her skirt, a silent anchor.

She forced herself to exhale, "Noah, this is a boundary we can't cross."

He stepped back, his expression conflicted but intense. "I know. I'm sorry," he said, his voice dropping to a whisper. "But I don't think I'll ever stop feeling this way."

Eve's fingers brushed the edge of her notebook as she watched him retreat. The door closed softly behind him, and she reached for her phone. Her fingers trembled slightly as she typed: *Meeting ran late. Don't wait up.*

Noah had just stepped into the dimly lit hallway when she called him back. "Noah, wait."

He stopped, turning slowly, his heart hammering in his chest. Eve stood at the threshold of her office, her hand resting lightly on the doorframe. She knew that she didn't look like the composed therapist he had been pouring his heart out to for weeks. There was something different in her expression now—unreadable, almost vulnerable.

"Dr. De la Gardie?" he asked, his voice tentative.

"Eve," she corrected softly, stepping into the hallway. Her heels clicked against the tile as she approached him, her movements deliberate but unhurried. "Can I make an unorthodox suggestion?"

Noah blinked, his brow furrowing. "Please."

Eve tilted her head, her lips curving into a faint smile. "I was thinking...maybe we could continue this conversation. Somewhere less formal."

His stomach flipped. "You mean...like, now?"
"Why not?" she said, her voice casual, as if she weren't breaking every rule she had set for herself. "There's a bar a few blocks from here. It's quiet. Discreet."

Noah didn't know what to say. His therapist—Eve—was asking him out. "Are you sure?" he asked, his voice catching slightly. "I mean, I don't want to...cross any lines."

Her smile deepened, her eyes glinting. "Consider it an exercise in perspective. No titles, no boundaries. Just two people talking."

Noah's hesitation melted and his eyes widened with surprise. "Okay. Yeah. That sounds…great."

Eve reached for her coat, draping it over her arm as she gestured toward the elevator. "I'll meet you there. Fifteen minutes."

Noah nodded, his pulse racing as he turned and headed toward the exit. The disbelief was written all over his face, but so was something else—anticipation.

Noah was already at the bar when Eve arrived, his knee bouncing nervously as he nursed a glass of water.

He stood abruptly, his movements awkward but endearing. "You came."

"I told you I would," Eve replied, her smile teasing as she slid onto the stool beside him. She draped her coat over the back of the chair, revealing the delicate line of her shoulders.

"I, uh…wasn't sure," Noah admitted, his cheeks coloring. "You know, with the…circumstances."

Eve tilted her head, her hair falling over one shoulder. "Think of it this way—sometimes, breaking routine is necessary for growth."

He laughed nervously as the bartender approached. Eve ordered a glass of red wine, her tone smooth and unhurried. Noah fidgeted slightly, his earlier confidence in the session faltering under her presence.

"So," he said, lifting his glass, "Dr. De la Gardie—uh, Eve—what's the protocol here? Do we pretend you're not my therapist, or…?"

Her lips curved into a faint smile as she swirled her wine. "What would you prefer?"

He leaned in playfully. "How about we drop the therapist-patient thing for a little while? Pretend we just met."

Eve chuckled softly, her eyes glinting with amusement. "Alright, Noah. What would you say to me if we had just met?"

He paused, considering his words carefully before responding. "I'd say I don't usually meet women like you."

She arched an eyebrow, taking a sip of her wine. "And what kind of woman am I?"

"Smart. Beautiful. Intimidating," he said, his voice gaining confidence. "The kind of woman who makes a guy forget what he was going to say."

Eve leaned back slightly, her gaze steady. "You don't seem like the kind of man who's easily intimidated."

"I am when it comes to you," he admitted, his grin softening into something more earnest. "You've got this way of making me feel like I can say anything. Like I don't have to pretend."

"Maybe that's because you're finally starting to see yourself the way others can."

The tension between them thickened, the unspoken electricity crackling in the space between their words. Noah leaned forward, his voice dropping. "I think I'm starting to see a lot of things."

Eve met his gaze as she swirled the dark liquid in her glass. "Good. That's the point."

They had eased into the drinks, starting with light conversation, but the wine was loosening both of them up, drawing out things neither had said before. He asked her about her favorite movies, her favorite cities, even her least favorite clients. She dodged the last one with a laugh, but the openness in his tone was disarming. Noah's laughter came easier, and Eve found herself leaning closer with each word, her lips curling into a smile that felt less rehearsed.

"You're not what I expected," he said, his voice steady but softer now. His second drink sat half-empty in front of him, but his attention was entirely on her. "When I walked into your office the first time, I thought you'd be...different."

Eve tilted her head, feigning curiosity. "Different how?"

"More clinical. Distant. But you…you see people. Really see them." His hand lingered near his glass before he reached for it and took another sip. "It's intimidating, but also…kind of incredible."

Eve chuckled softly, her gaze warm but assessing. "You're giving me too much credit, Noah. I'm just doing my job."

He shook his head, leaning in slightly. "No, you're not. You're doing more than that. You make people feel like they matter. Like they're not invisible."

She let the moment hang, swirling her wine again before taking a slow sip. "And yet, here you are. Not invisible."

Noah smiled, his confidence building with the steady rhythm of their banter. He took a long sip of his drink, setting the glass down with deliberate care. "Can I say something without it getting weird?"

Eve glanced down at his hand, then back up, her pulse quickening despite herself. She didn't move away. Instead, she leaned closer. "That depends on what you're hoping to accomplish."

He laughed nervously, his fingers tapping the table. "I really like that skirt on you. It accentuates the lines of your body."

Eve didn't respond immediately. When she finally spoke, her voice was softer, almost a whisper. "The moment has its risks."

The air between them thickened, their gazes locking as the unspoken tension coiled tighter.

Noah hesitated for only a moment before leaning forward, his hand brushing against her leg. "Some risks," he murmured, "are worth taking."

Eve's heart raced as she felt the warmth of his hand, her body leaning instinctively closer before she caught herself.

Noah held her gaze, his hand lingering for just a moment longer before he withdrew. "I think I'm okay with that."

"We should probably call it a night," she pulled back slightly, her voice steady but tinged with something unspoken.

They stood together, gathering their coats, the weight of the evening pressing against them. As Eve turned toward the door, Noah reached for her hand, stopping her mid-step. She turned back, surprised, but before she could speak, he stepped closer, his other hand brushing against her waist.

"I can't let you leave without doing this," he said, his voice husky and deliberate.

Eve barely had time to process his words before his lips pressed on hers. The kiss was bold, breaking every rule she'd carefully constructed, and yet she didn't pull away. Instead, her fingers gripped the front of his jacket, drawing him closer as her body betrayed her resolve. She could feel his hard-on pressed against her.

The world outside the dimly lit bar seemed to vanish. His hand slid from her waist to the curve of her hip, his grip firm but reverent, like he was afraid to shatter the moment. Her body tightened as his lips moved with a fervor that made her feel simultaneously powerful and undone.

When they finally parted, it wasn't a clean break. Her lips lingered dangerously close to his, her fingers still tangled in his jacket. His forehead rested against hers, their breaths mingling in the narrow space between them.

"Eve…" he murmured, her name a whisper that carried more weight than it should have.

"Don't," she said softly, her voice trembling with both warning and invitation. Her hand grazed the side of his face, placing her finger on his mouth. Her touch was as much a caress as it was a signal to step back. "This…this never happened."

Noah's lips curved into a slow, almost defiant smile. "You're the one who said we could break the rules."

Eve let out a shaky laugh, pulling herself away at last, though her body felt like it was fighting every step. She adjusted her coat, her fingers brushing her lips briefly as though she could erase the moment—or savor it.

"We'll talk soon," she said, her voice calm despite the storm inside her. She turned and walked out, the sharp click of her heels on the pavement echoing in the cool night air.

As she slipped into the driver's seat of her car, her hands gripped the steering wheel tightly and her mind began to race. *The thrill of his kiss, the audacity of her actions—it was intoxicating.* She pressed her fingers to her lips again and straightened herself in her seat.

She felt herself ignite—quietly, completely—and she didn't stop to think of what it might destroy.

Chapter 7

House of Cards

"I found another hit!" Eddie's voice was loud enough to turn heads in the hallway, but he didn't care. He stormed into Audrey's office, a manila folder clutched in his hand, his face a mixture of urgency and frustration.

Audrey barely looked up, her tone clipped. "What now?"

Eddie slapped the folder onto her desk, flipping it open. "Second victim—Constantine Giannopolous. New York City, a year and a half ago. Strangulation, no defensive wounds, another damn Tarot card. This time, it's the King of Wands.

"Analyst down at VICAP flagged it last night," he added, tapping the top corner of the report. "They've been combing through old cases for anything symbolic—this one finally pinged."

Audrey's brows furrowed as she scanned the report. "King of Wands. And Anthony had Cups. That makes three murders, three cards."

"The first case from fourteen years ago had the King of Pentacles," Eddie clarified, tapping the report. "Pentacles, Wands, Cups. Three suits."

Audrey set the file down, her fingers drumming against the desk as her mind raced. "Someone wants us to notice the details. But why these men? Why this pattern?"

Eddie sighed, running a hand through his hair. "That's what we're trying to figure out, isn't it?" His tone was clipped, the weariness in his voice hard to miss.

Audrey glanced up, catching the edge in his words. "Eddie, what's going on with you?"

"What's going on with me?" Eddie repeated, leaning back in his chair. "You've been hovering over everything I do today like I can't handle it."

Audrey's eyebrows shot up. "Hovering? I'm trying to make sure we don't miss anything."

Eddie gestured toward the stack of files on her desk. "Yeah, and in the process, you're acting like I need you to hold my hand."

Audrey opened her mouth to respond but hesitated. She realized the tension between them had been simmering all day— her curt responses, the way she'd double-checked his work without thinking. It wasn't intentional, but Eddie wasn't wrong to feel slighted.

"I didn't mean to," she said carefully, softening her tone. "This case has us all on edge." Audrey's jaw tightened. "I'm doing what I have to do to keep us on track."

"No, you're doing what you think you have to do to prove yourself to Reynolds," Eddie shot back. "And in the process, you're forgetting that this is supposed to be a partnership. I'm not your punching bag," he said finally, his tone softer but still edged with frustration. "I've got my own crap going on. My landlord's threatening to evict me, my sister won't stop calling about her divorce, and now we've got a serial killer leaving playing cards at crime scenes. So yeah, I'm at my limit too."

The words hit like a freight train. Audrey froze, her chest tightening as Eddie's gaze bore into her. She'd been so consumed by the case, by her own stress, that she hadn't even noticed Eddie's mounting struggles. She couldn't remember the last time she'd asked him about his life—or even bothered to check in

"Eddie…" she began, her voice faltering. "Why didn't you tell me?"

He shrugged, his expression weary but resolute. "Because it's not your problem. And I didn't need it to be. But if we're going to do this—if we're going to catch this guy—I need you to act like my partner. I can't do this if I'm just another cog in your machine."

The lump in her throat grew as his words sank in. *He's right*, she thought. *I've been so wrapped up in everything that I've treated him like a tool, not a person.* Her dad's steady advice to value those who have her back echoed in her mind, along with her mom's fondness for Eddie. *He's reliable, funny, and charming*, her mom had often said, hinting at potential beyond work. Audrey didn't see Eddie that way, but the thought only deepened her guilt. She hadn't even been treating him like the partner he was..

"I'm sorry," Audrey said finally, her voice cracking. "You're right. I haven't been fair to you."

Eddie studied her, his jaw tight, but he must have noticed the sheen in her eyes because his tone softened. "I'm not looking for an apology. I just need you to remember I'm on your side."

Audrey nodded, blinking rapidly to push back the tears threatening to spill. "I do. I will."

Eddie exhaled, his stance relaxing slightly. "Good. Now, let's figure out what the hell this killer's trying to tell us before we both lose our minds."

Audrey couldn't help but let out a faint, humorless laugh. Their conversation was still heavy but tempered by his honesty. For the first time in weeks, she felt a sliver of clarity.

Eddie studied her for a moment, his eyes searching hers. Finally, he gave a faint nod. "Good. Now, can we call Larkin before I lose my mind completely?"

Audrey didn't immediately reach for her phone. Instead, she gestured toward the file. "Before we do that, let's look at what we actually have. Three cards—Cups, Pentacles, Wands. That's three suits in Tarot. The killer's building a pattern."

"And it's creeping me out," Eddie muttered. "You think it's occult stuff? Rituals, magic, some kind of cult?"

Audrey tilted her head. "It's possible. The cards are symbolic—emotion, material stability, control. But why use something so public and accessible? It's not like these decks are hard to come by."

Eddie sighed. "I already asked Forensics about the deck. Mass-produced. Nothing unique about it."

"Which makes it harder to trace," Audrey murmured. "But the choice of cards still feels deliberate. The killer wants us to see them as part of the message."

Eddie frowned. "Then what's the message? 'Hey, I have a Tarot deck, and I know how to use it'?"

Audrey rolled her eyes but smiled faintly despite herself. "We need someone who can actually read these symbols, not just catalog them. I'll call Larkin. He's been researching this deck and the meanings behind it."

As she dialed, Eddie leaned against the wall, his arms crossed. "If this guy's playing by Tarot rules, does that mean we've got one more card to go?"

Audrey paused mid-dial, her stomach tightening. "It's possible. But we're not going to wait to find out."

Her thoughts wandered as Eddie stormed out of the office. The mention of Tarot cards triggered a vivid memory of high school—her and Sydney's goth phase. Sydney, naturally, had taken it to the next level. It had been a whirlwind of black nail polish, chokers, and endless reruns of *The Craft*. While Audrey dabbled, Sydney dove in headfirst. Her fascination with Nancy, the film's unpredictable and magnetic anti-hero, was borderline obsessive.

"She's not afraid of the flames," Sydney had said once, sprawled out on Audrey's bed with a deck of Tarot cards in hand. "She takes control. She doesn't let anyone walk over her, even if it destroys her in the end."

Audrey had laughed at the time, brushing off Sydney's dramatics, but now the memory felt sharper. Sydney had been the expert back then, always the one weaving intricate stories from the cards while Audrey half-heartedly shuffled her own deck.

Grabbing her phone, Audrey scrolled through her call history until she found Sydney's name. It had been a while since they'd talked, but if anyone could shed light on the Tarot angle, it was her.

Sydney picked up after a few rings, her voice dripping with playful suspicion. "Well, well. If it isn't my long-lost twin flame. You actually called me instead of texting like a coward. Who died?"

Audrey snorted. "Oh, just a couple of people. You free?"

Sydney let out a mock gasp. "I assume this is a sign of the apocalypse. Should I start hoarding canned goods?"

Audrey rolled her eyes. "You still have that old Tarot deck?"

There was a beat of silence before Sydney laughed. "That's what this is about? You, of all people, suddenly giving a damn about Tarot again? What happened, did the universe finally bitch-slap you with the fool card?"

Audrey nodded. "Something like that. You still have it or not?"

"Of course I do. It's the same one I had in high school—the one you made fun of but still begged me to do readings with."

"I did not beg."

Sydney let out a dramatic sigh. "Mmm, let's review. You swore you didn't believe in 'that woo-woo crap,' but if I so much as touched the deck, you'd be all, 'Just shuffle them for fun. Not that I believe in it. But shuffle them.'"

Audrey huffed. "Okay, fine. Maybe I was curious."

"'Curious' is a nice way of saying you had a full-blown identity crisis in the tenth grade. You went from pastel sweaters to black lipstick and a 'fuck the world' attitude in a week. Honestly, it was beautiful."

Audrey chuckled despite herself. "Yeah, well, you were worse. You fully committed. I had a phase. You were practically an oracle."

"Damn right I was." Sydney's voice took on a teasing edge. "I had the aesthetic *and* the knowledge. You just liked the eyeliner."

"Yeah, well, I never had your dedication," Audrey admitted, leaning back in her chair. "You actually understood all that stuff."

Sydney's voice shifted slightly, still teasing but laced with curiosity. "Okay, spill it. Why the sudden interest? You're not about to tell me you finally pulled the Death card and freaked out, are you?"

Audrey shook her head. "I'm working a case. Tarot cards keep showing up at crime scenes. I need to know what they mean."

Sydney hummed, intrigued. "You're telling me someone's leaving Tarot cards at murder scenes? That's bold. What kind?"

"All Kings—Cups, Pentacles, and Wands."

Sydney whistled low. "Damn. That's not random. That's *deliberate*."

Audrey tapped her pen against her notepad. "I figured as much. But why these cards? What do they mean?"

Sydney didn't answer right away, and for a second, Audrey could picture her—curled up somewhere with a cigarette between her fingers. "You remember what I used to say about the Kings?" Sydney finally asked.

Audrey searched through her memories. "That they were the most powerful cards?"

Sydney snorted. "That's *basic*. No, I said that the Kings represent people more than anything else. They're not just concepts—they're personalities. If someone's choosing them on purpose, it's because they see those traits in their victims."

Audrey straightened. "Explain."

"The King of Pentacles? That's your classic power player. Wealth, stability, control—think doctors, CEOs. People who've built an empire and aren't afraid to protect it. But the shadow side? Greedy. Possessive. Obsessed with keeping what's theirs."

Audrey's pen didn't stop moving.

"First victim was a surgeon. Top of his field. Controlled everything—his time, his patients, his life."

"Exactly," Sydney said. "Then you've got the King of Wands—charisma on steroids. Big ideas, big presence. He's not chasing money—he's chasing legacy. The kind of person who can walk into a room and own it. Think entrepreneurs, public figures, high-level execs."

"Second victim was a big-shot executive," Audrey confirmed. "Investment firm. Controlled millions. Had a reputation for taking risks."

Sydney nodded like a teacher who was pleased that her student was catching on. "And last—King of Cups. That's emotional mastery. Wise, compassionate...but also manipulative as hell when he wants to be. People in finance, therapy, counseling—the ones who act like they're guiding you but keep everything close to the chest."

Audrey tapped her pen against the notebook. "Third victim worked in finance."

"Fits," Sydney said, sitting back with a look that was half-satisfied, half-haunted. "Whoever this is—they're not just killing at random. They're playing with archetypes. With power. And they know exactly what they're doing." Sydney sighed. "Jesus, Aud. Listen, if you really want to get into the symbolism, I can dig up my old books. I still have them somewhere."

"You kept those?"

"Hell yeah. I keep *everything*. I'm sentimental."

Audrey scoffed. "You are *not* sentimental."

"Fine. I'm a hoarder of aesthetically pleasing knowledge."

Audrey hesitated, her mind drifting to her mother, the way she used to talk about Polish superstitions, about how the old ways weren't just stories but warnings. "Do you remember when my mom used to talk about Tarot?"

Sydney let out a dry chuckle. "Oh yeah. You pretended not to care, but I know you loved those stories. Something about the Death card always freaked you out."

Audrey tapped her fingers on her phone. "It wasn't the Death card. It was the Tower. My mom always said that was the real bad omen."

Sydney hummed. "She wasn't wrong. Tower means destruction, everything crumbling down. But the thing people forget? It also means revelation. It means you *see* things for what they are."

Audrey felt a chill creep down her spine.

Sydney's voice was lighter again but still knowing. "I'd say buckle up, bitch. Sounds like you're already in the middle of a Tower moment."

Audrey shook her head, unable to stop the small smile tugging at her lips. "Thanks for the vote of confidence."

Sydney echoed. "Sounds like life hasn't slowed down for you."

Audrey hesitated. "What about you? What's going on?"

There was a long pause before Sydney sighed. "My mom had a fall. Nothing too serious, but it shook her up. I'm flying back to Chicago tomorrow to help out for a bit."

Audrey sat up straighter, her chest tightening. "Sydney! Why didn't you tell me? I would've helped. You know your mom was like my second mom."

Sydney's laugh was softer now, almost apologetic. "Audrey, you've got a lot going on. I didn't want to distract you."

"That's not the point," Audrey said, guilt creeping into her voice. "I could've done something. I should've known."

"You're doing the whole guilt thing again, aren't you?" Sydney teased gently. "It's fine, Aud. You're in the middle of a huge case. I didn't want to interrupt."

Audrey's throat tightened. "I'm so glad you're coming back. I'll check in on her tomorrow evening. And... I'll ask my mom to call her, see if there's anything she needs right away."

Sydney chuckled. "Your mom, huh? Still running your life?"

Audrey snorted. "Every day. But she means well, and in this case, she can actually help."

"Thanks, Aud," Sydney said, her voice softening. "It means a lot."

Audrey swallowed hard, gripping the phone tighter. "It's the least I can do. And I'm really glad you'll be here."

"Me too," Sydney replied. "We'll catch up soon, okay?"

"Okay," Audrey said softly.

Audrey sat in silence after hanging up the phone, her grip on it tightening until her knuckles turned white. The guilt weighed heavier than she expected. *How could Sydney not tell me? How did I miss this?* Her mind flashed back to all the times Sydney's mom had treated her like one of her own—letting her crash at their house, sneaking her cookies before dinner, covering for her when she and Sydney were up to no good.

She's always been there for me, Audrey thought. *And now I'm too buried in my own chaos to even notice when she needs me.*

The room felt too small, the walls closing in as the phone call replayed in her head. Sydney had laughed it off, but Audrey knew better. She'd been so focused on the case, so consumed by chasing clues and managing Eddie, that everything else had fallen to the wayside. Her pulse quickened as her thoughts spiraled. *If I'm already dropping the ball here, what else am I missing?*

She pushed herself out of her chair, pacing the room in tight circles. The room swelled, its corners pulsing like a heartbeat, growing until it consumed her, until it swallowed the very air from her lungs. and she reached for her coffee mug, only to find it empty. *When was the last time I ate? Or slept more than five hours?* She couldn't remember, and that realization only made her chest tighten further.

Her father's voice echoed in her mind, steady and calm as always. "You've got to slow down, Audrey. You can't be everywhere at once. Even superheroes take a day off." *I don't have time to slow down,* she argued silently. Not with a serial killer out there. Not with Sydney coming back to a crisis. Not with Eddie waiting for me to fall apart so he can say I told you so.

She pressed her hands against her temples, squeezing her eyes shut. She could feel the heat rising in her face, a prickling sensation creeping up her neck. *Get it together. Get. It. Together.* She repeated the mantra like a lifeline, willing herself to calm down.

A sharp knock on the door startled her, and she spun around, her heart racing. Eddie poked his head in, his expression softening as he took in her pale face and tense posture.

"You okay?" he asked, his tone laced with concern. Audrey straightened, forcing a tight smile. "Fine.
Just…following up on a lead."

Eddie didn't look convinced, but he nodded slowly. "Alright.
Larkin's going to call. I'll meet you in the conference room."

She nodded, waiting until he disappeared down the hall before collapsing back into her chair. Her hands clenched the armrests as she took a deep, shaky breath. *You're fine. You're fine.*

But even as she told herself that, the crack in her armor felt wider than ever.

Audrey sat at the table, her mind replaying the earlier confrontation with Eddie. He leaned against the wall, arms crossed, his jaw clenched—a silent testament to the unresolved tension between them.

The laptop on the table pinged, signaling the incoming video call from Dr. Larkin. Audrey clicked to accept, waiting as the connection attempted to stabilize. The screen flickered, showing a loading symbol, then went black.

"Did he get lost in the digital void?" he quipped.

Audrey shot him a look. "Give it a second."

Eddie checked his watch. "It's been five seconds. Five too many."

A muffled voice crackled through the speakers. "Damn it. Hang on. I think my camera's..." Static. More fumbling. "Are you getting a video feed on your end?"

Audrey exchanged a glance with Eddie. "Nope. Can you check your settings?"

Larkin let out a frustrated sign. "I did. Twice." A brief pause. "It's just...not working. Give me a second..."

Eddie mouthed "tech genius" to Audrey.

The loading icon spun mockingly before vanishing, leaving nothing but Larkin's initials on the screen.

Eddie huffed. "Tell me again why we're trusting a guy who can't even turn on his webcam? I mean, it would be ironic if we discussed murder investigations in the dark."

Audrey rubbed her temple. "We can still hear you, Dr. Larkin. Let's just proceed."

A moment of silence, then Larkin's voice came through, slightly exasperated but composed. "Fine. Let's get to it."

Eddie leaned forward, flipping open the case file. "Another day, another dead body, another Tarot card. This time, it's the King of Wands. And for added flair, the killer left behind a pair of cufflinks—real high-end stuff. Nothing our victim would've owned."

"Interesting," Larkin murmured. The sound of keys clicking filtered through the speaker. "And the victim's cause of death?"

"Strangulation," Audrey supplied. "Same as the others. The cufflinks don't match anything the victim owned. They're expensive, personal. It's like the killer is dressing up his crime scene."

Larkin was silent before responding. "So far, we have the King of Cups, the King of Pentacles, and now the King of Wands. That leaves only one—"

"The King of Swords," Audrey finished.

"Correct. And that card represents authority, intellect, and control. The selection of these cards isn't random—it's a psychological blueprint. The killer is assigning roles. These men aren't just victims; they're characters in a narrative of his design."

Eddie leaned back, a thoughtful expression replacing his usual sarcasm. "If this perp sees himself as the orchestrator of these roles, assigning identities to his victims, it's like he's casting himself in the lead role of this twisted production."

Audrey's eyes narrowed as she considered Eddie's observation. "The Magician," she murmured.

Larkin's voice sharpened. "Pardon?"

Audrey straightened. "The Magician in Tarot is more than a performer. He's a manipulator. He has all four suits—the Cups, Wands, Pentacles, and Swords—laid out in front of him. He doesn't just influence the game. He *creates* it."

Larkin adjusted his glasses, a quiet hum of understanding in his tone. "The Magician is associated with power, influence, and the ability to manifest one's desires. If the killer identifies with this archetype, it suggests a need to assert control and demonstrate superiority."

Audrey tapped her pen against the table. "He's not just assigning roles—he's placing himself at the center of this macabre play."

Eddie's lips curled into a grim smile. "The Magician. Has a certain ring to it."

Dr. Larkin nodded. "It's a fitting moniker, considering the symbolism and the killer's apparent self-perception."

Audrey sat forward. "Then let's use it. We'll refer to him as 'the Magician' in our communications and the media. It might provoke a reaction, give us an edge."

Eddie raised an eyebrow. "You think naming him will draw him out?"

"It's possible," Larkin interjected. "If he sees himself as the Magician, acknowledging that could either satisfy his ego or challenge him, depending on his psyche."

Audrey exhaled, her mind racing. "But why these men? What's the connection?"

Larkin hesitated. "The victims may embody traits the killer identifies with or opposes. This indicates a perpetrator who is intelligent, methodical, possibly with a background in psychology or the arts—someone who views these acts as a form of expression."

Eddie's lips twitched into a sardonic smile. "Fantastic. A flair for dramaturgy."

Larkin continued, unfazed. "Historically, some killers have left symbolic items at crime scenes to convey messages or taunt authorities. For instance, during the D.C. sniper attacks, a Tarot 'Death' card was found at a crime scene, inscribed with the words *Call me God*. This act was intended to instill fear and assert control."

Audrey's eyes narrowed. "So, our killer might be using these cards to communicate something specific—to us or to themselves."

"Precisely," Larkin confirmed. "The deliberate choice of Tarot cards as calling cards suggests a desire to convey a message or fulfill a personal ritual."

Eddie's sarcasm faded, replaced by a steely resolve. "So, what's the play? Wait for them to deal the next card?"

Larkin's voice held firm. "We need to anticipate their next move. If the pattern holds, the King of Swords is next. We should consider potential targets who embody authority and intellect."

Eddie pushed off the wall, the earlier tension between them momentarily set aside. "I'll start pulling records. We're looking at someone who's playing a game only they understand. How the hell do we beat that?"

Audrey opened her mouth to respond—then the video feed abruptly turned on.

For a brief moment, Larkin's image flickered onto the screen. The camera focused downward, capturing only his hand hovering near the laptop, fingers twitching slightly. His posture was rigid, the subtle movement of his wrist shifting like he wasn't sure what to do with it.

Then, just as suddenly, the call disconnected.

Eddie blinked at the now-black screen. "Well...that was weird."

A strange unease settled over Audrey. "Yeah."

Eddie leaned back, stretching. "Guess technology isn't his thing."

Audrey's mind raced, considering the possibilities. "We need to cross-reference individuals who fit that profile with any connections to the previous victims. They're building to something, and they're not going to stop until the deck is complete."

Eddie nodded. "We should also brief the press and make 'the Magician' known. Maybe it'll force his hand."

As they prepared for the media announcement, the clock ticked down to the Magician's next move.

The conference room buzzed with restless energy, reporters shifting in their seats, murmurs rippling through the crowd like static. Bright camera lights illuminated the podium, casting harsh glares against the polished wood, but Audrey remained off to the side, out of view. She stood near the back, against the wall, her arms crossed loosely, close enough to hear every word but far enough to avoid the spotlight.

Chief Reynolds adjusted the microphone, clearing his throat as he watched the gathered representatives of the press. The city's expectations sat squarely on his broad shoulders, but he remained composed, his salt-and-pepper hair neatly combed, his sharp eyes scanning the room with practiced authority. The moment he stepped forward, the murmurs died down. The chief never had to demand attention—it was given.

"Good afternoon," Reynolds began, his voice even, deliberate. "We are here today to address an ongoing homicide investigation that has drawn significant concern from the public and the media. We've identified two previously unsolved cases that now appear to be connected to a recent homicide. The similarities suggest we may be dealing with a serial offender— one who leaves behind a deliberate and symbolic pattern at each scene."

A ripple of movement swept through the room as journalists leaned forward in their seats. Camera shutters clicked. Audrey's hands curled into fists at her sides, anticipation twisting in her gut.

"The details of these cases remain classified, but we can confirm one recurring element," Reynolds continued, his jaw tightening. "The suspect leaves behind a Tarot card at each scene. Because of this, our investigative team has assigned the moniker 'the Magician' to this individual."

A wave of whispers surged across the press pool, but Reynolds pressed on, unwavering.

"We believe this name reflects the perpetrator's self-perception—an individual who seeks power and control over their victims. We are treating this as a highly organized, methodical offender, and we are dedicating every resource to stopping them."

Audrey studied the faces in the crowd, watching how the words landed. Some leaned in, intrigued; others tensed, their pens moving frantically across their notepads. She could already predict the headlines: *Tarot Killer Strikes Again.*

"This investigation is our highest priority," Reynolds emphasized, his gaze scanning the room. "We urge the public to remain vigilant and report anything suspicious—no matter how small it may seem. We will not allow fear to take hold of this city."

A reporter shot up, not waiting to be called. "Chief Reynolds. does this mean you have no suspects?"

"We are actively investigating multiple leads," he replied smoothly.

Another journalist's voice rang out. "Are the killings linked to the occult?"

Audrey's chest tightened. That was the question she had been dreading.

Reynolds didn't flinch. "There is no current evidence to suggest these crimes are ritualistic. We are analyzing all possibilities, but at this time, we are focused on concrete forensic and psychological profiling."

More hands shot up, questions firing in rapid succession.

"How many victims do you expect?"

"What's the meaning behind the Tarot cards?"

"Is Chicago safe?"

Audrey's pulse ticked higher, but Reynolds remained a fortress, deflecting speculation without revealing more than necessary. It was exactly why he had been chosen as the public face of this case.

"Thank you," he said, cutting through the chaos with finality. "We will provide updates as new information becomes available."

The room was still buzzing as Reynolds stepped away from the podium. Reporters murmured, phones flashed, voices layered over one another in a discordant hum.

Audrey's heart pounded and her mind was racing. She exhaled as she made her way down to the back of the room. She watched the reporters hungrily dissect the information, twisting it into whatever narrative would sell. The Magician was real now, a public figure. The question wasn't whether the name would draw him out—it was how he'd respond.

The press conference had gone exactly as planned—controlled, strategic, giving the media just enough information without compromising the case. And yet, as she watched the scene unfold, an uneasy feeling pressed against her ribs.

Her gaze drifted across the crowd, scanning faces—reporters scribbling, photographers clicking away, expressions of morbid curiosity flickering in their eyes. But then, her attention caught on two familiar figures near the back of the room.

Sydney.

She hadn't seen her in months, but there she was, standing with effortless confidence, exuding the kind of presence that turned heads without even trying. Sydney had always been that way—bold, sharp-edged, magnetic. Even in the dim light of the precinct's briefing room, her jet-black hair framed her face in sleek waves, her crimson lips stark against her porcelain skin. The fitted leather jacket, the tailored black top, the high-waisted trousers—it all added to the air of someone who had stepped off the cover of a noir crime novel.

And Eddie had noticed.

Audrey could see it in his posture, the way he leaned toward Sydney, hands in his pockets but alert, engaged. There was something in his expression that she hadn't seen in a while—that easy, natural pull toward someone.

Their banter was animated, sharp, filled with amusement that neither of them had with her lately. Audrey recognized the look on Sydney's face—the one that said she was thoroughly enjoying herself.

Audrey wasn't sure why it bothered her.

It wasn't that she and Eddie weren't close anymore. If anything, he was the one person she trusted most. The person she could count on to have her back, to keep things light when the weight of the job pressed too hard. Their camaraderie had never wavered—except, maybe, on her end.

Maybe, after Josh, she had started to see Eddie differently—not as someone who had changed, but as someone who was safe. The one constant that she didn't have to worry about losing.

She never wanted to risk messing that up.

So maybe she had put up some distance. Maybe she had let the lines of their friendship blur into something strictly work-focused while she sorted herself out.

And now?

Now, she was standing on the sidelines, watching Eddie and Sydney slip into an easy rhythm, watching Eddie's eyes light up with something playful, intrigued.

And it hit her.

She had never seen him look at her like that.

Because she had never let him.

She had shut that door, locked it without ever acknowledging she'd done it, and now, here Sydney was—storming in, completely unaware of the walls Audrey had built, and Eddie was walking right through.

Her grip tightened on the edge of the column, her nails pressing into the wood.

She should be relieved. Eddie deserved someone fun, someone who could match his wit, someone who wasn't completely consumed by this case. And Sydney? She'd always been the kind of woman who could walk into any room and become the most interesting person in it. Of course Eddie would be drawn to that. Who wouldn't be?

But as she stood there, watching the effortless rhythm of their conversation, she felt an unexpected pang of something.

Not jealousy.

Not regret.

Just…a realization.

She had spent so much time compartmentalizing, so much time prioritizing the case, her career, her own fears, that she never stopped to consider what she might have lost along the way.

What did she have to show for it? A half-eaten dinner in her fridge. A growing distance between her and the people who once knew her best. And a case that still wasn't making any goddamn sense.

She forced herself to move.

As she stepped toward them, Sydney was already entertained by whatever exchange had just happened.

"What's so funny?" Audrey asked, her voice sharper than intended.

Sydney turned, lazily shifting her weight onto one hip as she met Audrey's gaze. "Oh, nothing," she drawled. "Just catching up with your partner here."

Eddie, standing next to Sydney with his arms crossed, tilted his head toward Audrey, eyes glinting with amusement. "Yeah, we were just discussing how you undersold your best friend."

Audrey frowned. "Undersold?"

Sydney quipped. "You made Eddie sound like some unshakable, no-nonsense detective. And here I find out he's actually got jokes."

Eddie shot Sydney a wink. "She did make me sound kind of terrifying, didn't she? Like I eat crime reports for breakfast and scowl at people recreationally."

Audrey huffed. "I do not—"

Sydney cut her off, holding up a hand. "It's fine, I like a surprise. He's at least mildly tolerable."

Eddie feigned offense, clutching his chest. "Wow. Mildly? You don't just go throwing compliments around, do you?"

Sydney's lips quirked. "Not unless they're earned."

Audrey's gaze flicked between them. She should be amused. She should even be grateful—Sydney wasn't easy to win over, and Eddie was…well, Eddie. She should be relieved they weren't at each other's throats.

So why did it feel like she had just walked into a conversation she didn't quite belong in?

Sydney arched a brow. "Eddie here has been filling me in."

Audrey stiffened. "Filling you in?"

Sydney's smile deepened. "Relax. Nothing scandalous. Just about your case, your ridiculous caffeine intake, and your unwavering ability to pretend you're fine when you're really not."

Audrey shot Eddie a look. He shrugged. "She got it out of me. She's kind of relentless."

Sydney gave a slow, knowing nod. "It's a skill."

Audrey exhaled, crossing her arms. "You two really hit it off fast."

Eddie's chest puffed up. "I know, right? It's almost like I have actual charm, despite your slanderous descriptions."

Sydney chuckled. "I wouldn't go that far."

Audrey wanted to chime in—to throw in some biting remark, something to remind Eddie that they had their own unspoken language. But before she could open her mouth, she hesitated.

And that hesitation was all it took. Now it was unfolding in front of her, only she wasn't part of it. She was the observer.

Before she could untangle that feeling, Eddie clapped his hands together. "So, before Audrey interrupts, I was just about to ask Sydney if she wanted to grab a drink later."

Audrey did not flinch. Not at all.

With a flicker of amusement, Sydney glanced back and forth. "Bold."

"Confident," Eddie corrected.

Sydney made a thoughtful noise before finally shrugging. "Sure. Why not?"

Eddie's smile widened. "Really? That easy?"

Sydney leaned in just slightly, lowering her voice. "Don't push it, Detective."

Audrey really didn't need to witness the tension crackling between them. She cleared her throat, leveling Sydney with a look. "Glad you two are getting along. But if we're done with the flirting, we have actual work to do."

Eddie and Sydney exchanged a glance.

A glance.

Audrey ignored the tightness in her chest and turned on her heel.

As they walked out together, Eddie was still grinning, and Sydney?

Sydney was watching him like she'd just found something unexpectedly interesting.

And Audrey?

Audrey wasn't sure when she had become the third wheel in her own goddamn life.

Chapter 8

Marked by the Magician

The Magician

The figure sat at a sleek, modern desk, their fingers deftly tracing the edges of a Tarot deck. The cards were fanned out, carefully arranged—Kings of Cups, Pentacles, and Wands laid in a row. Together, they formed an incomplete tableau, the missing King of Swords a silent promise of what was yet to come.

They paused, tilting their head as if listening to something just beyond perception. Their hand lingered on the deck, the pads of their fingers grazing the cards' surfaces in a rhythmic motion, as though the touch itself provided clarity.

The final act was taking shape in their mind. The deck had been their constant companion, a tool to guide their focus, to channel their purpose. They thumbed through the remaining cards, the motion slow and deliberate, until the King of Swords emerged. The card's sharp lines and commanding presence seemed to pulse under their touch.

For a fleeting moment, they allowed themselves to savor the thrill. The high after the last act had been…unexpected. There was power in the act, a surge of control pulsed through their veins long after the deed was done. It had not been part of the plan—this visceral reaction—but now it added a layer of anticipation to what came next.

But there was also conflict. A weight they had not expected. They had always sought control, to ensure the chaos of the world never tainted what was theirs. Yet now, the thought of losing that control lingered like a whisper at the back of their mind.

Their grip tightened on the deck as their thoughts shifted. There had been…signs. A breach of trust. A fleeting connection between what was theirs and something that didn't belong. It gnawed at them, the threat of losing what they had fought so hard to protect.

Their jaw clenched, and they placed the King of Swords in the empty space at the end of the row. *The tableau was complete now,* at least in their mind. They exhaled sharply, the sound cutting through the quiet. They didn't want to finish the deck—not yet. Not unless they were forced to. There was still time to keep everything intact, to ensure that no more lines were crossed.

"Not yet," they murmured, their voice low, carefully devoid of identifying tones. The words lingered in the air like smoke, curling and dissipating into the silence.

They rose, their movements fluid but purposeful. The cards were gathered and placed back into their box with precision. The lamp clicked off, plunging the room into darkness. They stood still for a moment before turning and vanishing into the shadows.

Somewhere, the Magician prepared their next act. The game continued, its outcome still unwritten.

Chapter 9

Fault Lines

Eve set the table with quiet precision, aligning the plates and silverware with a meticulousness she didn't entirely understand. Across the kitchen, Rory perched on a stool, her elbows resting on the counter as she scrolled through her phone, one foot swinging lazily in the air. Her dark hair framed her face in sleek waves, her neatly trimmed bangs accentuating the sharp, knowing eyes that always seemed two steps ahead of her age.

"Why do we even do this?" Rory asked, her voice laced with mock exasperation. "Family dinner feels like a 1950s social experiment. And don't say it's prep for Thanksgiving—I'm already bracing for the performative gratitude and dry turkey."

Eve slid a casserole dish into place. "It's not an experiment. It's called bonding."

"Bonding?" Rory quirked an eyebrow. "You make it sound like we're sticking our feelings together with Gorilla Glue."

Leo walked in, balancing a tray of roasted chicken. "Let me guess. Rory's lobbying to abolish family dinners again?"

"I'm just trying to get ahead of the Thanksgiving performance next week," Rory said, dramatically. "Same forced smiles, just more carbs."

Eve shook her head, biting back a laugh. "Sit. Eat. Mock us after dessert."

The meal began on a light note, with Rory's dry humor filling the silences. She described her latest school project—an art installation on "the absurdity of the mundane"—which Leo predictably teased her about and claimed it was pretentious.

"And how, exactly, does one make an art installation out of laundry lint?" Leo quipped, carving the chicken with a theatrical flourish.

"It's called commentary, Dad," Rory shot back. "You'd know that if you weren't trapped in the Stone Age."

Eve chuckled, pouring herself a glass of wine. "Leave your father alone. His Stone Age wisdom built this house."

Just as the laughter settled, the television in the adjacent living room flickered to life, its volume rising just enough to catch their attention.

"We interrupt your programming for an update on the case authorities are calling 'the Magician.'"

Leo, mid-reach for the serving spoon, turned toward the TV. Before anyone else at the table could react, he grabbed the remote from the counter and clicked the power button, cutting the broadcast off in an instant.

Rory, who had just twisted in her chair to look, let out a noise of protest. "Hey—what was that?"

Leo barely looked up as he reached for his wine glass. "News," he said offhandedly, taking a sip. "No need to listen to all that over dinner."

Eve, still setting down her fork, barely had time to register what had happened.

Rory, arms crossed, gave Leo a pointed look. "You could've at least changed the channel. Now I *definitely* want to know what it was."

Leo exhaled through his nose, reaching for another serving of chicken. "Rory, the last thing you need is another crime story keeping you up at night."

"That's a *you* problem," Rory shot back. "I sleep great."

Eve, reaching for her wine, finally spoke. "It *is* all over the news lately. Leo, you know Jordan at the practice—he's taking the lead on this one. It's his first case like this."

Leo gave a low chuckle, shaking his head as he sliced into his chicken. "Good for him. Seems like you've got a lot of confidence in the kid. I would've thought you'd leave something like this with O'Connor. Didn't you spend years trying to get O'Connor on board? Break into police investigations?"

Eve lifted a brow at his choice of words. "I didn't *spend years*—I built a partnership," she corrected lightly. "And O'Connor's still there when I need him, but Jordan shows a lot of promise. He's meticulous. Dedicated. It makes sense to let him take the lead on this."

Leo hummed in response, swirling the wine in his glass before taking a sip. "Huh. *Meticulous.*" He rolled the word over his tongue like he was tasting it, his tone unreadable. "And this is about... What? Training him up? Or are you already thinking about succession planning?"

Eve's grip on her glass didn't falter. "I'm considering *options*," she replied smoothly. "You of all people should appreciate a well-thought-out strategy."

Something felt offbeat—too controlled. "A strategy, huh?" He leaned back in his chair, the wine glass balanced effortlessly between his fingers. "Didn't realize you were already mapping out your legacy."

Eve set her glass down with a soft *clink*, tilting her head. "Legacy's a strong word," she said, watching him carefully. "It's about the future. Making sure things are in the right hands when the time comes."

Leo exhaled through his nose, amusement flickering in his eyes. "Sounds like you're planning your exit."

Eve gave a short laugh, shaking her head. "I'm planning for *contingencies*. That's how leadership works."

There was a beat of silence, something unspoken hanging between them.

Then Rory, sensing the slight shift in mood, cut in. "Okay, so *now* I *really* have to Google this guy."

Leo groaned dramatically, raking a hand through his hair. "Please don't."

Rory, completely unfazed, took an exaggerated bite of mashed potatoes.

Eve chuckled, letting the moment slide, but the exchange lingered in her mind. Leo rarely questioned her decisions like that—especially not her work. She wasn't sure why this conversation felt different.

For the briefest second, she wondered if he was *testing* her.

Her phone buzzed against the table.

For a second, she ignored it. But then she caught the name flashing across the screen.

Noah.

Her stomach tightened.

She hesitated for only a moment before flipping the phone face down, pretending she hadn't seen it.

But she had.

And now, as she sipped her wine, she could feel the text burning through the screen, a silent weight pressing against her consciousness.

The conversation carried on around her, but she felt like she was watching it from outside herself, like a camera panning back from a dinner scene. The food, the warmth, the easy family banter—it was all happening, but her mind wasn't there.

As the meal wound down, Rory studied Eve with a rare moment of seriousness. "Mom, are you okay? You've got that look."

Eve paused, startled by the question. "What look?"

"The 'I haven't slept in a week' look," Rory replied.

Eve smiled faintly, reaching over to brush a strand of hair from Rory's face. "I'm fine. Really."

Rory didn't seem convinced, but she didn't press further. "Just...don't forget to take care of yourself. You always tell me that, you know."

Leo jumped in, his tone light but firm. "Alright, that's enough worry for one night. Your mother knows how to pace herself."

Rory rolled her eyes but let the subject drop, returning to her usual sarcasm. "Fine. But don't expect me to pace myself when dessert comes out."

The room filled with laughter again, though Eve's mind lingered on Rory's words.

"I'll be in my office," she told Leo and Rory as she gathered the last of the dishes. She forced a smile, though her mind was already on the pile of notes waiting for her.

"Don't work too late, Mom," Rory called after her, her voice playful but tinged with concern. "Remember your beauty sleep. Not that you need it, of course."

Eve laughed, grateful for Rory's humor, but her steps felt heavier as she retreated to her sanctuary.

She barely glanced at the text from Noah before slipping her phone into her pocket.

She wouldn't respond.

Not yet.

But she also wouldn't delete it.

And that, she knew, was its own kind of decision.

Eve slipped into her office, the door clicking shut behind her. The second she was alone, her pulse quickened from anticipation.

Her phone sat on the desk, screen dark. The text from Noah was waiting. It had been waiting since dinner. She had deliberately ignored it, had forced herself to sit through the meal, to listen to Rory's jokes, to respond to Leo with just enough presence to seem engaged. But now, with the door closed and the rest of the world shut out, she allowed herself this moment.

She picked up the phone, heart pounding just a little too fast as she tapped the screen.

Noah: *Don't tell me I've already been forgotten.*

Eve typed quickly.

Hardly. Some of us have to maintain a facade of responsibility.

The dots appeared, flickering with their own kind of electricity.

You? Responsible? Now that's adorable.

Eve bit her lip. He always knew how to pull her in. It was effortless, the way he fractured her foundation, crack by crack.

Eve: *Careful. I might take that as an invitation.*

Noah: *You should.*

The warmth spread through her, curling low in her stomach.

Noah: *So, what's my ranking?*

Eve laughed softly, shaking her head.

Eve: *Bold of you to assume you're even on the list.*

Noah: *Oh, please. If I'm not first, we've got a problem.*

She hesitated a second too long before responding, fingers hovering over the keyboard.

Eve: *Confidence is attractive.*

Noah: *Confidence? I'd call it certainty.*

Eve swallowed.

Her thumb hovered over the keyboard, but before she could type another word, her phone lit up with an incoming call—Lilah.

Damn it.

She exhaled, willing the heat in her chest to settle, forcing herself to push Noah to the back of her mind as she answered.

"Lilah," she greeted, schooling her voice into something composed.

"Brace yourself. Please, darling, just surrender." Lilah's voice was all champagne and mischief. "The gala! It's practically crying out for you to be the star. I've already decided you'll be the highlight of the evening. My *pièce de résistance!* You're the perfect combination of elegance and intrigue."

Eve chuckled, shaking her head. "Elegance and intrigue, is that so?"

"Absolutely. And might I add, intrigue is in short supply these days. These socialites bore me to tears with their endless chatter about hedge funds and Peloton classes."

Eve barely heard her. Her mind was still stuck on Noah, on the certainty in his words, on the warmth in her skin that hadn't quite faded.

"Lilah, what exactly are you planning to do with me?"

"Well, first, you'll give a little speech. Nothing too stiff—just enough to remind everyone why I'm the genius who brought you into my orbit. And second, Maximillian is dying to design for you."

"Maximillian?"

"Don't pretend you don't know him. The man's a fashion sorcerer. He made me look like Cleopatra reincarnated at Harold's yacht christening last spring."

Eve joked, "I thought that gown nearly sank the yacht with all the gold embroidery."

"*Opulence, darling...opulence,*" Lilah corrected, unfazed. "And now, Maximillian will work his magic on you. Something sleek, something powerful—like a Bond villain with Grace Kelly's cheekbones."

The words hit differently this time. Eve barely noticed Lilah's chatter, her mind wandering. Not to Leo. But to Noah.

The dress.

The gala.

For a fleeting moment, she wasn't picturing herself stepping out of the car on Leo's arm, smiling for photographers with the perfectly curated poise of a politician's wife. No, in this vision, the lighting was different. Warmer. Sharper.

She imagined Noah seeing her in it. The way his eyes would darken, the way his breath might hitch just slightly. He'd say something cocky, low-voiced, just for her—

Let me guess—top three?

A rush of heat bloomed in her chest.

"Eve?"

She blinked, refocusing.

"Hmm?"

Lilah sighed dramatically. "You *have* to pay attention when I'm designing your entrance, darling. What's the point of throwing you into the lion's den if you're too distracted to revel in the spectacle?"

Eve forced a small laugh, leaning back against her desk. "Sorry. Just a long day."

"I *know*. That's why you need this." Lilah's voice softened slightly. "You've been buried in work. It's time to remind them who you *are*."

Eve exhaled slowly.

Wasn't that the problem?

She wasn't sure she knew anymore.

"By the way," Lilah continued, breezing past her momentary lapse, "we're going bold for the theme. None of this pastel nonsense Harold loves. Think *chartreuse, magenta, lapis*— something that demands attention."

"Subtle," Eve quipped.

"Subtlety is for the timid, darling. You're not timid. You're iconic."

Eve's mouth tilted in mock amusement. "And speaking of icons?"

"Ah! Yes." Lilah's tone turned conspiratorial. "Harold wants to sponsor a mental health initiative through the gala. Isn't that just deliciously noble?"

Eve tilted her head, intrigued. "Mental health? That's...a good cause."

"Of course it is. Harold insists it's close to his heart. And you, my brilliant, stunning friend, will be the face of it for one *glorious* night."

Eve couldn't argue with that. If she could lend her voice to a cause she believed in while adding to her professional profile, all the better.

"Alright, Lilah," she said. "I'll see what Maximillian has in mind. But no thirty-five-foot trains."

Lilah gasped. "Blasphemy! Fine. We'll keep it under twenty."

"Fifteen."

"Deal," Lilah said with mock solemnity. "Now, promise me you'll let Maximillian turn you into a masterpiece. This is your night as much as it is mine."

Eve's phone buzzed in her hand again.

Noah: *Still waiting on my ranking.*

She swallowed, pulse kicking up again.

Lilah's voice carried on in her ear, but Eve wasn't listening anymore.

This is dangerous.

She knew that.

And yet—

Her thumb hovered over the keyboard.

Eve: *You might be higher than you think.*

Noah's response was immediate.

Noah: *Finally. I was starting to think you were playing hard to get.*

Eve's lips parted slightly.

God, what was she doing?

"Lapis it is," she murmured absently, only half-answering Lilah as she set her phone down, her mind still lingering on Noah's words.

As much as she resisted Lilah's whirlwind at times, she couldn't deny the peculiar comfort it brought. In Lilah's world, everything sparkled, and for one night, Eve would allow herself to sparkle too.

But she knew the truth.

The sparkle wasn't for the cameras.

It wasn't for the cause.

And it sure as hell wasn't for Leo.

It was for *him*.

And that realization was the most dangerous one of all.

The house had sunk into stillness, the kind that felt heavier than it should. Outside, wind scraped dry leaves against the windowpanes—a late November chill that hinted at snow, though the sky hadn't yet delivered. The faint scent of cinnamon still lingered from Rory's attempt at a Thanksgiving "test pie" earlier that afternoon. Rory's TV murmured faintly upstairs, an occasional burst of laughter filtering through the vents. The clink of ice in Leo's glass punctuated the silence between them.

Eve sat curled at the opposite end of the couch, her posture relaxed—her mind anything but. The heat from her laptop pressed against her legs, but she hadn't touched the keyboard in over fifteen minutes.

Her phone was inches away. Noah's text still burned behind her eyes.

Sweet dreams, gorgeous. I'd say I wish I was there, but I think we both know I'd keep you up all night.

She hadn't replied. She hadn't needed to. The warmth between her thighs told her she had already answered.

Now, Leo was watching her. She could feel it. His gaze steady. Assessing.

It made her skin prickle, though she couldn't tell if it was from guilt or something else.

"Hard to believe Thanksgiving's in a few days," Leo said, his voice low, thoughtful. "You'd never know it with how quiet this place feels lately, and you're awfully quiet tonight." He swirled his wine, watching her over the rim of his glass. "Even for you."

Eve exhaled, steady, controlled. She offered a small, easy smile. "Long day."

Leo tipped his head, studying her. "You've had a lot of those lately."

She shrugged. Didn't react. "Casework."

A pause. A slow sip. "Right. Casework."

She didn't like the way he said it. Like he was trying to decide if she was telling the truth—or just seeing how much he could let slide without calling her on it.

Then, suddenly she heard, "You're beautiful, you know that?"

Eve blinked, startled by the abruptness of it. By the way his voice softened, just slightly.

She looked up, finding his gaze locked onto hers. Unwavering. Unreadable.

"Still, after all these years?" she tried to tease, but her voice felt thinner than she meant it to.

"Always," he said. He reached for her knee, his fingers brushing against the edge of the blanket. "And I don't say it enough, but I'm proud of you. The book deal. Your practice. Everything you've built."

She should have felt something deeper, something warmer. But all she could manage was polite gratitude.

So, she kissed him. Trying. Trying to meet him halfway. Trying to remind herself that this was real. That he was real. That they were real.

Leo responded immediately, his hand sliding to her hip, pulling her in.

His lips moved against hers—familiar, steady, certain.

Too certain.

She forced herself to relax, to lean into him.

But then—

Noah.

His hands. His grip. The sharp pull of oxygen from her lungs.

A memory she hadn't invited. Hadn't wanted. Hadn't asked for.

But it was there, curling beneath her skin. Searing.

Her breath hitched—not from pleasure, but from something dangerously close to panic.

Leo's hold on her tightened.

His hands slid lower, pressing against the curve of her spine. Stronger than she remembered. His fingers locked her against him, guiding her onto him like this was muscle memory.

Leo was always patient.

But tonight—tonight, he wasn't waiting.

His grip shifted, firm, knowing. There was no hesitation in his movements—he was leading, claiming.

A heat spread across her skin—not desire, but the raw, breathless knowledge that she wasn't in control of this moment anymore.

Her body stiffened, but Leo only pulled her closer, stronger, like he didn't notice. The heat of his breath at her jaw. The certainty in his touch.

The expectation.

"You're always moving," he murmured, lips brushing her throat. "Always running."

His hands curled around her thighs, fingers pressing into her skin like he could anchor her. Like if he just held on tight enough, she wouldn't slip away.

Her pulse was racing, but not for him.

Leo's grip adjusted, just slightly. Not forceful. But not asking either.

Eve's stomach twisted.

His fingers ghosted beneath the hem of her top, trailing heat in their wake. "You're tense," he murmured against her lips. "I can fix that."

No.

Noah had been a slow-burning fuse, the kind that coiled, pulled, teased her open.

Leo's touch was certainty. Grasping. Sure. Unshakable.

A slow, practiced motion. One they'd done a hundred times.

A hundred times before everything started to feel different.

She had to stop this. Now.

Eve pressed her palms against his chest, pushing back—not hard, not aggressive, just enough.

Leo stilled.

His grip lingered at her waist, fingers flexing once, like he was debating something.

Then—finally—his hands dropped away.

The air between them was thick. Dense. Something unspoken balancing at the edge of a knife.

"I just..." Eve inhaled, careful. Controlled. "I think I'm getting cramps."

Silence.

Too much silence.

Leo leaned back, exhaling through his nose. Slow. Deliberate.

"Cramps," he repeated, his voice unreadable.

Eve hated how her stomach twisted at his tone.

She climbed off his lap too quickly, retreating before she could think better of it.

Leo studied her. His expression should have shifted. He should have made a joke. Should have thrown out some sarcastic remark, something light to brush off the moment.

That's what he always did.

But tonight?

Tonight, he just sat there.

Watching.

Eve smoothed her top. Cleared her throat. "I'm going to check on Rory."

Leo picked up his wine glass, swirling the deep red liquid.

His expression didn't change.

But something in his silence made her pulse hitch.

"Yeah," he said finally, voice quiet. Measured. "Goodnight."

Eve turned quickly, walking out of the room before she could feel the full weight of his eyes on her back.

She didn't see the way his fingers curled, tight, around the stem of his glass.

Didn't see the slight tick of his jaw.

Didn't see the way he finally, slowly, took a drink—long, measured, unhurried.

Like he had all the time in the world.

Chapter 10

One Step Behind

The newsroom montage on the precinct's mounted TV was relentless. The voices of the anchors bled together—grave, electric, and unshakable.

"The Magician has struck again."

"Three victims so far, each tied to a mysterious Tarot card left at the scene..."

"The city is gripped with fear as police race against the clock..."

A chipper Thanksgiving jingle played low under the anchor's voice, promising *gratitude, gravy, and the gift of togetherness.* Audrey blinked at the screen, feeling hollowed out by the absurdity. People were panic-buying pie crusts while a serial killer arranged corpses like centerpieces.

The words burrowed under Audrey's skin like splinters.

Her eyes flicked to the crime scene photos. The Magician's signature taunted her, clawing at the edges of her mind. Even when she blinked, she saw Tarot cards burned into the backs of her eyelids—mocking her, seeping into her thoughts like a virus.

It felt personal. Like the cards weren't just for the investigation. Like they were meant for her.

Across the room, the chief of detectives, Gordon Reynolds, stood before the TV, arms crossed, his face red, his jaw so tight she could see the muscle jump near his temple. The newsroom continued its slow, gleeful dismantling of the department's failures.

"No leads."

"No suspects."

"Another body."

"Turn that damn thing off," the chief barked. A rookie fumbled with the remote, fingers shaking.

Audrey exhaled sharply, pulling her gaze away from the screen, forcing herself back to reality. Eddie caught her moment of detachment before she even registered it herself. He didn't say anything, but she felt his stare. He had noticed. He always noticed.

The chief shouted suddenly, "Holliday, Chan. My office. *Now!*"

Audrey entered first, her spine straight despite the fatigue dragging at her every step. Eddie followed, trying to downplay the tension with a sarcastic look, but even he couldn't mask his unease.

Inside the chief's office, the air was thick with frustration, tension coiled tight like a storm ready to break. The desk lamp cast sharp shadows across the walls, making the exhaustion in the chief's face even more pronounced.

"You two need to get this under control," he started, pacing behind his desk. "This psycho's got the city by the throat, and every goddamn reporter in town thinks they're a profiler now.

Tarot cards? The Magician? What's next—cocktail specials named after him?"

Audrey stepped in, her voice flat but firm. "We're working every angle. He's careful. No breadcrumbs. We're trying."

"Yeah, well, the public doesn't care about trying. They care about results. And if I don't give them some, the mayor's gonna start asking if I've got the right people on this case. *You* want that?" His voice was like a hammer, each word striking its mark.

Audrey's jaw tightened, her fingers curling into fists at her sides. "Understood."

Eddie raised a lazy hand. "For the record, I have full confidence in Audrey to save your job, Chief."

"Out," the chief snapped.

The precinct crackled with tension. Officers murmured, keyboards clicked, and somewhere outside, a siren howled like a wounded animal. The silence wasn't empty—it was waiting.

Eddie tossed a pen in the air, catching it absent-mindedly, his eyes flicking toward Audrey. "Don't take it personally. He's just mad he got called out for the bald spot on Channel 7."

Audrey didn't laugh. She just shook her head. "He's not wrong. We're running in circles."

Eddie leaned back, tossing his pen onto the desk. "At least we're still doing better than the psychics. Imagine how many palm readers are cashing in on this mess."

Audrey's lips curled slightly. "You think they've cracked the case yet?"

"Bet they're blaming Mercury retrograde."

The humor was a momentary relief—too brief, too fragile. Audrey dragged her hands down her face, rubbing away the exhaustion that was settling into her bones.

The problem wasn't just the lack of leads. It was how much this case was burrowing into her. Seeping into her routine, her sleep, her *brain chemistry.*

Eddie must have picked up on something in her face, because his expression softened. "We'll get him, Aud. He's smart, yeah, but nobody's smarter than you."

Her lips parted—ready to thank him, to make some deflective remark—but she hesitated.

A small part of her wasn't sure if she believed him anymore.

Audrey flipped to another page in her file, her eyes scanning the same lines she'd read a dozen times already. "I'm going to grab coffee. Want anything?"

Eddie sat up, stretching. "I'm good, thanks. But grab me some of those little creamer pods if you see any. I'm working on a tower."

Audrey sat at her desk, rubbing her temple, the dull throb of a migraine pulsing behind her eyes.

Tarot cards. Blood. Lifeless eyes. The same details, over and over, rearranging themselves in her mind like a cruel puzzle.

Eddie, chewing gum too loudly, flipped through a report with infuriating ease. "You're staring at those like the guy's about to jump out of them."

Audrey didn't answer. Her jaw was locked tight. She'd read every detail of the case files a dozen times. A hundred. And yet, nothing.

The sharp trill of the phone shattered the quiet.

"9-1-1, precinct desk," a young officer answered, his voice thin, nervous. The color drained from his face almost instantly. "Wait—sir, slow down—" He fumbled with the receiver, eyes darting wildly. Then, voice cracking, he called out, "Detective Holliday!"

Audrey snatched the phone so fast the cord nearly snapped. "This is Detective Holliday. Who am I speaking to?"

Static hissed. Then—a voice. Low. Wheezing. Amused.

"You're always one step behind, Detective."

Audrey's pulse spiked. "Who is this?"

A chuckle. "You tell me."

Too calm. Too deliberate.

"You've been looking for me, haven't you? Guess what? I've been looking for you too."

Audrey's grip on the phone tightened. Across from her, Eddie's chair creaked as he sat up straight, his eyes locked onto her.

She shot a look at the tech on duty. *We better be tracing this,* she mouthed. He nodded, fingers flying across the keyboard

"You want to find me, don't you?" The voice dripped with amusement. "I'll give you a clue. I'm closer than you think."

"Where are you?" Audrey demanded, her voice sharp as a blade.

A wheeze of laughter. Then—*click.* The line went dead.

The room exploded into motion.

Audrey's knuckles whitened around the receiver as she slammed it down. "Talk to me," she barked at the tech.

The tech whirled around. "Got him! Signal came from 238 Willow Street. Quiet neighborhood, two miles out. Looks legit."

Eddie grabbed his coat, already moving. "Then let's make this guy wish he picked another hobby."

Sirens blazed a crimson path down empty streets as the convoy of police cars snaked toward Willow Street. Audrey gripped the wheel, jaw set, Eddie uncharacteristically silent beside her. The address loomed on the navigation screen—a nondescript two-story house. Porch light off. Curtains pulled tight.

"Doesn't feel right," Eddie murmured as they pulled up. The SWAT team fanned out. Shadows melting into the dark.

Audrey ignored him. *You think it's nothing until it's something. Let's move.*

The team fanned out as flashlights sliced through the dark. The chief's orders crackled through radios: "Breach on my count. One...two..."

The explosion of wood and hinges was deafening. Splinters rained down like shrapnel as SWAT poured inside. A split second of quiet. Then chaos.

A dog barked—sharp and frantic. From the second floor, a woman's scream echoed, raw and terrified.

Audrey's instincts kicked in. "Eddie—downstairs! I've got the upstairs!"

She bolted for the stairs, flashlight bouncing across the cracked banister. Halfway up, movement flashed—a shadow darting toward the back of the house.

"STOP! POLICE!"

The figure crashed through the window screen, disappearing into the yard below.

Audrey didn't hesitate. She vaulted down the stairs and into the night, adrenaline thundering through her veins.

The chase unfolded in a blur of gravel and grass. Audrey's flashlight bobbed wildly as she sprinted after the runner—a wiry shape in a hoodie. The pounding of their footsteps echoed through the quiet neighborhood, louder than it had any right to be.

"STOP!" she shouted, but he didn't.

The figure glanced back, his foot catching on his untied shoelace. He tumbled forward with a sickening thud, his face slamming into the concrete.

Audrey was on him in seconds, pinning him down. "Don't move!" she yelled, cuffing his wrists. She flipped him over with a rough yank, shoving his shoulder into the pavement.

Her flashlight hit his face.

A kid. Teenager. Acne. Wild, terrified eyes. A busted lip from the fall.

But she didn't see a kid at first.

All she saw was a suspect. A liar. Another ghost slipping through her fingers. Her grip on his wrist tightened—too tight. The boy whimpered, squirming beneath her.

"What the hell were you doing?!" Audrey snapped, her voice sharp and cutting.

She jerked him upright, one hand locked around his bony forearm, the other gripping the collar of his hoodie.

The kid cried out, "Please—please don't hurt me! It—it was a joke!" he stammered, eyes wide. "I didn't think you'd actually show up!"

Her breath was too fast. Her pulse pounded in her ears. A flicker of hesitation. Then—Eddie's voice.

"Aud!"

She barely registered the warning in his tone.

Eddie's hand came down over hers, firm but steady. "Let him go."

Audrey blinked. The haze lifted and her fingers unclenched. The boy sagged in relief.

Eddie didn't say anything right away. He just gave her a look. The kind that said, *You're losing it. And I'm not letting you go down like this.*

Back at the house, the chaos had settled into something more surreal. The boy's parents—barefoot and in pajamas—were yelling at the officers.

"You busted into my house because of a prank call?" the father roared, his face crimson. "He's just a kid!"

The mother sat on the couch, sobbing, hands shaking around a teacup someone had thrust into her grasp.

Audrey stood off to the side, staring blankly at the scene. The flashlights. The broken door. The dog barking upstairs, still rattled. The father's rage was white noise in her ears.

Eddie appeared at her elbow. "You okay?"

She didn't answer. The tension finally cracked as tears stung her eyes. She turned slightly, her voice a cracked whisper. "This is too much, Eddie. We could've shot him."

Eddie placed a hand on her shoulder, his tone uncharacteristically soft. "We didn't."

"That's not the point," Audrey said, her voice rising. "We're chasing ghosts. This kid thought it was funny because the Magician is a *headline,* not a *person.*"

Eddie nodded, his humor tempered into something gentler. "I get it, Aud. I do. But you're not chasing ghosts. You're chasing answers. And you're closer than you think."

Audrey looked at him, disarmed by the sincerity in his tone. "You really believe that?"

He ran a hand over his face. "Yeah. So we should call it a night before you punch a dad in the face."

Audrey exhaled a shaky laugh, swiping at her eyes. "You're ridiculous."

"And you're stuck with me," Eddie shot back. "Now come on. Let's go explain this disaster to the chief before he sees it on the news."

The heavy tension of the false lead still hung in the air as Audrey and Eddie followed Chief Reynolds into the conference room. His temper had been bad before, but now? It was a live wire waiting to snap.

Eddie muttered under his breath, just loud enough for Audrey to hear, "If this is about that SWAT mess, I vote we say the kid was the next Houdini."

Audrey shot him a look, her patience worn thin. "Just don't talk."

Chief Reynolds planted himself at the head of the table, the overhead light casting sharp angles across his already severe face. His fingers tapped against the desk—deliberate, controlled, but the tension in his jaw gave him away.

"Thank you, Dr. Larkin, for joining on short notice," the chief began, his voice carrying the weight of too many sleepless nights. "We've got public panic on one side, City Hall breathing down our necks on the other, and the department looking like a bunch of clowns chasing shadows."

Eddie opened his mouth to retort—because of course he did—but Audrey kicked him beneath the table. Hard.

He shot her a look but wisely stayed quiet.

The chief exhaled through his nose, eyes narrowing at the two of them before shifting to the speakerphone sitting in the middle of the table. Larkin's voice crackled through, groggy but composed.

"This better be good," Larkin muttered. "I don't usually take calls in the middle of the night unless it involves a suicide attempt."

Chief Reynolds shot back, "You've done good work, Larkin, but I need more. The mayor's already making noises about pulling resources, and I can't have this department looking incompetent." He leaned in, his tone dropping to something sharper. "O'Connor's been profiling for this department for years and we didn't have these issues. We need to know who this son of a bitch is before he escalates. I don't care what it takes."

Larkin sighed on the other end, the rustle of sheets and a faint, irritated mumble in the background. His girlfriend, probably. Must be nice—to be able to sleep.

"Chief, I agree. The Magician is operating on a psychological plane that requires deeper analysis. His control, his theatrics— it's calculated. But to predict his behavior accurately... I believe we need a fresh lens."

The chief gave a curt nod, like he'd been waiting for that answer. "Exactly. That's why I need you to bring in your boss."

Larkin said, "I agree. Eve De la Gardie is my superior at Obsidian. If anyone can help us map this guy's next move, it's her. I'll send her everything in the morning. If she signs off, she'll be all in."

Audrey stilled at the unfamiliar name, but Eddie's curiosity was quicker. "De la Gardie? I've heard that name somewhere before."

The chief turned his glare on Audrey and Eddie, leveling a finger at them. "You two—coordinate with Larkin. Get Dr. De la Gardie fully briefed on the case."

Audrey's voice was calm, masking the frustration knotting in her chest. "Understood, Chief. We'll make sure she has everything she needs."

Chief Reynolds cut a sharp glance between them. "Get out."

They got out.

The weight in Audrey's chest hadn't lessened. If anything, it was heavier. Every lead felt colder than the last. The chase felt futile. They were playing the Magician's game, and he was winning.

Across from her, Eddie stretched, cracking his neck. "Welp, I'd say that went well."

Audrey scoffed, shaking her head. "We got benched."

Eddie, with a gleam in his eye, quipped. "*Delegated*, technically. To an expert. Which, by the way, means less paperwork for us, so—"

"Shut up, Eddie."

His eyebrows raised slightly. "Alright. Damn."

Audrey slammed her hand against her desk. "We're running in circles. Chasing shadows. And now? Now we have to sit on our hands and wait for some outsider to explain what we already know?" She let out a sharp, humorless laugh. "Yeah. This is bullshit."

Eddie studied her, his easygoing demeanor shifting into something more serious. "Aud, I get it. I do. But losing your shit isn't going to solve anything."

"Oh, is that what I'm doing? Losing my shit?" She shoved back from her desk, her chair scraping against the floor. She rounded on Eddie, eyes burning. "Tell me, Eddie, what's your grand plan? Another joke? Maybe a bet on who's next? Or do you just like watching me come apart?"

Eddie's expression darkened. "That's not fair."

Audrey knew it wasn't. But it didn't stop the words from coming. "You're just fine, aren't you? Cracking jokes, living your damn life, while I'm over here *drowning* in this." She jabbed a finger at the case files, her voice climbing. "Do you even care about this? Or are you just here because you like the thrill of it?"

The moment the words left her mouth, she regretted them.

Eddie's jaw clenched. "Wow," he said, voice quieter now, but no less sharp. "You really think that little of me?"

Audrey swallowed hard. "Eddie—"

"No, it's fine." He stood, grabbing his coat with deliberate ease. "Maybe you're right. Maybe I do have a life outside of this. Maybe you should get one too."

That one stung. More than she wanted to admit.

She exhaled sharply, frustration bubbling up. "And what do you suggest? A spa day? Maybe a damn nap? Because unless you've got the Magician hiding under your desk, I don't have time for a break."

Eddie studied her. "I was thinking of something more drastic." He leaned against her desk, just barely making a comeback. "California."

She blinked. "Excuse me?"

"Sydney," Eddie repeated. "Go visit her in California when she's back home."

Audrey scoffed. "I don't have time—"

"Make time," Eddie cut in, his tone firmer now. "This case is eating you alive. You're seeing ghosts where there aren't any. Take a few days. Reset."

Audrey hesitated, her arms still crossed. "I can't just leave."

"Why not?" Eddie challenged. "Larkin's bringing in De la Gardie. That gives us a window to step back before we run ourselves straight into a wall."

Audrey opened her mouth. Closed it. Then sighed.

"I'll think about it," she muttered.

Eddie gazed toward her. "That's all I needed to hear."

Then, after a beat, he added, "Speaking of Sydney…"

Audrey's eyes narrowed. "What about her?"

Eddie feigned nonchalance, but there was something playful in his expression. "We've been…chatting."

"Chatting?"

"FaceTiming."

Audrey folded her arms tighter. "And?"

Eddie grinned. "She's…something else."

A strange, twisting feeling settled in Audrey's stomach. Sydney was family. So was Eddie. The idea of them becoming something more…it unsettled her.

"Just…be careful," she said slowly. "I care about you both."

Eddie's expression softened. "I get it, Aud. I promise, I'll tread lightly."

Audrey hesitated, then sighed. "Alright."

Eddie nudged her shoulder. "So, about California…"

She rolled her eyes. "I said I'd think about it."

"Uh-huh." He slung his coat over his shoulder, stepping back. "I'll pack your bags."

Audrey huffed, shaking her head, but as she glanced back at the case file, the details lingered.

It was fleeting. But it was there. A fragile urge to let it all slip from her grip.

Chapter 11

Letting Go in Blue & Gold

The convertible sliced through the highway, the ocean stretching endlessly beside them, a mirror of blue and gold. Audrey turned her attention to the coastline, where the waves crashed against jagged rocks, sending white foam spiraling into the air. The scene was idyllic, a world away from the gray skies and relentless pressure of Chicago. And yet, something itched at the back of her mind.

She glanced at the road sign they just passed, catching only a blur of red and gold before it disappeared in the rearview mirror. It wasn't a Tarot card. It wasn't anything. But for a fraction of a second, her mind had filled in the gaps—had painted an image of something familiar where it didn't belong.

Her fingers curled against her thigh. This trip was supposed to be an escape, so why did she feel like the case was following her?

"I can't believe you let me convince you to come," Sydney said as she pushed her oversized sunglasses higher on her nose. "You, willingly taking time off—what's next, dogs running for congress?"

Audrey grinned sideways, but the usual sharpness wasn't behind it. "I didn't have much of a choice, did I? You practically dragged me to the airport."

Sydney waved her hand dismissively. "Semantics. I'm just impressed you're not wearing one of those power blazers. You look almost…human. Like someone who might actually enjoy a weekend off instead of cataloging murder suspects."

Audrey glanced down at her linen blouse, rolling the fabric between her fingers. No badge. No gun holster pressing against her ribs. No cold precinct air-conditioning making her shiver. The realization sat strangely in her chest.

"It's just clothes," she muttered.

Sydney shot her a look. "Yeah? Then why do you look like you just realized you left your identity back in Chicago?"

Audrey didn't answer. Instead, she leaned her head back, letting the warm sun soak into her skin.

Letting go was harder than she thought.

Sydney tapped her manicured fingers against the steering wheel, her voice casual—but Audrey knew her too well. Beneath the teasing, there was something heavier waiting.

"So, are we going to talk about it?"

"About what?" Audrey feigned ignorance, turning her gaze toward the waves.

"Oh, I don't know," Sydney mused, flicking her blinker on as they pulled into the driveway. "Maybe the fact that you've been running on fumes for months. That you look at crime scene photos like they're love letters. That your whole life has turned into one long chase scene, and you haven't even stopped to ask why."

Audrey tensed, fingers curling slightly in her lap. "Sydney—"

"No, just—hear me out." Sydney shifted the car into park and turned to face her fully, her expression uncharacteristically serious. "You think you're chasing a killer, but what if you're actually running from yourself?"

The words landed with a weight Audrey hadn't expected. A slow, sinking sensation settled in her chest, as if something had cracked, just slightly.

Her expression warmed. "That's deep. When did you start moonlighting as a therapist?"

Sydney gave her a knowing look. "Don't deflect, Aud. You know I'm right."

Audrey swallowed hard, opening the door before Sydney could push further. She wasn't ready to answer that question— not yet.

Sydney's bungalow was perched atop a hill with a view of the ocean. The scent of jasmine and salt filled the air as they stepped out of the car, with Sydney immediately grabbing their bags from the trunk. "Come on, Detective Workaholic. Time to relax."

As Audrey followed her inside the bungalow, Sydney's curated world of chaos and charm was evident immediately. Gold mirrors and black-and-white framed photos adorned the moody charcoal walls. A crimson velvet couch with clawed wooden legs dominated the living room. Beyond, the kitchen was ultra-modern with stainless steel appliances, ebony wood cabinets, and a stunning gold-veined onyx countertop. The entire space felt like a perfect balance of Gothic drama and sleek sophistication—entirely Sydney.

Sydney plopped onto the couch and gestured for Audrey to join her.

"So, what's the plan?" Audrey asked, arching an eyebrow.

"The plan," Sydney said, "is to do absolutely nothing serious. Starting with cocktails and gossip, followed by a beach day tomorrow. You're in California now, babe. Relaxation is mandatory."

Audrey sank into the couch, the weight of her exhaustion beginning to lift and she allowed herself to exhale fully. "Alright. Surprise me."

Sydney stood, sauntering toward the kitchen with a dramatic flick of her hair. "Alright, Detective. Time to see what I can conjure up. You like tequila, right?"

Audrey sank into the lush couch, letting her head fall back as her eyes traced the patterns on the black-painted beams above. Sydney was tinkering in the kitchen, a comforting rhythm of cabinet doors and the occasional clink of glass. For a fleeting moment, the chaos of Chicago felt distant, as though she'd stepped out of her life entirely.

But her thoughts refused to stay still. The Magician case lingered in the back of her mind, its dark details pressing against her attempts to relax. The Tarot cards, the cryptic connections, the growing public fear—each piece of the puzzle felt more personal with every passing day. And then there was the chief's constant pressure, a weight she carried with the same precision she carried everything else.

Sydney returned with the drinks.

Audrey's fingers curled around the margarita glass, the salt catching the light.

She took a slow sip. It helped, but it didn't erase the memories.

Josh. The cabin. That velvet box. She'd said yes—not because it felt right, but because she thought it should. He wanted the kind of life she admired in theory but had never truly wanted for herself. *You're amazing, Audrey, but you're always somewhere else*, he'd said one night, his voice heavy with frustration. *I need someone who's here, someone who isn't consumed by a job or a case.*

She'd argued at first, insisting she could be both—a dedicated detective and a supportive partner. But the truth was, she couldn't give him what he needed. And she hadn't fought him when the engagement ended, not because she didn't care, but because deep down, she'd known he was right.

Audrey leaned forward, setting the glass on the coffee table. Her eyes lingered on the salt-rimmed glass, the golden hue of the margarita catching the soft light. The drink was refreshing, vibrant, and deceptively simple—much like the façade she wore every day. She was always the one people leaned on, the one who never faltered under pressure. But lately, she felt like the ice melting in her glass—steady on the surface but slowly breaking apart underneath.

Her mind shifted to her own boundaries—ones she upheld so strictly yet questioned in moments like these.

Had she built walls to protect herself, or to keep others out?

Her recent choices, her willingness to push herself into exhaustion, to stay tethered to a job that demanded more than she could always give, made her wonder if she was running toward something—or simply running away.

She sighed, her gaze falling to the ornate rug beneath her feet.

She didn't know how to turn off the part of her that analyzed, that sought control.

Yet here she was, hundreds of miles from Chicago, trying to prove to herself that she could let go, even for just a weekend.

The sound of Sydney's voice broke through her reverie. "You look like you're solving a murder case over there," she teased. "Come on, Audrey. You're in California. That intense brooding thing doesn't work with all this sunshine."

Audrey smiled faintly. "Old habits," she murmured.

"Time to break them," Sydney said, plopping onto the couch beside her with dramatic flair. "And I mean it. We're going to give you the full California reset—beach, sun, cocktails, maybe even a cute surfer or two. You know, proper relaxation. You've got two options: stew in your own thoughts or let me force some fun on you."

Audrey chuckled despite herself. "I think I'm afraid of what your idea of fun entails."

"Good." Sydney gave her a look. "That means I'm doing it right."

The beach stretched endlessly, a painter's palette of vivid blues, golden sands, and the glistening white of foaming waves. Sydney led the way, her oversized sunglasses and dramatic hat making her look like a celebrity dodging the paparazzi.

"Why do I feel like I'm about to star in a sunscreen commercial?" Audrey quipped, adjusting the straps of her tote bag. The vibrant energy of the beach, with its cacophony of laughter, splashing water, and distant guitar music, was both alluring and slightly overwhelming.

"Because you're in California, darling," Sydney replied, spinning around with a grin. "And today, you're the leading lady. Now come on. The crew's waiting."

Audrey followed Sydney to a cluster of colorful blankets and umbrellas where her friends lounged in an arrangement that seemed effortlessly curated. Sydney's grand arrival caused an immediate stir.

Audrey tried to let the scene wash over her—the sunlit chatter, the carefree ease of these people who weren't weighed down by a job that demanded every ounce of them. But her mind refused to stay still. It kept circling back, grasping for control, for purpose. If she wasn't the detective, the responsible one, then who was she?

A sip of her margarita burned down her throat, its sweetness doing little to mask the taste of uncertainty.

"You're thinking again," Sydney accused, watching her over the rim of her glass. "Stop it."

Audrey exhaled sharply. "I'm just—"

"You're just trying to hold on," Sydney cut in, her tone light but her gaze serious. "Even here, even now, you're gripping the reins like someone's going to take them away."

Audrey opened her mouth, instinctively reaching for a deflection, but Sydney held up a hand.

"Aud," she said, quieter now. "What's the worst that happens if you let go?"

The words hit deeper than Audrey wanted to admit. She rolled them over in her mind, letting the question linger longer than she normally would.

"Look who finally decided to show up!" a voice rang out, belonging to a striking man who practically glided to his feet. His tan was flawless, his tank top clung just enough to leave a little to the imagination, and the look in his eye could only be described as wicked. "Audrey, right? I'm Casper. Style icon, gossip guru, and influencer."

Audrey blinked, unsure how to respond to the whirlwind introduction. "Um—nice to meet you?"

"Of course it is," Casper said, tossing his towel around his neck theatrically before collapsing back onto the blanket. "Sydney told me you were pretty, but she left out the whole enigmatic thing. I'm intrigued."

"Casper," Sydney warned.

"Please," he huffed. "They're lucky to bask in my glow."

"Speak for yourself," said a young woman with porcelain skin and deep red lipstick, peeking out from under an oversized sunhat. "Blair, but you can call me B. Aspiring Oscar winner, part-time diva, and full-time victim of terrible directors." She gestured toward Casper. "And an occasional babysitter to this one."

"Guilty," Casper admitted, holding up his drink.

Nearby, a shaggy-haired surfer raised his beer in greeting. "Chase," he said simply. "Marine biologist. They make me hang out with people sometimes."

"You love it," Sydney teased.

"Only because the ocean's too loud to hear Casper," Chase deadpanned, earning a loud laugh from Blair.

A quiet man seated cross-legged on a woven mat gave a small wave. "Eli," he said. "I'm in tech. Not as interesting as Casper, I'm afraid."

"Understatement of the century," Casper interjected. "He's a Silicon Valley king. The kind who makes apps and who I wish was my sugar daddy."

Eli rolled his eyes. "I make data systems. Hardly glamorous. Oh...and you wish!"

"You pay for brunch," Blair pointed out. "That's glamorous enough."

Audrey took another sip of her drink, letting the tangy sweetness linger. She had expected to feel awkward, but the group's easy banter was disarming.

"Alright, Miss Chicago," Casper said, his eyes gleaming. "Sydney says you're a big deal back home. Some hotshot detective? Spill the tea. What's the craziest thing you've seen?"

Sydney raised a hand like a referee. "She's on vacation, Casper. Let her decompress."

"Oh, fine," Casper said with exaggerated resignation. "But I'm filing a formal complaint. You know I live for juicy crime drama."

Audrey smiled faintly, the warmth of the group's energy melting away some of her initial apprehension. "You're not what I expected," she admitted.

Blair arched an eyebrow. "And what did you expect?"

Audrey shrugged. "I don't know... Something more predictable? But you're all—"

"Brilliant, sexy, and a little unstable?" Casper quipped.

"Sure," Audrey said, laughing softly. "Let's go with that."

Chase cracked open another beer, lounging lazily on the blanket. "Welcome to the circus. We're harmless. Mostly."

The conversation flowed effortlessly as the group shared stories. Casper launched into a vivid story of a yacht party gone wrong—one that involved an inflatable unicorn and a very drunk billionaire named Harold. Blair described the horror of filming an emotional scene in a freezing rainstorm, only for the director to scrap it entirely. Even Eli, who had been quiet, contributed an amusing anecdote about a company retreat that involved an obstacle course and a very angry CEO.

Audrey found herself laughing more freely than she had in weeks. The margarita helped, but it was the camaraderie that felt like a balm. These people weren't her colleagues or witnesses or suspects. Their ease was contagious. And in their presence, she let her guard drop, just enough to feel like herself again.

Sydney nudged her playfully. "See? I told you. California magic."

Audrey raised her glass, the salt on the rim a pleasant contrast to the sweetness of the drink. "You might be onto something."

The sun began its descent toward the horizon, casting a golden glow over the beach. The energy of the group remained vibrant; their laughter carried on the warm breeze. But Audrey found her focus drifting. The sound of the waves was soothing, yet her thoughts pulled her elsewhere—back to Chicago, back to the badge she carried, back to the Magician.

The Tarot cards flashed in her mind—their intricate designs and haunting implications. She imagined the King of Cups placed so deliberately at the scene, a silent taunt meant to unsettle. The symbolism still danced in her thoughts, their meaning elusive but insistent. Her fingers tapped rhythmically against the rim of her glass, an unconscious tell Sydney immediately caught.

"Stop." Sydney's voice cut through the noise, sharp but not unkind. Audrey blinked, startled, as her friend fixed her with a pointed look. "You're mentally cataloging suspects again, aren't you?"

Audrey hesitated, then sighed, a faint smile tugging at her lips. "Is it that obvious?"

"Painfully," Sydney said, leaning back on her elbows with dramatic flair. "Come on, Audrey. You're at the beach. There's literally no room for serial killers here unless they're hiding under the sand."

Blair, perched nearby, overheard and added with mock seriousness, "If there's a killer around, let me know. I've always wanted to try method acting for a crime drama."

Casper joined in, shaking his head. "I refuse to be in a Lifetime special. Too many unflattering close-ups."

Sydney laughed before turning back to Audrey, her tone softening. "Seriously though. You need to unplug, babe. Just for a little while. You're too good at your job, and that's not a compliment right now."

Audrey exhaled, the tension in her shoulders easing slightly under Sydney's insistence. She nodded, though her thoughts remained tangled. "I'll try."

"Good," Sydney said firmly, handing her another drink. "Start with this. It's scientifically proven that margaritas improve relaxation."

Audrey laughed despite herself, taking the glass. She watched the group, their carefree ease like a foreign language she was trying to learn. Blair and Casper were debating the merits of vintage fashion, while Chase and Eli exchanged quiet words about surfing conditions. It was all so light, so unburdened.

Something inside her stirred—an ache, not for their lives but for their freedom. She wondered what it would feel like to drop the weight she carried, even just for a moment. To act without planning, to speak without rehearsing, to let the tide take her wherever it wanted.

Her thoughts turned inward, unearthing memories she'd long buried. She had always been the responsible one, the planner, the protector. Even in her personal life, she had held herself to impossible standards. It was why her relationship with Josh had faltered—his frustrations with her control, her inability to let go, had widened a gulf between them until it swallowed everything.

And yet, here she was, on a beach surrounded by strangers, feeling the stirrings of something new. A spontaneity she rarely allowed herself to indulge, a recklessness that didn't seem to fit her carefully constructed image. It felt…familiar though. As if it had always been there, waiting.

Sydney's voice broke through her reverie. "You okay?"

Audrey met her gaze and nodded. "Yeah. Just thinking."

"Stop that," Sydney said with a crooked smile tugging at her lips. "Thinking is overrated. Be bold for once. Do something crazy. Shock me."

Audrey laughed, a sound that felt lighter than she expected. She watched the sun dip lower, painting the sky with streaks of pink and orange, and for the first time in a long while, she let herself consider it. The possibility of stepping outside her lines, just to see where it might take her.

As she sipped her drink, the edges of her mind began to blur, the constant churn of her thoughts slowing to something softer. There, in the warmth of the setting sun and the laughter of new friends, she began to feel the faintest echo of another life—a life that wasn't hers but somehow felt connected.

The idea was fleeting, a whisper on the wind. But it lingered, and for a moment, Audrey allowed herself to wonder.

Who might she be if she let herself break the rules, even just once?

Audrey and Sydney stepped out of the cab into the glittering chaos of the California nightlife. The club was already teeming with energy—a massive line snaked along the velvet ropes, the bass vibrating through the pavement. The neon sign above the entrance flickered with moody elegance, casting a kaleidoscope of color on the stylish crowd below.

Audrey instinctively straightened her posture, brushing invisible lint from her sleek black jumpsuit. She looked good—different, even. But as she stepped forward, a chill skated down her spine, a phantom sensation, like being watched. She shook it off. No one was watching her. Not here.

Sydney—ever the picture of confidence—strode forward like she owned the place. The bouncer, a towering man with arms thicker than tree trunks, gave her a subtle nod of recognition.

The dim glow of the blue lighting rippled over dark walls. Ornate glass fixtures caught the light like reflections on water.

Blue and silver. The same hues as the King of Cups card left at the last crime scene. The same cold, liquid shimmer. She exhaled sharply, forcing the image away.

Audrey raised an eyebrow. "You come here often?"

Sydney slid hand to her hip. "Let's just say I know people. And people know me."

The moment they stepped inside, Audrey felt her breath catch again—too tight, too sudden. The club shimmered in deep blue and silver, the lighting soft and fluid, casting reflections across the polished floors like ripples on water. It was elegant. Serene. *Wrong.*

The colors—the glint of mirrored walls, the soft, liquid gleam of glass beading across the VIP chains—reminded her, again, of the King of Cups card left at the last crime scene. Calm on the surface. Darkness waiting underneath. For a split second, the club seemed to tilt, warping at the edges like light bending beneath water. A chill swept over her, seeping beneath her skin, tugging her into memory—the blood-streaked walls, the eerie stillness of that room. Audrey's stomach flipped. Her breath came sharp. Then, just as quickly, she shoved the sensation down, gripping onto reality like a lifeline. *Not here. Not tonight.*

She exhaled sharply, blinking the illusion away. Just a club. Just another night. The music shifted as "Sweet Dreams" by the Eurythmics pulsed through the speakers. She let out a small, humorless laugh. The song felt like a taunt, a whisper from the past. Of course it would be playing now.

Audrey froze, mid-step.

And then she saw it.

A playing card on the floor. Face-down. It wasn't a Tarot card—it couldn't be. But the moment she bent down to pick it up, a flash of memory hit her like a gut punch—the last victim, his glassy eyes staring up, the King of Cups laid carefully beside him.

She let go of the card like it burned. It was nothing. Just a random club discard.

But the panic sat in her chest, sharp and unshakable.

"Oh my God!" Sydney squealed, grabbing Audrey's hand and pulling her toward the dance floor. "This is our song!"

Audrey forced a smile, letting Sydney pull her into the crowd. She wasn't going to let things get to her. But her pulse refused to slow.

Sydney's enthusiasm was impossible to resist. They moved with abandon, singing along to every word. Audrey felt alive— almost.

A server approached them with a tray, and Sydney snapped up two drinks without missing a beat. She handed one to Audrey, raising her glass in a toast. "To breaking free."

Audrey hesitated. Just for a second.

Sydney noticed. She always noticed.

"Jesus, Audrey," she said, exasperated but not unkind. "It's a drink, not a damn life commitment."

Audrey sighed, taking the glass. "I know. I just—"

"You just don't know how to let yourself have something that doesn't come with consequences," Sydney finished for her. "Even when you want to."

Audrey's jaw tightened. "That's not—"

"Isn't it?" Sydney arched a brow. "Because I'm pretty sure you've been white-knuckling your entire life since the moment you got your badge."

Audrey exhaled through her nose, gripping her drink tighter than necessary. "I know how to have fun, Syd."

"Prove it." Sydney clinked her glass against Audrey's, meeting her gaze head-on. "One night. One drink. No second-guessing. Just let yourself exist."

As the song shifted to an upbeat remix, she found herself laughing harder, her body loosening with every sip.

She didn't notice him at first—leaning casually against the bar, his sharp eyes fixed on her. He was striking in his simplicity: a tailored black blazer over a white t-shirt, his posture relaxed but confident. His dark eyes held a magnetic intensity that sent a thrill up her spine.

It wasn't that he was staring—it was how patient he looked. Still. Collected. Like he had all the time in the world.

And yet…something tugged at her. A flicker of familiarity, just out of reach.

Audrey frowned slightly, tilting her head as if looking at him from another angle might unlock the memory. *Do I know you?*

The thought vanished as quickly as it appeared. It was the drink. The dim lighting. The way attraction sometimes tricked the mind into *believing* recognition.

Sydney, ever the wingman, nudged her subtly. "Tall, dark, and brooding at your three o'clock. I think he likes what he sees."

Audrey rolled her eyes but couldn't suppress her smile. The heat of his gaze didn't falter, and for a fleeting moment, she felt the weight of the breakup with Josh lift. It felt good—liberating—to be noticed again.

The man leaned casually against the bar, the soft gleam of his watch catching the low light as he lifted his drink. His scent reached her before his words did—a mix of warm cedar and something faintly spiced, like the ghost of a lit cigar. Not overpowering. Just enough to linger.

His voice was the same. Low. Unhurried. The kind of voice that made you lean in, even when you knew better. "You seem like you're having fun," he said, finally closing the space between them.

Audrey raised her drink, tilting her head. "I guess I am. For once."

"For once?" he echoed, curiosity flickering across his features.

"Long week," she said simply.

He smiled. "Well then, you're overdue." He extended a hand. "Jack."

Audrey hesitated—just for a second. Something about the way he held himself, the way he was completely at ease, made her pulse quicken.

"Jack?" she repeated, arching a brow. "That's my dad's name."

He chuckled, unfazed. "And is that a dealbreaker?"

"Depends," she said, shaking his hand. His grip was warm, firm—the kind that told her he was used to being in control. "Audrey."

Jack's fingers lingered a beat longer than necessary before releasing. Not a test. A promise.

"Nice to meet you, Audrey." The way he said her name sent heat curling low in her stomach.

They began to dance, the space between them electric but unpressured. Jack was confident but not arrogant, moving with her in an effortless rhythm. As they swayed to the music, Audrey noticed how he watched her—not with the intensity that suffocated, but with a quiet magnetism that made her feel seen.

Another round of drinks appeared in Sydney's hands, and she pressed a glass into Audrey's. "Keep it going, girl!" she shouted over the music.

Audrey threw back half the drink, the alcohol dulling the edges of her control, making everything feel looser, warmer. She caught Jack's eye again and let herself sink into the moment. No second-guessing. No analyzing. Just…feeling.

The music slowed, bass thrumming through the floor, wrapping around them. Jack leaned in, voice low and deliberate. "You've got an energy about you."

"That so?" Audrey asked, tilting her head.

"Yeah." His gaze never wavered. "Something that makes it hard to look away."

A thrill coiled through her—not just from his words but from the freedom of this moment. She wasn't Detective Holliday here. She wasn't a walking case file.

She let her fingers trace the rim of her glass.

"Come on," Jack murmured, a challenge in his tone. "Let's get out of here."

Audrey hesitated.

Her mind flickered back to Chicago, to the never-ending weight of her badge pressing against her hip, to the quiet of her apartment where sleep never came easy. The crime scene photos she still saw when she closed her eyes. The promises she never kept to herself.

She had spent so long holding her life in a vise-grip, afraid that if she let go, even for a second, everything would fall apart.

Maybe it already had.

Maybe letting go was the only thing she hadn't tried.

She met Sydney's gaze across the dance floor. Her friend tilted her head, waiting. Daring her.

Audrey took a breath, let it fill her lungs, then exhaled— letting something uncoil in her chest as she turned toward Jack.

"Not yet," she said softly. "Stay a little longer."

As the night deepened, the club's energy only seemed to heighten. Audrey let herself get lost in it—the music, the lights, the easy flow of conversation with Jack. For the first time in what felt like forever, she wasn't defined by her job, her breakup, or the weight of expectations. She was just…Audrey.

Sydney caught her arm as they took a breather at the bar. "I told you," she said with a knowing grin. "California works wonders."

Audrey glanced over her shoulder at Jack, who was waiting patiently with a fresh drink in hand. A flicker of excitement and uncertainty coursed through her, but for once, she let it linger without trying to name it.

"Maybe you're right," she said, her smile genuine.

The crowd had thinned just enough to give the club a slightly more intimate feel, and Audrey found herself perched on one of the plush barstools near the edge of the room. Jack leaned against the counter beside her, his hand loosely cradling a whiskey glass, his focus entirely on her.

"So, what brings you to California?" he asked, his voice pitched just above the music. The question was casual, but his tone carried genuine curiosity.

Audrey swirled the last sip of her drink, her fingers toying with the rim of the glass. "Escaping," she admitted, her voice softer now, less guarded. "Needed to get out of my head for a bit."

Jack nodded, his dark eyes steady on hers. "Work?"

"Life," she corrected with a faint smile, though she didn't elaborate. "What about you? You don't seem like the type to blend into a crowd like this."

He chuckled, taking a slow sip of his drink. "Guilty. I'm more of a spectator than a participant, but tonight felt...different."

Audrey raised an eyebrow. "Different how?"

His gaze flicked to hers and the playful mask slipped, revealing something more raw, more real. "You."

A single word hung between them, and Audrey felt her pulse quicken. Her usual instinct was to deflect, to push away anything that felt too real, too personal. But here, in the haze of the music and the alcohol, she let herself lean into it.

"Careful," she said, her tone teasing but her expression serious. "I might believe you."

Jack's lips curved into a small smile, but he didn't respond immediately. Instead, he reached for her hand, his touch light but deliberate. "Would that be such a bad thing?"

The question lingered, and Audrey felt the pull of the moment—the way the air seemed heavier, charged with a kind of electricity she hadn't felt in a long time. She didn't answer. Instead, she stood, her hand still in his, and gave a small tilt of her head toward the door.

He didn't hesitate. As they began to weave their way toward the exit, Audrey caught Sydney's eye from across the dance floor, lifting her drink slightly in a silent farewell. Sydney, ever the mischief-maker, chuckled and mouthed, *Behave*—though her wink suggested she hoped otherwise. Audrey let out a breathy sigh, slipping her phone from her purse and typing a quick message.

I owe you brunch for this one. Don't wait up.

They left the club, stepping into the balmy night, the neon glow fading behind them. The street hummed with life—distant laughter, the occasional honk, the rhythmic bass still reverberating from inside. But as they walked, the noise melted away, replaced by something quieter. Something heavier.

The boardwalk stretched ahead, the wooden planks warm beneath their steps. Beyond it, the beach opened into a silvered expanse under the moonlight, the tide rolling in with a rhythmic hush.

Jack's footsteps were oddly quiet for someone his size. Audrey glanced down, but the sand barely held any impression. Probably nothing—just the breeze playing tricks. She didn't like how easily her brain tried to explain it away.

"You're not used to this, are you?" Jack's voice was low, but there was no teasing in it.

Audrey glanced at him. "Used to what?"

Jack studied her, eyes glinting in the half-dark. "Letting go."

She huffed a quiet laugh. "That obvious?"

Jack smiled, shaking his head. "It's not a bad thing. But even now—you're holding onto something."

Audrey hesitated, gaze drifting to the horizon.

The air smelled like salt, thick with ocean mist.

She knew he was right. She had spent so long gripping control so tightly, she barely knew what it felt like to just…exist.

"It's complicated," she finally said.

"It always is," Jack murmured.

For a beat, neither of them spoke. The waves lapped at the shore, and a few late-night wanderers dotted the sand in the distance, their laughter blending with the wind.

Jack exhaled, shifting his weight before reaching for her hand. Not forceful. Not demanding. Just offering.

Audrey stared at his hand for a second too long. His touch was warm. Familiar. Too familiar? She blinked, shaking off the ridiculous thought. She didn't know him. Not really. But something about the way he looked at her made her wonder if he did.

Then, before she could think herself out of it, she slipped her fingers into his.

The Uber ride back was quiet, but not uncomfortable. Audrey's pulse thrummed in her wrists, her chest. The tension sat between them, unspoken, crackling under the hum of the radio. Jack's thumb traced slow, absent-minded circles against her skin, and she let it happen.

She didn't let go when they stepped out of the car either.

Sydney's bungalow sat perched on the hillside, porch light dimmed. The stillness of the neighborhood contrasted the rush of adrenaline still coursing through her veins.

Jack's hand brushed against hers again, deliberate now. Audrey felt the heat of it through her skin, the charge buzzing at the edges of her restraint.

She exhaled. Then, making a decision she wouldn't let herself overanalyze, she led him toward the side entrance.

The gravel crunched beneath their steps, the night air thick with jasmine and ocean breeze. The darkness only heightened the awareness curling in her stomach, the weight of his gaze on her as they reached the door.

Audrey turned the handle, stepping inside.

The warm glow of the lamp flickered on, casting soft shadows across the room. Jack lingered in the doorway for half a second before following, his eyes drinking her in like he was memorizing every detail.

He stepped closer.

Audrey's pulse skipped.

Then, with deliberate ease, Jack reached out, brushing a strand of hair behind her ear. His fingers barely ghosted against her skin, but the sensation sent a shiver down her spine.

Something in her stilled.

And when she met his gaze again, she knew—this was a choice.

Their lips met, slow at first—a question, not an answer.

Jack's fingers brushed against her jaw; his touch deliberate but waiting. Audrey felt the moment stretch too long—just enough for hesitation to creep in.

He noticed.

"You always this careful?" Jack's voice was quiet, but there was something else underneath—something that made her stomach tighten.

Audrey exhaled sharply, her grip tightening on the fabric of his shirt. "I don't do this."

Jack studied her, his thumb trailing just beneath her chin. "Then do it anyway."

She didn't know if it was the challenge in his voice, the tension coiled tight between them, or the fact that for once, she didn't want to be careful.

Audrey leaned into him, exhaling softly as he pulled her closer. His body was firm against hers, heat radiating between them, something slow and deliberate in the way he kissed her.

His hands slipped down to her waist, fingers curling over the fabric of her jumpsuit a quiet ask before moving lower. She pulled him closer, feeling his hard cock beneath his clothes, the way he felt solid—real—against her.

Audrey slid her fingers under his jacket, pushing it from his shoulders. It landed somewhere behind them, forgotten. She made quick work of the buttons on his shirt, feeling the ridges of his stomach as she dragged her hands over bare skin.

Jack's fingers traced the hem of her jumpsuit, lowering it inch by inch until somehow it was pooling onto the floor.

She didn't think. Or, at least, she tried not to.

For half a second, something wavered inside her—a whisper of caution, of everything she was supposed to be.

Detective Holliday wouldn't do this.

But right now, she wasn't just Detective Holliday. She was a woman who wanted to feel something other than responsibility.

And so, she let herself fall and get lost in the press of his body, the rasp of his breath against her collarbone, the way his lips followed the path of her pulse.

As they broke apart for air, Jack's eyes locked onto hers, burning with a fierce desire. "I want you," he whispered, his voice low and husky.

Audrey felt a surge of excitement at his words, her body responding to the raw hunger in his voice. She nodded silently, helplessly drawn into the night, pulled toward him as if by an unseen force. This time there was no need for words—their bodies spoke louder than any language could express. With a quiet growl of satisfaction, he swept Audrey into his arms, lifting her off the ground and depositing her gently back into the bed.

His hands cradled her curves, and Audrey's body tensed as the back of her legs hit the edge of the bed. In the darkened space, she let herself surrender. Their bodies moved in sync, a slow push and pull—like the tide rolling against the shore, relentless and consuming. The world outside receded further still, leaving only the two of them lost in this whirlwind of sensuality.

With each passing moment, their movements became more urgent, more primal. They were two people consumed by desire, driven by a hunger that could only be sated by each other.

The faint sound of birds chirping filtered through the curtains, mixing with the warm glow of the early morning sun. Audrey stretched in bed, the memories of the night before unfolding in her mind like a dream. She felt light—untethered. She glanced over at the empty pillow beside her, hearing soft footsteps and the faint creak of the side door.

Jack was an expert in quiet escapes—or so he thought.

As he eased the door open, barefoot and shirt half-buttoned, Audrey heard Sydney's voice cut through the silence like a gunshot.

"And where exactly do you think you're going, Loverboy?"

Audrey leaned up in bed and looked through the partially open door. She saw Jack stiffen, then exhale, shaking his head as he turned around.

"Jesus, you nearly gave me a heart attack."

Sydney, perched against the porch railing, coffee in one hand, phone in the other, stared like she'd been *waiting* for this moment. "Good. Consider it a test. If you were really gonna sneak out on my best friend, you at least need to have the decency to fail at it."

Jack chuckled, rubbing the back of his neck. "Not sneaking out. Just…avoiding the awkward morning-after interrogation."

Sydney arched a brow. "Oh, sweetheart, *this* is the interrogation."

Jack sighed, running a hand through his hair. "Alright. Hit me with it."

Sydney took a slow sip of coffee, watching him over the rim of her mug before casually asking, "So…where'd you say you're from again?"

"Here and there." He shrugged. "I move around a lot."

Sydney hummed. "Funny. You don't have an accent."

Jack barely laughed. "Not everyone does."

Sydney's gaze sharpened. "Right. And what do you do again?"

He took a beat too long before answering. "Consulting."

Sydney's lips curled like a cat who smelled a lie. "Vague. Mysterious. Classic."

Jack flashed a grin. "You should be a cop."

Sydney grinned. "That's Audrey's job. You should be less suspicious."

For the briefest moment, Jack's knuckles tightened where they rested on the doorframe. Then, he relaxed. Too quickly.

Jack grinned. "Do I get to leave now, or is there an exit fee?"

Sydney took another sip of coffee. "Yeah. You owe me an oat milk latte, and if I ever see you again, you'd better be bringing flowers." Sydney watched him go, a quiet *hmm* escaping her lips.

Jack gave her a mock salute, shaking his head as he walked off, leaving Sydney smirking to herself as she turned back toward the house.

In the bedroom, Audrey sat back in bed and ran her hand over the empty pillow, her fingers tracing the fabric absently before catching herself. *Stop it.* Sydney was the one overanalyzing things this morning. She was letting it all go.

This wasn't a thing. This wasn't her.

Except, maybe…it was.

Still, her body had tensed when she heard the front door click shut. It was fine—normal. But the quiet that followed felt too complete, like something had been erased.

So why was she still thinking about him? She didn't even know what he did for work. Or if Jack was even his real name. That should've bothered her more.

Audrey sighed, reaching for her phone as it buzzed.

Sydney: *Morning, sunshine. Hope Loverboy wasn't too disappointing.*

Audrey rolled her eyes.

Sydney: *Also, just so you know, he tried to sneak out. Like a damn teenager. You're welcome.*

Her stomach did a slow flip as she told herself it was just leftover adrenaline. But the way Jack had slipped out...it didn't feel like someone she was done with.

Moments later, Audrey emerged from her room, her hair tousled and a soft, almost dreamy smile lingering on her lips.

She stopped short when she saw Sydney lounging on the crimson velvet couch, sipping her coffee with the air of someone preparing to drop a bombshell. "So? Spill. Was it worth breaking your 'no fun' streak?"

Audrey sat down, grabbing one of the throw pillows and hugging it to her chest. "It was...liberating," she admitted, the words feeling strange but good on her tongue. "I didn't overthink it. I just let myself—"

"Feel?" Sydney finished for her, her tone uncharacteristically gentle. "Good for you, Aud. About damn time."

Audrey laughed, tossing the pillow at her.

"But seriously, I'm proud of you. Not just for last night. For letting go. You've been carrying so much for so long. You deserve a break," Sydney said, catching the pillow effortlessly.

Audrey leaned back, her laughter fading into a softer smile. "I don't know who I was last night, but I think I liked her."

Sydney raised her coffee mug in a mock toast. "To the new Audrey—bold, fearless, and apparently a magnet for guys that have names starting with the letter J."

Audrey laughed, shaking her head. "It's funny though. I never thought I'd do something like this. It's not...me."

Sydney tilted her head, studying her friend. "Maybe it is, and you're just starting to figure that out. Or maybe it's just a side of you that you don't let out often enough. Either way, own it."

As they sat in the sunlight filtering through the living room windows, Audrey felt a strange mix of empowerment and curiosity. The spontaneity of the night had cracked open something inside her—a part of herself she rarely let breathe.

And though she couldn't put her finger on it, there was an odd sense of connection in the air, as if this new version of herself wasn't so new after all, but something she'd always been on the edge of discovering.

Later that night, the patio glowed under a string of warm fairy lights, their soft illumination mirrored by the stars scattered across the California sky. The ocean breeze whispered through the potted plants and wind chimes.

Sydney leaned back in the oversized wicker chair, her wine glass cradled in one hand, while Audrey curled up on the cushioned bench, staring at the night sky.

"You really know how to create a moment," Audrey murmured. The night felt like a balm, but her thoughts still had edges, sharp enough to cut.

Sydney swirled her wine. "Please, this? This is just a Tuesday. Wait until you see what I pull out next time."

Audrey let out a quiet chuckle, but Sydney's gaze lingered, studying her in the flickering light. Then, softer: "It's strange," Audrey began, her voice quiet. "You think you know someone, and then one day it all feels...hollow."

Sydney tilted her head, observing her friend with a mix of curiosity and concern. "You're talking about your ex-fiancé?"

Audrey nodded, a faint smile tugging at her lips. "I thought Josh and I were building something solid, you know? We had plans—our own place, a wedding, the works. Then suddenly, it's like he wasn't the man I knew anymore."

"Or maybe he was always that man, and you just didn't want to see it," Sydney said, her tone blunt but not unkind.

Audrey glanced at her, startled, then let out a soft laugh. "You don't pull punches, do you?"

"Why should I? You deserve better than some guy who couldn't keep up." Sydney leaned forward, her expression softening. "You're a hurricane in heels. Some men see that and run because they can't handle the storm."

"It wasn't just him," Audrey admitted, her voice faltering. "I wasn't exactly easy to live with. The late nights, the case files all over the house, me snapping at him because I was too exhausted to talk. It wore him down."

Sydney shook her head, her dark hair spilling over her shoulder. "Josh might've been a decent guy, but if he couldn't see past all that to who you are, then screw him."

Audrey chuckled, a genuine laugh this time. "That's what I told myself when I pawned the engagement ring."

Sydney's mouth fell open in mock shock. "You didn't."

"Oh, I did. Got a decent payout too. I used it to pay for a weekend getaway. I figured if he could ruin my future plans, I could at least ruin his."

Sydney burst out laughing, nearly spilling her wine. "That's my girl. Ruthless when it counts."

Audrey's laughter faded into a contemplative smile. "I don't know, Syd. Sometimes I wonder if I'm the problem. If I expect too much from people."

Sydney sat up, her expression turning serious. "You're not the problem. You're just...complex. And maybe that intimidates people. But it doesn't mean you should settle."

Audrey looked down at her glass, her fingers tracing the rim. "I miss him sometimes. Not the fights or the tension—just...having someone who cared."

"You have me," Sydney said, her voice teasing but warm. "Granted, I'm not husband material, but I've got charm for days."

Audrey laughed, the sound soft but genuine. "That you do."

Sydney teased. "Maybe we should pull a Tarot card for you."

Audrey exhaled sharply, not amused. "Please don't."

But Sydney was already reaching into her bag, pulling out a travel-sized Tarot deck with a flourish. "It's fate, babe. I brought them with me."

She shuffled lazily, then plucked a single card from the deck, holding it up between two fingers. "Well, well."

Audrey didn't want to look. But she did.

The Hanged Man.

The figure dangled upside down, suspended by one foot, his expression eerily serene. Audrey's stomach twisted.

"Suspended between two worlds, waiting for clarity," Sydney mused, sipping her wine. "That sounds about right, doesn't it?"

Audrey swallowed, her mouth suddenly dry. It was just a coincidence. Just Sydney screwing around.

And yet, she couldn't shake the feeling that the card had chosen her.

Audrey scoffed, but there was something in the way her grip tightened on her wine glass.

"You're afraid of what happens when this case is over, aren't you?"

Audrey froze. The words hit deeper than she expected.

"You think if you stop running, you'll have to actually feel it," Sydney continued, voice quieter now, stripped of its usual mischief. "The exhaustion. The grief. The fact that you don't even know what a life outside of this job looks like."

Audrey lifted her wine glass. "Damn. That's a little heavy for beachside philosophy."

"That's a little heavy for you," Sydney corrected. "And you hate heavy. That's why you keep diving headfirst into a case you can't solve, into a job that eats you alive, into…" She paused, tilting her head. "Men who don't matter."

Audrey's jaw tightened. "You don't know that."

Sydney sighed, setting her glass down. "I know that if Jack wasn't a distraction, you wouldn't be arguing with me right now." Her laughter played at the corners of her mouth. "Alright. So let's talk about someone who actually keeps up with you."

Audrey raised an eyebrow. "Oh God. Who?"

"Eddie."

Audrey scoffed, a little too quickly. "Eddie? Please."

Sydney just watched her, taking a slow sip of wine before speaking again. "You ever notice how he looks at you?"

Audrey shifted in her seat, feigning indifference. "We're partners. That's it."

Sydney tilted her head, studying her like a scientist watching an experiment unfold. "So if I went for him, you wouldn't care?"

Audrey snorted, lifting her glass. "Do whatever you want."

"Huh," Sydney mused, swirling the wine in her glass. "You say that like you mean it. But your face just twitched."

Audrey's grip on the stem of her glass tightened. "No it didn't."

Sydney grinned like a shark that had detected blood. "Oh, babe. It so did."

Sydney watched her for a beat longer, like she was waiting for something. But when Audrey didn't take the bait, she just clinked their glasses together.

"Good to know."

Chapter 12

The Mirror Between Us

The entrance to Obsidian Health Group exuded the same understated sophistication that defined its head, Dr. Eve De la Gardie. The sleek black-and-silver lettering stood out boldly against the frosted glass doors. Floor-to-ceiling windows framed an overcast skyline, diffusing soft light across the modern but inviting space. Leather chairs were arranged in careful symmetry, and a faint scent of lavender lingered in the air—a curated calm Audrey immediately distrusted. This space was clearly designed to soothe even the most troubled minds.

Audrey stepped through the doors first, her sharp gaze sweeping the lobby with practiced efficiency. Despite her exhaustion, she carried herself with that unflinching confidence that came from years on the force. Eddie trailed behind, less graceful but no less observant, hands shoved into the pockets of his coat as his eyes flicked around.

"Swanky joint," Eddie remarked, nudging her elbow. "You think their therapist couches are fancier than ours?"

Humor laced Audrey's tone. "We don't have couches, Eddie. Just that chair in the corner that smells like someone's leftover lunch."

The receptionist was a poised young woman who offered an efficient greeting then led them down a hallway lined with polished hardwood floors and framed degrees.

"Dr. Larkin will see you now."

They followed her through the quiet corridors, the air carrying faint traces of lavender and mint. The farther they walked, the more Eddie's usual chatter died down, replaced by an unspoken tension. The Magician case hung over both of them like heavy fog, but there was something else—something intangible that Audrey couldn't quite place.

The receptionist pushed open a door to reveal Dr. Larkin standing behind a polished mahogany desk, his hands resting on an open file. Beside him stood Eve De la Gardie.

Audrey's didn't move.

It was her.

Not someone who resembled her. Not someone with a vague likeness. This was her face—staring back at her from across the room. But her blonde hair swept back into a chignon. Her asymmetrical black dress, accented with gold buttons along one side, screamed fashion and money.

Eve turned, an iPad in her hand, her gaze sharp and observant. Her professional smile was carefully composed, but the moment her eyes locked onto Audrey, the iPad slipped from her fingers.

Her professional smile faltered. Audrey saw her own shock reflected back at her, like an emotion she wasn't ready to claim. Her stomach flipped, her body bracing instinctively, like she was in danger—except she wasn't. This wasn't a threat.

It was a revelation.

Audrey's breath came shallow and sharp. Her vision narrowed, the room blurring at the edges. This wasn't just seeing someone who looked like her—it was seeing herself outside of her own body. A crack in reality.

Not a mirror. Not a trick. A person.

Audrey's fingers twitched at her side, but she didn't move.

"Uh…" Eddie's voice shattered the silence. "Did I drink something weird, or are there two of you?"

Audrey elbowed him. "Shut up, Eddie."

No one said a word. The room seemed to contract, the air thickening as Audrey and Eve stared at each other. The identical features—the same sharp jawline, high cheekbones, and piercing eyes—created a mirror neither woman had ever expected to see.

Eve's sharp, analytical eyes widened in disbelief as she stared at Audrey—her reflection, standing across the room. Only Audrey's hair was slightly tousled from her day, her features lined with fatigue.

Dr. Larkin recovered first, glancing between them with bewilderment. "You two…you're—"

He couldn't finish the sentence.

Eve took an involuntary step forward, her typically steady hands trembling as she reached out. "This…can't be real," she whispered, the words barely audible.

Audrey couldn't move. The logical part of her mind screamed for answers—*Who is this woman? Why does she look exactly like me?* But all she could do was stare as Eve's hand brushed, almost reverently, against her cheek. It was as if Eve needed physical confirmation that Audrey was flesh and blood.

The tension shattered as Eddie let out a low breath. "Okay, what the hell is going on here?" He looked back and forth between Audrey and Eve, his usual wit subdued. "Someone want to explain this, or are we all just going to stand here like statues?"

Eve drew her hand back sharply, as if burned. Her mask returned, though cracks showed through.

"This...doesn't make sense," Eve murmured, her brows furrowing. "Are we—" She cut herself off, as if afraid to say the word.

Audrey flinched at the contact, her eyes filling with tears she hadn't expected. "Twins?" The words cracked through her throat, her voice splintered with awe and confusion.

Eve blinked, her throat bobbing as she swallowed. "I—I don't know."

Eddie blinked, processing, then muttered under his breath, "This is some serious *Parent Trap* shit."

The joke landed like a pin in a grenade. Dr. Larkin shot Eddie a glare that could peel paint, but Lydia, who had quietly entered the room moments earlier, spoke up. "I've seen this on TikTok," she said, her tone somewhere between fascination and disbelief. "People meeting their long-lost siblings. It always ends in ugly crying."

Audrey let out an unsteady breath that could've been a laugh—or a sob—while Eddie gave Lydia a look. "You're not helping, lady."

"I'm serious!" she insisted, though her voice softened.

Eve turned sharply away, her back to the room as she braced herself against the desk.

Dr. Larkin, ever the professional, cleared his throat to regain control of the room. "There...clearly needs to be a conversation. But perhaps this isn't the time or place—"

Eve straightened abruptly, cutting him off. "O'Connor will take over the case," she said, her voice clipped but unsteady. "I—I can't—" She turned toward Audrey again, and though her expression was blank, her eyes betrayed her turmoil. "This is too much."

Audrey's throat tightened. Every instinct screamed for her to demand answers—to demand Eve stay and explain—but the look in Eve's eyes stopped her. It was like staring into her own reflection and seeing her most fragile self exposed.

"Eve," Audrey whispered, the name strange on her tongue.

Eve looked away, her professional mask slipping further. "I need some time," she murmured before brushing past them toward the door, leaving the room heavy with everything unsaid.

Audrey watched her leave, her heart pounding as though she'd just run a marathon. Her thoughts were a storm— questions piling up faster than she could process. Who was Eve? Why hadn't they known about each other? And what did this mean for her own identity?

Eddie's voice finally broke the silence.

"Well... I don't know what the hell that was, but I'm pretty sure it wasn't in the case file."

Audrey turned toward him, but her gaze was distant. "We need to talk," she murmured to herself, her voice soft but certain. "Soon."

The café Eve had chosen was almost laughably over the top. Polished marble counters, gold accents, and glass pastry displays so pristine that Audrey wondered if fingerprints were considered a crime here. It was the kind of place where a latte cost enough to make you question your life choices—and exactly the kind of place Audrey imagined Eve would pick.

Eve sat primly across the table, her back straight, hands curled around a porcelain cup. Her immaculate appearance made Audrey feel more disheveled in her jeans and oversized winter jacket.

As Eve stirred her latte absently, eyes narrowed over the rim of her cup, Audrey approached. Eve's sharp gaze tracked her movements, narrowing slightly.

"You're late," she observed, though her tone lacked judgement

Audrey plopped into the chair with zero grace.

"Traffic," she deadpanned. "And I needed time to psych myself up for the sticker shock of this place. Do they charge for oxygen too?"

Eve's lips twitched, the corner of her mouth threatening to curve into a smile. "You seem far more concerned with the menu than meeting your long-lost twin."

Audrey lifted a brow with amusement. "I can multi-task."

Her gaze flickered to Eve's cup. "Let me guess—something herbal. Chamomile, maybe?"

Eve raised an eyebrow, clearly assessing her. "You strike me as a 'coffee, black, with too much sugar' kind of woman."

Audrey feigned offense. "Not even close. I'm a latte girl. It's all about the froth." She leaned in conspiratorially. "But I'm sweet enough as it is."

A small, dry laugh escaped Eve, breaking through her practiced exterior. She lifted her cup pointedly. "Well, we have one thing in common. I'm a latte girl too."

Audrey blinked, surprised. "Seriously?"

Eve took a measured sip and shrugged with an air of mock nonchalance. "A little sweetness and froth go a long way."

Audrey snorted, unable to help herself. "Well, you just got about ten percent more likable."

Eve tilted her head, her lips quirking. "I'll take that as a win."

Audrey paused, something tugging at the edges of her memory. "You know, this isn't the first time I've been near you."

Eve frowned slightly. "What do you mean?"

Audrey leaned back, shaking her head. "A couple of months ago, I was at a café—probably just as ridiculous as this one—and the barista mentioned someone who looked just like me had been there. I laughed it off, figured I was sleep-deprived and she was messing with me."

Eve's brows furrowed. "Wait…the café on LaSalle?"

Audrey snapped her fingers. "That's the one."

Eve's eyes widened. "I was there that day. That's my usual spot after therapy sessions."

Audrey's voice tinged with something reflective. "You walked out right before I got there. I remember because the barista said something about how striking you looked. And I remember catching this faint whiff of orange blossom when I stepped inside."

Eve blinked in surprise. "My perfume. Orange blossom and neroli—it's been my signature for years."

Audrey tilted her head, a flicker of something warm passing through her. "Funny. That's one of my favorite scents too."

For a beat, neither of them said anything, both caught in the weight of the strange connection.

Audrey finally broke it. "I guess we should just...say it out loud. This is insane, right?"

Eve met her gaze, her carefully composed mask faltering slightly. "Insane would be an understatement."

For a moment, neither of them spoke. Audrey's eyes traced Eve's face—her face—searching for flaws, differences, anything to ground her in some reality. But the resemblance was staggering: the sharp cheekbones, the slope of the nose, the shape of their mouths. It was like looking in a mirror that reflected an alternate version of herself.

"I never thought I'd have a twin," Audrey said quietly. "Never even crossed my mind."

Eve's fingers tightened subtly around her cup. "Me neither. I mean, biologically, I always knew I was adopted, but my parents...they were clear there were no siblings. Or so they said."

Audrey swallowed hard, her voice brittle. "Mine too."

A beat of silence passed, both women grappling with the implications. Audrey leaned back, her arms crossed, a defensive barrier forming as she stared at the table. "So, what now? We just...pretend this didn't happen?"

Eve exhaled sharply, her fingers tracing the edge of her saucer. "I don't know what happens now. But pretending isn't an option, is it?"

Audrey shrugged, her voice dipping. "It's worked for thirty-some years so far."

The tension broke with Eve's soft laugh—dry but genuine. "That's one way to look at it." She sobered quickly, fixing her sharp gaze on Audrey. "We should get a DNA test. It's the logical next step."

Audrey's stomach twisted at the suggestion, though she wasn't sure why. "You think I need proof?"

"No," Eve said quickly. Her voice wavered with something raw, something real. "But this isn't just about us, Audrey. If this is true, there's a bigger question here—if we're identical…then someone made a choice to separate us. A deliberate one."

Audrey looked away, fingers curling into the sleeves of her jacket. "I don't know if I'm ready for those answers."

Eve tilted her head slightly, studying Audrey. "You're a detective. Isn't digging for answers what you do?"

"That's different," Audrey shot back, her tone sharper than she'd intended. "This isn't some case file. This is my life. Our lives."

Eve paused, her composed veneer cracking. "Do you think I want this? My entire life has been built on a foundation I thought I understood. Now…" She trailed off, searching for words. "Now I'm questioning everything—my parents, my choices…who I even am."

Something in Eve's voice softened Audrey's defenses. She sighed, her shoulders sagging slightly. "Fine. We'll do the test."

Eve's brows lifted in faint surprise. "You're sure?"

"No." Audrey let out a small, humorless laugh. "But I think we'd regret it if we didn't."

Eve nodded once, locking in the decision. "I'll arrange it. Discreetly."

Audrey arched a brow. "Everything you do is discreet, isn't it?"

"It's a habit." Eve took a sip of her latte, her hand steady again, though her eyes were anything but calm.

"Rough around the edges?" Audrey offered.

"Grounded," Eve corrected, surprising her.

Audrey blinked, caught off guard. "Oh. Well, that's thanks to my dad. He was a cop. Tough as nails, but he cared." A small, wistful smile touched her lips. "He taught me that showing up for people matters more than anything. Even when it's hard."

Eve stared at her, processing the words with an intensity that made Audrey shift in her seat. "He sounds...remarkable."

"He is." Audrey hesitated, then returned the volley. "What about you? What were your parents like?"

Eve set her cup down carefully, her voice quieter now. "They loved me. In their way. But expectations were everything in my house. Grades, achievements...appearances." She paused, as if debating whether to say more. "It wasn't warm, but it was stable. I guess I learned to excel because it's what they valued most."

Audrey studied her. "So that's why you turned out so... polished."

Eve gave a wry smile. "And you turned out so...unpolished."

For a moment, they both stared at each other, then burst out laughing—soft, almost fragile, but real. The sound startled Audrey with how natural it felt, like they'd shared it for years instead of minutes.

"God, this is weird," Audrey muttered, wiping at her eyes.

Eve smiled faintly, a warmth in her gaze that hadn't been there before. "It's beyond weird. But...maybe it's a good weird."

Audrey met her gaze, something unspoken passing between them. "Yeah. Me too."

The café had mostly emptied by the time their conversation shifted again, leaving only the faint clink of dishes behind the counter. Audrey watched Eve across the table—the perfect latte art in her cup long forgotten as she stared absently into the foam, her brow drawn tight.

It had been a lot to process. For both of them.

"You know what's funny?" Audrey said suddenly, breaking the quiet. "You."

Eve's head snapped up, her sharp gaze landing on Audrey. "What?"

Audrey gestured between them. "For someone so put together, you seem a little rattled."

Eve's lips twitched in a faint attempt, but her voice was measured, controlled. "It's not every day *Sweet Valley High* becomes a reality."

Audrey leaned back, crossing her arms. "I loved that show! But this—you and me—it's more than just looks, isn't it?"

Eve tilted her head, studying her twin in a way that seemed to look straight through her. "What do you mean?"

"I mean this." Audrey motioned vaguely between them. "It feels…natural. Like we've known each other forever, even though we just met. Don't tell me you don't feel it too."

Eve's polished mask faltered. She looked almost startled—like Audrey had voiced something she'd been unwilling to admit even to herself. "I do." The admission came quietly, almost reluctantly. "It's strange, isn't it? Like some part of me always knew you were out there."

Audrey's heart squeezed at the question, hearing the acknowledgment lurking beneath Eve's calm exterior. For her, it had been different. Her adoptive parents had given her a warm, steady life—no secrets, no suspicion. Her parents were her parents. End of story.

Still, Eve's question struck something deep. "I never thought to question it," Audrey admitted softly. "My parents loved me so much that I didn't need to. They were my family. But…"

"But what?"

Audrey hesitated, her thoughts spiraling. She felt a tug of that same curiosity Eve had voiced—a deeper, darker itch to understand the truth. "Maybe that's something we can ask our parents."

Eve froze, her eyes narrowing slightly. "Ask them?"

"Yeah," Audrey said carefully, watching Eve's reaction. "We should talk to them. Both our families."

Eve's entire posture tensed, her hands going still on the table. "Audrey, no."

"Why not?"

"Because," Eve snapped, her voice hard before softening into something more controlled. "Because it's opening a door we might not be ready to walk through."

Audrey studied her, folding her hands slowly on the table. "Sometimes doors don't stay shut, no matter how much you want them to."

Eve looked away, silent for a long beat before she finally spoke, her voice low. "You don't know my parents. They're…complicated. If we bring this to them, it's going to break apart everything."

Audrey's brow furrowed. "And that's a bad thing?"

Eve shot her a sharp look. "Yes, Audrey. It is. Not all families are like yours."

Audrey blinked, stung. "And what's that supposed to mean?"

"Just that yours was warm. Stable. Loving," Eve said quietly. "Mine was different. Expectations. Appearances. If I tell them something like this…" She trailed off, shaking her head.

Audrey softened at the admission, her voice gentler now. "I get it. But don't you think we need answers? Even if they're messy?"

Eve looked up, meeting her gaze with an intensity that surprised Audrey. "Do you really want those answers? Because I'm not sure I do."

Audrey was silent. She searched Eve's expression. "Yeah," she said finally, her voice resolute. "I do."

Eve exhaled, long and slow, before finally leaning back in her chair. "Fine. But we do it my way. My house. My rules."

Audrey was confused. "Your house?"

Eve's lips quirked faintly. "You want answers? I want control. If we're doing this, we're doing it on my terms."

Audrey watched her for a beat, then let out a small laugh. "You're a control freak, you know that?"

"Somebody has to be," Eve replied dryly.

A genuine smile tugged at Audrey's lips, unexpected but welcome. "Alright, fine. We'll do it your way." She paused, her gaze softening. "But I'm calling my parents. You call your parents. Deal?"

Eve hesitated, then nodded slowly. "Deal."

The tension in the room eased just slightly, the invisible thread between them pulling tighter in a way neither of them could fully explain. Audrey grabbed her coat, shrugging it on as she stood.

Eve stood too, surprising her. Neither of them moved. Then, Audrey extended her arms awkwardly.
"We're doing this, right? Might as well make it official. Come over to my house. We'll do dinner with everyone."

Something softened in her face. Slowly, she stepped forward, and the two women embraced—tentative, stiff at first, but then unexpectedly natural.

When they pulled apart, Eve's expression was softer than Audrey had ever seen. "I'm glad we found each other," she said quietly. Then, after a brief pause, "You know, I have a daughter."

The words landed like a punch Audrey hadn't expected. A lump formed in her throat, though she covered it with a smile. "Yeah? What's she like?"

"She's amazing," Eve said, a hint of pride in her voice. "Smart, confident—more than I ever was at her age."

Audrey smiled faintly, though something in her chest ached unexpectedly. *A daughter.* The thought stung in a way she couldn't name. She was happy for Eve—she really was—but it pulled at something deeper. A quiet ache for what she didn't have.

"She sounds incredible," Audrey said softly.

"She is." Eve's voice was warm, unguarded, and for a moment, they simply stared at each other—two strangers, two sisters, two halves of a whole.

Audrey broke the silence first, forcing a smile. "Let's just hope this dinner doesn't end in disaster."

Eve quipped, "We'll see."

As Audrey turned to leave, she glanced back, her voice softer. "We need to know the truth, Eve. All of it."

Chapter 13

Where Our Paths Cross

The doorbell rang, its chime crisp and deliberate, echoing through Eve's immaculately styled home. Eve glanced at Leo, whose calm demeanor betrayed no sign of the tension she felt coiling in her chest. He placed a reassuring hand on her back before she walked toward the door.

When Eve opened it, Helen and Jack Holliday stood framed in the doorway, the winter air trailing in behind them. Helen stepped forward immediately, her arms cradling a container of food. "Pierogi," she said, her voice soft but trembling with emotion. "I always bring something to share."

Eve hesitated before reaching out, her fingers brushing Helen's as she took the container. The small, unintentional touch seemed to break something in Helen—her lips parted, and her breath caught audibly. Her eyes, a warm hazel tinged with blue, roamed Eve's face with an intensity that almost made Eve look away.

"My God," Helen whispered, tears welling in her eyes. "You're—" Her voice broke as she pressed a trembling hand to her mouth, tears spilling down her cheeks. "You're her."

Jack, just behind her, stood frozen in place, his sharp green eyes scanning Eve's features. His typically stoic face softened as he finally spoke, his voice low and reverent. "Eve," he said, his tone catching slightly. "It's like…looking at Audrey. The resemblance is uncanny."

Helen began sobbing openly, her tears cascading down her face. She reached out instinctively, as if needing to touch Eve to confirm she was real. "How could we not have known?" she choked out, barely coherent. "How could we not have found you?"

Eve froze. Her walls cracked under the power of Helen's raw emotion. She had spent a lifetime managing other people's feelings, but this—this was overwhelming. The container of pierogi trembled in her hands as she tried to steady herself.

Jack, ever the anchor, placed a firm but gentle hand on Helen's shoulder. "Let's sit down," he said, his tone even and steady. He guided her toward the nearby couch, where she sank down, her hands clutching her knees as if to ground herself.

Helen wiped at her eyes, trying to compose herself. She reached for Eve's hand, her fingers trembling slightly.

"You…you're so beautiful," she whispered, her voice raw but steadier now.

Before Eve could respond, rapid footsteps echoed down the hall. Rory burst into the room, holding her iPad. "Mom! Can I—" Her voice faltered when she saw the scene before her. Her wide eyes darted from Helen to Jack to Eve before landing on Audrey, who had quietly entered the room.

Rory blinked at Audrey, then slowly tilted her head. "Okay…so how does this work? Do I get double the rules or double the Christmas presents? Because one of those sounds way better than the other."

Helen's teary face lit up as she turned toward Rory, her maternal instincts kicking in. "You must be Rory," she said warmly, her voice steadying. "You're...you're wonderful."

Rory raised an eyebrow, glancing between Helen and Jack. "Sooo...does this mean I'm, like, extra-grandparented now? Because I don't think that's a thing, but I'm open to negotiations."

Helen's eyes filled again as a smile spread across her face. "I suppose so," she said softly, her tone tinged with wonder. "And you're exactly what I imagined a grandchild might be."

When Eve was ten, a girl in her class lost her father. At recess, everyone huddled around, whispering about how sad she must be. Eve had walked up, unsure what she was supposed to do. She copied the others—tilted her head, softened her voice. "I'm so sorry," she had said.

The girl had thanked her, but her eyes flickered. Like she could tell.

Like she knew Eve wasn't actually feeling it.

Eve hadn't thought about that moment in years. But now, looking at Helen's tear-streaked face, she felt it again. The distance. The way emotion should be there—but wasn't.

Helen turned toward her, expectant. "Eve?"

So she did what she had learned to do. She mimicked the response. "I...I'm glad you're here."

Rory declared, her eyes flicking between Helen and Jack, "Do you guys like jokes? Mom says I'm the funniest person in the family."

"Absolutely," Jack said, his stern face softening as a faint smile curved his lips. "Let's hear one."

Rory beamed. "Okay. Why did the scarecrow win an award?"

Jack leaned forward slightly. "Why?"

"Because he was outstanding in his field!" Rory threw her hands up dramatically and laughter bubbled through the room.

But Eve's laughter stalled—because she was still watching Audrey.

The way they both reached for their drinks at the same time. The way Audrey tilted her head just slightly—just like Eve had a moment before. It was like seeing herself reflected in a distorted mirror.

The room felt smaller suddenly.

How much of her was really her? And how much of her was just…coincidence?

Helen reached out, brushing Rory's arm gently. "You're even better than I imagined," she said, her voice trembling with warmth.

Leo, standing just behind Eve, remained uncharacteristically quiet. Too quiet.

Eve wasn't looking at Audrey anymore. She was looking at him.

His gaze had drifted toward Audrey again, his expression still unreadable, but there was something…off. He wasn't just observing. It was like he was studying her.

Eve's fingers twitched at her side. A prickle of unease crawled up her spine.

Why are you looking at her like that?

Eve reached for her glass, but her fingers brushed against Leo's wrist.

He flinched. A fraction of a second. Barely enough to notice. But Eve did.

Leo doesn't flinch.

Her eyes lifted, but his expression was already smooth again, unreadable. A faint smile in place. Too faint. "Just taking it all in," he said, his voice even.

Eve exhaled softly, forcing a laugh, but something in her stomach coiled tight.

What aren't you saying?

Audrey finally spoke, her voice light but tinged with awe. "It's surreal, isn't it? Seeing the two of us together."

Jack nodded, his blue eyes still wide with disbelief. "I've seen a lot in my years, but this…" He trailed off, shaking his head. "It's something else."

Helen reached for Eve's hand, her touch hesitant but full of longing. "Thank you for inviting us," she said softly. "It means more than you know."

Eve hesitated before squeezing Helen's hand gently. "I…I'm glad you came."

Rory leaned back in her chair with a dramatic sigh. "Grandma Helen, tell me something. At what age am I finally allowed to touch the fancy plates? Because I'm pretty sure I have the motor skills of a functional human."

Helen laughed through her tears, standing slowly. "I'd love to help, sweetheart."

Audrey watched the scene unfold, a warm smile playing on her lips. Her parents' instinctive connection to Eve and Rory filled her with a quiet sense of hope. For all the chaos, maybe this was the beginning of something good.

But in the corner, Leo's eyes lingered on Audrey for a moment longer, his mind racing.

The sound of the doorbell echoed through the house, silencing the warm chatter that had begun to flow between the Hollidays and Rory. Audrey and Eve exchanged a brief, loaded glance—equal parts anticipation and trepidation. Audrey felt her stomach tighten, and Eve, ever the composed one, stood a little straighter, her shoulders squaring as she moved toward the door.

"I'll get it," Eve said softly, her voice calm but laced with tension.

Leo, ever attentive, stepped up beside her. "I'll join you," he murmured, offering a reassuring nod.

When the door opened, Vera and Oliver Field stood framed by the soft glow of the porch lights. Vera, impeccable as ever, wore a tailored navy coat over a silk blouse and pencil skirt. Her salt-and-pepper hair was pinned back in an elegant chignon, her piercing green eyes scanning the entryway with the precision of a surgeon. Beside her, Oliver stood tall and confident in a dark suit, his polished shoes clicking softly as he stepped inside. His sharp gray eyes flicked between Eve and Audrey almost immediately.

"Eve," Vera greeted, her voice cool but unmistakably affectionate. "You look lovely, as always." Her gaze shifted to Audrey, and for a brief moment, the mask slipped, her composure faltering. "Oh…"

Oliver, more accustomed to keeping his emotions in check, placed a steadying hand on Vera's arm. His own eyes widened, betraying his surprise as they settled on Audrey. "It's like seeing double," he said quietly, his usual charm tempered by awe.

Audrey stepped forward, extending a hand. "Audrey Holliday," she said, her voice firm despite the butterflies swirling in her stomach.

Vera hesitated for half a second before taking Audrey's hand. "Vera Field," she replied, her tone softened by the moment. "It's…an honor to meet you."

Oliver's handshake was warm and deliberate, his eyes searching Audrey's face. "You've made quite an impression already, Ms. Holliday," he said with a faint smile. "I've heard a great deal about you."

From behind Audrey, Helen and Jack rose from their seats, their presence drawing the Fields' attention. Helen, still wiping the remnants of her tears, stepped forward with an awkward but genuine smile. "You must be Eve's parents," she said, her Polish accent faint but unmistakable. "I'm Helen. Audrey's mother."

Jack followed closely, his imposing frame softened by his warm smile. "Jack Holliday," he said simply, extending a hand to Oliver.

The two men shook hands, a moment of silent assessment passing between them. "Oliver Field," Oliver said, his tone even. "A pleasure to meet you."

Eve watched the interaction with a faint smile, but her eyes darted to Vera, who seemed to stiffen slightly, her posture rigid. Audrey noticed it too and decided to break the ice.

"Let's all sit," she said, gesturing toward the living room. "We've got a lot to talk about."

As everyone settled into their seats, the contrasts between the two families became more pronounced. Helen perched on the edge of the couch beside Jack, her hands folded tightly in her lap, while Vera sat primly in an armchair, her back straight and legs crossed at the ankles. Oliver leaned slightly forward, his hands clasped as he surveyed the room with practiced ease.

Leo remained in the background, his gray eyes darting between Audrey and Eve. He stood near the wall, his posture relaxed but watchful, as though he were cataloging every detail.

"So," Jack began, his voice steady but warm, "this is quite the reunion."

"Quite," Vera agreed, though her tone was more measured. She glanced at Eve. "Have the DNA results come in?"

Eve nodded. "They did. A perfect match." She hesitated, then added, "There's no doubt."

The room fell silent. The revelation settled over them like a thick fog.

Helen broke the quiet, her voice trembling but firm. "It was a closed adoption," she said, her gaze flicking between Audrey and Eve. "That's why we didn't know. We weren't told."

Jack nodded, his brow furrowed. "We didn't even think to ask. At the time, it wasn't something that crossed our minds."

Vera's lips pressed into a thin line, her sharp green eyes narrowing slightly. "It was the same for us," she admitted reluctantly. "We were told Eve had no siblings. No family."

Audrey leaned forward slightly. "Doesn't that strike you as strange? That both of you were told the same thing?"

Oliver cleared his throat, his voice low and deliberate. "It does. But adoption agencies were…different then. Records were sealed, and parents were often given incomplete information."

Each person got lost in their own thoughts. What had been stolen from them hung heavy in the air.

Rory, sensing the tension, leaned over to Helen and whispered loudly, "Does this mean we're having pierogi for dinner?"

The question broke the solemnity, drawing soft chuckles from both families. Helen reached over, patting Rory's hand. "Only if you help me in the kitchen, sweetheart."

As the laughter faded, Vera glanced at Audrey, her sharp gaze softening slightly. "I don't know how we begin to unpack all of this," she said quietly. "But I hope we can try."

Audrey nodded, meeting her gaze with steady determination. "I think we have to. For all of us."

The dining table buzzed with conversation, dishes being passed around as the families found their rhythm. Plates of pierogi, roasted vegetables, and fresh bread filled the space, the air warm with the scent of Leo's cooking.

Helen looked across the table, her eyes settling on Oliver. She tilted her head, her expression curious. "You know, Oliver, your face has been bothering me."

Oliver quirked an eyebrow. "Bothering you?"

Helen laughed, waving her hand dismissively. "Not in a bad way! I've been trying to place it. I worked for your company years ago as a secretary."

The room fell into a stunned silence. Audrey froze, her fork halfway to her mouth. Eve's eyes widened, her gaze snapping to her father.

"You...worked for my father?" Eve asked, her voice a mix of curiosity and disbelief.

Helen nodded, her tone light. "I did. Back when Jack and I were first married. Small world, isn't it?"

Oliver leaned forward, his sharp gray eyes narrowing slightly as he studied her. "Remarkable. I had no idea. You must have been in one of the other divisions."

"Accounts," Helen replied, her voice tinged with nostalgia. "It's been years, but I remember the company well. Who would've thought?"

Jack chuckled, breaking the tension with a warm laugh. "It seems we're all more connected than we realized."

Before anyone could respond, Rory looked up from her plate and beamed at Helen. "Grandma, can I have more pierogi?"

Vera's head snapped toward Rory, her eyes wide with surprise. "Grandma?" she repeated, her tone sharp.

Helen grinned, leaning toward Rory with an exaggerated whisper. "Don't mind her, darling. She's still warming up to me."

The table erupted in laughter, Rory giggling as she nudged Helen playfully. "You're funny, Grandma. I think I like you."

"I like you too, sweetheart," Helen replied, her voice warm and animated as she squeezed Rory's hand. "You've got good taste."

Eve's gaze flicked to Leo, expecting to see him watching the lively conversation unfold. She had been married to Leo for years. She knew his expressions like muscle memory. She could predict when he was about to smile before his lips even moved. But tonight—something was off.

It wasn't just the way he watched Audrey. It was how still he was.

Leo always filled a room, but right now, he was shrinking into the edges, observing. Waiting. Calculating.

Eve's fingers curled against her palm.

"You've been quiet," she said, keeping her voice light as she touched his arm.

Leo blinked, as if shaking himself from a thought. Too late. His smile was a fraction of a second too slow. "Just taking it all in," he repeated.

Eve nodded absently, but her stomach twisted.

Why does it feel like you're lying?

Helen's cheerful voice broke through the moment. "Rory, do you like animals? Audrey, tell them about Elvira!"

Audrey lit up, her discomfort momentarily forgotten. "Elvira's my cat," she explained, smiling at Rory. "A Siamese. She's a diva."

Helen chimed in, "Audrey's always had a soft spot for animals. When she was little, she begged us for a dog, and when we got one, she immediately started asking for a cat."

"That's not true," Audrey protested, laughing. "I waited at least six months before I started asking."

Jack chuckled. "You always wanted more, Audrey. And we couldn't say no to you."

Eve leaned forward, her smile faint but genuine. "Some things never change."

Audrey's expression shifted as a memory struck her. She turned toward Leo, tilting her head. "Wait... I know your name. Leo De la Gardie."

Leo stiffened slightly, his fingers curling around the armrest of his chair. "You do?"

Audrey nodded, excitement sparking in her eyes. "You're the coroner! My partner Eddie and I met with you on the Magician case."

Leo's grip tightened on his glass. A fraction of a second too long.

Then he realized Eve was watching him. And he smiled. That same slow, practiced smile that had always convinced her he was in control.

But tonight, it didn't work because Eve wasn't convinced.

He recovered quickly, his usual smooth demeanor sliding into place. "I handle a lot of high-profile cases."

Eve frowned.

She was used to reading people, to knowing when someone was holding something back. It was like a muscle memory at this point—seeing the tension before it even registered on a person's face.

Eve's voice broke the moment, her tone light. "Well, now that everyone's connected, let's hope the surprises are done for the evening."

Jack laughed. "Knowing this group? I wouldn't count on it."

Eve watched Leo just a second longer than she normally would.

He should be relaxed now, laughing with the rest of them. But instead, his grip on his glass was a little too tight. His shoulders, usually so composed, held a hint of stiffness.

He was trying to seem normal.

And Eve had no idea why.

It started with the water glasses.

Audrey and Eve both reached for their glasses at the exact same time, their movements uncannily synchronized. The room fell silent, all eyes darting between the two of them.

"Okay, now I'm officially freaked out," Rory announced, breaking the silence with a dramatic hand to her forehead. "Are we sure there isn't a third one?"

Audrey quirked her lips into a half-grin. "If there is, I hope she's better at remembering birthdays."

Eve quirked an eyebrow. "And hopefully she doesn't have your habit of being late."

The family burst into laughter, the twins' playful digs setting a lighter tone. Rory, however, wasn't done.

"Hold on. This is too good," she said, pulling out her phone. "We need to test this."

"Test what?" Audrey asked, leaning back in her chair.

"How identical you really are!" Rory gestured for them to stand on either side of the doorframe. "Come on!"

Helen clapped her hands together, her face lighting up. "Oh, I love this! Do it!"

Audrey groaned but got up, rolling her eyes. "Alright, but only because I'm trying to win the 'favorite aunt' award."

Eve followed, smoothing her skirt as she stood. "Let's see what you've got."

Rory positioned Audrey and Eve on opposite sides of an open doorway, standing just far enough apart that they couldn't see each other.

"Okay, question one," Rory announced, bouncing excitedly. She turned to Helen and Jack and flashed three fingers. "How many fingers am I holding up?"

Audrey and Eve hesitated for the briefest moment—then, at the same time, they both lifted three fingers.

Rory crossed her arms, giving them a skeptical once-over. "Okay, weird. Either you're telepathic or just both equally good at guessing." She turned to Jack. "What do you think? Should we call a scientist or a magician?"

Jack chuckled, leaning back in his chair. "I am starting to feel like I'm in a magic show."

Helen waved a hand. "Do another one! This is fascinating."

Rory bit her lip, thinking. "Alright, flip your hair. Go!"

Both women tossed their hair over their shoulders in the exact same manner.

The room buzzed with laughter, but Eve's focus had narrowed.

Leo wasn't watching the game. He wasn't watching Rory's excitement or Helen's amusement. His eyes were locked on Audrey.

And his smile…it wasn't quite right.

It was there, but only on the surface. Like he was watching something he didn't know how to process.

"Alright," Rory said, barely containing her glee. "Last one. Make a face like you just ate something sour."

Eve scrunched her nose and puckered her lips. On the other side of the door, Audrey mirrored the expression perfectly.

Rory doubled over laughing. "I can't! This is too much. You're like—what's the word—symbiotic or something."

Helen dabbed at her eyes, laughing so hard she was crying. "Oh, I needed this. You two are incredible."

Even Vera, seated stiffly at the table, allowed a small smile to creep across her face. "It's...intriguing," she admitted.

Audrey stepped back into view, gesturing to Rory. "Okay, experiment over. You're not posting any of this online."

Rory pouted dramatically. "Fine. But only because I like you."

Eve glanced at Leo. He was watching Audrey.

His expression should have been amused, but it wasn't.

His smile had faded, just barely, his jaw tightening just slightly. Most people wouldn't have noticed. But Eve did.

A strange thought crept into her mind before she could stop it.

You've never looked at me like that.

The game was supposed to be funny. A joke.

But knowing Audrey moved like her—exactly like her—Eve felt something tighten in her chest.

It wasn't just mimicry. It wasn't just a coincidence.

It was something else.

Something she wasn't sure she liked.

Eve couldn't help eavesdropping as her mother and Helen cleared the plates. Helen carried a platter toward the kitchen, her movements quick and purposeful. Vera, ever composed, followed with a small stack of dishes.

"You don't need to do that," Helen said over her shoulder, glancing back at Vera. "I've got it."

"It's fine," Vera replied, her tone cool but polite. "I find hosting to be...tiring."

Helen paused, turning with a raised eyebrow. "Tiring? Try hosting a Polish family. You haven't seen chaos until your cousin drinks all the vodka before dinner starts."

Vera's lips curled up. "That does sound...colorful."

"Colorful doesn't even begin to cover it," Helen replied, laughing. "You'd be amazed at how quickly they can turn a quiet evening into a polka party."

Vera chuckled softly, the sound surprising even herself. "Perhaps we'd make a good team then."

Helen set the platter down on the counter. "Careful, Vera. I might just take you up on that."

Their exchange, though brief, carried a warmth that hadn't been present earlier. The divide between their worlds seemed to narrow. Even if only slightly. Eve felt a mixture of relief and something more complicated.

Audrey leaned back playfully and folded her arms. "Alright, Eve. Let's settle this. Do you think we've got one of those twin telepathy things?"

Eve raised a skeptical brow. "Audrey, we've known each other for, what, two days? I think it's a little early to be reading each other's minds."

Audrey grabbed a throw pillow and placed it in front of her face, shielding her mouth. "Alright, let's test it. I'm going to say something in my head, and you guess."

Eve crossed her arms, looking unimpressed. "Fine. But if you're thinking about food, I'm walking out."

Audrey grabbed her phone and typed out a random word, keeping it hidden.

Eve tapped her chin, feigning deep concentration before blurting, "Froth."

Audrey gasped. "No way!"

Eve finally broke into genuine laughter, the sound warm and disarming. "Alright, I admit it. That one was a guess. But froth seems like your vibe."

"On another note, uh...I found something," Audrey began, her tone casual but betraying a hint of guilt.

Eve lowered her cup, her eyes narrowing. "What did you find?"

Audrey sighed, setting her phone aside and facing Eve directly. "I ran a background check."

Eve's eyebrows shot up, her voice sharpening. "You did what?"

"I know, I know," Audrey said quickly, holding up her hands in defense. "It's against the rules. Technically illegal. But this isn't just some random case. This is us."

Eve stared at her. "You used your work resources to dig into our birth mother?"

Audrey shrugged, guilt flickering in her eyes. "I needed to know, Eve. I couldn't just sit around and wonder if she was even still alive."

Eve pinched the bridge of her nose, exhaling sharply. "Audrey, do you realize the risk you're taking? If anyone finds out—"

"No one will find out," Audrey interjected firmly. "I was careful. And it's not like I haven't bent the rules before."

Eve's lips pressed into a thin line. "That doesn't make it right."

Audrey leaned forward, her voice softening. "Look, I get it. You're pissed. But I couldn't just sit here and wait for some miracle. I found her, Eve. She's in Oregon."

Eve froze, the information hitting her like a freight train. "Oregon," she repeated, her voice barely above a whisper.

Audrey nodded, her tone resolute. "She's alive. And we have a name, an address. This is our chance to find her."

Eve's composure faltered, her hands trembling slightly. "And what if she doesn't want to be found?"

Audrey's expression softened. "Then we'll deal with it. But at least we'll know we tried."

The only sound was the ticking of the clock on the wall. Eve stared at her twin, a mix of frustration and gratitude warring in her eyes. Eve shook her head, but a faint smile tugged at her lips. "You're lucky we're related."

Audrey leaned back, her grin widening. "That's the spirit. So…road trip?"

Eve groaned, covering her face with her hands. "For better or worse, we're in this together now. God help me."

Audrey grabbed a blanket from the couch and tossed it toward Eve. "Here. You look cold."

Eve caught it, her brows lifting slightly. "Thanks."

"It's funny," Audrey said, sitting down again. "I always do that for my friends. Never thought it was a twin thing."

Eve chuckled, wrapping the blanket around herself. "Or it's just a 'being nice' thing, Audrey."

Audrey gave a wry smile. "Don't ruin the magic, okay?"

As the laughter faded, a hush settled between them. The warmth of the evening still lingered, but something heavier curled at the edges of the silence.

Eve stared at Audrey, really stared, as if seeing her for the first time. The candlelight cast flickering shadows across their faces, but no matter how the light wavered, their features remained the same. Mirror images. A perfect split in the universe.

Eve swallowed hard, suddenly aware of the cold weight pressing at her ribs. She laced her fingers together, her grip tightening.

"I've always felt it," Eve murmured.

Audrey's eyes flickered, then faded. "Felt what?"

Eve exhaled, slow and unsteady. "That something was missing. And not just in a 'what's my purpose?' kind of way. It was…deeper. Like a space in my life I couldn't name."

Audrey's expression shifted. She knew exactly what Eve meant. Because she had felt it too.

That gnawing emptiness. The inexplicable ache. Like a song playing too far away to hear, a word on the tip of her tongue that never fully formed.

All these years, they had been looking for something, reaching for something, never knowing what. Never knowing it was each other.

Audrey inhaled sharply, her hand twitching against the couch. "Jesus." Her voice barely made a sound.

Eve let out a quiet laugh, but it was hollow. "I thought if I just worked harder, achieved more, that feeling would go away. But it never did."

Audrey nodded slowly, her hands gripping the hem of her sweater like she needed to hold onto something solid. "Yeah," she whispered. "Me too."

Eve's jaw clenched, her mind racing back to every restless night. Every inexplicable feeling of loneliness that made no sense. The way she would sit in a crowded room and feel like she was waiting for someone who never arrived.

A strange, electric awareness buzzed in the air between them. Like two magnets finally aligning.

Audrey let out a breathless, nervous chuckle. "Is this…normal?"

Eve huffed a small laugh, shaking her head. "Nothing about this is normal."

Audrey's lips parted, like she wanted to say something more, but the words never came. Instead, she reached forward, hesitating for just a second before grabbing Eve's hand.

The second their fingers touched, the world seemed to still.

Neither of them breathed.

Something ancient and unspoken settled in the space between them.

Audrey's fingers curled around Eve's—a grip that felt like it had existed before they were born.

Eve shivered but didn't pull away.

Audrey swallowed, her voice breaking slightly. "So what now?"

Eve's throat tightened, and for a long moment, she said nothing.

Then—finally, with great difficulty—she exhaled.

"Now," Eve whispered, "I think we start over."

Audrey's lips quirked, just slightly. "Together?"

Something inside Eve uncoiled. Like a shadow retreating, a fracture sealing shut. A sliver of something else crept in alongside it.

Fear.

Because for all the ways Audrey completed her, for all the gaps she unknowingly filled—

Eve still wasn't sure who she was without that emptiness.

Chapter 14 (The Magician)

The Tower is in Play

December 18th. 7:01 p.m.

Audrey hadn't noticed them—no one ever did.

They moved in the cracks of the world, in the in-between places where people never looked. Not a person, not a shadow, but something in the air itself.

Their breath was slow. Measured. They had followed her from the moment she left the precinct. Her every movement— the way her head tilted slightly when she was thinking, the unconscious way her fingers flexed when she was uneasy—was a script they had memorized.

She had glanced back twice.

She hadn't seen them. But she felt them.

Good.

The Magician shifted slightly, their form blending into the rhythm of the sparse foot traffic. They had perfected the art of being seen but not noticed. The kind of presence people's brains discarded the second they turned away.

A cab passed, its headlights flaring across the damp sidewalk. The Magician didn't move.

Audrey lingered at the door for just a second too long before stepping inside.

Hesitation.

The Magician crossed his arms with a knowing look.

You're starting to feel it, Audrey. The storm is already in motion…and you're standing in its eye.

The door shut with a heavy thunk behind her.

A tenant exited moments later, holding the door open without a second glance. People were too trusting. Too willing to assume.

They stepped inside, their movements so fluid, so natural, that they might as well have belonged there. The scent of the building changed here—warmer, full of human traces. Perfume, old carpet, the faint lingering of a late dinner from someone's apartment.

They lingered near the row of brass mailboxes.

Audrey Holliday.

Their fingers ghosted over the engraved plate, a fraction of a second longer than necessary.

So predictable. So certain of her place in the world.

The hallway stretched ahead—dimly lit, quiet. The Magician inhaled slowly.

Her scent was here.

Faint, beneath the artificial detergent of freshly cleaned floors. A hint of citrus, the lingering trace of shampoo.

The things people left behind without thinking.

From their pocket, they pulled a single Tarot card.

The Tower.

Its edges were worn, the ink smudged from years of handling.

They knelt, slow and deliberate, and slid the card under her door.

A message. A promise.

The soft scrape of paper on tile was barely audible.

They lingered. Listening.

The faint shuffle of movement inside. She was there. So close.

They closed their eyes and inhaled. The smell of food. Of warmth. Of home.

She didn't know.

You'll think of me, Audrey. Every breath you take. Every choice you make.

They straightened, their expression unreadable.

Then, with quiet precision, they slipped down the hall, vanishing into the city's pulse.

The Tower was in play.

And the storm had only just begun.

Chapter 15 (Audrey)

In a Mother's Silence

December 18th. 9:45 p.m.

The streetlights flickered faintly, their orange glow reflecting off wet pavement as Audrey jogged the final stretch to her apartment. Her breath came in short, visible clouds in the crisp night air.

The city hummed around her—the distant wail of a siren, the muffled bass from a passing car, the quiet shuffle of footsteps behind her.

She slowed as she passed the turnoff near Obsidian Health Group, her gaze lingering on the shadowed building. The facade loomed, its dark windows revealing nothing. But something about it felt different tonight—as if it were watching her back.

A prickle of unease crawled up her spine. Not fear exactly. Awareness.

Like a thread tugged too tight, a vibration at the base of her skull. It had been there all evening, an instinct she couldn't quite name.

She picked up her pace. Just nerves.

She reached her building and scanned the street out of habit.

Nothing looked out of place, but that meant nothing.

The shadows pooled deep in the alley beside her complex— too dark, too still.

Still, her fingers hesitated over the keypad, the weight of an unseen gaze pressing between her shoulder blades.

December 19th. 6:35 a.m.

Audrey stirred her coffee absent-mindedly, her mind still racing from the unease of the night before.

Her foot brushed against something on the floor near her front door.

She frowned, glancing down.

A card.

The breath caught in her throat as she picked it up.

The Tower.

Her pulse spiked.

The edges were worn, the ink slightly smudged. It wasn't new. It had been touched. Handled. Kept.

She turned it over.

No message. No clue.

Just silence.

Her phone buzzed on the counter, jolting her back. Eddie.

"You okay?" his voice crackled over the line, casual but edged with concern.

"Yeah," she lied.

Her fingers tightened around the card.

"The Magician left a card under my door. I'll tell you about it when I get there."

As she ended the cal

l, her thoughts tangled.

The Tower wasn't random.

Someone had chosen it for her.

But why?

Her stomach tightened. A flicker of memory—Anthony McCall's case. The coroner's report. The way the wounds were almost ritualistic.

Her fingers moved before her brain caught up, dialing Sydney.

"Hey," came Sydney's voice, drowsy but alert. "Did you get abducted by aliens or something?"

Audrey let out a breath she didn't realize she was holding.

"Not yet. Listen, I need you to tell me something."

"Uh-oh." A pause. Sydney waking up fast now. "Okay. Hit me."

Audrey hesitated, turning the card over in her palm again.

"The Tower. In Tarot. What does it mean?"

Sydney made a low sound, like she had just been punched in the gut.

"Shit."

"Not the response I was hoping for."

"Dude." A pause. "That's one of the worst ones you can get. It's not like…a little bad luck. It's collapse. Big. Like, losing everything you thought was stable."

Audrey's grip on the phone tightened.

Sydney's voice softened. "Audrey, why the hell are you asking me this?"

She swallowed.

"Because someone slid it under my door last night."

A long beat of silence.

Then, all drowsiness was gone from Sydney's voice: "Where are you? Are you alone?"

Audrey glanced around her apartment, the morning sunlight casting deceptive warmth over everything.

Her gaze returned to the card.

You'll think of me, Audrey. Every breath you take.

She exhaled, slow and steady.

"I'm fine. Just needed to hear your take."

Sydney wasn't buying it. "You need to tell Eddie about this."

"I already did."

"…And?"

"And I don't know yet."

Another silence. Then Sydney's voice softened again.

"Audrey, this isn't a joke. If someone picked the Tower, they're not just screwing with you. That card means something."

Audrey nodded, even though Sydney couldn't see her.

"I know."

But what?

She ended the call, her mind already spiraling back to the case.

The Magician. The crime scenes. The surgical precision.

No. Not just surgical precision.

Familiarity.

A shiver traced her spine.

Whoever was doing this knew exactly how a body broke. How it bled.

Her eyes flicked toward her kitchen counter.

The coroner's report sat there, waiting.

Waiting for her to see what she'd missed.

December 19ᵗʰ. 9:33 a.m.

The morning light filtered through the precinct's blinds, casting long shadows across Eddie's cluttered desk. Audrey stood beside him, tapping the edge of the Tarot card on the surface with restless fingers.

Eddie stared at the card as though it might reveal its secrets if he glared long enough. "The Tower," he murmured, reading the title. "So this is what you found under your door?"

Audrey nodded. "Yeah. Slid it right under. I don't think it's just a coincidence, Eddie. The Magician wants me to know something."

Eddie leaned back in his chair, his expression darkening. "Or they're targeting you."

"That's what I'm worried about," Audrey admitted, crossing her arms tightly. Her voice dipped lower. "But this case… It's personal, Eddie. Too personal to let it slide."

Eddie ran a hand through his hair, clearly torn. "We'll dig into this. But what's your plan in the meantime? Hiding in your apartment?"

Audrey hesitated. "Actually, no. I'm leaving for Oregon. Today."

Eddie's eyes widened. "Oregon? What's in Oregon?"

"My birth mother," Audrey said simply. "I found her."

Eddie sat up straighter. "Wait, what? How?"

Audrey exhaled. "I ran a background check. Not exactly by-the-book, but…" She trailed off, shrugging as if to say, *What other choice did I have?*

He exhaled sharply. "Audrey, I get it. Believe me, I do. But running off while we've got a killer targeting you? That's risky, even for you."

"It's not just about me," Audrey said, her voice rising. "This is bigger than a case file or a Tarot card. This is my life, Eddie. My family's life. It's not running," she countered. "It's getting space. And maybe it's what I need to think clearly. You're staying here, working with Dr. O'Connor, digging into this case. You're the best detective I know. If anyone can crack this, it's you."

Eddie's gaze softened, her words sinking in. "You really think this trip is what you need?"

"I do," Audrey said firmly. "And it's not just for me. It's for Eve too. We need answers about our past if we're going to make sense of any of this."

He nodded slowly, his reluctance clear but his trust in her unwavering. "Alright. Go. But promise me, if anything feels off—*anything*—you'll call me. I don't care if it's the middle of the night."

Audrey gave him a faint smile. "I will. And, Eddie? Be careful. Whoever this is…they're not playing by the rules."

The sound of rain filtered through Audrey's window, mingling with the soft rustle of Elvira shifting on the couch. The upcoming trip gnawed at her nerves. Eve, perched elegantly on the worn couch, exuded an aura of unshakable control. Her phone was a blur of motion as she rattled through travel confirmations, her voice crisp.

"I booked the earliest flight to Portland," Eve announced, her eyes still glued to her phone. "We'll land at 8:15 a.m., rent a car, and drive to Astoria. The hotel is…well, quaint, but it's the best option available on such short notice."

Audrey straightened, walking over and holding out a hand. "Let me see."

Eve handed her the phone without hesitation. Audrey scanned the screen, her brows rising. "This is…beautiful. That's your definition of quaint?"

Eve shrugged. "Perspective."

Audrey rolled her eyes, handing the phone back. "Perspective, sure. You call it charming. I'd call it something I'd need to budget for a year."

Eve glanced at her, one brow arching. "You're welcome. Now, here's the plan. We check into the hotel and meet her the following morning. I've blocked off the entire day for it. Afterward, we can reassess how we're feeling and either stay longer or head home."

Audrey leaned back, frowning. "You sound like you're preparing for a business meeting."

Eve's expression softened, and for a moment, the ever-efficient psychiatrist gave way to something more vulnerable.

"What would you rather do? Wing it? Show up at her door unannounced?"

Audrey shrugged, her arms crossing defensively. "I don't know. Maybe. This is just…so surreal. What if she doesn't want to see us? What if she regrets everything?"

Eve hesitated, her phone still in her lap. "I've thought about that too. But we won't know until we try. And if she doesn't want us there…" She exhaled slowly. "We leave."

"You make it sound so simple," Audrey muttered, her fingers drumming against the armrest.

"It's not simple," Eve admitted quietly. "But fear doesn't solve anything. Action does."

Audrey let out a humorless laugh. "You sound like a motivational speaker."

"Therapist," Eve corrected. "Close enough."

The tension eased slightly, and Audrey's lips twitched in spite of herself. "What if she opens the door and faints?"

"At least you're CPR-certified," Eve replied dryly, earning a soft chuckle from her sister.

Elvira stretched again, this time nudging Eve's hand with her head. Eve hesitated before scratching behind the cat's ears. Audrey raised an eyebrow.

"She never warms up to people this fast," Audrey remarked. "It's kind of freaking me out. Are you two conspiring against me?"

"Maybe she recognizes a kindred spirit," Eve said lightly, running her fingers through Elvira's fur. "She has good taste."

Audrey snorted. "Don't let it go to your head."

Eve glanced at her sister, her expression unreadable. "Too late."

The rhythmic thrum of the airplane filled the silence between them. Audrey stared out the window, their reflections faintly visible against the endless expanse of clouds. Seeing their identical profiles side-by-side still sent a shiver down her spine.

"I've been thinking about the Magician," Eve said suddenly, her voice low.

Audrey turned sharply, her body tensing. "We're seriously doing this now? Talking about murder at 30,000 feet?"

"It's a theoretical discussion," Eve replied, unruffled. "You're a detective. I'm a psychiatrist. I think we can handle it."

Audrey hesitated, then sighed. "Fine. What do you think?"

"They're not killing randomly," Eve began, her brow furrowing. "There's a pattern—a narrative. It's calculated, but there's chaos in the details. A need to disrupt, to dismantle. It feels personal."

Audrey frowned. "You say that like it's admirable."

Eve's gaze flicked to her sister, her expression clinical. "Not admirable. Methodical. There's a difference."

Audrey's unease deepened, her fingers gripping the armrest. *She talks about it like it's a game. Like she's analyzing moves on a chessboard.*

"You think it's connected to us somehow?" Audrey pressed cautiously. "The timing, the escalation…"

"I don't know," Eve admitted, her voice softer now. "But the timing is…interesting."

Audrey turned back to the window, her reflection merging with Eve's. She felt her sister's words settling in her chest, mingling with her own doubts.

"Do you think she'll regret seeing us?" Audrey whispered after a long silence.

Eve didn't answer immediately. Her voice, when it came, was quieter than Audrey expected. "I think she'll regret the circumstances. Not us."

The wheels touched down, jolting them both slightly. Audrey watched as Eve straightened in her seat, her polished mask slipping back into place.

The twins sat in silence, the engine off but the faint metallic tick of cooling metal filling the silence. Through the windshield, the house stood like a relic of another era, its charm dulled by decades of salty air and rain.

Eve leaned back in the passenger seat, her arms folded across her chest. Her calm facade was betrayed by the tension in her tightly crossed legs, her slightly bouncing.

Audrey drummed her fingers on the steering wheel, her tension visible in the taut set of her jaw. "So…this is it," she muttered, her voice low as though the house might overhear.

Eve tilted her head, her eyes narrowing as she scrutinized the property. "It's smaller than I imagined," she said, her tone distant.

Audrey shot her a glance. "What were you expecting? A mansion?"

"No," Eve replied faintly. "But I wasn't expecting something out of a Nicholas Sparks novel either. All it's missing is a lighthouse and some tragic backstory."

Audrey huffed a laugh, her nerves flickering into humor for a moment. "Well, we've got the tragic backstory covered."

"Are we just going to stare at it all day?" Eve asked, her gaze fixed on the weathered front porch.

Audrey let out a shaky exhale, her eyes glued to the house. "I just…need a second," she murmured, her voice quieter than usual.

Her gaze traveled to the curtains framing the windows, the wind chimes swaying gently under the eaves. The house looked ordinary, humble—nothing like the picture she had carried in her head for weeks. It was almost too normal, too rooted in reality for the magnitude of what they were about to do.

Audrey's heart pounded as she took in the faded blue shutters, the patch of garden overrun with wildflowers. "I thought it would feel…different," she confessed. "Like I'd just know."

The sound of a car engine broke their reverie, and both twins snapped their attention forward. A silver sedan pulled into the driveway, the rumble of its engine briefly interrupting the rhythmic crash of the waves. The driver's door opened. A woman stepped out, balancing a canvas bag of groceries against her hip. Her hair, streaked with gray, was pulled into a low bun, and her face, though lined with age, held a quiet beauty. She wore simple clothes—jeans and a weathered sweater—practical and unassuming.

The woman paused at the door, fumbling with her keys, and for a fleeting moment, she turned her head toward the street. The twins ducked instinctively, their hearts pounding.

The air in the car grew heavier.

Eve studied Audrey's profile, her twin's expression a mix of determination and doubt. "You think that's her?" Eve asked softly, her voice dipping into unfamiliar uncertainty.

Audrey's lips pressed into a thin line as her eyes darted over the details of the house. "I don't know." she admitted. Her fingers tightened on the wheel. "But then again, what did I expect? A neon sign saying, *Here's your mother?*"

Humor sparked behind Eve's eyes, but her amusement was short-lived. "She does look a little like us," she ventured. "Maybe in the cheekbones?"

A heartbeat of silence.

The woman disappeared into the house, the door closing with a soft creak. The twins sat frozen, neither willing to move, the reality of the moment pressing down on them like a weight.

"She doesn't know," Audrey murmured, more to herself than to Eve.

"No," Eve replied, her voice barely above a whisper. "But she's about to."

The silence that followed was filled with the distant sound of the waves and the occasional cry of a seagull overhead. Audrey finally unbuckled her seatbelt, her movements deliberate but hesitant.

Eve's voice cut through the tension. "We can sit here all day, but it's not going to get any easier."

Audrey turned to her twin, her expression raw. "What if she slams the door in our faces? What if she doesn't want to see us?"

Eve softened, her therapist's voice slipping in naturally. "Then we deal with it. But we can't let fear keep us in this car forever. She deserves to know. And so do we."

Audrey exhaled, nodding slowly. "Alright," she said, her voice steadier than she felt. "Let's do this."

They stepped out of the car together, their synchronized movements a testament to their growing bond. The late afternoon sun cast long shadows across the pavement as they approached the front door. Each step felt heavier than the last, their breaths shallow, their hearts pounding in unison.

Audrey hesitated at the doorstep, her hand hovering over the doorbell. She looked at Eve. Determined. Afraid.

Eve stepped forward, brushing past her twin. Without a word, she pressed the doorbell, the chime echoing faintly from within.

Nothing happened. Then…footsteps. Slow. Deliberate. Drawing closer.

The door creaked open. And there she was—the woman who had given them life but never known them. Her gaze swept over their faces, pausing as recognition dawned. Her hand clutched the doorframe for support as her mouth opened and closed, but no sound emerged.

Audrey found her voice first. "Are you Camille Hayes?" she asked, her tone trembling but clear.

Camille nodded. Her lips parted…but no words came.

"We're your daughters." Eve's voice was calm…but underneath, something cracked. "May we come in?"

Camille led them into her modest living room, the faint scent of lavender and aged wood lingering in the air. The space was simple yet inviting—framed photos of landscapes hung on the walls, a hand-knit throw draped over a chair, and a small bookshelf crammed with well-worn paperbacks. A ticking clock punctuated the silence, each second dragging as if time itself had slowed for this moment.

She gestured toward the couch, her hand trembling visibly. "Please, sit. Can I get you something? Tea? Water?"

Audrey shook her head, the moment pressed on her chest. Eve, ever composed, offered a polite nod. "Tea would be nice, thank you."

Camille disappeared into the kitchen, leaving the twins alone. Audrey turned to Eve, her voice low but urgent. "She looks so normal. Like someone you'd pass on the street and never think twice about."

Eve's gaze didn't waver from the doorway. "That's the thing about trauma. It hides in plain sight." Her voice was calm, but Audrey noticed the slight tension in her sister's fingers as she clasped them in her lap.

When Camille returned, her composure had begun to collapse. The teacups rattled slightly on the tray as she set them down, and her shoulders sagged as she sank into the armchair opposite the twins.

"I always wondered," she began, her voice barely above a whisper. "But I never thought this day would come."

Audrey leaned forward, her hands clasped tightly. "We have so many questions."

Camille managed a faint smile that quivered at the edges. "You must have."

The room fell silent except for the ticking clock, its rhythm relentless. Camille's eyes darted between the twins, as if searching their faces for some tangible proof of connection.

"It happened when I was nineteen," she said at last, her gaze dropping to her clasped hands. "I was walking home from work—just a short walk, but it was late. He came out of nowhere."

Audrey felt a jolt of anger flare in her chest. As a detective, she'd heard stories like this before, but never one that felt so close. She tightened her fists until her nails bit into her palms, her jaw clenching to keep from speaking.

Eve, meanwhile, sat perfectly still, her expression calm yet alert. Inside, her mind raced, cataloging the signs of trauma— Camille's trembling hands, her uneven breathing, the way her gaze darted away from direct eye contact. She could see the toll of decades spent carrying this weight, and it made her heart ache in ways she hadn't expected.

Camille continued, her voice breaking. "I tried to fight. I screamed. But he was stronger. Afterward, I just lay there, staring at the stars, trying to pretend it wasn't real. That if I didn't move, it wouldn't be true."

A tear slid down Eve's cheek, surprising even herself. Audrey's throat tightened painfully, her professional detachment crumbling as she imagined the scene—the cold ground, the darkness, the terror.

"When I found out I was pregnant," Camille said, her words trembling, "I didn't know what to do. I was raised Catholic. Abortion wasn't an option for me. But every time I felt a kick, every time I craved something, it was like he was there, haunting me all over again."

Her voice cracked as sobs overtook her. "I loved you. Both of you. But I couldn't give you the life you deserved. Not when I was broken."

Audrey glanced at Eve, her sister's calm mask slipping just slightly as she reached out to place a hand on Camille's knee. "You did what you thought was right," Eve said softly, her voice steady despite her glistening eyes. "You gave us a chance. That matters."

Camille shook her head, her tears flowing freely now. "I thought I was doing the right thing. But the guilt…God, the guilt never left. Every day, I wondered if you were safe, if you were happy."

Audrey finally spoke, her voice raw with emotion. "Why didn't you tell the families that there were two of us?"

Camille's head fell forward, her hair slipping out of its loose bun. "It was a closed adoption. They wouldn't let me. They said it was for the best, that you'd never have to deal with…with what I went through."

Audrey's stomach twisted. It was a reasonable answer—one she might even accept in a case report. But something about it didn't sit right. She never fought to know if they were together? Was it really just the system keeping them apart, or had Camille been too afraid to dig?

Eve must have sensed her doubt because she shifted slightly beside her, but she didn't challenge Camille. Audrey held her tongue too. Now wasn't the time.

Audrey swallowed hard, the lump in her throat nearly unbearable. She glanced around the room, her gaze drifting over the walls before settling on a mantle lined with framed photographs. She stood, drawn by one in particular—a family portrait. A man, two teenagers, and Camille smiling in a sunlit yard.

Her heart sank. "You…you have other kids?" she asked, picking up the frame.

Camille wiped her face, nodding. "They don't know about you. And neither does my husband. I buried that part of my life because I didn't think I'd survive if I didn't."

Eve studied the photo, her psychiatrist's mind parsing the complexity of Camille's dual life. She saw the pride in the mother's eyes, but also the strain, the cracks in the facade.

Audrey set the photo down, her hands trembling. "So what happens now?"

Camille looked at them both, her voice trembling with a mix of hope and fear. "I don't know. But I'd like to know you—if you'll let me."

The twins exchanged a glance, their identical expressions reflecting the storm of emotions swirling within them.

Eve broke the silence, her voice soft but firm. "We'd like that too."

Audrey nodded, the weight of the day settling over her. "But we have to take this one step at a time."

Camille reached out hesitantly, her hands closing over theirs. "Thank you for finding me. Thank you for giving me this chance."

Tears streamed down all three faces as the clock ticked on, its rhythm a reminder that time, no matter how heavy, could not erase the bonds that had finally been uncovered.

Audrey's eyes drifted around the room, absorbing the modest, lived-in space. Camille, seated in an armchair by the window, seemed smaller than the towering figure Audrey had imagined. There was a fragility about her, but also a quiet strength that hinted at untold stories.

"I don't even know where to begin," Camille said softly, her fingers nervously twisting the edges of a knitted throw draped over her lap. Her eyes flickered between the twins, a mix of longing and trepidation in her gaze.

Eve leaned forward slightly, her voice steady but tinged with curiosity. "Maybe...tell us about the family. Where we come from."

Camille's teeth flashed as she nodded. "Of course," she said, her voice trembling. "Your great-grandfather, Wallace, was an engineer. He helped build the railways that connected Chicago. He always said those tracks were like veins—pulsing with life and bringing people together."

Audrey glanced at Eve, her brow furrowing slightly. "An engineer? That's...impressive."

Camille's demeanor grew wistful. "He was brilliant, but humble. And then there was Constance, your great-aunt. She and her identical twin sister, Eleanor, were known all over the city for their writing. Constance worked for the *Chicago Times*—her columns could stir the city into action. She always said the pen was her sword."

Eve's expression warmed. "Identical twins run in the family then."

Camille chuckled softly, the sound warm and unexpected. "Yes, it seems to be a theme. I'll have to find a picture of them for you—they were striking, just like you two."

Audrey shifted in her seat, her voice hesitant. "And what about you? What was your life like?"

Camille's expression faltered, a shadow passing over her face. "It wasn't always easy," she admitted, her voice thick with emotion. "But there were moments of beauty. I loved books— stories were my escape. I even thought about becoming a librarian once, but life had other plans."

Camille hesitated, then rose from her chair. She crossed the room, moving toward a small wooden cabinet. With a breath that seemed to steady her, she unlocked the drawer and pulled out a journal—its leather cover aged and worn, the edges softened from years of handling.

She turned back to the twins, clutching it to her chest. "I wrote about you," she said finally, her voice thick with emotion. "For years. It was the only way I could hold onto you."

Audrey leaned forward, her gaze softening. "What did you write?"

Camille opened the journal to a ribbon-marked page, her breath catching as she began to read. Her voice quivered, but the words flowed steadily, raw and unfiltered.

"Dear girls," she started, her voice breaking slightly. "Tonight, I sat alone in the dark, staring at the stars. They looked so far away, like tiny promises I'd never be able to keep. I wondered if you could see them too, if you felt as small and lost under their light as I do. I wondered if you're safe, if someone is holding you the way I long to hold you, if you've felt joy—real, boundless joy—yet."

She pressed her fingers to her lips before continuing. "Every kick I felt was a miracle and a reminder of him at the same time. Every time I craved something, I hated myself for the joy it brought. How could something so pure and perfect come from something so dark and vile? And yet, you were the light in my darkness.

The only thing that kept me breathing. The day you were born, I cried tears I didn't know I had left. You were so small, so beautiful. I didn't think it was possible to feel so much love and so much pain all at once. They told me it was for the best. That you'd be better off. But when I kissed your tiny heads and said goodbye, it felt like my heart was being ripped from my chest.'"

Camille's voice cracked, and she paused, wiping at her tears with trembling fingers. "'I used to dream of the life you might have. Were you loved? Were you happy? Did you know each other? I prayed every night that you'd find each other someday, that you'd look into each other's eyes and know the truth of who you are. My greatest hope was that you'd find the strength to love yourselves in a way I couldn't love myself.'"

The room was heavy with silence, broken only by Camille's quiet sobs. She looked up at them, her tear-streaked face etched with decades of longing and guilt. "I didn't think this day would ever come," she said, her voice thick with emotion. "But I wrote to you as if it might, because it was the only thing that kept me going."

Audrey swallowed hard, her throat tight. "And...what about now? Do you think you'll tell them—your family?"

Camille's expression faltered. "I don't know. Sophie and Matthew...they're still so young. And Henry...he doesn't know how to handle this yet. But I'll figure it out. I want them to know you. I want them to know who you are."

Eve's voice was quiet but firm. "We want to know them too. When the time is right."

Camille reached out, her trembling hands grasping theirs. "Thank you," she whispered. "Thank you for finding me. For giving me a chance to know you."

As they stood to leave, Camille held onto them for a moment longer, her grip firm despite her trembling hands. "This isn't goodbye," she said, her voice resolute. "This is only the beginning."

Outside, the cold air nipped at their faces, but the twins barely noticed. Audrey glanced at Eve, her thoughts swirling in a tangled storm of disbelief and understanding. Her breath fogged in the night air as she spoke. "I didn't expect...any of that."

Eve nodded, her gaze fixed on the dark horizon as if searching for something solid in the vast uncertainty that now stretched before them. "It changes everything," she murmured, her voice steady but fragile.

They slid into their seats, shutting the doors in near unison. The night pressed down on them, thick and unrelenting. For a long moment, neither of them spoke; the only sound the distant rustle of leaves and the soft ticking of the cooling engine.

Then Audrey broke the silence, her voice trembling. "She wrote to us," she whispered. "All those years...she never stopped thinking about us."

Eve turned to her, and for the first time, the composure she'd been holding onto so tightly shattered. Her shoulders shook as tears spilled down her cheeks—silent at first, then wracking her body with the force of a dam breaking.

Audrey reached for her without hesitation, pulling her into a tight embrace. And suddenly, it wasn't just Eve's grief—it was both of theirs. The love, the anger, the relief, the profound sadness of what could have been—it all poured out in a tidal wave neither of them could hold back.

They pulled back just enough to meet each other's eyes, their identical features reflecting the same exhaustion, the same raw vulnerability.

In that moment, there were no walls. No masks. No carefully constructed defenses. Just two halves of the same broken soul, clinging to each other in the darkness—for the mother they had only just met, for the years they had lost, and for the harsh reality of the world that had brought them here.

Audrey wiped her face with the sleeve of her jacket, her laugh breaking through the lingering silence like a fragile, unexpected gift. "You know," she said, voice thick with emotion, "crying this much really works up an appetite."

Eve blinked, her tear-streaked face tilting toward her sister in confusion before a small, incredulous laugh escaped her. "Are you serious?"

Audrey's tired eyes shone red. "I mean, if we're going to unravel our entire existence, we might as well do it over burgers, right? There's gotta be a 24-hour diner somewhere around here, right?"

Eve shook her head again, but this time, a faint smile lingered on her lips. "Burgers it is," she said softly.

Chapter 16

Beneath the Garland and Glitter

As the evening progressed, the room dimmed slightly, the chandeliers casting soft golden halos across snow-dusted centerpieces—the delicate shimmer of artificial flakes catching the candlelight in flickering glass votives. Eve watched the musician, her gilded harp shimmering faintly in the low glow, the notes she coaxed from its strings so delicate they seemed spun from air. The music weaved through the room like memory—half-remembered, almost ghostly.

Lilah stepped onto the softly illuminated stage, her floor-length gown a shimmering silver-white, reminiscent of frost on moonlit glass. Fine crystals caught the light like falling snow as she turned, the velvet train trailing behind her like a shadowed snowfall.

"Ladies and gentlemen," Lilah began, her voice smooth and commanding, "I know you're all here for the glitz, the glamor, and, of course, the open bar. But tonight, we're also here to honor a truly remarkable woman. Dr. Eve De la Gardie isn't just a celebrated author and psychiatrist—she's someone whose insight reminds us that behind every sparkle, there's a story. And trust me," she added with a conspiratorial smile, "Eve knows how to keep us spellbound. Please join me in welcoming the brilliant Dr. De la Gardie."

As the applause died down, Lilah returned briefly to the stage, raising her glass toward the back of the room. "And can we take a moment to thank the divine Cordelia for that breathtaking music tonight?" she said, gesturing toward the harpist in her icy blue gown, seated beside the candlelit tree. "She makes me want to write poetry, or at least attempt something more refined than a martini order."

Light laughter followed. The harpist gave a graceful nod, her fingers never still as she continued weaving quiet enchantment through the air.

Eve rose gracefully from her seat, her diamond necklace catching the light like a constellation of its own. She ascended the stage with the poise of someone who was no stranger to commanding attention but carried an aura of modesty that drew people in. She steadied herself at the podium, her fingers brushing the edges as she took a breath. She had addressed crowds like this before, but tonight felt different. Heavier. The truth she was about to share wasn't just her own—it belonged to Audrey, to her mother, and to every silent voice burdened by the trauma.

"Thank you, Lilah, for that warm introduction," Eve began, her voice steady but carrying an undertone of something deeper—something raw. "And thank you all for being here tonight. It's truly a privilege to share this evening with so many people who care about making a difference."

She paused, her gaze sweeping the audience as she allowed the moment to settle. "Tonight, I want to share something personal—something I, until recently, hadn't fully processed myself."

The room seemed to hold its breath.

She paused, letting her gaze sweep over the crowd. Confidence radiated from her, but a glimmer of vulnerability softened her presence.

"I'm thrilled to announce I've just signed a deal for my second book," she continued, her words met with a ripple of murmured excitement. "The title is still under wraps, but I can share that it explores the psychological effects of trauma and how it shapes not only our minds but also our relationships, our choices, and even our sense of self. Recently," she said, her voice softening but gaining an emotional resonance that drew the audience in, "I discovered that I have an identical twin sister. For my entire life, I believed I was an only child. But fate, as it often does, had other plans. Meeting Audrey has been one of the most profound experiences of my life."

She smiled faintly, her composure quivering ever so slightly. "But with that discovery came another truth. One that has reshaped how I view my own story and, ultimately, my work."

Eve steadied herself at the podium, fingers tightening against the smooth surface as she let the moment settle over her. The room was silent, expectant. Hundreds of eyes watched her, waiting for the next carefully curated words to leave her lips.

But suddenly, the words she had prepared felt like glass in her throat.

She had spoken on stages like this before. She had delivered keynote addresses, held panels, led discussions on the human mind and all its complexities. But tonight was different. Tonight, the words she was about to speak didn't come from research or theory—they came from something raw, something real, something she hadn't even had time to fully process.

Her gaze flickered to the front row, where Lilah sat poised, her usually playful expression softened with something like quiet encouragement. Beside her, Leo watched intently, his brow slightly furrowed, concern laced in his otherwise unreadable expression.

Eve's stomach clenched.

The memory of their mother's shaking hands, the tear-streaked face of a woman who had buried decades of pain, flickered through Eve's mind. Camille had fought to leave the past behind, had carefully constructed a life where this part of her story no longer existed. If she were in the audience tonight, would she feel exposed? Betrayed?

Eve's fingers curled against the podium.

She had been sworn to confidentiality hundreds of times as a psychiatrist. She knew what it meant to hold someone's pain with reverence. Was she crossing a line now?

But then, her mind shifted—to that small, leather-bound journal Camille had clutched in her lap the night they met. The pages filled with words Camille never had the courage to say out loud. The prayers, the pleas, the love she had poured into ink, hoping that one day—somehow—her daughters would know they had always been wanted.

Eve had spent years telling people that healing wasn't found in silence—it was found in the courage to face what was broken and choose to speak anyway.

How could she stand here now and refuse to do the same?

She inhaled sharply, steeling herself.

Her voice, when it came, was softer than she intended. "My sister and I," she began, the weight of each syllable pressing against her chest, "are the adopted daughters of a woman who survived unimaginable trauma." She hesitated, allowing herself a moment to steady her breath before continuing.

"Our mother was a rape victim who, despite everything, chose to carry us and give us the chance at life she might not have believed we could have. That choice came at a cost—one she bore alone for decades."

A ripple of hushed whispers spread through the audience, some hands instinctively covering mouths. Eve let the silence linger, let them sit in the gravity of those words. Her own heart pounded in her chest.

She had said it.

And now, there was no turning back.

Eve's voice wavered, but she pressed on, the vulnerability in her tone drawing everyone into her world.

"Trauma," she said, her voice trembling slightly, "isn't just something that happens to you—it's something you carry. It weaves itself into your life in ways you can't predict. And while it doesn't define us, it shapes us. Trauma is not something that respects time. It doesn't fade simply because years pass or circumstances change. It finds ways to weave itself into the fabric of our lives, often when we least expect it."

She paused, her voice catching as tears welled in her eyes. "And yet, it's in those moments—those raw, unfiltered moments of reckoning—that we have the opportunity to redefine what strength looks like. It isn't about erasing the scars, but learning to carry them with grace."

Around the room, guests dabbed at their eyes, some openly shedding tears. Lilah, seated near the front, looked stunned, her perfectly glossed lips slightly parted as she absorbed the revelation. Even Leo's composure faltered, his expression softening into something deeper—concern, perhaps, or simply an awe-struck silence.

Eve reached for a glass of water on the podium, her fingers trembling slightly. She inhaled deeply, regaining her composure before continuing. "I'd like to share a passage from my upcoming book that speaks to this very idea. It's about the moments where pain intersects with hope—where our darkest shadows become the source of our greatest light."

She opened a small leather-bound notebook, her hands steadying as she read aloud:

"'Trauma is not the end of the story, though it often feels that way. It is a chapter—one that changes the arc of who we are but does not define the entirety of our narrative. Healing does not mean forgetting; it means learning to live with what once broke us. And in that space, in the fractures and the seams, there is beauty.'"

Eve's voice quivered on the final word, and for a moment, the room was utterly silent. Then, like a wave, the applause began—soft at first, but building into a thunderous ovation.

She closed the notebook, blinking away tears. "Before I finish, I'd like to share one more piece of news. My husband, Leo, and I have made a $25,000 donation tonight to a non-profit that supports survivors of sexual violence—providing counseling, advocacy, and vital resources. This cause is no longer just important to me. It's personal."

Eve stepped back from the podium, her head held high despite the tears that shimmered in her eyes. She felt a wave of exhaustion wash over her. Speaking the truth had been cathartic, but it had also laid her bare. And tonight, of all nights, she wasn't sure she could handle being seen so clearly.

The applause thundered around her, punctuated by the occasional sob or sniffle from the emotionally charged audience. Whispers of amazement and tearful conversations rippled through the room like an unstoppable current, creating a palpable energy of shared humanity.

Lilah shot to her feet, her sequined gown catching the light like a constellation in motion. Tears streamed down her impeccably made-up face as she dramatically pressed a hand to her chest, her tiara slightly askew from the abrupt movement.

"Eve!" she exclaimed, her voice a mix of awe and emotion. She grasped Eve's free hand with both of hers, her grip firm but trembling. "That was…beyond words. If I wasn't wearing my tiara, I'd be on the floor weeping!" Lilah sniffled, dabbing at her eyes with the corner of her crystal-encrusted clutch. "You've made me cry and question my life choices all in one evening. If that isn't brilliance, I don't know what is."

Eve offered a faint smile, her composure wavering as her gaze met Lilah's. "Thank you, Lilah," she whispered, her voice raw with emotion.

Lilah nodded fervently, her usual theatrics tempered by genuine admiration. "You're extraordinary. Truly extraordinary," she said, her voice breaking slightly as she let Eve go and sank back into her chair, still dabbing at her eyes.

Eve turned toward her seat and squared her shoulders. Leo stood as she approached, his expression an intricate blend of pride, concern, and something she couldn't quite name.

"Why didn't you tell me?" Leo asked, his voice low but firm as she sank into her seat. His fingers wrapped around hers—steady but probing—his eyes searching for something she wasn't ready to offer.

Eve's composure cracked just slightly. "I couldn't," she whispered, the words barely audible over the applause still echoing through the room. "Not yet."

Leo exhaled slowly, nodding, though the crease in his brow lingered. He leaned closer, his voice softer but weighted. "You don't have to carry it alone, you know."

A shadow and a light seemed to envelop not only their table, but the entire room. Lilah, seated nearby, glanced at them both, her sharp eyes glistening with unshed tears as she adjusted her tiara and straightened her posture.

"Well," she murmured to no one in particular, brushing a tear from her cheek. "If that doesn't deserve another glass of champagne, I don't know what does."

The remark drew soft chuckles from the surrounding guests, breaking the tension just enough to allow the evening to breathe again.

Eve sat with Leo, her diamond necklace catching the dim light as it shifted subtly with her movements. Her face held the serene mask she had perfected, but the emotional weight of her speech still pressed heavily on her chest. Around her, guests mingled and whispered, their tearful reactions to her revelation rippling through the room.

A woman in a deep emerald gown approached their table, her eyes glistening. "Dr. De la Gardie," she said softly, her voice trembling, "I just wanted to say how brave you are. I can't imagine… I don't even know how you find the strength to speak about it."

Eve turned to her, her practiced smile warm yet measured. "Thank you," she replied gently. "But I believe strength often comes from the places we least expect."

The woman nodded, dabbing at her eyes with a handkerchief. "You've given so many people hope tonight. Truly."

As Eve offered a gracious nod, she settled back into her seat, her body still thrumming with residual adrenaline from her speech. The murmurs around her table swirled in a hazy blur—congratulations, praise, admiration—but she barely heard them. Her thoughts were too tangled, her emotions too raw.

She reached for her champagne flute, needing something—*anything*—to steady herself. But as she lifted it to her lips, her gaze flickered across the room and—

Her breath caught.

Noah.

He was standing at the bar, a champagne flute in hand, looking so at ease it made her stomach twist. His dark hair was neatly styled, his white dinner jacket crisp against the warm glow of the chandeliers. He looked like he belonged here.

But he shouldn't be here.

Eve stiffened, gripping her glass tighter. Panic coiled in her chest. He couldn't have just happened to be here—not at this event, not when she was the headlining speaker. Was he a donor? A last-minute guest? Or had he come for her?

Noah turned, as if sensing her gaze. Their eyes met across the ballroom, and for the briefest moment, everything else vanished.

Then he smiled.

Just a quiet, unreadable curve of his lips—one that sent a slow, creeping heat through her. He lifted his glass in silent acknowledgment, as if they were merely two acquaintances exchanging pleasantries.

She felt the fragile balance she had carefully cultivated begin to shift. The control she prided herself on seemed to slip through her fingers, replaced by something darker—desire mingled with guilt, power muddled with vulnerability.

Leo shifted beside her, brushing her hand lightly. "Everything all right?" he asked, his voice warm but edged with curiosity.

Eve forced a smile, her voice steadier than she felt. "Of course," she said, glancing at him briefly before returning her attention to the glass in her hand. "Just...taking it all in."

Leo nodded, his concern fading as he turned back to the conversation at the table.

Eve, however, couldn't shake Noah's gaze. Against her better judgement, she glanced toward the bar again, only to find him still watching her, his expression unreadable but intent.

Her mind buzzed with conflicting emotions—how easily she could walk across the room, the way his presence seemed to pull her, how wrong it all was, and yet how much she wanted it anyway. She ran a finger along the edge of her necklace, the cool metal a sharp contrast to the heat pooling in her chest.

When Noah tipped his glass again, this time with a subtle tilt of his head, her breath caught. She couldn't decide if he was daring her to approach or simply reminding her of what they'd shared. Either way, the tension in the air was unbearable.

"Eve," Leo said, his voice pulling her back. She blinked, turning to him, her composure slipping for just a moment before she smiled again.

"I'm fine," she lied, reaching for her water glass to steady herself. She sipped it slowly, keeping her focus on the table, but her mind was already racing, the memory of Noah's touch still burning in the back of her mind.

It would be better to ignore him. But the idea of him watching her all evening, their shared history unspoken and unresolved, felt equally unbearable.

"I need to stretch my legs," she said suddenly, interrupting a comment from one of their tablemates. Her voice was calm, her tone breezy, but she avoided meeting Leo's eyes as she pushed her chair back and stood.

"Do you want me to come with you?" Leo asked, his hand resting lightly on her arm.

"No, it's fine," she replied quickly, offering a faint smile. "I won't be long. Just a bit of air."

He hesitated, his brow furrowing slightly, but then nodded, releasing her arm. "All right. Don't be too long."

Eve strode down the gilded hallway, her heels clicking against the marble—sharp, deliberate. Pine garlands and white lights traced the archways, their quiet glow casting soft shadows. From one corner, a small sprig of mistletoe hung—unassuming, almost easy to miss. The city lights beyond the windows shimmered like frost, but she barely noticed.

She needed space—space to breathe, to think, to stop feeling watched.

But the second she rounded the corner near the coat check, she froze.

Noah.

He was standing there, waiting.

The air thickened around her. He leaned against the wall, hands in his pockets. His white dinner jacket was still crisp under the chandeliers, offset by a deep green velvet bow tie that hinted at festive indulgence.

She felt the pull of his presence like a phantom touch on her skin.

This wasn't a coincidence.

She swallowed hard, forcing her voice into something resembling control. "Why are you here?"

Noah pushed off the wall, moving with the same controlled ease that had always unnerved her. His lips curved into a slow, unreadable smile. "I could ask you the same thing."

Her pulse pounded in her ears. "I'm the guest of honor."

"And I'm a donor," he said smoothly. "Very last-minute, in case you're wondering."

Eve's stomach flipped. "You—" She stopped, realization crashing over her. "You donated just to be here?"

His expression didn't change, but something flickered in his eyes. "A friend suggested I attend."

"A friend?"

Eve's jaw tightened. This was a choice. Noah had chosen to be here, and that was worse than any accidental encounter.

"I didn't come to cause trouble," he murmured, taking a step closer.

She stepped back automatically. "Then why did you come?"

A beat of silence stretched between them. His gaze never wavered.

"You already know why, Eve."

Her heart slammed against her ribs.

His thumb traced the inside of her wrist, pressing against the frantic beat of her pulse.

She should pull away. She should say his name like a curse, like a warning.

Instead, it came out like a confession.

"Noah."

Somewhere, in the fractured edges of her mind, she saw Leo's face.

Saw Audrey's wary gaze.

Saw the woman she used to be.

This is wrong.

But then Noah's hands were on her hips, dragging her closer, and every coherent thought burned to ash.

Recklessness surged through her, an intoxicating rush. She bit down on his lip, half in anger, half in surrender.

"You love playing with fire, don't you?" he responded with a low growl.

Her laugh was breathless, near hysterical. "And you love watching me burn."

This wasn't just an affair. This was destruction.

She could stop this. Right now. Turn and walk away. But she didn't. She couldn't. Because the flames felt too good.

Noah smelled like expensive cologne and bad decisions. Logic blurred, the ground beneath her shifting.

She wrapped her legs around his waist, pulling him in deeper. Eve's fingers dug into his shoulders, pulling him closer as pleasure coiled tight within her. Each thrust sent a wave of pleasure through her body.

As Noah's lips claimed hers, their kiss deepened, a fiery passion that ignited a burning desire within her. His touch was electrifying, sending shivers of anticipation coursing through her veins as his fingers brushed against her thighs, tracing the curve of her legs with a slow, deliberate caress. Sweat beaded on his forehead, a testament to the intensity of their passion.

With a gentle yet firm touch, Noah pulled up her gown, exposing her panties. He hooked his fingers under the elastic, pulled them down, and his eyes widened as he felt her wetness.

Eve's face flushed with excitement, her body aching for his touch.

"Noah," she gasped, pulling away to catch her breath.

"Yes?" His voice was low, his eyes locked on hers, his gaze dark with desire.

"I want you." The words tumbled from her lips, raw and desperate.

Noah's face inched closer, lips brushing softly against hers again. "I want you too."

She reached down, her hands trembling with anticipation, and unzipped his pants. Her fingers wrapped around his hard cock, feeling its thickness and warmth. Noah groaned, his eyes closing in ecstasy, as she stroked him, her touch sending shivers down his spine.

As they stood there, the tension between them became unbearable.

With a quiet gasp of surrender, Eve said, "I want you to fuck me, Noah." The words hung in the air like a challenge or a promise.

Noah's eyes flashed with desire as he pulled her closer. "Here?" he asked, his voice low and husky.

Eve nodded, barely able to speak. "Yes."

Noah lifted Eve up, holding her against the wall, his hands grasped her ass, spreading her legs apart. He positioned himself beneath her, his cock pressing against her, and with a swift motion, he thrust inside her.

Eve gasped, her body arched into his touch, as he filled her completely. Noah's hands held her in place as he began to move, his strokes deep and intense. Eve's hands dug into his shoulders, pulling him closer, as she felt herself being pulled into a vortex of pleasure.

The sound of their heavy breathing filled the air, mingling with the scent of sweat and desire. Noah's body trembled with restraint as he tried to hold back, but Eve's wetness and warmth were too much, and he gave in, his thrusts becoming more rapid, more intense.

"I'm going to come." Her voice was barely audible over the sound of their heavy breathing.

As they reached the peak of their passion, Eve's body convulsed and her muscles contracted around Noah's cock as she came, her pleasure mingling with his. Noah's body shuddered, his arms wrapped around her like a vise, holding her close, as he released himself inside her.

As they stood there, wrapped in each other's arms, panting heavily, Eve knew that she had crossed a line. She had given in to her desires and risked everything for a moment of passion with Noah. But as she looked into his eyes, she saw something there that gave her pause—a spark of connection, a sense that this was more than just a fleeting moment of lust.

Eve stepped back to regain her composure, her breath unsteady as reality crashed over her like a cold wave. The quiet alcove now felt suffocating, every shadow a reminder of what they'd just done. She averted her gaze, her hand brushing against the wall as though seeking balance.

"Noah," she began, her voice barely a whisper. "This…this can't happen again."

He studied her, his expression unreadable but achingly familiar. "You keep saying that," he replied softly, "but here we are."

She shook her head, swallowing hard. "I have to go," she said, her voice steadier now, though her hands trembled as she smoothed her gown. She glanced toward the hallway, her mind racing with how to make her return to the ballroom seem effortless.

Noah reached for her hand, stopping her just as she turned away. His touch was gentle, but the weight of it anchored her in place for one more moment. "Eve," he said quietly, his voice laced with something deeper. "You don't have to keep running from this."

Her throat tightened, but she didn't respond. Instead, she pulled her hand free, her gaze fixed firmly ahead as she stepped out of the alcove and headed to the women's bathroom.

Eve re-entered the ballroom. What she had done clung to her like perfume—undetectable to everyone but her. The guests mingled between courses, sipping spiced pear cocktails and mulled wine served in delicate etched glassware. Platters of sugared cranberries and ginger tarts shimmered beneath silver domes, their scents mingling with evergreen and citrus. Laughter rose in waves across the ballroom, a warmth that softened the winter night.

But Eve felt none of it.

Her pulse hadn't settled. Her lips still felt raw.

As she approached their table, her stomach twisted into knots so tight she thought she might be sick.

Leo stood when he saw her, a small smile playing on his lips. "I thought I lost you to the champagne fountain," he teased lightly, reaching for her chair to help her sit.

Eve forced a smile, sliding into her seat. "Something like that."

She waited for relief—waited for the comfort of familiarity to drown out the fire still licking at the edges of her mind. But it didn't come.

Leo was watching her. Not outright suspicion, not yet. But…something.

His eyes lingered on her a second too long, his fingers brushing hers when she reached for her water glass. She forced herself to take a sip, but the liquid felt thick in her throat.

She wasn't imagining it.

Leo was perceptive—always had been. He could read a room in seconds, shift a person's insecurities with one well-placed question. That skill had drawn her to him, made her admire him. But tonight, that same skill was a threat.

"Are you okay?" he asked, his voice warm, steady. The way it always was.

She nodded, too quickly. "I just needed a moment. It's a lot, you know? Speaking, all the emotions in the room."

Leo's expression didn't change, but she caught the small shift in his jaw, the way his fingers tapped once against the table before he stilled them.

Lying to him felt foreign. Heavy.

He was still watching her when Lilah's voice broke through the noise.

"Darling, that speech," Lilah said as she approached, glass in hand, her sequined gown catching the light like a thousand tiny stars. "You had me in tears. And I hate crying—it ruins my makeup."

Eve let out a breath of forced laughter, grasping onto Lilah's presence like a lifeline.

Lilah studied her, her perfectly glossed lips puckered. "But that's not what we need to talk about, is it?"

Eve stiffened. Lilah didn't ask. She *knew*.

Eve held her gaze, then glanced at Leo. He had turned to another guest, momentarily distracted.

"Let's step outside," Lilah said smoothly, her voice quiet but firm.

Eve hesitated. The last thing she needed was a conversation about *this*. Not now. Not when she hadn't even figured out what *this* was.

But Lilah was already moving, and Eve had no choice but to follow.

She followed Lilah toward the terrace, every step feeling heavier than the last.

The cold night air hit her like a reset button, crisp with the faint scent of juniper and distant woodsmoke from the outdoor heaters tucked along the terrace's edge. She inhaled deeply, snow-dusted garlands lining the balustrade glinting faintly under the moonlight—but the weight pressing against her ribs didn't lift.

Lilah leaned casually against the railing, her sequined gown glittering even in the dim light. Eve stayed near the door, arms crossed over her chest, resisting the urge to rub her hands over her arms, as if she could scrub the night off her skin.

Lilah's voice was softer now, but unyielding. "Eve."

She froze.

The warmth in Lilah's voice was deceptive—light, casual, but intentional. Eve turned, forcing a smile, but the second she met Lilah's gaze, she knew.

The knowing glint. The slight tilt of her head. Lilah saw too much.

Eve's pulse quickened. "What?" she asked, aiming for nonchalance, but her voice was thinner than she intended.

Lilah sighed, lips curving into something both amused and disapproving. "That look," she murmured, giving Eve a slow once-over. "It's the kind you only give to a man who makes you forget your better judgement."

Eve stiffened. "Lilah, I don't—"

"You don't have to say anything," Lilah interrupted.

Eve glanced around quickly, scanning the room for Leo, for Noah, for anyone who might see her unraveling. She let out a slow breath, gripping the railing as she willed herself to steady.

Lilah crossed her arms. "You're unraveling."

Eve bristled. "I'm fine."

Lilah scoffed. "You're a lot of things, sweetheart. Fine isn't one of them." She studied Eve for a beat, her sharp gaze missing nothing. "You're slipping, and people are starting to notice."

A cold chill slithered down Eve's spine. "No one noticed anything."

Lilah arched a perfectly sculpted brow. "Didn't they?"

Eve clenched her jaw. She wanted to argue, to dismiss it, but the unease in her stomach refused to subside.

Lilah stepped closer, her voice softer now. "I know that look. The one that says you just did something you shouldn't have."

Eve's fingers curled against the railing, gripping the metal so tightly it bit into her skin.

Lilah exhaled, shaking her head. "You need to be careful, Eve. Whatever this is—whoever this is."

Eve scoffed, shoving down the panic rising in her throat. "I don't need a lecture."

"You need a wake-up call," Lilah countered, her voice sharper now. "Do you even realize how close you are to losing control? To losing everything?"

Eve turned sharply, her eyes flashing. "You don't understand."

Lilah's eyes darkened. "Then make me understand." A beat passed. Then her voice softened, but not in the way that let Eve off the hook. "Tell me what you're really chasing."

Eve's throat tightened. Her nails dug into her palm as she forced herself to meet Lilah's gaze. "I don't know," she admitted, the words trembling as they left her lips. "I just...I need to feel something."

Lilah let out a slow breath, her gaze shifting toward the city lights beyond the terrace. "Yeah," she murmured. "I know that feeling."

Eve glanced at her, the shift in Lilah's voice catching her off-guard.

Lilah smiled wryly, but there was no real humor in it. "I married a man twice my age because I thought it would fix me. I thought money, status, all of it would fill the gaps. But it didn't. And every time I stepped out of line, every time I chased something that felt real, I paid for it."

Eve stared at her, stunned. She had known Lilah for years, but she had never seen this part of her. The part that wasn't glittering under chandeliers or framed by designer gowns.

"Why didn't you ever tell me?" Eve asked quietly.

Lilah's lips twitched, but it was a sad, tired smile. "Because I'm Lilah. The fabulous one. The one who makes everything look effortless. You don't want to see the mess behind the glitter. No one does."

Eve didn't have a response. So she reached for Lilah's hand, squeezing it tightly.

"I don't know how to stop," she admitted, her voice barely above a whisper. "I feel like I'm unraveling, and I don't know how to hold it together anymore."

Lilah turned to face her fully. "Then let me help you," she said. "Let someone help you. You're not alone, Eve. You've got people who love you—people who would do anything to see you happy. But this?" She shook her head. "This isn't the way."

Eve closed her eyes and inhaled deeply. "Thank you," she whispered. "For always being there."

Lilah squeezed her arm before stepping back. "Promise me something."

Eve hesitated. "What?"

Lilah leaned in slightly, her tone almost maternal. "Promise me that whatever you're chasing...whatever this thing is—it doesn't take more than you're willing to give. Because if you let it, it will. And I can't stand by and watch you destroy yourself."

Eve swallowed hard, the truth of Lilah's words slamming into her like a cold wave.

Her voice was barely above a whisper. "I don't even know who I am anymore."

Lilah touched her heart lightly. "That's because you keep looking out there." She gestured vaguely toward the city. "But the truth? It's all in here. You just have to be brave enough to face it."

Eve let out a shaky breath, a tear slipping down her cheek.

Humor sparked behind Lilah's eyes. "Now, come on. Let's get back inside before the bridge club starts whispering that we're plotting to steal their husbands and their jewels."

Eve let out a quiet laugh. But as she followed Lilah back inside, she realized she was running out of time.

Chapter 17

The Empress, The Priestess and

The Moon

Audrey hesitated at the threshold of Eve's office, fingertips grazing the smooth wood of the door. She had been inside the practice before—but never here.

This wasn't just an office. This was Eve's world.

The thought unsettled her more than it should.

"Come in," Eve called from inside, her voice warm, effortlessly controlled. "What brings you by? Hope this isn't a professional visit. I've been keeping my nose clean, Detective."

Audrey stepped inside. "Nothing like that. Just thought it was time I got a look at your world."

Eve sat perched on the edge of her desk, one ankle crossed over the other, looking effortlessly poised in a way Audrey never could. The room mirrored her: polished, composed, every detail curated. The bookshelves stood in flawless order, not a title out of place. A sleek desk gleamed under the soft light, the only imperfection—a vase of white peonies, too delicate against all that control.

Everything about it was deliberate.

Audrey whistled low, shoving her hands into her pockets. "Not bad, Doc. I was expecting something a little more...clinical."

Eve tilted her head. "I try not to terrify my patients the second they walk in." She pushed off the desk and gestured around the room. "But I guess I should've known you'd do a full detective-level analysis the second you walked in."

Audrey snorted. "Old habits."

She turned slowly, letting herself take in the space, absorbing the carefully arranged books, the sleek furniture—until her gaze snagged on something behind Eve's desk.

She froze.

A framed display of three Tarot cards.

The Empress. The High Priestess. The Moon.

The air in the room shifted. Tightened.

Eve followed her gaze, and a small, knowing smile played on her lips. "Beautiful, aren't they?"

Audrey swallowed, stepping closer. The cards were bold, vibrant. Too bold. Too vibrant. They didn't belong here, among all this order.

"Didn't peg you for a Tarot person."

Eve leaned against her desk, arms folding loosely. "Everyone has their secrets."

Audrey's pulse thrummed in her ears. "Do you use them in your practice?"

Eve chuckled, shaking her head. "No. Just a personal thing. These three always meant something to me."

"Meaningful how?"

Eve analyzed her expression. It was thoughtful but unreadable. Then she stepped forward, gesturing to the first card.

"The Empress," Eve murmured, trailing a finger along the first card's gilded edge. "She nurtures, but she doesn't bend. Creation. Power. Strength in vulnerability."

She moved to the next card without breaking stride. "The High Priestess—intuition, secrets. The space between knowing and unknowing."

Audrey's mouth felt dry.
"And the Moon?" she asked, though something deep in her gut told her she already knew.

Eve's lips curved slightly. "Ah. The Moon is deception wrapped in beauty. The whisper of doubt when everything seems clear. Fear. Illusion. And the truths we bury so deeply, we convince ourselves they never existed."

The words hung in the air like smoke.
Audrey's stomach twisted. The room felt smaller. The walls, closer.

Eve wasn't speaking as a casual collector. She wasn't even speaking as a psychiatrist. She was speaking like someone who understood these cards on a level that made Audrey's skin crawl.

It was too precise. Too measured.

Not just something she'd read.

Something she'd lived.

Audrey forced a chuckle, but it came out thin. "Didn't know you were into this kind of thing. Thought you'd be more...I don't know, logic and science."

Eve brushed a strand of blonde hair behind her ear. "When I was a teenager, Tarot was my escape. My parents had expectations—success, achievement, discipline. There wasn't much room for anything else." She gestured at the cards. "This was my rebellion. A quiet one."

Audrey huffed out a small laugh. "I had a witchy phase too. Spells, runes, Tarot—you name it."

Eve's brows lifted slightly. "Really?"

Audrey shrugged. "Yeah. Mom thought I was summoning demons in the basement."

That pulled a real laugh from Eve. A genuine moment. A sliver of connection.

Audrey should have held onto it. But her gaze flicked back to the Tarot cards, and just like that, the moment was gone.

Eve didn't miss it.

Her eyes sharpened. Just slightly. She tilted her head, studying Audrey with that same practiced intensity she probably used on her patients.

"You're quiet," she said. Somewhere between a question and not a question.

Audrey forced a smirk. "You always this nosy?"

Eve's lips quirked. "Occupational hazard. But also…it's you. You were relaxed when you walked in. Now you're different."

Audrey swallowed, forcing her posture to stay casual. "Just thinking."

Eve watched her. "About?"

Audrey hesitated, her heart pounding against her ribs. The words came out before she could stop them.

"How two people can be raised worlds apart…and still end up staring at the same ghosts."

A pause. A beat too long.

Eve's expression didn't change, but something in the air did.

Audrey wasn't sure if Eve was studying her—or dissecting her.

Finally, Eve exhaled softly. "Strange, isn't it?"

Audrey nodded. "Yeah."

She forced herself to hold Eve's gaze.

Strange.

That was one way to put it.

The crisp evening air wrapped around Audrey as she stepped out of Eve's office building, but it didn't cool the heat rising beneath her skin.

She couldn't shake it.

The feeling that something inside that office had shifted—or maybe she had.

Her fingers tightened around the car door handle. The metal was solid, grounding. The streetlights above buzzed faintly. A car drove past, headlights flashing over the pavement. Normal things. Routine. But everything around her felt wrong.

Her thoughts circled those three Tarot cards.

The Empress. The High Priestess. The Moon.

"The Moon is deception wrapped in beauty," Eve had said, her voice steady. "The whisper of doubt when everything seems clear."

At the time, it had been nothing more than a poetic musing. Now?

Now it twisted into something else.

A shiver crawled up Audrey's spine.

Eve had been too poised. Too measured. Like she had rehearsed it.

Was that how she spoke to patients? Smooth, practiced, pulling the exact right words at the exact right moment?

Or was it how she spoke to a detective?

Audrey squeezed her eyes shut, inhaling sharply. Facts over feelings. Evidence over instinct.

But instinct had saved the Miller boy.

The memory hit her like a fist to the ribs.

Ten years old. Missing for three days.

She could still feel his small hands, clawing at her jacket, gripping like she was the only thing keeping him tethered to the world.

"Please don't leave me."

That case had nearly broken her.

Everyone else had stopped believing he was alive. The search had turned into a retrieval mission, not a rescue.

Her chief told her to let it go. "It's been three days, Audrey. The odds are what they are."

But she had felt it—something in her gut, screaming.

The cabin had been at the edge of a dead-end road, nestled between trees so dense they swallowed the moonlight. The air had smelled like rotting wood and cigarette smoke.

She had kicked in the door, gun raised, not knowing what she was about to find.

And there he was.

Curled in the corner, eyes too big for his face, shaking so violently she thought his body might snap in half.

And behind him—Markham.

John Markham.

Audrey could still see the wild grin stretched across his face as he turned toward her, arms raised like he was inviting her to take a shot.

"Funny, Detective," he had said. "You talk like you knew I was gonna be here."

Because she had.

Because she had trusted herself.

Because she had been right.

But now?

Now that same instinct was screaming at her—and she didn't know if it was leading her to the truth or dragging her into a lie.

Her pulse hammered.

She climbed into her car, gripping the steering wheel so tightly her knuckles ached.

The reflection in the rearview mirror wasn't the detective who had saved a boy.

It was a woman unraveling.

And then—

The world stopped.

Not literally. Cars still moved. The streetlights still hummed. The city still pulsed with life.

But for Audrey, everything inside her froze.

Because Markham's words—the ones that had been nothing more than a taunt at the time—came back.

"You talk like you knew I was gonna be here."

But then he had leaned in and lowered his voice as though he had already won.

"Maybe you knew me because we're the same."

The words ripped through her like a blade.

At the time, she had ignored him. Because Markham was a liar, a manipulator, a predator.

But now?

Now those words felt like an open wound.

"Maybe you knew me because we're the same."

The same.

She had spent her career hunting men like him. Like Markham.

And now she was staring at Eve—her own flesh and blood—and wondering if she was looking at one of them.

Her stomach twisted.

She swallowed hard, trying to steady her breathing, but she couldn't shake it.

She and Eve shared the same DNA. The same eyes. The same hands.

If Eve was capable of something unthinkable—

Then what did that mean for Audrey?

Her phone buzzed.

Eddie.

Her fingers hovered over the screen.

She should pick up. She should tell him—

But what could she even say?

"I think my sister might be a killer."

The thought made her physically ill.

The call went to voicemail.

Audrey stared at the screen, pulse thundering in her ears.

She needed to move. To do something—anything—before the walls closed in on her.

Without another thought, she threw the car into gear and drove.

The glow of Audrey's laptop bathed the room in pale light. The apartment was silent, but her mind wasn't.

On the screen, half-typed search queries blinked accusingly:

Psychological traits of killers…

Twin empathy myths…

Can two people share the same darkness?

She hadn't clicked on a single one.

Her fingers hovered over the keyboard, her pulse hammering in her ears.

She was a woman who trusted her gut. That had always been her edge. She wasn't afraid of the dark—she thrived in it. The chase, the puzzle, the unraveling of a person's secrets…it was exhilarating.

But this wasn't some criminal.

This was Eve.

And she might have to destroy her.

A knock at the door.

Audrey stiffened.

Eddie.

Audrey exhaled slowly, forcing the tension from her shoulders before opening the door.

Eddie stood there, tall and solid, his broad frame filling the doorway. He wasn't just big—he was the kind of presence that made a room feel smaller when he walked in. Today, he had a black hoodie slung over a fitted t-shirt, jeans that had just enough wear to look intentional. Hands in his pockets, jaw set.

But it was his eyes that made her stomach twist.

He was looking at her—really looking.

Audrey braced herself for a joke, some cocky remark to cut through the weight pressing down on her. But it didn't come.

Instead, his brow furrowed, his expression unreadable. His usual teasing personality was nowhere to be found.

"You look like you haven't slept in days," he said finally, his voice quieter than usual.

Audrey blinked, caught off guard.
It hadn't even been a full day since she'd seen Eve, but it felt like she'd been untangling for longer. Maybe because she could see it on herself now.

The reflection in the microwave behind Eddie showed everything she was trying to ignore—her loose sweatshirt wrinkled at the hem, leggings creased at the knees, makeup smudged beneath her eyes from where she'd rubbed them too many times. Her ponytail, once neat, was now slipping loose, stray blonde strands framing her face in a way that wasn't intentional.

And she hated that she suddenly cared.

She stepped aside without a word.

Eddie walked in, the scent of pizza trailing behind him. Not just any pizza. She spotted the white box in his hands, red lettering unmistakable. Pequod's.

Sausage and giardiniera.

Her favorite.

Her stomach tightened. She hadn't even realized she was hungry.

Eddie's gaze flicked to the laptop still open on the table, the half-typed search queries glaring in the dim afternoon light.

"You're off today." His brow furrowed. "I don't know what happened, but you look like you got hit with something heavy."

She wanted to brush him off, make some sarcastic remark, but the weight in her chest was too much. Instead, she sighed and rubbed her temples.

"I've just been…stuck in my head."

Eddie tilted his head slightly, studying her. "Is it Eve?"

The name hit her like a fist to the ribs.

Her throat felt tight.

Eddie had been her friend long enough to know when something was off.

She swallowed hard. "It's complicated."

Eddie studied her for a long beat. Then, without another word, he turned and set the pizza box down on the counter, flipping it open.

The scent of caramelized crust and spicy sausage hit her full force.

He grabbed a slice and took a bite, chewing like this was just another ordinary afternoon.

"Don't make me be the only one eating," he muttered between bites. "It's bad for my ego."

Audrey hesitated.

She wasn't sure what made her reach for a slice—hunger or the fact that Eddie wasn't asking her for answers.

Either way, she took one, the cheese stretching as she pulled it free.

Eddie nodded approvingly. "See? Better already."

They ate in silence, the TV murmuring in the background. Audrey barely registered what was playing, but Eddie stretched out beside her on the couch, his arm draped lazily along the back. Casual. Easy.

She let out a slow breath.

It didn't make sense, the way his presence settled her.

Her knee brushed his, and for a fleeting second, she felt him go still.

Not uncomfortable. Just…remembering something.

A moment that had passed years ago.

Eddie had once had feelings for her. She knew that. It had never been spoken aloud, but it didn't have to be. They'd just moved past it—shifted into something else. Something stronger.

Still, there was something in the way he stayed. The way he never pushed but always showed up.

A moment of quiet stretched between them, familiar but weighted.

Eddie broke it first, reaching for the remote. "You know, you're never this quiet unless something's eating at you."

Audrey didn't respond.

Eddie didn't push.

The pizza was half-eaten, the TV still murmuring in the background, when Eddie finally stretched, making a show of yawning.

"Well, I should go before you start crying on me," he teased, standing up. "I'm bad with emotions. It ruins my brand."

Audrey lifted a brow with amusement. "You don't have a brand."

"I do, actually." He grabbed his jacket, slinging it over his shoulder. "It's effortless cool with a hint of sarcasm. You wouldn't get it."

She rolled her eyes, standing too, but something in her chest ached as he walked toward the door.

Eddie lingered for a beat before pulling it open.

"You know where to find me," he said, voice unreadable.

She nodded.

And then, he was gone.

The apartment felt colder.

Audrey turned back to her laptop.

And finally, she clicked.

Chapter 18

Before It All Came Undone

The door to Eve's office clicked shut with a muffled finality, and Noah's measured steps seemed to echo louder than they should have in the serene space. Eve looked up from her desk, her pen pausing mid-motion, and observed him carefully. Tonight, there was something almost magnetic about him—his tailored shirt, a deep blue that offset his warm complexion, clung to his shoulders in a way that accentuated his frame. There was a sharpness to his movements, a quiet confidence that seemed to grow with every session.

"Noah," she greeted, her voice calm yet laced with curiosity. "You seem...different today."

He smiled faintly, his confidence unmistakable as he adjusted his cuffs before sinking into the chair across from her. "Maybe I am," he replied, his tone even but charged with an undercurrent of something unspoken. "I've been feeling stronger lately. Like I'm finally stepping into who I am."

Eve felt her pulse quicken as he spoke, and her mind involuntarily flashed to their stolen moment at the gala. The warmth of his hand on her waist, the unrestrained intensity of his kiss—memories that lingered far longer than they should have. She forced herself to refocus. "That's good to hear," she said, leaning forward slightly. The motion was instinctual, the silk of her blouse catching the warm light and momentarily drawing Noah's eyes. He averted them quickly, but not before she noticed.

He hesitated for a moment, then let out a soft chuckle. "I took charge at work. A meeting that I would've let someone else dominate a few months ago—I owned it. People listened to me. And it felt...different. It felt good."

"That's real progress, Noah," Eve said with a faint smile, her pen resting lightly against the notepad. "You've earned that feeling."

Noah leaned forward, elbows resting on his knees, his gaze locking onto hers. Outside, the last slivers of daylight faded through the window—the city shifting from afternoon into evening.

"I think it's because of you," he said, his voice quieter now, brimming with intensity.

The air between them seemed to thicken, the tension crackling like static. Eve's pulse quickened as his words hung in the air.

She forced herself to respond evenly. "You've done the work, Noah. I've only provided the space."

"No," he said, shaking his head slightly. "It's more than that. You've...seen me. And that's changed everything."

Her fingers tightened around the pen she held, her grip betraying her inner turmoil. "Being seen is powerful," she murmured, her voice almost a whisper.

"And being kissed by someone who sees you," Noah added softly, "is even more powerful."

The words landed between them like a spark, igniting the room with unspoken electricity. Eve's chest tightened as his meaning sunk in. She opened her mouth to respond but found herself at a loss.

"Noah," she began, her voice trembling slightly, "what happened at the gala—"

"—felt right," he interjected smoothly, his tone steady but laced with vulnerability. "It wasn't just a kiss, Eve. You know that as much as I do."

She inhaled sharply, her mind racing to rationalize, to undo the moment. "It was a lapse in judgement," she said, her voice firm but brittle. "And it can't happen again."

Noah leaned forward, his elbows resting on his knees as his gaze pinned her in place. "You keep saying that," he said quietly, "but your actions keep saying something else." His eyes dropped briefly to her hands resting on the desk before flicking back to her face. "You make it easy," he said softly, the words carrying a weight that felt both grounding and dangerous.

The silence that followed wasn't empty—it was charged, thrumming with the unspoken. Eve's resolve wavered, and she felt the familiar pull, that intoxicating mix of danger and desire. She should redirect him, reestablish the boundaries she had already let blur far too many times. But instead, she allowed the moment to stretch, each second eroding the professional wall between them.

"You've come a long way, Noah," she said finally, her voice steady but hollow. "That kind of transformation takes strength."

He tilted his head, his lips twitching into a small smile. "It's because of you," he repeated, his voice firmer now.

"Noah," she began, her voice steady but trembling beneath the surface, "what you're feeling right now—it's natural. But it's important to understand the difference between what's real and what's transference."

He stood suddenly, the movement fluid, almost predatory. Eve tensed as he crossed the small space between them, his presence overwhelming. The air seemed to shift with his proximity, the calm of the office giving way to a charged atmosphere that set her nerves alight.

"I know what this is," he said, his voice low but resolute. "And it's not just transference. Don't tell me you don't feel it too."

Eve opened her mouth to respond, but the words caught in her throat. He was too close, the heat of him radiating like a second skin. Her pulse thundered in her ears as she struggled to summon the professionalism she knew she had to maintain.

"Noah," she tried again, but his name came out as a whisper, her voice betraying the internal war she was losing.

He reached out, his hand brushing against hers, tentative but deliberate. She didn't pull away. "This isn't…" she began, but her voice faltered.

His other hand rose, his fingers grazing her jawline, tilting her face toward his. "Tell me to stop," he murmured, his voice a mix of plea and command.

"You said it yourself," he continued, his voice dropping lower. "You see me. And I see you, Eve."

The name fell from his lips like a secret, and her resolve crumbled. His fingers grazed her jawline and tilted her chin toward him. "Tell me to stop," he repeated. She didn't.

His lips found hers, and the world outside the office disappeared. The kiss was deep, searching, and consuming. Her hands gripped the edge of the desk, her knuckles white as she fought the war raging within her. His confidence, once tentative, now surged, and his touch grew bolder, tracing the curve of her neck to her waist.

The world outside the office seemed to fade away, leaving only the two of them locked in a moment that felt both dangerous and inevitable. His touch was gentle but insistent, his fingers trailing from her jaw to the curve of her neck. She leaned into him, her resolve shattering under her own desire.

For a fleeting moment, Eve allowed herself to surrender. To the pull of his touch, the intoxicating thrill of crossing every line she'd sworn to uphold. But as his hands slid to her waist, reality crashed down around her like a cold wave.

"Noah," Eve said sharply, stepping back like she'd been burned. Her breath came in short, uneven gasps as she pressed a hand to her lips, as if she could erase the moment.

"This—" She forced the words out, each syllable dragging across her throat like gravel. "This is over."

Noah's chest rose and fell, but his eyes stayed locked onto hers, unrelenting. "You don't mean that."

"I do," she said, forcing steel into her tone. "And you need to hear me."

His jaw clenched. "You felt it too."

Eve exhaled sharply, forcing herself to meet his gaze head-on. "It doesn't matter what I felt. It doesn't matter what either of us felt. This was a mistake, and it will not happen again."

Something flickered in Noah's expression—hurt, maybe, but he masked it just as quickly. "And my therapy?"

She hesitated. For a fraction of a second. Then she lifted her chin. "You'll need to find another therapist."

That landed.

Noah inhaled slowly, his Adam's apple bobbing as he processed the words. His fingers flexed at his sides like he wanted to reach for something—maybe her, maybe the moment itself—but he didn't. He swallowed, jaw set, shoulders squared.

Then, after a long silence, he gave a single nod. "Okay."

No argument. No plea. Just acceptance.

Eve didn't let herself exhale. Not yet.

Noah stepped toward the door, pausing with his hand on the knob. "I meant what I said," he murmured. "I don't regret it."

Eve's stomach twisted, but she didn't let it show. She refused to give him anything else.

Instead, she lifted her chin. "Goodbye, Noah."

A beat of silence.

Then, finally, Noah turned the handle and walked out.

The door clicked shut.

Eve locked it. Twice.

And then, slowly, she exhaled. The room was too quiet, too still. The air should have felt lighter. It didn't.

She sank into her chair, gripping the arms like they were the only thing keeping her upright. Her pulse still thundered in her ears, drowning out the silence.

This was the right thing. The necessary thing.

Then why did it still feel like something had come undone?

An hour later, the evening news barely registered over the clinking of dishes and the soothing rhythm of running water. Rory sat at the dining table, arms slumped over her iPad. Leo's footsteps echoed briefly as he descended to the basement, leaving Eve momentarily alone in the tranquil chaos of domestic life.

"Anthony McCall, identified as the latest victim of the Magician…"

The plate slipped from Eve's hand, shattering on the tile floor with a piercing crash that split through the air. She stood frozen, her breath caught between a gasp and a cry, her heart hammering as the name ricocheted in her mind.

Anthony. His name echoed with the weight of memory—of trust, of vulnerability, of intimacy.

Her body locked, every muscle rigid, every nerve screaming, because that name—that name—wasn't supposed to be here.

The blood drained from her face.

Her pulse roared.

Her trembling hands reached for the broken shards. The moment her fingers closed around a jagged edge—pain bloomed.

The noise startled Rory. "Mom!"

Eve barely registered Rory's alarmed cry. Her vision blurred, not from the pain in her hand but from the image flashing on the television. Anthony's photo—a face she knew intimately—filled the screen, his smile was both haunting and heartbreakingly familiar. It wasn't just a face on the news; it was a face she had known in moments of quiet, of passion, of vulnerability.

Frozen in time. A news photo—one she recognized, one she had traced with her fingertips in the quiet, in the dark. His easy, lopsided smile. The warmth in his eyes, caught in a moment of careless charm.

But his face wasn't supposed to be on the news. It wasn't supposed to be among the dead.

Anthony—laughing, head tipped back, fingers brushing over her wrist as if he could hold her there forever.

Anthony—telling her she was the only person who ever truly saw him

Anthony—walking away before she could figure out what he really meant.

And now—

Anthony—gone. Something inside her splintered.

The plate shards blurred under her feet. Her fingers clenched around the porcelain instinctively, and pain sliced deeper, but she hardly felt it.

Her chest constricted as the memories crashed over her in waves, each one sharper, more vivid than the last. It wasn't just Anthony she saw—it was the moments they had stolen, the pieces of herself she had allowed him to carry. And now, those pieces lay scattered, broken, just like the shards of the plate at her feet.

"Eve."

Leo's voice. Firm. Grounding.

Then—his presence.

He was suddenly there, crouching beside her. Warm hands closed around her wrists, steadying her.

She flinched.

Not from the pain—from being pulled back into the moment.

Leo's eyes flickered between her face and the mess on the floor, assessing, calculating.

"What happened?"

Eve's pulse thundered.

Anthony is dead.

"I…I dropped it."

Her voice cracked, brittle, barely above a whisper.

Leo's gaze flicked back to her hands, his jaw tightening.

Without a word, he pulled her to her feet.

The faucet roared to life. Ice-cold water rushed over her palm, stinging, but she barely reacted.

Leo worked in silence, rolling up his sleeves as he rinsed the blood away. His grip was firm but careful, his touch efficient. The rough pad of his thumb brushed against her wrist as he turned her hand beneath the stream, his warmth grounding, solid.

"I'm fine," Eve insisted weakly, but the words rang hollow, even to her. She flinched as he guided her hand under the cool stream of the faucet, the sting of the water sharp but grounding.

"This isn't 'fine,'" he muttered, his voice edged with irritation but laced with something else—something harder to name.

Eve swallowed, her throat tight.

She wanted to tell him to stop looking at her like that.

Like he could see too much.

Like she wasn't as put together as she pretended to be.

He grabbed the first-aid kit, peeling the gauze apart with quick, precise movements. "You're not okay," he countered, watching her. Not just her hand. Not just the cut.

Her.

Eve's fingers curled into a fist as he wrapped the bandage around her palm.

Leo's gaze didn't waver.

"You should sit down."

She nodded absently, stepping away from the kitchen.

The television flickered in the corner of her vision.

Anthony's face lingered.

Rory hovered nearby, watching with wide, worried eyes. "You're bleeding," she said, her voice barely above a whisper.

"I'm okay, sweetheart," Eve lied.

Leo's gaze flicked up to her as he cleaned the wound, his brow furrowed. "You're shaking," he observed, his tone softening. "What's going on?"

"It's nothing," Eve snapped, the sharpness in her voice more reflex than intention. She looked away, her gaze catching on the television screen again.

Anthony's face stared back at her, haunting and accusatory. Her chest tightened further, a hollow ache radiating outward as her mind spun. *How could I not have known? Larkin has been working this case for weeks. How did I miss it?*

Her thoughts swirled chaotically, like leaves caught in a violent windstorm, whipping through fragments of logic and emotion with relentless fury. She thought of the countless times she had poured over Larkin's notes, the late-night updates she had received about the Magician case, the brief mentions of victims—all without ever putting Anthony's name in the mix. It was impossible. It was unforgivable.

Images of Anthony tangled with her thoughts, vivid and unrelenting. His voice—a mix of hope and despair—telling her she was the only one who saw him. The scent of his cologne lingering on her skin after their last encounter. His hand brushing against hers as he'd looked at her with a longing she hadn't dared to acknowledge too deeply. Now his voice was silent, his touch gone forever. The noise of her mind crescendoed, a cacophony of guilt, confusion, and the creeping realization that she had failed in ways she couldn't yet fully comprehend.

Leo's voice broke through her spiraling thoughts. "Eve." His tone was firmer now, pressing.

She turned to him sharply, meeting his gaze. "I said it's nothing," she repeated, but her voice wavered.

His dark eyes narrowed slightly, searching hers. "Is it work?"

"Yes," she lied again, forcing the single word through clenched teeth. "It's always work."

But it wasn't just work. Anthony's laugh echoed in her mind, the way he'd thrown his head back during their late-night conversations, his hand brushing against hers as if the smallest contact would ground him. Anthony's touch lingering on her skin, the low timbre of his voice as he whispered her name in the dim glow of his bedroom. The way he had looked at her—like she was a lifeline in a world intent on swallowing him whole. He ended things so abruptly.

And now, Anthony was gone. The man who had once looked at her like she held the stars had become nothing more than a headline. The Magician's latest victim.

Rory tugged at her sleeve. "Mommy, are you sad?"

Eve's heart clenched. She knelt, forcing a smile that felt paper-thin as she cupped Rory's cheek with her uninjured hand. "No, baby. I'm just tired," she whispered, her voice trembling under the weight of her lie.

Leo finished bandaging her hand, his movements deliberate but tinged with an edge she couldn't place. "You should sit down," he said.

She nodded absently and retreated to the living room, the familiar space suddenly foreign and oppressive. Her eyes drifted back to the television screen, where Anthony's photo lingered, his face frozen in time.

Her pulse a relentless drumbeat in her ears as she stared into the depths of her wine glass. The liquid swirled darkly, its crimson hue a cruel mimicry of the blood she had seen tonight —on her hands, on the shattered ceramic. She couldn't escape the feeling that she was complicit in some way, that her secrets had spilled into a world she couldn't control.

The wine glass trembled in her hand, and for a fleeting moment, she thought about smashing it against the wall, letting the shards scatter like the fragments of her mind. But instead, she set it down, her hand shaking so violently the glass nearly toppled.

"You've been out here a while."

Eve tensed.

He stood in the doorway, arms crossed, watching her.

Eve forced a nod, her movements slow, deliberate. "Just needed a minute."

Leo didn't move.

Didn't believe her.

His eyes flicked to the television.

To Anthony's face.

Then—back to her.

The weight in her chest pressed heavier, sharper.

Finally, he exhaled, his expression unreadable.

"Alright," he said simply.

But he didn't leave.

His gaze lingered.

Then, at last, he turned and disappeared down the hall.

The room felt colder.

Quieter.

More dangerous.

Eve pressed her hand to her forehead, trying to breathe.

Trying to pull herself back.

But the silence pressed in, suffocating.

And Anthony's face never left the screen. Her mind swirled, thoughts of him and the Magician colliding with flashes of her own misdeeds. Noah's face intruded, unbidden—his gaze burning with desire, his words heavy with admiration. Her boundaries collapsed under the reckless pull of their affair. That trust had felt like power, intoxicating and dangerous, but now it felt like a noose tightening around her neck. The threads of her control unraveled, leaving her exposed and vulnerable to the storm she had created.

Was she responsible? Had her actions, her failures, her choices, drawn this chaos into her life? Or worse—had she been part of it all along, without even knowing?

The silence pressed in, heavier and darker, until the final, chilling thought seeped into her consciousness. *What if I'm already too late to stop what's coming? What if this isn't the end?*

Sometime past midnight, the clock on the wall ticked softly—steady, rhythmic, suffocating. Eve sat slumped at her desk, exhaustion pressing her down. Anthony's file stared back at her, thick with unspoken accusations. The dim glow of the desk lamp barely pushed back the shadows, and beneath its pale light, she looked different. Older. Less like a person, more like something unraveling in slow motion. Her fingers drifted over the notes she had taken during Anthony's sessions—structured, clinical, precise. She had spent hours listening to him, observing him, analyzing every hesitation in his voice. And yet, she hadn't seen this coming.

Then—her hand stilled.

A doodle. A Tarot card.

The Magician.

She froze, her stomach twisting. *She hadn't even realized she had drawn it.* But there it was, inked in the margin in sharp, confident strokes. Not Anthony's hand—hers. She had drawn the card absently, her pen scratching at the margins during one of his sessions. The lines were unmistakable: the infinity symbol above the figure's head, the wand pointing skyward, the table strewn with symbols of power. Her gaze snapped to the framed Tarot cards hanging on the far wall. They had been there for years—silent, unmoving. A relic of a past self. A fascination she had long since buried.

Or had she?

The cards seemed to loom now, larger than they had any right to be, the muted gold of their borders catching the faint flicker of the lamp's light. Her chest tightened. Why had she drawn it? Had it been unconscious? A meaningless sketch born from idle hands? Or was it something deeper? Her breath quickened as she stared at the lines, the edges of the drawing now etched into her mind like a brand.

The questions circled her like vultures, each one pecking away at her composure. *Had I known?* Her pulse thrummed in her ears as her thoughts spiraled, a cacophony of doubts, fears, and half-formed memories clawing at her.

The lamp flickered. The glow pulsed—a heartbeat, alive and watching. The edges of her vision blurred, her exhaustion pulling her under. The pen slipped from her fingers and her head tilted forward.

She didn't realize she had closed her eyes until she was already dreaming.

And then—

Darkness.

Something exhaled in the room with her.

The air around her turned cold, damp, heavy. Eve opened her eyes—or thought she did—but the darkness was absolute. The desk lamp was gone, the soft hum of the office replaced by an oppressive silence that pressed against her skin. Her breath fogged the air as she took an uneasy step forward, her heels clicking against a surface she couldn't see.

A pulse of light beneath her feet—faint, flickering. When Eve looked down, her stomach lurched.

Magician Tarot cards. Hundreds of them. Stretched in a path before her, each card identical. Staring up at her. Again and again and again.

As she walked, the cards crunched under her steps, their glossy surfaces smeared with what looked like blood.

A voice—

Not a whisper. Not a scream. Something in between.

"Eve."

She turned, every muscle seizing.

Anthony stood at the far end of the path, his face pale and gaunt, his eyes shadowed and glassy. Blood dripped steadily from his hands, pooling around his feet and staining the cards beneath him. He didn't move. He simply stood there, his gaze fixed on her, unblinking.

Her heart pounded as she tried to speak, but her voice was trapped, caught somewhere between her chest and her throat. She stepped closer, her feet reluctant but driven by an unseen force.

"You knew," Anthony whispered, his voice hollow and disembodied.

"I didn't—" Eve stammered, but the words died in her mouth.

The path of cards began to shift, curling and bending like something alive. They slithered, twisting beneath her feet, forming a bridge that led directly to Anthony's feet. The blood dripping from his hands began to spread, running in rivulets that pooled into strange, swirling patterns. The whispers grew louder, overlapping, chaotic.

"You knew…" Anthony repeated, his voice now layered with others. "You always knew."

The scene shifted violently. The ground tilted, and Eve fell, her hands scraping against the now-slick cards. She scrambled to her feet, only to find herself in a dimly lit room. Candles flickered along the edges, their flames unnaturally still. Tarot cards littered the floor in a perfect circle, and in the center, Anthony lay sprawled, his body contorted unnaturally, his lifeless eyes wide open and fixed on her.

Her breath came in short gasps as the Magician card floated up from the pile, spinning in the air like it was taunting her. It stopped abruptly, hovering inches from her face. The figure on the card seemed alive now, its infinity symbol pulsing, its hand reaching out toward her. She stumbled back, tripping over

Anthony's body, her hands landing in a warm, sticky puddle. Blood. So much blood.

The whispers grew into a deafening roar. The Magician swelled, its borders pulsing like a heartbeat, growing until it consumed her, until it swallowed the very air from her lungs.

Mirrors.

A thousand reflections surrounded her, each one shifting, distorting—wrong.

The Eve staring back wasn't her.

Her eyes were feral. Her lips curled in a smile that wasn't hers.

And her hands—oh God, her hands.

A knife. A syringe. A coil of rope.

"Take it," the figure commanded, its voice deep and distorted, reverberating through the void.

Eve shook her head, stepping back. "No...no..."

"It's yours," the figure intoned, its voice a guttural growl. It thrust the card toward her, and Eve felt an invisible force pull her forward. She clawed at the ground, desperate to escape, but her body betrayed her, dragging her closer and closer. The card's light burned brighter, searing into her mind.

The figure's laughter filled the space, a sound so low and cruel it made her stomach turn. "You can't run from it. You never could."

"No!" she screamed, her voice finally breaking free, raw and desperate. "I didn't do this! I'm not—"

The figure lunged. Its hand gripped her throat, ice-cold and unrelenting.

She gasped, clawed, fought. But the darkness swallowed her whole.

Eve jolted awake, her chair screeching against the floor as she scrambled to right herself. Her chest heaved with ragged breaths, her heart hammering as though it would burst from her ribcage. The file on her desk lay open, the Magician doodle staring back at her like an accusation.

The clock read 3:17 a.m., the only sound in the room the faint ticking that now seemed unbearably loud. Her fingers curled into fists as she shoved the file away, but the whisper slithered through the silence, wrapping around her like a noose: *It's yours.*

The next afternoon, the house was suffocating and pressed in on Eve from all sides, thick as humidity before a storm, curling into her lungs, weighing down her limbs. The television murmured in the background, its flickering light carving restless shadows along the walls.

Rory curled against Leo's side, giggling softly at something on the screen, a sound so normal it felt like a foreign language. The scent of popcorn lingered in the air. The soft hum of the furnace kicked on.

All of it ordinary. All of it unbearable.

Eve stared at her phone.

A single line of text burned against the glow of the screen.

We need to talk.

Her thumb hovered.

Type. Delete.

Type. No, too defensive. Delete.

Type again. Too needy. Delete.

Each version sat there for a fraction of a second before being erased, as though any response would somehow make it real.

Leo shifted, his arm draped over the couch. "Eve, are you even watching?"

She flinched. The screen swam into focus—black-and-white, sharp strings carving through the air. Hitchcock, maybe. She couldn't remember which one.

"Yeah," she lied.

She hadn't heard a single word.

Her phone buzzed in her palm, the vibration thrumming through her bones. She didn't look at it. Not yet.

Leo's gaze flicked toward her, assessing. He was too good at reading between the lines.

Then—Rory turned, blinking up at her. "Mom, you forgot my lunch today."

The words cut clean through her, sharper than they should have been.

Leo's brows lifted. "She forgot?"

"I—I'm sorry, sweetheart." The apology came out too fast, breathless. "I'll make it up to you tomorrow."

Rory shrugged, unfazed. "It's okay. My friend shared her sandwich."

Her chest constricted.

Her phone buzzed again.

Leo caught the shift in her posture—how tightly she gripped the device, how her shoulders tensed.

"Who keeps blowing up your phone?" he asked, tone light, but threaded with something sharper.

Her pulse jumped. "Work," she said automatically. "Just follow-ups."

Leo didn't respond. He didn't need to. The silence was enough.

The walls were closing in.

"I have to take this," she said abruptly, rising from the couch. "It's urgent."

Rory's small voice followed her. "Where are you going?"

Eve hesitated. She forced a smile—too tight, too thin. "Just a quick call, sweetheart. I'll be right back."

She stepped into the hallway, out of sight.

Pressed her back against the wall.

Finally exhaled.

Her fingers hovered over her screen. The message stared back at her.

I'll explain everything when I see you. Tonight at 8.

A tremor rippled through her.

She shouldn't do this.

She should go back to the couch, pretend everything is fine, force herself to be the version of Eve she was supposed to be— the wife, the mother, the composed professional.

Instead, she typed.

I'll see you tonight.

The streetlights stretched long shadows over the pavement, their glow weak against the night. The cold air curled around her like a whisper, slipping beneath the collar of her coat, pricking at the nape of her neck.

Eve sat rigid behind the wheel, her fingers locked around the leather like it was the only thing tethering her to the present.

She shouldn't be here.

The thought pounded through her, insistent, desperate, the last defense against the magnetic pull of inevitability.

She could still leave.

She could press her foot against the gas, watch his house shrink in the rearview mirror, convince herself this was nothing—a fleeting impulse, a moment of weakness, an illusion of need.

The rational part of her begged her to listen.

But the rest of her—the part that had clawed its way out of the wreckage of today, the part still raw and bleeding—refused to move.

The night pressed against the windshield, distorting reflections in the glass. Every house darkened, their windows like vacant stares, lifeless and watching. The only thing that felt real was the dim glow of Noah's porch light—a single, flickering tether to something human.

What was she doing?

Then, before she could think herself out of it, before she could give in to the screaming voice telling her to go home, she moved.

Her finger pressed the doorbell.

A heartbeat.

Then—Noah.

He filled the doorway, silhouetted against the warm glow inside, dark eyes scanning her, searching, dismantling her, piece by piece.

"You're late," he said, stepping aside.

"I know." Her voice was raw, uneven. "I almost didn't come."

She stepped inside hesitantly, her presence at odds with the room's quiet order. Noah, in a fitted gray sweater and dark jeans, looked as put-together as his surroundings. Even here, he exuded quiet confidence—the image of a man who had found his footing. Or so he wanted to believe.

Eve's gaze flicked around the room, unfocused. The warm lighting, the scent of cedarwood—none of it seemed to register. She stopped near a chair and set her bag down with stiff, mechanical movements.

Noah's brow furrowed in concern. "Eve," he said, measured. "What's going on?"

She let out a short, brittle laugh. "I don't even know where to start."

Her hands trembled as she ran them through her hair, a nervous tic he hadn't seen before. She watched as he realized that the Eve he knew—strong, poised, unshakable—was gone.

"Then don't," he said, stepping closer. "You don't have to explain. Just...be here. I'm not going anywhere."

Her lips pressed into a thin line. "I shouldn't have come," she muttered, wrapping her arms around herself. "I don't know what I was thinking."

Noah hesitated, then reached out, his fingers grazing her arm. Slow. Careful. Like she was something delicate, breakable—but not fragile.

"You came because you needed someone," he said, voice softer now. "And because you know I won't walk away."

Her gaze lifted, a mix of defiance and despair. She started to speak, then faltered. When the words finally came, they were rushed, uneven.

"Anthony's dead."

Noah blinked. "Anthony?"

"Yes. A patient." Her voice wavered, composure slipping. "But he was more than that."

Her confession hung between them, heavy and unspoken. Noah's chest tightened. "You and Anthony..."

Her nod was sharp, almost defiant. "We had an affair. He ended it months ago. And now he's gone, and I can't stop thinking about it. About him. How I didn't see it coming."

Noah stepped back, his presence shifting, absorbing what she had just said. His fingers twitched at his sides, like he wanted to reach for her but wasn't sure if he was allowed.

Eve barely noticed.

The room felt too small. The walls too close. The air too thick, pressing against her ribs like it wanted to squeeze her lungs shut. She tried to swallow, but her throat locked.

She'd said the words out loud.

Anthony is dead.

And just like that, they became real. The weight of them crashed down.

She wrapped her arms around herself, fingers digging into the sleeves of her coat as though she could hold herself together through sheer force. "The news," she rasped, her voice brittle, cracking. "The Magician."

Noah's expression barely flickered, but she saw the way his Adam's apple bobbed. "Anthony was his latest victim?" His posture stiffening, like someone had just yanked the floor out from under him. "The Magician...the serial killer?"

Eve nodded. Her jaw locked. She clenched it so tightly that the pressure rang in her ears.

His face flashed in her mind—Anthony's easy, lopsided smile. The feel of his breath against her cheek, the way his fingers would skate along the inside of her wrist when no one was watching, the way he had looked at her that last time—

No.

She shoved the memories down before they could surface, but her stomach churned violently.

"It was over," she said, but even as the words left her lips, they felt wrong, like she was reciting them from someone else's script. A truth she had rewritten so many times it had started to feel real. "He ended it, then disappeared. And now he's dead, and I—" Her breath faltered, her pulse hammering so violently it felt like her ribs might crack beneath it.

She swallowed hard, forcing herself to finish. "I can't stop thinking about it. About him. About how I didn't see it coming."

The last words came out strangled, nearly lost to the silence that followed.

Noah's fingers twitched at his sides, curling into a fist before flexing open again. His expression was controlled, but tension coiled in his stance, like he was bracing himself.

"You couldn't have known," he said, steady but clipped. Like he was trying to convince her. Or himself. "Eve, you're not a mind reader."

A brittle, splintered laugh broke from her throat and the terrifying part was she couldn't seem to stop it.

"That's the problem, Noah," she whispered, the words laced with something sharper than grief.

Guilt.

"I should have seen the signs."

The confession felt like an admission of something unforgivable.

"I was his therapist," she said, barely above a breath. "For God's sake."

Her stomach twisted, nausea rising hot and acidic. She squeezed her eyes shut, but it didn't stop the memories from crashing over her. His case file—buried under others. Reports she barely skimmed. Details she should have caught but didn't.

She sucked in a shaky breath. "My team—my subordinates—they were working the case. I wasn't involved, not directly. I signed off on things, but I trusted them. I thought everything was handled."

A humorless scoff slipped out. "I told myself I was being professional, keeping my distance—but I was avoiding it. Avoiding him. Avoiding anything that made it real."

Her fingers dug into her arms, her nails pressing through fabric to the skin beneath. "And then, suddenly, it wasn't a file on my desk anymore. It wasn't notes I could skim. It was his face on the news."

"I saw the name before I saw the photo, and I—I actually thought, 'God, what are the odds?'"

She let out a ragged exhale, shaking her head. "And then I saw his face, and my whole body just—stopped."

Noah stayed silent, watching her. His stillness only made it worse—like he was letting her spiral, letting her lay out the full, ugly truth.

Eve dragged a trembling hand through her hair. "I let myself believe I had it under control." Her laugh was hollow. "And then I didn't."

She forced herself to look at Noah, and his expression was unreadable—but his eyes weren't.

She expected judgement.

She found something else.

A tension she couldn't name.

"You're human," he said finally, his voice firmer now, but quiet. "You don't have to carry this alone."

She wished she believed him, but she turned her face away sharply, like she could deflect the words before they reached her.

He didn't understand.

She had spent years carrying this alone.

Being the one everyone leaned on. The one who had the answers. The one who didn't fall apart. Because falling apart meant failure.

She let out a sharp exhale, fingers pressing against her temples. "I've always had to keep it together," she muttered. "My parents drilled that into me—falling apart wasn't an option. And now—"

Her voice broke.

A fracture. A crack in the foundation.

Noah stepped forward, and she didn't stop him.

His hands landed on her shoulders—gentle, deliberate, like he thought she might shatter beneath his touch. His fingertips barely pressed into her skin, his warmth bleeding through the thin fabric of her coat. A question lingered in his touch, an unspoken plea for permission.

"Hey," he said, voice low, steady. A whisper meant just for her. "You're not alone. I'm here."

She hated how much she wanted to believe him.

The words coiled around something fragile inside her, something she had spent years burying beneath poise and precision, beneath all the carefully constructed walls that kept her standing.

Her gaze lifted to his, searching.

But all she saw was him. His eyes locked onto hers, steady and certain, like he'd already decided she was worth the risk. Like whatever she was about to give—or take—he'd accept it without hesitation and stay present for her.

Something inside her caved.

Slowly—too slowly—she let herself lean into him. The movement felt unnatural at first, her body resisting the comfort, but exhaustion won out.

God, she was so tired.

Her forehead found his chest, the fabric of his sweater soft against her skin, warm from his body heat. His scent wrapped around her, threading through her senses, tugging her deeper into the moment.

Her ribs tightened around the air she struggled to take in. She could feel the way her body held itself—rigid, on the verge of flight, like a bird too used to cages to recognize an open door.

His arms curled around her, pulling her firmly into him, not forceful, not demanding—but protective. Grounding.

She sucked in a sharp breath as his embrace settled around her like an anchor.

"Then I'll keep you afloat."

A promise.

The words shouldn't have mattered.

But they did.

They pressed into the hollow spaces inside her, the places where guilt and doubt had carved out something too raw to name. They filled the fractures she refused to acknowledge, seeped into the cracks she had spent so long convincing herself didn't exist.

The moment stretched, heavy with something dangerous.

The silence between them wasn't empty. It was charged, thick with unspoken things—a line she wasn't sure she had the strength to redraw.

Noah's heart beat beneath her cheek—a slow, steady rhythm. Certain.

Unlike hers.

Eve's didnt move. Her lips parted slightly, but she said nothing, her mind at war with her body's impulse to pull away. Instead, she stayed.

And that was the most dangerous thing of all.

The quiet drive home had done nothing to untangle the knots in her chest.

Now she sat across from Leo, the room steeped in low amber light, shadows pooling in the corners like things half-asleep. His gaze cut sharply through the quiet stretching between them.

Leo lounged back against the couch, casual in posture, deliberate in everything else. His voice sounded soft—almost bored—but she knew better.

"You've been on edge since learning about Anthony's death."

Her breath faltered—just for a beat. *Patient.* The word echoed in her skull like it should mean distance. Detachment. But it didn't. She forced herself to meet Leo's stare, lips curling into something cool, composed. "He was a patient, Leo. It caught me off guard. Anyone would be shaken." Not a lie. But not the truth either.

His head tilted—not quite convinced and not fooled. The smallest flicker of interest curled at the edge of his mouth. Watching her. Weighing her.

"Mmm," Leo hummed. "Seems like more than that."

A test.

Her pulse tightened in her throat. "Let it go, Leo."

It wasn't a plea. It was a warning.

Leo didn't push, but she could feel him turning the pieces over in his mind.

She rose, smoothing her palms over her thighs—a gesture meant to look effortless, but nothing felt effortless anymore.

The hallway stretched before her, dark and empty, but it felt occupied. Heavy. Like something unseen was pressing against the walls, watching. The bathroom light flickered on with a quiet click, the sudden brightness stabbing at her eyes. Eve exhaled slowly and shut the door behind her, bracing against the weight of the house, the night, the silence.

The moment she was alone, her breath stuttered out of her like she'd been holding it for hours.

She caught the edge of the sink and gripped it as if anchoring herself to the real, the solid, the now.

Cold water roared against the porcelain. She splashed it over her face—once, twice—as though it could wash away what clung to her skin. A tangled ruin of memory, grief, and guilt.

The mirror caught her in its grip. She swore her reflection lagged behind. Like it wasn't quite her.

Her hair hung in uneven strands, her skin ghostly, the shadows under her eyes carving deep hollows. But it was the way she looked at herself that sent a shiver down her spine—drawn, hollowed, unfamiliar. Like she was staring at a stranger who had borrowed her face.

She looked like a woman unraveling.

A sharp knock against the bedroom wall made her stomach lurch.

Leo.

Eve squeezed her eyes shut.

He would follow soon. She knew him. Knew his patterns, his instincts. He was already suspicious. Already watching her movements, cataloging every misstep, every second she spent in here.

Her hands moved on autopilot, twisting bottle caps, reaching for serum, for moisturizer, for anything to make it look like routine instead of escape.

But she fumbled.

A bottle slipped from her fingers, clattering against the counter. Frustration burned through her ribs as she clenched her jaw, fingers curling into fists.

Eve shut off the faucet. Her movements slowed, deliberate, as if she had to will each one into existence. She met her own gaze in the mirror, staring—searching. Then, without a word, she flicked off the light and stepped into the hallway.

Leo was already in bed, but he wasn't resting. He lay still, too still, arms crossed behind his head in a way that was almost studied, like he was positioning himself to appear relaxed. But his eyes tracked her, careful, waiting—like he was watching a suspect, not his wife.

She didn't acknowledge him.

Not because she wanted to be cruel—but because she wasn't sure if she could meet his gaze without betraying everything.

The silence thickened.

She peeled off her clothes, swapped them for pajamas in stiff, mechanical movements, then slipped under the covers. The mattress dipped under her weight; the warmth of her body just close enough to remind him how far apart they were.

Eve lay beside him, back turned, breath uneven. He hesitated, then reached out, fingertips grazing the curve of her waist—testing the waters.

Her entire body went rigid.

"Eve." His voice was gentle. Cautious.

She squeezed her eyes shut.

For a second, she considered leaning back. Letting him pull her into his warmth. Letting him make this feeling go away even, if only, for a moment.

But she couldn't.

She edged away, her body curling into itself, retreating to the farthest sliver of the bed.

A beat of silence. Then, slowly, his hand withdrew.

But the absence of his touch didn't ease her—it made her hyperaware of herself. Of the way her breath shuddered unevenly. Of the restless twitch in her fingers. Of the unbearable tightness in her ribs, like she was trapped in her own body, unable to breathe, unable to escape herself.

Her throat clenched around something thick, suffocating. The pressure built, rising, rising—until her breath broke in a small, trembling sound. A sniffle. Too quiet, but enough.

Leo heard it. She knew he did.

She could feel his presence behind her, his thoughts spinning, circling, cataloging.

He was still watching. Still piecing together the cracks she thought she had concealed.

The silence stretched, pressing against her ears until it was deafening.

She couldn't breathe.

The sheets pinned her in place. The air pressed against her ribs. She could feel her own pulse behind her eyes, hammering, drowning out Leo's steady breath beside her.

Don't move. Don't let him see.

But her body betrayed her. A sharp, uncontrollable lurch surged up from her core. The moment she moved, it was a mistake. The air turned thick, the sheets twisting around her legs, tightening, trapping. Her chest caved in.

She needed out. Now.

Her limbs fought against her, barely carrying her to the bathroom before she slammed the door behind her.

Leo sat up instantly, alarm flashing across his face as she stumbled toward the bathroom, her feet barely registering the cold floor.

The moment the door shut behind her, she gripped the counter and squeezed her eyes shut.

Breathe.

The nausea rose quickly, burning through her throat.

She lurched forward.

The retching sound barely made it past her lips before her stomach clenched, violently rejecting what little she had eaten.

The water roared to life again as she rinsed her mouth, as if she could erase the remnants of this moment, as if she could wash it all away.

A creak from the bedroom.

Leo.

She braced herself.

A second passed. Then another.

The second she stepped into the bedroom, the air shifted.

Leo's eyes tracked her, steady. Unhurried. Too calm. Like he had already drawn his own conclusions and was waiting to see if she'd confirm them.

Eve's pulse slammed against her ribs, but she kept her movements steady—mechanical—as she crossed the room and slipped back beneath the covers.

The sheets were cold, but Leo's gaze was warm. Too warm.

Like he was waiting for something.

Her pulse hammered.

"Eve," he murmured, barely above a whisper.

She didn't let him finish. "I'm fine."

But she turned her back to him before he could press further, curling into herself, her body a fortress of tension and exhaustion.

Leo didn't speak again.

But she could feel it—his thoughts winding tighter and tighter and his stare heavy against her back.

She could feel the moment he turned onto his back, the shift of the mattress beneath him.

Could feel the way his breathing slowed, controlled.

She knew he wasn't asleep.

Neither was she.

And neither of them spoke the words that hung between them, thick as smoke.

But the moment she closed her eyes, she saw Anthony's face.

Waiting. Watching. Accusing.

Chapter 19

A Tapestry of Murder

Victim 1 - Ryan Williams (14 Years Ago)

Leo hovered at their apartment door, juggling a bag of groceries while fishing for his keys. As he stepped inside, Eve's voice floated through the space—low, melodic, laced with a playfulness he hadn't heard in months.

"Of course I remembered," she said, her tone almost flirtatious. A pause. "Next time? We'll see."

Leo froze, the bag slipping lower in his grasp. His stomach twisted. Then—the sharp snap of her phone shutting. Silence. He took a step forward, the sound heavier than intended. Eve appeared in the doorway, momentarily startled before smoothing her face into that effortless, practiced smile.

"Hey," she said, breezing past him toward the kitchen. She poured a glass of water, her movements casual. "You're back early."

"Who was that?" Leo asked, keeping his voice even.

"Just a patient," she said, sipping her water. "Quick follow-up."

He nodded, but doubt had already rooted itself deep.

A few days later, while Eve was at work, curiosity—no, paranoia—got the better of him. He rifled through her desk, his pulse hammering as he sifted through papers and files. His fingers halted on a small, leather-bound notebook—familiar. He flipped it open. Clinical notes.

At first, the entries seemed innocuous, detailing her sessions with various patients. But then he saw the name: Ryan.

His breath caught as he scanned the lines.

Session 6: Noted progress. He craves praise, bends under affirmation. It's thrilling to see how easily he bends to my suggestions.

Session 8: The line blurred today. I moved first. He followed without hesitation. The power is intoxicating.

The notebook slipped from Leo's trembling hands, his mind reeling. She hadn't just been unfaithful—she had used her skills, her intelligence, to manipulate someone into her orbit. His Eve, the woman he adored, had toyed with another man like he was a pawn in her game. He felt like the ground beneath him was crumbling. They were engaged, planning a life together, their days filled with excitement and their nights often stolen by the demands of their budding careers. But even in the midst of this shared ambition, Eve had found time for someone else—a patient, no less. The thought sent a wave of nausea rolling through him.

That evening, Leo sat on the couch, a movie playing in the background, waiting for Eve to come home. When she finally arrived, she slipped off her heels and unfastened her hair, her face glowing with the satisfaction of a good day. She kissed him lightly on the cheek, her smile perfunctory, before she breezed into her office. Her focus was elsewhere, her eyes flickering to her phone every few minutes.

"You've been busy," he said, his tone light but probing. "How's work?"

"It's good," she replied absently. "Lots of new patients."

His gaze hardened. "Anyone stand out?"

She finally looked at him, her brow furrowing slightly. "Not really. Why?"

"Just curious," he said, forcing a smile. But inside, his resolve hardened. She wouldn't admit it—she would never admit it. If he wanted answers, he'd have to find them himself.

Later, as Eve prepared for bed, Leo found her sitting at her desk. She opened the drawer where her Tarot cards were stored, pulling down the worn deck with care.

"You still use those?" Leo asked, his voice deceptively casual as he leaned against the frame.

Eve glanced back at him, startled but not suspicious. "Not really. They're more for decoration these days." She held the deck in her hands, running her fingers over the intricate designs on the back. "I guess they remind me of a simpler time."

Her tone softened, taking on a wistful quality he hadn't heard in months. "My parents hated them," she said with a small laugh. "Thought they were too mystical, too rebellious. But I always loved how beautiful they were. And the meanings behind them...they always felt like stories waiting to be told."

She began to shuffle the cards, her movements absent-minded but practiced. A few moments later, she paused, selecting three cards and setting them aside: the Empress, the High Priestess, and the Moon. "These were always my favorites," she murmured, almost to herself. "The stories they tell, the power they hold—it's beautiful, really." After a moment, she gathered the rest of the deck, tucking them neatly back into their box, leaving the three selected cards on the desk as if still contemplating them.

Leo's gaze locked on the cards as her words hung in the air. Beautiful. Powerful. Was that how she saw herself? The thought tightened his chest. She was his—his fiancée, his future wife— and yet, these cards, these symbols, seemed to hold a piece of her he could never reach.

She didn't notice the storm brewing in his eyes as she tucked the cards neatly back into their box. "They're just stories," she said with a shrug, breaking the silence. "But I always thought they had a kind of magic."

She spoke so fondly of the cards, so reverently, while her betrayal sat unspoken between them like a poison. Did she think of her patient this way? Did she see him as magic?

An idea simmered, dark and insidious, taking shape in his mind.

Later that night, as Eve slept soundly beside him, Leo sat at her desk, the Tarot cards spread out before him. The three she'd chosen sat at the top, their imagery vivid and unsettling: the Empress, a figure of nurturing and creation, embodying both strength and vulnerability; the High Priestess, a symbol of mystery and hidden power; and the Moon, shrouded in illusion and intuition, pulling on the threads of the subconscious.

His fingers hovered over the rest of the deck, flipping through them one by one until his gaze caught on the King of Pentacles. The card radiated authority, stability, and dominance. It was a mirror of what he wanted to be—the foundation Eve could rely on, the anchor in her chaos. But now, it felt like something more. It felt like justice.

The words in her patient notes replayed in his mind, each one like a needle piercing his chest. She had manipulated this man, pulled him into her orbit, and then discarded him like he was nothing. And Leo was supposed to just stand by and let it happen?

No. If Eve wanted control, he would show her what it truly meant.

Ryan was easy to track. Leo had memorized every detail from Eve's notes—his coffee shop, his gym, his commute. For weeks, he followed, his rage simmering beneath the surface. Ryan moved through life blissfully unaware, oblivious to the shadow stalking his every step.

The night of the murder was cold. Rain slicked the pavement, turning the alley into a mirror of neon and shadow. Ryan barely registered the movement before Leo's fist cracked against his jaw, sending him sprawling into the alley wall. Leo didn't hesitate. He wouldn't stop now. Ryan staggered, dazed. Leo moved fast, slamming him onto the wet pavement. His hands closed around Ryan's throat, fingers pressing deep. Ryan's eyes widened in horror; his gasps choked into silence as Leo squeezed tighter.

"You should've stayed away from her," Leo murmured, his voice steady, almost gentle. The menace was in the quiet. The satisfaction of hearing Ryan's labored breathing fueled Leo's resolve. He leaned closer, his face inches from Ryan's, and repeated, "You should have stayed away."

Leo's hands squeezed tighter, cutting off Ryan's air supply. He felt a sense of calm wash over him as he watched Ryan's face turn purple, his eyes rolling back in his head. The struggle was brief, but intense. Ryan's body bucked and convulsed beneath Leo, but he held firm, his grip unyielding.

Ryan's body went limp. Leo let go, watching the final shudder of breath leave him. He straightened, exhaling slow and steady. No regret. No remorse. Only a sense of satisfaction. Justice had been served.

Ryan crumpled. Leo crouched, sliding the King of Pentacles from his pocket. His fingers brushed the card's edge before pressing it to Ryan's chest—his mark, a quiet declaration only he understood.

Leo's eyes gazed down at the card, the image of the King of Pentacles staring back at him. He felt a sense of kinship with this king, this symbol of material wealth and earthly power. But Leo wasn't just playing the role—he *was* the king now. And kings didn't hesitate.

The ritual wasn't complete. Leo crouched beside Ryan's body, movements precise—clinical. The coroner in him knew every cut, every delicate extraction. From his jacket, he pulled a sterile kit from the morgue, flipping it open with practiced ease. From the kit, he retrieved a thin, curved instrument, designed for the delicate task at hand. With a steady hand, he made a small incision in the sclera, carefully prying the retina loose from its delicate moorings. The only sound was the soft clink of his tools against the metal kit. He placed the delicate tissue in a small vial filled with a clear preservative, sealing it with a twist of his wrist. Leo pocketed the vial, its weight grounding him.

Leo's eyes locked onto Ryan's, even though the man could no longer see. He believed that the eyes were the windows to the soul, and by taking them he wasn't just taking a life—he was claiming something deeper. A piece of Ryan. Reclaiming the piece of Eve Ryan had taken from him.

The city streets stretched out before him like a kingdom. Leo exhaled. He had done what needed to be done. To protect her. To protect them. He was the king. And kings did not bow.

As he walked, Leo couldn't help but think about the next King in his Tarot deck. The thought sent a shiver down his spine, a thrill of excitement mixed with anticipation.

He knew that he couldn't stop now. He had to keep going, had to keep protecting Eve from those who would seek to harm her. And so he walked on into the night, ready for whatever lay ahead.

Leo never showed up unannounced.

It wasn't his style.

And yet, here he was, standing in the sterile quiet of the practice Eve was finishing her residency at, holding a paper bag from one of her favorite cafés. The scent of rosemary and warm bread curled through the air, starkly out of place in a building that smelled like antiseptic and paper. A rare gesture—one that, under normal circumstances, might have earned him a flicker of a smile, a touch of appreciation.

But before he could ask the receptionist to call her down, he heard a name that changed everything.

"Dr. Field, someone's on the line about a former patient. Ryan Williams. His family says he's missing."

Leo's grip on the paper bag tightened, the waxed cardboard crinkling in his grasp.

Missing.

The word coiled through his mind, smooth and unhurried, settling in the space between his ribs. He didn't react. Not outwardly. Years of practice had made sure of that. He simply shifted his stance, casually scrolling through his phone, his posture so at ease that no one would guess he was listening.

Across the room, Eve went still.

It was subtle—the faintest hitch in breath, the way her hand stiffened around the disposable coffee cup before she set it down. A casual observer might not have noticed.

But Leo wasn't a casual observer.

He studied her. Cataloged the shift in her body language like ink spreading through water. The way her shoulders locked, then relaxed too deliberately. The way she smoothed a hand down the front of her blouse as if to ground herself before picking up the receiver.

Her voice, when it came, was measured. Smooth, practiced. Too practiced.

"This is Dr. Eve Field."

Leo turned off his phone screen and slid it into his pocket. His focus narrowed.

A woman's voice crackled through the receiver, raw and edged with controlled panic.

"Dr. Field," she exhaled, her breath shaky. "My brother, Ryan Williams… He hasn't been home. It's been days. He told me he was seeing someone at your practice. Did you—" A beat. A hesitation. "Did you notice anything unusual?"

Leo adjusted the bag in his hands, shifting just slightly for a clearer view of Eve's face.

Her fingers curled against the desk. Not clenched—not quite—but tense enough that he knew she was holding something back.

"I'm so sorry," Eve said smoothly, her voice even. "Ryan was…quiet. Introspective. I wish I could tell you more, but I'm sure you understand doctor-patient confidentiality."

Leo's gaze sharpened.

He knew that tone.

She was convincing herself.

A pause. The woman on the other end exhaled shakily. Defeat settled in her voice.

"Yeah…I understand. I just—" She swallowed thickly. "If you think of anything—"

"I'll let you know."

Lie.

Leo knew it the second the words left her mouth.

The call ended. But Eve didn't move. She sat at her desk, fingers drumming absently against a notepad, staring into nothing. The quiet stretched between them, wrapping around her shoulders like an unseen force.

She was thinking about something.

Something she wouldn't tell him.

Leo exhaled slowly, adjusting his grip on the café bag.

Interesting.

Maybe stopping by wasn't such a wasted effort after all.

Leo didn't bring up the phone call.

Not at first.

That wasn't how you got people to talk.

You let them think they were in control. Let them offer information. And if they didn't—well, that didn't mean you didn't already have it.

So he said nothing as Eve set the table, her movements crisp, too precise. Like she was moving through a script rather than a routine. That was the first sign. Normally, she took her time with things like this. Tonight, her hands moved too fast, like staying busy would quiet the thing gnawing at her thoughts.

Leo refilled her wine glass. She barely noticed.

He carved a bite of steak. Ate it. Watched her. Waited.

Finally, Eve set her fork down.

She exhaled—long, slow. The kind of breath people take when they've been holding something in for too long. Her thumb smoothed absently along the rim of her wine glass.

Leo knew what came next.

"One of my former patients is missing."

Leo didn't react.

He set his knife down, took a sip of his drink, tilted his head slightly—just enough. Not too much. Not too eager. Just…enough.

Now she was watching him.

"Missing?" His voice was a perfect note of concern—just enough curiosity, just enough restraint. "Since when?"

Eve ran her thumb over the stem of her glass.

"His sister called the office today."

Leo's expression shifted with just the right amount of weight. A husband should look concerned. But not too much. If you looked too worried, people stopped talking.

"Did you know him well?"

Eve hesitated.

Too long.

Then she caught herself, correcting too quickly.

"Not really. He was quiet. Introspective." A small shake of her head. "It's strange. His sister said he hasn't been home in days. It's like he just…vanished."

Leo set his glass down.

That was interesting.

People didn't just vanish. They left behind threads—fragments of themselves woven into the lives of others, their habits, their routines. Someone always saw them last.

And in Ryan Williams' case?

That person was Eve.

She didn't know that Leo already knew.

The air between them shifted. The flicker of a candle flame. The soft scrape of a fork against porcelain. Something unspoken curling between them, thick as smoke.

Leo let a small crease form between his brows, his expression reflecting the concern a husband should have—but not too much.

"I'm sure they'll find him," he murmured, reaching across the table.

His fingers curled around hers, warm, steady. The perfect touch of comfort.

She let him hold her hand. But she was already gone.

Already lost in thought.

Leo let his hand linger before pulling away.

To her, Ryan's disappearance was a tragedy.

Another story slipping into the folds of her busy life.

To him?

It was a masterpiece in progress.

Victim 2 –Constantine Giannopoulos (6 years ago)

Their life had settled into a rhythm—not effortless, but earned.

Eve and Leo were married and parenthood had shifted and stretched them. It softened some edges while sharpening others.

Eve thrived in her role as a psychiatrist. She had secured a small private office in a historic Gold Coast building—the kind of space that reflected her precisely: poised, thoughtful, quietly powerful. Sunlight streamed through the towering windows, suffusing the warm earth tones of the office that she had so carefully chosen; the framed artwork, the subtle textures designed to calm even the most guarded patient.

Leo watched her with fascination, the way she disarmed skeptics with a measured smile, how she could shift from warm to authoritative in a single breath. She had always been good at reading people—perhaps too good. He remembered one time in particular when she had met with a young couple who were struggling to connect with each other, and how she had listened attentively to their concerns before offering words of wisdom and guidance that seemed to resonate deeply with them.

"For the next week, I want you to focus on active listening. No interruptions, no rehearsed responses—just listen. Then, when you speak, try stepping into their perspective. Reframe the conversation as if their thoughts were your own. Try to schedule regular 'us' time—as a non-negotiable. Even something small, like making dinner together. Connection thrives on intention."

Leo admired her, even as he carved his own path. After years in the shadows of the city morgue, his precision had earned him a permanent role as a coroner. The work suited him. It was precise, orderly, and rewarding in a way that was hard to articulate. There was a strange kind of peace in uncovering the stories of those who could no longer speak; a quiet satisfaction in solving the puzzle of life's inevitable end. The work demanded discipline and detachment, qualities Leo had in abundance. It also required secrecy, which he learned to carry like a second skin.

Eve and Leo would often meet for lunch at Bella's Café, a charming little spot just down the street from her office, known for its fluffy pancakes and quiet ambience. It became their sanctuary, a momentary escape from their busy lives. As they sat across from one another, Eve would light up as she recounted her day—sharing stories of patients who had taken small but meaningful steps toward healing. Leo would listen intently, marveling at how effortlessly she connected with people, her intuition a seemingly endless well of insight.

But as much as he loved these moments, a faint unease began to creep into the edges of his mind. There were times when she seemed distant, her laughter not quite reaching her eyes. Her phone would buzz, and she'd glance at it before slipping it back into her bag without explanation. Once, she'd been distracted during lunch, absently stirring her coffee while her gaze lingered out the window.

Leo told himself it was nothing. They were both busy, both exhausted from their demanding careers. Yet, the whispers in his mind persisted, subtle but insistent. His mind would begin to swirl with scenarios of late nights at the office and if they were always filled with paperwork or if the warmth she offered her clients extended beyond professional boundaries.

Still, in quieter moments, Leo felt a distance he couldn't ignore. He remembered one night in particular Eve had slept beside him, her body turned slightly away, the faint glow of her phone dimming as it slipped beneath her pillow. A habit she never used to have. He had reached out to brush a strand of hair from her face, not out of tenderness but curiosity and suspicion.

Her hand twitched. Her fingers curled protectively against the pillow's edge as if she were guarding a secret.

It struck him then. Whatever she was holding onto…wasn't just the pillow.

Then, the moment he had been dreading arrived. A hotel receipt sat at the bottom of their bathroom trash bin, ink smudged from condensation. Leo picked it up, smoothing the paper between his fingers, his breath steady. Room 1724. One night. The date burned into Leo's mind like an open wound. It was time.

Leo saw the shift before she realized it herself. A hesitation before answering. A flicker of her eyes toward her phone when it buzzed. A subtle inhale, as if weighing her words before speaking. She thought she was careful. But Leo was always watching—always noticing the tiny fractures in her façade. The way she paused for just a fraction of a second too long. The way her fingers tensed before setting her phone aside. She was hiding something. And Leo's fascination grew.

He started to play a game with himself, testing his own powers of observation and deduction. He would ask her innocent-sounding questions about her day, all the while probing for any cracks. He would listen carefully to her responses, searching for any inconsistencies or tells that might reveal what she was really thinking.

He also started to pay attention to other details, such as Eve's schedule and routine. He would note the times she left for work and returned home, looking for any patterns or anomalies that might suggest she was meeting someone else. He would check her phone records and email accounts, searching for any suspicious messages or contacts.

At night, he would lie awake beside Eve, his mind whirring with theories and suspicions. He would replay their conversations in his head, searching for any inconsistencies or tells that might reveal what she was really thinking.

And yet, despite his growing obsession with uncovering Eve's secrets, Leo couldn't help but feel a twisted sense of admiration for her. She was so clever, so skilled at hiding behind her mask of innocence. It was almost as if she knew he was watching her all along.

The game had begun, and Leo was determined to win. But what exactly did winning mean? Was it uncovering Eve's secrets and claiming victory over her deception? Or was it something more sinister?

As he lay there in the darkness, listening to Eve's gentle breathing beside him, Leo smiled to himself. This game, this delicate dance, this endless pursuit—it had only just begun, and now there was only one thing left.

Leo had long accepted that Eve was skilled at deception. He just hadn't expected to be on the receiving end of it.

A conference in New York. That was her excuse. He had almost believed her. Almost. But there was something about the way she said it—too careful, too measured—that struck him as rehearsed. And Leo, of all people, knew the difference between truth and a well-practiced lie.

Leo followed her.

She hadn't gone to her conference hotel. Instead, she had taken a car to Constantine Giannopoulos' apartment.

Leo watched from a distance as she approached the entrance, as Constantine stepped forward to greet her—smiling, comfortable, familiar. The way he touched her arm, the way she leaned in, was intimate in a way that made Leo's breath slow, his fingers curling into fists at his sides.

Then came the moment that cemented everything.

Constantine opened the door for her. Not just as a courtesy, but with the ease of someone who had done it before. Someone who knew she would step inside without hesitation.

And she did.

She smiled—not her polite, practiced one, but the kind that reached her eyes. The kind Leo hadn't seen in years.

The door clicked shut behind them, locking Leo out.

She had chosen him.

And now, Leo had chosen him too.

But she wasn't staying here.

A black car pulled up to the curb an hour later. Eve and Constantine emerged together, moving with the ease of people accustomed to private spaces and whispered secrets. Their body language, subtle but intimate, spoke in a language Leo didn't need translated.

She leaned in. He touched her back.

They got into the car together.

Leo followed them to a hotel outside the city that was discreet. He didn't go inside. He didn't need to. He stayed back, watching as Eve and Constantine entered the lobby, his stomach curdling as the elevator doors slid shut behind them.

For hours, he waited.

Leo waited outside the hotel, his pulse a steady drum against his ribs.

Eve left sometime after midnight. He watched her slip into another car, her shoulders pulled tight, a lingering glance up at the hotel windows.

She was thinking of him.

Constantine.

Leo didn't follow her. He had no interest in Eve right now. She had already made her choice.

No—his attention was on the man who had touched what belonged to him.

His fingers hovered over his phone before pressing dial. His voice, smooth, controlled, carefully casual.

"Hi, I'm calling about something left in Mr. Giannopoulos' car—his last guest accidentally left an item behind. She was hoping he could check for it."

A lie. A calculated one.

A lie Constantine would believe.

It took less than five minutes.

Leo was already waiting when Constantine stepped into the parking garage. His gaze flicked left, then right—a habit of someone who was used to being watched. His shoulders were squared, confident. Wealth had made him that way. Untouchable.

But tonight, Constantine wasn't untouchable.

"Need something?"

Constantine's voice was low, casual, but his stance shifted slightly—a flicker of caution.

Leo smiled. Small. Calculated.

Then he struck.

The motion was quick—not perfect. Constantine reacted, his elbow jerking back—Leo hadn't expected that. A sharp crack of pain shot through his ribs. The first lesson of real violence: nothing ever went as planned.

Leo adjusted, his grip tightening. He forced Constantine against the car, pinning him, feeling the man's pulse hammering against his fingers.

Constantine struggled. A second mistake.

Leo had already won.

A quick jab to the throat. A shuddering gasp.

Then—a slow, withering collapse.

Leo stood over him, breathing heavily, his own heart racing, and yanked him backward into the car.

He drove in silence. The road narrowed, swallowed by towering trees, the shadows stretching long, skeletal fingers clawing at the last remnants of daylight. The full moon hung above like a voyeur, casting a cold glow over the desolate path.

His grip tightened on the wheel, his mind circling Eve and her lover.

The way she had accidentally mentioned "Costa" at home, quickly covering it up with a nervous laugh—*Costa Rica, I meant Costa Rica.* But Leo had known.

She wasn't talking about a place.

She was talking about a man.

Constantine.

Leo's jaw flexed. He had spent hours scouring the forest, searching for the perfect location to unleash his wrath. The scent of damp earth and decaying leaves filled the car, thick and pungent, a morbid perfume that fueled his madness.

This was his domain. A realm where he could be master of life and death.

A flicker of gold caught his eye.

A Tarot card rested on the passenger seat. The King of Wands.

Leo's gaze flicked to the rearview mirror, where Constantine's reflection sagged against the trunk's interior. The gag in his mouth muffled any pathetic attempt at resistance.

Leo exhaled, slow and measured.

Tonight, he was the hand of fate.

Leo removed him from the trunk and dragged him forward, his shoes gathering dirt from the wet grass. The first strike was controlled. Precise. The ritual unfolded with practiced precision. Leo withdrew the King of Wands. A fitting tribute—action, risk, ambition. Constantine had played his role, and now, the stage was set for his final bow.

As he began to strangle Constantine, his face twisted into a grotesque grin inches away from his victim's face. He observed Constantine's fading gasps, his terror-stricken eyes crying for mercy, and it only excited Leo's rage, fueling his mania. With every twitch and spasm, Leo felt his supremacy being confirmed. The woods were silent witnesses, holding secrets within, but even the trees seemed frozen in fear, as if they, too, were watching Leo's mastery over life and death.

When Constantine's body stilled, Leo exhaled slowly, the tension unwinding from his muscles. He adjusted his sleeves, brushing off the dirt as if nothing had happened. He was more assured now, more confident in his actions. He reached into his pocket, retrieved the small kit he had prepared for this moment, and began his meticulous work. With the ritual complete, Leo stood up, tucking the vial into his pocket.

The forest seemed to stretch out before him like a kingdom. Leo's vision became clearer. In this moment, only one thing mattered—Eve and keeping her safe from those who would seek to harm her. And if that meant killing anyone who got in his way, then so be it.

Victim 3 - Anthony McCall, weeks earlier.

As the sun set over the city, casting a golden glow over the streets, Leo's mind was consumed by a sense of excitement and anticipation. He could feel the familiar stirrings of restlessness within him. His eyes would often drift to Eve, watching her with a mixture of adoration and possessiveness. She was his prized possession, his family's matriarch, and he would do anything to protect her.

Rory had been a part of their lives for years now. She was proof, Leo thought, that he and Eve had once wanted the same things. Family. Stability. A life built together. But Rory grew. And so did the distance. Whatever tether Rory's birth had created between them had long since frayed. Leo had told himself for years that fatherhood—family—would be enough to ground Eve. To keep her his. But as the years stretched on, the cracks became impossible to ignore. The whispered phone calls, the secret meetings, the stolen glances—all of it pointed to one inescapable conclusion: Eve was having another affair.

This time, it was with Anthony. Leo had been tracking her movements for weeks, learning his routines and habits. He knew that they had selected an abandoned laundromat on the outskirts of town as their rendezvous point. The thought sent a shiver down his spine as he imagined the scene unfolding before him.

As Leo made his way to the laundromat, his heart pounded with excitement. He felt alive; he was a predator stalking his prey. The abandoned building loomed before him, its crumbling facade a testament to neglect and decay. He slipped inside, his eyes adjusting to the dim light within.

Anthony was waiting for Eve, his back against the wall as he checked his watch for what felt like the hundredth time. Leo emerged from the shadows, his movements swift and silent. Anthony never stood a chance.

The laundromat stood like a tombstone against the night, its rusted frame and grime-streaked windows a testament to years of abandonment. The faint remnant of a neon sign cast fractured shadows across the cracked pavement. Inside, the faint smell of mildew and motor oil lingered—a place forgotten by the world and perfect for what Leo had in mind.

He waited in the shadows, his eyes tracking Eve's every movement. She emerged from the laundromat, her face unreadable in the dim light. Leo's pulse quickened as she walked away, her heels clicking against the pavement, the sound growing fainter with every step. He stayed rooted in place, watching her silhouette vanish into the distance. Relief and exhilaration twisted together in his chest—she was gone, and now it was just him and Anthony.

Anthony sat slouched on a broken bench, oblivious to the storm about to crash down on him. The fluorescent light overhead flickered, throwing his shadow against the dingy wall in uneven bursts. He looked small, almost insignificant, surrounded by rows of rusted washers and dryers.

Leo stepped into the light, his movements slow, deliberate. The King of Cups card burned in his pocket, its edges worn smooth from his touch. The ritual had been playing in his mind all evening, a symphony of control and vengeance.

"She's mine," Leo murmured, the words barely audible, though they echoed loud enough in his head to drown out everything else. He repeated it silently, the mantra fueling his every step forward.

Anthony glanced up, his expression shifting from confusion to unease as Leo closed the distance between them. The laundromat seemed to grow quieter, as though the air itself held its breath. The machines stood like silent witnesses, their dull metal surfaces reflecting slivers of the dim light.

Leo stopped just a few feet away, tilting his head slightly, his voice cutting through the oppressive silence. "It's nothing personal," he said softly, his tone unnervingly calm. "But you should've known better."

Anthony opened his mouth, maybe to argue, maybe to plead, but the words never came. Leo's hands moved with practiced precision, grabbing him with a force that sent them both crashing against a row of machines. The clang of their impact reverberated through the empty space, a violent punctuation to Anthony's muffled protests.

Leo's grip tightened, his breath steady as Anthony thrashed, his fear palpable. For Leo, this wasn't chaos—it was clarity. Every movement, every decision felt like an affirmation of his purpose. He wasn't just taking a life; he was protecting Eve, securing their fragile world.

The struggle didn't last long. After Anthony's body went limp, Leo tilted his head slightly, angling it to access the eye more easily. With a deft touch, he claimed his prize and slipped it into the vial.

Reaching into his pocket, he retrieved the King of Cups and placed it on Anthony's chest, smoothing the card down with the flat of his palm. The card lay like a benediction, a quiet proclamation of his dominion.

Leo let the silence settle, absorbing it. The laundromat's stale air clung to his skin, the scent of mildew hanging thick. He adjusted his cuffs, straightened his posture. The moment was done. And yet, the rush still curled in his veins, coiling around his ribs, stretching him taller. He had restored order. He had made things right.

His gaze flicked to the door through which Eve had disappeared only moments ago. The image of her face flashed in his mind, her lips forming the smallest of smiles as she'd walked out into the night. Would she smile like that if she knew what he'd done for her? Would she understand?

He shook the thought away. It didn't matter. What mattered was that she was safe, that she would never know the depths he'd gone to for her.

He stepped back into the shadows, leaving the laundromat behind. This was different from the first two. It was quicker, rawer, more immediate—his love for Eve burned hotter, his sense of purpose sharper. Leo felt truly alive.

The morgue's cold, clinical atmosphere was just the way Leo preferred it. The sharp scent of antiseptic dominated the air, masking the faint, organic undertones that lingered beneath. As he adjusted his gloves with a precise snap, he reveled in the control this environment afforded him.

The double doors swung open, admitting Detective Eddie Chan and Audrey Holliday. Both were clad in full personal protective equipment: gowns, N95 masks, face shields, and gloves. This adherence to protocol was standard during active autopsies to prevent exposure to potential biohazards.

Leo greeted them with a measured nod, his voice steady. "Detectives," he acknowledged, then glanced at Audrey.

Eddie's eyes crinkled slightly above his mask, hinting at a smile. "Dr. De la Gardie, this is Agent Audrey Holliday."

Leo's gaze flicked to Audrey's eyes—for a moment, he recognized something, but he dismissed the thought.

"Agent Holliday," Leo acknowledged, gesturing toward the autopsy table. "Anthony McCall. Cause of death: strangulation. No defensive wounds, but there are faint restraint marks on the wrists, suggesting temporary binding."

Audrey stepped closer, her eyes narrowing as she examined the marks. "The precision of these ligatures indicates a methodical approach. The perpetrator may have experience restraining victims."

Leo adjusted his posture to appear contemplative. "Not sure." he said, careful to maintain his detached demeanor. "The marks aren't deep—could suggest they weren't used for long or weren't applied tightly. Still, they tell us something about the killer's methods."

The faintest hint of a smile tugged at Leo's lips, but he suppressed it, lowering his gaze as if in thought. He'd been meticulous, every detail calculated. The restraint marks had been applied with precision, just enough to hint at their presence without raising immediate suspicion. He relished the control it gave him—the ability to shape the narrative while standing in the very room where the truth should have unveiled.

Eddie's voice broke through his thoughts. "And the Tarot card? The King of Cups? It was found on the body at the laundromat. Any theories on that?"

Leo paused for effect, the silence stretching just long enough to feel deliberate. He shrugged, feigning a lack of insight. "Could be a calling card. Some killers like to leave a signature. Or it might mean nothing at all—just something the victim had on him." Inside, his thoughts churned, the thrill of the kill still fresh in his veins. He relived the moment he placed the card on Anthony's chest, the rush of power as he completed another chapter of his carefully constructed justice.

Audrey's gaze remained fixed on Leo, her eyes searching for something beneath his composed exterior. "Or it could symbolize the killer's perception of himself—a ruler of emotions, perhaps."

Leo met her gaze evenly, his mask hiding any reaction. "An interesting theory."

Leo tapped the wrist marks, drawing attention without seeming to. "If you'll notice here," he began, drawing attention to the evidence he'd planted, "there's an almost ritualistic quality to the way the restraints were applied. It's subtle, but it could suggest a methodical approach."

The tension in the room was palpable, but Leo thrived on it. Every question he asked, every piece of evidence they scrutinized—it only reinforced his own genius, his ability to stay ten steps ahead.

As the conversation wound down, Eddie lingered by the table, his gaze fixed on Anthony's lifeless face. "This doesn't feel random," he said finally, his voice quiet but firm. "It feels…personal."

"Perhaps," he said, his tone neutral, unbothered. "But we'll need more evidence to draw conclusions."

With that, Audrey and Eddie turned and the click of their shoes on the tile echoed in the stillness as they left the room.

Leo's gaze flicked to the evidence bag. The King of Cups glared back at him, its colors stark against the sterile backdrop. A quiet thread of satisfaction coiled in his chest. *They'll never understand,* he thought. *But she will. One day, she'll see I did it all for her.*

Leo stood alone in the morgue, the cold air brushing against his skin. He looked at Anthony's body one last time, his face impassive.

"Rest easy," he murmured under his breath, his tone laced with mock sympathy. "Your sacrifice wasn't in vain."

Once alone, Leo removed his gloves, the snap echoing in the sterile room. He allowed himself a brief, satisfied smile, knowing that his meticulous planning continued to elude their scrutiny.

Victim 4 – Unnamed, next.

The house held its breath.

Leo sat at the kitchen table, watching the steam coil from his untouched coffee, the aroma thick and sharp in the early morning hush. The overhead light flickered once, a pulse of artificial glow against the storm-darkened windows.

Eve had already left. Earlier than usual.

She'd kissed his cheek before stepping out, murmuring something about a morning session. Her perfume lingered in the air— orange blossom, familiar. But beneath it, something else clung to the fabric of her coat. Something faint. Masculine.

Leo hadn't said a word.

Not last night, when she came home just a little later than expected. Not when Rory mentioned—offhandedly—that Mom had picked her up from practice later than usual. Only ten minutes. Maybe fifteen.

And not when Eve placed her phone on the nightstand face-down before slipping beneath the covers.

She hadn't done that in a while.

Leo had turned off his bedside lamp and closed his eyes. But he hadn't slept. Not really.

Now, in the silence of the kitchen, he traced his finger absently along the ceramic rim of his mug, his pulse slow, steady.

He knew patterns.

They started small. A hesitation before answering. A flicker of her eyes toward her phone. A coat that smelled like something unfamiliar.

Alone in the house, with nothing but the hum of the refrigerator and the ticking of the clock, he let himself sit with it. Felt it settle into his bones.

Eve was slipping.

Not like before—not yet—but he knew the signs. He had seen them before Ryan. Before Constantine. Before Anthony.

This time, there was no name. No proof. Just a feeling.

Leo reached for the travel mug sitting untouched on the counter. Still full. Still warm.

She never forgot her coffee.

Outside, the storm clouds pressed low against the city, swallowing the skyline in a haze of slate and silver. Rain streaked the window, beads of water sliding in uneven paths, distorting the view.

He watched it fall.

And he waited.

Because the moment would come—that first undeniable crack in the facade.

And when it did, he would be ready.

Chapter 20

When the Thread Snaps

Late afternoon sunlight slanted through the sheer curtains, stretching long, spindly shadows across Audrey's living room floor. She paced, arms locked tight across her chest, her thoughts looping like a bad refrain.

Something is wrong with Eve.

The cracks in her sister's polished exterior were growing. Not just stress cracks—deep fractures. They didn't fit the woman Audrey had recently gotten to know, the woman who always seemed to be in control.

Eve had missed Sunday dinner, and while they hadn't been doing it long, it had become an unspoken expectation since their reunion. Skipping tonight felt different. Her excuse had been vague, something about a client emergency, but her tone had been off—strained, almost distracted.

Audrey could still hear her sister's voice on the phone. "I'm just tired. It's been a long day."

The memory was interrupted by a text notification on her phone. Eddie: *Dinner tonight? Bring your conspiracy board.* Leave it to Eddie to joke even when her silence must have been driving him insane.

She typed out a quick reply: *Maybe. Lots to unpack. Let me think.*

Her smirk faded.

The night before she hadn't planned on eavesdropping—just a quick check-in at Eve and Leo's house. But as she stood outside their door, hand raised to knock, their voices leaked through the wood, low and tense.

"I can't keep covering for you, Eve."

Leo's frustration pulsed through the words.

"You're not covering for me," Eve snapped back, her tone sharper than Audrey had ever heard it. "I'm handling it."

"Handling it? Like you handled the last time?" Leo's voice dipped dangerously close to a growl. "Don't forget, I know more than anyone else."

Audrey froze, her hand hovering over the door. She strained to hear more, but the voices lowered, the rest of the conversation dissolving into an indistinct hum. Her stomach churned with unease as she stepped back, her instincts warning her that something was deeply amiss. The cracks were widening.

Audrey stared at the phone in her hand, the screen glowing faintly in the dim light of her apartment. She hesitated, her thumb hovering over Eddie's name in her contacts. The room felt too quiet; her thoughts pressed down from all sides. She finally pressed *Call.*

He answered on the first ring, his voice warm and familiar. "Aud? You good?"

She swallowed hard, her throat tight. "Hey. Can you come over?"

There was a pause, then Eddie's tone shifted, tinged with concern. "Be there in twenty."

Twenty-five minutes later, Eddie was seated across from her at the dining table, his brows knit together as he studied her face. Audrey hadn't said much since he arrived, and the silence between them was uncharacteristically heavy.

"Alright," he said finally, leaning forward, his hands clasped on the table. "What's going on? You look like you've seen a ghost."

Audrey opened her mouth, then closed it again, struggling to find the right words. Her gaze dropped to her hands, her fingers twisting together in her lap. "It's Eve," she said quietly.

Eddie's expression softened. "What about her?"

She exhaled sharply, running a hand through her hair. "I think...I think she might be involved in the Magician case."

His brow furrowed, his confusion evident. "What are you saying? That Eve—?"

"I don't know!" Audrey interrupted, her voice rising before she forced herself to take a calming breath. "I don't know what I'm saying. But there are things—little things—that don't add up. And if I don't figure them out in time, someone else could end up dead."

Eddie sat back, crossing his arms as he regarded her carefully. "Okay. Start from the beginning. What's got you thinking this?"

Audrey hesitated, her mind racing. "She's been distracted. Missing family moments. She's tense, evasive. I overheard her and Leo arguing—something about him covering for her. And then there are the Tarot cards..." Her voice trailed off, her unease palpable.

Eddie raised an eyebrow. "Tarot cards?"

She nodded. "I found them in her office. They're framed— the Empress, the High Priestess, and the Moon. She explained their meanings, but the way she spoke about them...it felt rehearsed, calculated."

Eddie's expression tightened. "You think she's hiding something?"

Audrey shook her head, her frustration mounting. "It's not just that. It's everything. The way she talks about her work, the way she carries herself—it's like she's detached from reality. Like she's performing."

Eddie leaned forward again, his tone calm but firm. "Aud, do you hear yourself? You're accusing your sister—your twin—of being a murderer. Do you really think she's capable of that?"

The question hit her like a punch to the gut. She dropped her gaze, her voice barely above a whisper. "I don't know. But if I ignore it, and I'm right…what does that make me?"

Eddie exhaled sharply, dragging a hand down his face. "And what if you're wrong? You know what this could do—to her? To you? Once you cross that line, Aud, there's no coming back."

Audrey's chest tightened and a heaviness crept in. "I can't just turn it off, Eddie. I can't pretend I don't see the cracks."

The tension in the room was suffocating, the silence stretching between them. Finally, Eddie reached across the table, his hand covering hers. "I get it," he said softly. "You're scared. And you don't want to be blindsided. But if you're going to follow this, you need to be sure. Because if you're wrong…" He let the implication hang in the air.

Audrey looked up at him. Tears clung to her lashes, threatening to spill. Her voice was barely a whisper. "I don't want to be right, Eddie. I really don't. But if I am…" Her voice broke, and she pressed her palms against her eyes, trying to compose herself.

Eddie let out a long breath, his lips twitching in thought. He reached across the table and gently tugged her hands away from her face, his expression soft but laced with the kind of patience only he could muster. "Okay, Aud, let's play this out. Worst case, you're right—your sister's hiding something big, maybe even something awful. Best case?" He paused dramatically, his tone lightening. "You're totally losing it, and I can finally say 'I told you so.'"

Audrey let out a shaky laugh despite herself, tears slipping down her cheeks. She swiped at them hastily, her lips twitching into the ghost of a smile. "I'm glad you're finding this so amusing."

"Hey, if I didn't laugh, I'd cry. And we can't both be the hot mess in this room," he teased, sitting back and crossing his arms with exaggerated confidence. "You should thank me for keeping this friendship balanced."

She laughed again, this time a little stronger, shaking her head at him. "You're ridiculous."

"And yet, here you are, trusting me with your weird twin serial killer hunch." His grin faded slightly, and his tone softened. "Look, Aud, I know this is eating you up. But don't let it devour you whole. You've got that scary detective brain, always looking for patterns. Just don't forget—your sister's just as good at hiding them. You can't go all *True Detective* on me, okay? You're too pretty for existential dread."

Audrey's laugh broke through the tension like sunlight through a storm cloud. She reached out and shoved his shoulder lightly, a touch that was equal parts affection and mock exasperation. "Thanks, Eddie. Really."

He stood, pulling her into a quick but firm hug. "That's what I'm here for. Hugging, eating your snacks, and being the comedic relief in your high-drama life."

Audrey wrapped her arms around him, her trembling subsiding as she leaned into his familiar warmth. "You forgot being my favorite pain in the ass."

"See? You do appreciate me," he said, pulling back and winking. "Now stop crying before you give me the reputation of being a good guy. I've got an image to maintain."

She rolled her eyes, but her smile lingered as he grabbed his coat. "Call me if you need me, Detective Overthinker. But seriously, try to get some rest. And maybe eat something that isn't coffee."

Audrey watched him leave, her smile fading as the door clicked shut. The laughter had eased her nerves, but the weight in her chest returned almost immediately.

Her instincts were screaming at her, louder than ever. She walked to the window and stared at her own reflection. The city lights fractured her image in the glass, cutting it into jagged, unrecognizable pieces. Was she seeing clearly—or only what she wanted to see? Whatever this was—whatever Eve was hiding—she would find out the truth.

And this time, she couldn't afford to be wrong.

She traced her finger down the patient list from Eve's practice, her detective's instinct honed and focused. Officially, she had gained access to these records as part of the Magician case. Dr. Larkin and Dr. O'Conner had handed over the list to assist with her investigation, unaware that Audrey was scrutinizing it with far more personal intent.

Her pen tapped against the desk as she categorized the names. Most of the patients were ordinary—people dealing with grief, anxiety, or the echoes of past trauma. But when her eyes landed on one name, her hand stilled.

Noah Watson.

Audrey leaned back in her chair, scanning his file. Anxiety and depression. Recent sessions. Nothing outwardly suspicious. But Eve's slip-up had been small—too small. And Noah wasn't just another name on a list. He was something more. Her gut churned as she opened her browser and typed in his name.

His LinkedIn profile was the first hit. He was a tech executive in his late thirties. The photo showed that he was sharply dressed and well-groomed with striking features—dark, styled hair, a strong jawline, and a confident, disarming smile. The kind of man who didn't just blend into a crowd but commanded attention.

She clicked through his social media accounts. Photos painted the image of a man at the top of his game—events, parties, business dinners. But something about him stood out beyond the curated professionalism. The sharper his image, the more Audrey's gut twisted.

Noah wasn't just a patient. He was Eve's type. Her sister's cryptic behavior and now Noah—it all fit too well.

But she needed more. That's what led her to grab her coat and head toward Eve's office.

Her thoughts churned as she grabbed her keys. She was running out of time—if she was right, Eve's next move could already be in motion.

Audrey adjusted her coat as she lingered in the lobby of Eve's practice. The receptionist, a young woman with warm brown eyes and an eager smile, glanced up from her desk. She radiated the kind of friendliness that seemed effortless but calculated—perfect for this kind of office.

"Hi there," Audrey began, her voice light but purposeful. "I was hoping to catch Eve for a quick chat, but I think I might be a little early."

The receptionist's brows knitted momentarily, her gaze flicking over Audrey's face. "Oh, Dr. De la Gardie! I didn't realize your session was over so soon.

Audrey offered a breathy laugh. "Gotcha! You're actually looking at the other twin."

The receptionist's cheeks flushed. "Oh my gosh, I'm so sorry for the mix-up! I should've known."

Audrey chuckled, shaking her head. "Honestly, I'd be confused too. It's like one of those cheesy twin switch movies in real life."

The receptionist laughed, visibly relaxing. "I'll give you that. Well, Dr. De la Gardie is finishing a session. Would you like me to let her know you're here?"

Audrey leaned against the counter, keeping her tone casual. "Actually, I had a quick question while I wait. Have you noticed a patient named Noah Watson? Late-thirties, dark hair, sharp features, kind of polished-looking?"

Recognition flashed in the receptionist's eyes. "Oh, yes— Noah. Really handsome guy. He's been coming in regularly. And he's definitely sharp-looking. He's got that executive vibe, you know?"

Audrey nodded, urging her on.

"And the watch," the receptionist added with a small laugh. "I noticed it last week—it's the kind of thing you only see in magazines. Expensive, sleek. Every time he comes in, it feels like his outfits get more polished. Like he's dressing up for someone."

Audrey kept her smile polite, though her thoughts roiled. "Sounds like he's doing well."

The receptionist nodded. "Definitely. Quiet but nice. Memorable, for sure."

Audrey thanked her and moved to the seating area. Her stomach churned as she replayed the description in her mind. It wasn't just that Noah fit the profile. It was the way Eve operated—the way she could pull people into her world and make them feel chosen. And Audrey couldn't shake the feeling that Noah wasn't just another patient. He was something more.

When Eve finally emerged from her office, her polished smile widened at the sight of Audrey. "Audrey! I wasn't expecting you."

Audrey stood, her own smile tight, masking the storm of emotions roiling beneath the surface. "Thought I'd stop by. Do you have a minute?"

"Of course," Eve replied smoothly, gesturing toward her office. "Come on in."

Audrey followed her sister down the hall, her heels clicking against the polished floors. Each step felt heavier than the last, as her suspicions settled over her. She couldn't tell if she was walking toward clarity or deeper confusion.

Eve closed the office door behind them, motioning for Audrey to take a seat.

Audrey hesitated, her hands clasped tightly in her lap. She studied Eve's face—perfectly composed, not a hint of anything amiss.

"I just realized it's been a while since we've caught up," Audrey began, keeping her tone casual. "With everything going on lately, I thought it might be nice to check in."

Eve's polished smile softened slightly, her gaze drifting to the framed Tarot cards on the wall. "It has been hectic," she admitted. But the slight shift in her tone, the measured cadence of her words—Audrey knew this game. It wasn't honesty. It was control. "Balancing Rory, the practice, and everything else. It feels like spinning plates some days."

Audrey leaned forward slightly, her voice light but probing. "Rory and Noah must be good anchors for you."

Eve blinked, her lips parting slightly. "Rory and—" She paused, the faintest flicker of discomfort crossing her face before she quickly corrected herself. "Leo, of course. They both are."

Audrey's pulse quickened. The slip was minor, but it was enough to send her instincts into overdrive. She forced a chuckle, leaning back in her chair. "Sounds like you've got your hands full. How are your sessions going? Busy these days?"

Eve nodded, her smile easing into something more natural. "Always. There's no shortage of people needing help."

Audrey leaned casually into Eve's patient chair, her tone carefully neutral. "You know, I've been looking into the Magician case more closely. Larkin handed me a copy of your client roster to cross-reference with potential leads."

Eve glanced up from her desk, her brows knitting slightly. "My client roster? Audrey, I thought you were leaving that to Larkin and O'Conner?"

"I was," Audrey replied, shifting slightly in her chair. "But with everything going on, I thought it wouldn't hurt to double-check for any connections. The killer's been methodical—specific. I figured your client list might hold some insight."

Eve leaned back in her chair, her expression guarded but polite. "And? Did you find anything of interest?"

Audrey hesitated, her gaze steady. "A name stood out—Noah Watson." She waited for Eve's reaction. Silence could be as revealing as words, and Audrey had spent her career reading people under interrogation. But Eve wasn't just any suspect. She read people too—only, she was better at making them believe they had nothing to hide."

Eve's jaw tightened, her polished smile faltering for just a moment before she recovered. "Noah's a patient of mine. He's been dealing with a lot of stress, trying to balance his career and personal life. Why does he stand out to you?"

Audrey folded her arms, her tone casual but laced with intent. "His name popped up when I was reviewing the client list. It made me curious, especially considering how meticulous you are about the kind of cases you take on."

Eve tilted her head slightly, her eyes narrowing with subtle suspicion. "Curious about what exactly? Noah's a typical case—anxiety, some confidence issues. Nothing that should raise alarm bells."

Audrey leaned back in her chair, feigning a relaxed demeanor, though her pulse raced. "Sure, but his background stood out. Young, successful, attractive—he's not exactly the profile of someone struggling silently in the shadows. It made me wonder what brought him through your doors."

Eve's lips pressed into a thin line, her polished composure slipping just enough for Audrey to notice. "Audrey, I hope you're not suggesting there's anything unusual about Noah. He's a client, nothing more."

Audrey let the silence linger for a beat, watching her sister closely. "Maybe," she said finally, her voice soft but edged with something sharper. "But you have to admit, the timing is interesting. He fits the kind of person who might…attract attention, don't you think?"

Eve's expression darkened slightly, her professionalism shielding whatever flicker of unease she felt. "Audrey, if this is about the Magician case, I can assure you, Noah has no connection. If you're fishing, I'm not biting."

Audrey's jaw tightened as she considered her next words. "I'm not fishing, Eve. I'm trying to piece together a pattern. And maybe it's nothing, but I have to follow every thread."

Eve's gaze hardened, her tone cooling. "Well, let me save you some trouble—Noah's just another patient. A good man trying to work through some things. He's not part of any pattern."

The tension between them was palpable, each sister silently measuring the other's words. Audrey held her ground, her instincts screaming that Eve wasn't telling her everything, but there was no way to press further without tipping her hand completely.

"Well," Audrey said, standing and adjusting her jacket, "thanks for the insight. I'll let you get back to your day."

Eve rose as well, her polite smile returning, though her eyes were watchful. "Always happy to help. But, Audrey…tread carefully. Not every thread leads where you think it will."

Audrey nodded once, her heart pounding as she left the office. The cracks in Eve's facade were there—small, but undeniable. And Audrey couldn't shake the feeling that her sister's polished defenses were hiding far more than she dared admit.

Audrey hunched over her desk at the precinct, eyes burning as she scrolled through Eve's practice records.

The timestamps weren't adding up.

Eve had claimed she was working late. Yet, her practice's billing software told a different story. Noah Watson—always the last appointment of the day.

Audrey dug deeper. A quick search of her own department's database turned up nothing unusual on Noah himself. But where did he fit into all of this? Audrey leaned back, her mind racing, before an idea struck her.

She quickly drafted a request for camera footage from nearby businesses and traffic cams around Eve's practice. Using the timestamps from Eve's sessions, Audrey and Eddie sifted through hours of footage until she saw it: Eve and Noah walking into a hotel just a few blocks from her office.

Her heart sank as she played the footage again, this time noting the ease between them. It wasn't just professional—they moved with a familiarity that made Audrey's chest tighten. She rewound to another night's footage, the same timestamp from another late session. There they were again, Eve in her fancy coat, Noah trailing close behind, his hand brushing against hers as they entered the hotel.

Audrey stared at the footage on her laptop. Eve and Noah had entered the boutique hotel twice in the past two weeks. He wasn't just a client. He was something more. But was he Eve's next victim...or her accomplice?

Each time, the time of arrival had been eerily consistent— early evening, just after Eve's supposed last session of the day. But two instances weren't enough to guarantee they'd catch them in the act again. She needed a stronger lead. Audrey called the hotel to inquire about a reservation under Noah's name. Her heart skipped a beat; there was a pending reservation. A reservation for the following evening.

She stared at the screen, heartbeat thudding in her ears.

Noah Watson. Hotel. Tomorrow.

Audrey exhaled slowly, a single word slipping from her lips. "Gotcha."

Audrey hunched over her laptop, eyes locked on the boutique hotel's booking system they had been granted access to. Eddie stood beside her, arms crossed, skepticism woven into every line of his face.

Her voice was steady, but her pulse wasn't. "Room assignment happens at check-in."

Eddie exhaled sharply. "And? We can't just barge in and knock on every door."

Audrey's pen tapped against the desk. "We don't have to. Tonight, we will scout the hotel. Entrances. Exits. Stairwells. Then, when Noah checks in, I track his room while you cover the outside. I'm scoping out Eve in the morning. I need to see what she's wearing—if I match her look, I might be able to move unnoticed if things go sideways."

"And if we don't get the room number before they go in?" Eddie asked.

Audrey's lips pressed into a thin line. "We wait and watch for movement. If Eve shows up, we'll know. Either way, we'll get what we need."

Eddie tilted his head, his brows furrowing. "You're banking a lot on this."

Audrey's gaze hardened. "Because this isn't a coincidence. Same nights. Same hotel. The last time Eve got distant, people ended up dead. I don't believe patterns are that neat unless someone's making them."

A beat of silence. Then Eddie sighed, shaking his head. "Fine. But I swear to God, if this turns out to be a rom-com and not a crime scene, you owe me dinner."

Chapter 21

Kingmaker

Leo stood in the dimly lit hotel room, the air thick with the scent of sweat and something metallic.

Noah lay crumpled near the bed, his body twisted in the aftermath of a struggle he had had no chance of winning. The pristine sheets were pulled askew, the bedside lamp tilted at an odd angle, casting fractured light across the room.

Leo exhaled slowly, measured. His pulse had already steadied. He peeled off his gloves with practiced ease, folding them neatly before slipping them into his coat pocket.

He turned to the mirror. A quick once-over. Not a hair out of place. His jawline was smooth, his blue eyes clear, unaffected.

Good.

Leo tilted his head slightly, observing his work with the faintest trace of satisfaction. Order restored. The King of Swords was now neatly placed on top of Noah. A seal. A message. Leo's methodical nature masked the storm of emotions beneath—rage, possession, and a twisted sense of control.

He slid his hands into the pockets of his coat and stepped toward the door. The metal handle was cool beneath his fingertips.

Click.

He slipped into the hallway, the muted hum of the hotel swallowing him whole. Shadows clung to the edges of the corridor, wrapping around him like a silent escort as he strode toward the elevator.

Ding.

The doors slid open. Leo stepped inside, turning just as Audrey and Eddie emerged from the stairwell down the hall.

For half a second, his dark eyes flickered toward them. But they were too focused on their destination to notice him.

The doors glided shut.

Leo smiled.

Victim 4 – Noah Watson

Leo's eyes scanned the room, his gaze settling on Eve as she laughed and chatted with a group of people. They were at the gala and Leo had accompanied her, dressed in a tailored tuxedo and trying to make small talk with the other guests. He couldn't help but feel a sense of pride and possession. She was his wife, his partner, and he loved her more than anything.

As the night wore on, Leo's mind kept wandering back to the flowers that Eve had brought home from her office a few days ago. The massive bouquet of birds of paradise and other exotic flowers had been a beautiful addition to their living room, but now it seemed like a potential clue to something more sinister.

Eve had barely acknowledged them. "Just a client." She hadn't even noticed the small envelope that had slipped between the petals.

Leo had.

Thinking of you. Just three words, written in an unfamiliar hand.

At the time, Leo hadn't thought much of it. He assumed it was just a kind gesture from one of Eve's clients. But now, as he thought back to that moment, he wondered if there was more to it than that. Who could have sent those flowers, and what did they mean by *Thinking of you?*

Leo's mind was racing with questions and doubts. *Who sent them? Why now? And why did Eve look so guilty?*

His jaw tensed. He needed answers, but he wasn't sure where to start or what he would find out.

Lost in thought, Leo's eyes drifted back to Eve. She was laughing and chatting with someone across the room, oblivious to his concerns. But he couldn't shake off the feeling that something was off, that there was more to Eve's life than she was letting on.

And then, his eyes landed on an email on her phone—an older message, timestamped from yesterday afternoon, now pushed to the top by a reply. It was from someone named "N" and all it said was: *Can't wait to see you.*

Leo's mind went into overdrive as he tried to process this new information. Who was "N," and what did they want with Eve? And why did Eve seem so preoccupied tonight?

Leo's eyes gleamed as he slipped into the attic, a space that was rarely used by Eve. The air was thick with dust and the smell of old clothes, Rory's old toys, and forgotten memories. Leo had converted this space into a makeshift lair, a place where he could plot and plan without fear of discovery.

He had been watching Eve for weeks, studying her every move and habit. He knew that she was hiding something from him, and he was determined to find out what it was. One day, while she was sleeping, he used a sticky sheet to lift her fingerprint from her phone. He had then used the fingerprint to create a mold, which he had used to access her computer.

It wasn't long before he discovered Noah's name. He found an email that Noah had sent to Eve, one that made it clear they were having an affair. Leo's anger and jealousy boiled over as he read the words on the screen.

He spent hours gathering more information about Noah, using his knowledge of psychology and human behavior to anticipate every possible move that Noah might make. He created a detailed map of Noah's daily routine, noting his habits and patterns.

The King of Swords Tarot card sat on top of the trunk, staring up at Leo like a cold and unforgiving eye. This card represented clarity and precision, two qualities that Leo admired greatly. But as he gazed at it now, he saw something more—a symbol of his own madness and desperation.

As he pored over his research, Leo's mind worked overtime to plan the perfect murder. He was a master of manipulation, using his knowledge of anatomy and psychology to anticipate every possible outcome.

He began to experience strange visions—dark shadows dancing on walls, whispers echoing through empty corridors. His grip on reality started slipping further away.

With shaking hands, Leo scribbled notes in journal pages. *Must protect her. Must keep her safe. Only I can do this.* The words became a mantra, repeating over and over in his mind as he planned his next move.

In this secret space, hidden away from Eve's prying eyes, Leo was free to indulge his darkest fantasies. He was a monster, driven by a desire to protect Eve at all costs. And he would stop at nothing to achieve his goal.

The attic creaked and groaned around him, the old wooden beams seeming to whisper their approval of his plans. Leo felt a sense of comfort in this space, surrounded by the shadows and secrets that only he knew. It was here that he could be himself, without fear of judgement or discovery. And it was here that he would plan the perfect murder.

Again, Leo found himself following Eve to a hotel and as he lurked in the shadows outside the elevator, his eyes fixed on the door and his pulse steady as he watched them. Eve and Noah, deep in conversation, their heads close—too close. This wasn't their first meeting, but it was different. Urgent.

Eve had even left a message—something about needing to talk.

Leo had been waiting ever since—tracking their meetings, studying their movements, anticipating their every step.

Now, he waited for Eve to leave.

As soon as she walked out of the room, Leo sprang into action. He slipped inside. He knew exactly what to do this time, exactly how to move.

He crept up to the room where Noah was sitting, every sense on high alert. He could hear Noah's breathing, slow and steady, and he knew that he was completely unaware of the danger that was lurking nearby.

Leo burst into the room, his eyes locking onto Noah's with a fierce intensity. They just stared at each other, frozen in time.

The air was electric with tension, and Noah's eyes widened in terror as he realized he was staring into the face of madness.

And then Leo struck, his body propelling itself forward like a coiled spring unleashed. The two men clashed. Their bodies crashing into each other with a sickening thud. Leo was fueled by adrenaline, his strength surging through him like a tidal wave.

In a flurry of punches and kicks, Noah tried to defend himself but Leo was too powerful. He grabbed Noah's throat and squeezed tight, his fingers digging deep into the skin as he strangled him with every ounce of strength he possessed.

Noah's body twitched once…twice and finally the last breath rattled from his throat, his hands clawing weakly at Leo's wrists before falling limp.

Leo didn't let go. Not yet.

He held firm, feeling the final shudder of life slip away beneath his fingers. He had never felt so powerful, so untouchable.

His lips parted, a whisper at first, then a murmur that grew into a triumphant declaration.

"I am master."

He lifted his chin, the word sinking into the walls around him. "King."

As Leo stood over Noah's lifeless body, he heard the sound of the elevator doors opening in the distance. He froze, his heart racing with anticipation. He knew he had to get out of there, and fast, before he was discovered.

With a burst of adrenaline, Leo turned and ran toward the door. He flung it open and sprinted down the hallway, his footsteps echoing off the walls. He could hear the sound of voices behind him, growing louder with every step.

Leo didn't dare look back. He kept his eyes fixed on the exit sign at the end of the hall, his legs pumping furiously as he ran toward it. He burst through the door, gasping for breath.

He didn't stop running until he was several blocks away from the building. Finally, he slowed to a stop, his chest heaving in the frigid air. He looked around cautiously; no one was in sight.

Leo let out a sigh of relief and leaned against a nearby wall, trying to catch his breath. He had made it out alive, but he knew this was far from over and too close for comfort. His eyes narrowed. "I am master," he whispered to himself once again. "King."

Chapter 22

Room 710

Audrey parked a block away from Eve's house, her heart pounding as she leaned back in the driver's seat. The early morning light cast soft shadows across the quiet suburban street.

A flicker of movement.

The front door swung open, and there she was—Eve. She emerged from the front door, dressed in a sexy all-black outfit. Her blonde hair was in magazine-worthy loose waves. The kind of look meant to be noticed.

Audrey's jaw clenched.

She watched, memorizing every detail. The fabric. The accessories. The exact shade of Eve's lipstick.

"Alright, sis," she muttered. "Let's see how you like being followed."

Audrey and Eddie parked a block from the boutique hotel, the building's soft glow radiating quiet opulence.

Audrey stepped out, tugging her coat into place. The outfit was identical to Eve's from that morning—sleek, deliberate.

Eddie eyed her, lips quirking. "Subtle."

Audrey arched a brow. "That's the point."

The hotel lobby was sleek and intimate, with polished marble floors and a concierge desk flanked by comfortable seating. Audrey and Eddie moved in sync, their practiced ease masking their true purpose.

Audrey's eyes darted to the reception desk, where a cheerful attendant was checking in a couple.

Eddie grabbed a brochure, flicking through it absently. "So what's the move?"

Audrey kept her voice low. "Entrances, exits, staff areas. We need to know how they move in this place."

They noted the side doors—key card access. The discreet stairwells. The *Employees Only* hallway. Cameras positioned with careful intent.

Audrey's eyes flicked upward. "Surveillance isn't bad. We'll need to stay in the gaps."

Eddie nudged his chin toward a lounge tucked off to the side. "That should give you a clear line to the front desk."

"Alright," she said, her tone resolute. "Tonight, it's all about timing. If Noah checks in and goes straight to his room, I'll tail him discreetly."

Eddie's skepticism edged into his voice. "And if it goes sideways?"

Audrey's gaze didn't waver. "Then we adapt."

Eddie observed her before nodding. "Alright. Let's do it. But for the record, you owe me a drink after this."

Audrey nodded. "I'll station myself here. When Noah checks in, I'll figure out his room number."

"And me?" Eddie asked.

"You cover the exterior," Audrey said. "If Eve doesn't come through the lobby, she'll have to use one of the side entrances. Keep an eye on anyone matching her description—or mine."

Eddie raised a brow. "This whole twin thing is starting to mess with my head."

Audrey's lips twitched. "You and me both."

Audrey adjusted her scarf, stepping into the hotel lobby with her earbuds snugly in place. Eddie's voice was a quiet hum in her ear. She scanned the room, taking in the muted elegance of the guests checking in and out.

"Still nothing," she muttered.

"Relax." Eddie's tone was calm, focused. "We've got time. In the footage, Noah's always the early bird in these scenarios, right?"

"That was the plan," Audrey said, her eyes flicking toward the glass doors.

Then her breath caught.

Eve.

She strode in, a vision of control, her black coat cinched tight. Leather skirt flashing beneath. Knee-high boots clicking against marble.

"She's here," Audrey hissed, her pulse quickening. Audrey tracked Eve's effortless movement. No hesitation. No check-in. Just a smooth step into the elevator.

"What?" Eddie's voice sharpened. "I thought Noah was supposed to show first."

"Apparently not," Audrey muttered. "She's already heading up."

"Alright," Eddie said, his voice steady but urgent. "What now?"

Audrey said faintly, "We wait. Then I get the room number. Watch and learn."

"Copy that," Eddie said, and then added with a teasing lilt, "By the way, Syd never mentioned this side of you. Leather skirt?

Knee-high boots? Audrey, is this the real you, or is Eve secretly rubbing off on you?"

Audrey rolled her eyes. "It's called blending in, Eddie. Try to focus."

"Oh, I'm focused," he shot back, his tone dripping with mock admiration. "I just didn't realize you had this...femme fatale energy. Very noir detective of you."

Audrey rolled her eyes, suppressing a laugh. "Don't get used to it. You're not exactly pulling off 'international man of mystery' over there."

"Hey," Eddie replied with mock indignation, "just because I'm not rocking knee-high boots doesn't mean I'm not nailing this stakeout."

Audrey stifled a laugh as she leaned against the far wall. "Keep it up, and I'll make sure Sydney knows about the time you cried during *The Notebook*."

Eddie chuckled. "Touché, Detective De la Gardie 2.0. Touché."

Audrey glanced at the clock and gave it another ten minutes, letting Eve's presence settle before moving toward the reception desk.

She took a deep breath as she approached, her leather boots clicking softly against the marble floor. Her scarf was snugly wrapped around her neck, and she adjusted it as if to shield herself from the faint chill in the lobby. She glanced around, ensuring no one was paying her undue attention.

Eddie's voice crackled in her ear. "Alright, Aud, go for it. And sell it. You're Eve —charm, confidence, and just a touch of superiority."

"Thanks for the coaching, Eddie," Audrey muttered under her breath, her lips barely moving.

The receptionist, young and efficient, barely glanced up before offering a professional smile. "Good evening. How can I assist you?"

Audrey returned the smile, warm but slightly distracted. She tucked a stray strand of hair behind her ear and leaned casually against the counter. "Hi. I left my room key upstairs. Could I get a spare?"

"Of course, ma'am." Fingers tapped against the keyboard. "May I have your name?"

"Eve De la Gardie," Audrey said without hesitation.

The receptionist's smile brightened in recognition. "Ah, Ms. De la Gardie. Room 710, correct?"

Audrey nodded, adjusting her coat as if cold. "That's right."

The receptionist reached for a keycard, her movements swift and precise. She swiped it, then slid it into a branded paper sleeve with the room number written neatly on the front. "Here you go. Let us know if there's anything else you need."

Audrey slid the keycard into her coat pocket, offering a practiced smile. "Appreciate it."

She pivoted, movements smooth, measured—just another guest in an expensive coat.

Her pulse steadied.

She reached the far side of the lobby, leaned casually against the wall, and murmured into her mic, "Room 710. I've got it."

Eddie's voice was calm but tinged with tension. "Copy that. I'll keep an eye on the exits. You heading up?"

"Not yet," Audrey replied, leaning against the wall to appear casual. "Give it a few minutes. Don't want to raise suspicion."

"Smart move," he said, pausing before adding with a teasing lilt, "Gotta say, you're nailing this whole 'undercover twin' thing. You're pulling off Eve a little too well. Should I be concerned?"

Audrey gave a wry smile. "Relax. This is a one-night-only performance."

She adjusted her coat and took a step toward the elevator bank. Her reflection caught her eye in the glass doors. For a split second, it wasn't her own face she saw. It was Eve's.

She inhaled sharply, turning away before the thought could sink its claws in. She wasn't her sister. She wasn't.

Eddie's voice crackled in her ear. "Heading up?"

"Almost," she murmured, scanning the lobby one last time. Then, impact.

A man balancing a tray of drinks turned too sharply in her path.

"Whoa, oh no!" he exclaimed as the tray wobbled, cups of water and coffee tipping over and cascading onto Audrey's coat and skirt. She froze mid-step, the splash soaking into her carefully coordinated outfit.

The man's face turned crimson as he scrambled to set the tray down on a nearby table. "Oh my God, I am so, so sorry!" he stammered, reaching for a stack of napkins. "I didn't see you there. Are you okay?"

Audrey forced a tight smile, brushing at the damp spots. "It's fine. Really."

"No, no, it's not fine," he insisted, practically thrusting the napkins into her hands. "I've ruined your outfit! Please, let me pay for dry-cleaning. Or—I don't know—buy you a new coat or something."

Audrey dabbed at her coat with a napkin, trying to keep her composure. The last thing she needed was a scene, but the man's mortified expression only made the situation more awkward.

"I'll just go clean up in the bathroom," she said evenly, glancing toward the receptionist, who had momentarily paused her work to watch the commotion.

"But still," the man continued, clearly flustered. "I feel terrible. You look so…stunning." His words tumbled over themselves, his cheeks flushing deeper.

Audrey arched a brow, folding the damp napkin and tossing it onto the table. "I appreciate the sentiment," she said dryly.

The man's gaze flicked over her outfit, and he gave her an almost sheepish smile. "Honestly, I think I've just made it worse. You look amazing—like, seriously—and here I am, the clumsy idiot who managed to mess that up."

Audrey sucked in a breath. "You're very persistent," she said, her tone wry.

He laughed nervously, scratching the back of his neck. "It's a talent. But really, let me make it up to you."

"It's fine," Audrey cut him off, her patience thinning but her voice still polite. "Really. No harm done."

Eddie's voice crackled in her ear, laced with amusement. "Who's your new friend, Aud? He sounds smitten."

Audrey pressed her lips together, ignoring him as she adjusted her coat. The man took a small step back, still holding the remaining napkins as if unsure what to do with them. "Well, if you're sure..." He hesitated, his gaze lingering a moment too long. "For what it's worth, I wasn't kidding—you look stunning."

Audrey's smirk returned, this time with a sharper edge. "Thanks."

The man gave her a sheepish grin before retreating back toward the lobby bar, leaving Audrey to refocus. She glanced toward the receptionist, who was already back at her computer.

Eddie's voice came through her earbuds again, dripping with mockery. "Well, well. Looks like you've still got it, Detective."

Audrey rolled her eyes, running her fingers along her damp coat. "Save it, Eddie. I'm going to hit the bathroom and clean up. Take point in the lobby while I'm gone."

"Copy that," Eddie replied, his tone still laced with amusement. "But hurry back. Wouldn't want your new admirer to think I'm your jealous husband."

"Funny," Audrey muttered, scanning for the nearest restroom sign. She made her way through the lobby with purpose, keeping her movements casual yet deliberate.

Audrey leaned against the sink, the cool porcelain grounding her. She met her own gaze in the mirror, but the longer she looked, the less she recognized herself. This disguise—it wasn't just external. She was stepping into Eve's shadow, inch by inch. And it terrified her.

She let out a shaky breath, gripping the edge of the sink. "Focus," she murmured, shaking her head as if to dispel the thought. She couldn't afford any distractions, not when so much was riding on this night.

In her ear, Eddie's voice broke her concentration. "Our receptionist buddy just got a fresh coffee delivery. Guess that means you've got some time to perfect your look."

Audrey tossed the crumpled paper towel into the trash. "Stay focused, Eddie. I'll be out in two."

"Take your time," he quipped. "I'll hold down the fort."

True to his word, Eddie moved into the lobby, leaning casually against a column near the seating area. His sharp eyes scanned the room, noting the comings and goings of guests and staff alike. He kept one ear on Audrey's occasional updates, his attention snapping to the elevator every time the doors slid open.

The elevator chimed softly, its polished metal doors sliding open to reveal a corridor cloaked in muted luxury. Thick carpet dulled her footsteps, but the weight in her chest did not ease. The air felt different up here—denser, heavier. A space not meant to be disturbed.

Audrey's fingers brushed the keycard in her pocket, its cool edge grounding her, but her thoughts churned. Room 710 loomed ahead, its brass numbers glinting under dim sconces. She slowed, each step deliberate, her pulse thrumming. Her earpiece crackled, breaking her concentration.

"Audrey, hold up," Eddie's voice came through, urgent but low. "I've got something. Back exit. Someone just slipped out."

"Describe." Eddie's voice sharpened.

"Thigh-high boots. Long black coat." A pause. Then, quieter, "Wait. Audrey, where are you?"

Audrey stilled, her fingers tightening around the keycard. "Outside Room 710. Why?"

Eddie cursed under his breath. "It's not you. It's her."

Audrey's stomach dropped. "Eve?"

"Has to be," Eddie muttered. His mind raced through the possibilities. The figure had moved with a familiar gait, disappearing before he could get a clear look.

If Eve was already leaving, then what was she walking away from? Noah?

Eddie shifted on his feet, his gaze locked on the alley. The cold air stung his cheeks as he leaned against a lamppost, keeping his silhouette inconspicuous. His eyes darted to every flicker of movement, scanning for the figure he'd seen moments before.

The streetlamp buzzed above him, casting fractured light over the pavement. The figure was gone, swallowed by the darkness, but the nagging sense of familiarity lingered.

Then—a sound. A faint shuffle of footsteps in the gravel. Eddie's spine straightened, his hand instinctively brushing the badge on his belt.

The figure emerged again, slipping toward the edge of the alley. Eddie's pulse jumped as he caught a better glimpse—then froze.

Something was off.

"Eddie?" Audrey's voice cut through his thoughts. "What's happening?"

Eddie's voice crackled. "I lost her. She's gone."

Audrey froze mid-step, her breath hitching. "Gone? What do you mean, gone?"

"I mean she just—" He ran a hand over his face, forcing down frustration. "She was right there, then she wasn't. It was her, Aud. I swear it."

A sick feeling churned in her gut. "What about Noah? Did you see him?"

Eddie exhaled sharply. "No. Just her—or someone who looked like her. Damn lighting made it impossible to be sure."

A pause.

His voice softened slightly. "Aud, I think we're missing something big here."

At this point, Eddie knew that there was no way he could catch the figure. He decided to make his way to elevator. If there was anytime that his partner needed support, it was now.

Eddie saw Eve standing down the hallway. A wave of protection ran over him. It was during times like these his humor went out the window and, he knew, Audrey was a tough and capable woman but she wouldn't be able to tackle someone on her own.

Eddie stood beside her, shifting his weight, his hand resting on the grip of his holstered gun. His voice was steady, low. "Whatever's behind that door, we handle it. You and me."

Audrey tightened her grip on the keycard, her knuckles aching from the pressure. The plastic bit into her palm. She couldn't shake the image of Eve slipping out of the hotel and blending into the night. If Eddie was right, then time was slipping away.

She nodded. "Together."

Audrey swallowed hard, feeling the lump in her throat. "Okay."

She slid the keycard into the slot. The lock clicked, and the sound felt deafening in the otherwise silent hallway. Eddie pushed the door open, his movements cautious but deliberate, and the two stepped inside together.

The room was eerily quiet, the air still and heavy. Eddie scanned the space, his body tense and ready, but it was Audrey who spotted Noah first. The room was a snapshot of something terrible—a moment frozen in the aftermath.

The silence in the room felt unnatural, as though the space itself had been holding its breath. Audrey's eyes moved quickly, cataloging details the way training had taught her to—bed, curtains half drawn, a glass of water sweating on the nightstand.

On the far side of the room, shadows pooled near the bed. Something in the room felt wrong—too still, too final—as if whatever had happened here had only just settled into silence.

Noah's body lay crumpled on the floor near the bed, his face pale, his neck marred by the faint red indentations of a violent struggle, and there, resting on his chest like a sick trophy, was the King of Swords card.

Audrey's knees nearly buckled. She crouched, her hand hovering over Noah's shoulder, her fingers trembling but never touching.

Too late.

The card mocked her, its placement deliberate, its message clear.

"Jesus Christ," Eddie muttered, his voice hoarse as he stepped beside her. His eyes darted between the body and the card, his jaw tightening. The placement wasn't careless. It was deliberate—centered, almost ceremonial. Whoever had done this hadn't rushed. They'd wanted the message seen. Wanted it understood.

Audrey's voice wavered, barely above a whisper. "It's her. She's the Magician."

Her pulse roared in her ears. She should have been faster. Should have stopped this. Her sister's face flickered in her mind—poised, unreadable.

She pulled out her phone, her hand shaking slightly as she dialed.

Her voice came out even, mechanical. "We've got another Magician murder. Room 710. Strangulation. The killer left evidence."

Eddie caught the muffled response from the chief, expletives mixed with orders. Audrey's face was set, her grip on the phone iron-tight.

But Eddie saw the cracks. The barely perceptible tremble in her fingers. The way her chest rose too sharply with each breath. She wasn't breaking down—she was holding herself together with sheer force of will.

His hand found her shoulder. A solid, grounding weight. "Audrey," he murmured, voice firm but quiet.

She exhaled sharply, her shoulders sagging. "I should've stopped this," she said, her voice breaking. "Noah didn't deserve this."

Eddie's chest tightened. He knew she'd carry this like a scar, whether it was fair or not. He stepped closer, his grip on her shoulder firm but comforting. "This isn't on you, Audrey."

Audrey's eyes glistened, but she nodded, the smallest crack of vulnerability showing through her hardened exterior. "Thanks, Eddie."

"Always," he said simply, his voice steady and sure. And in that moment, he wasn't just her partner in the investigation, he was her anchor.

The car was silent, except for the faint tick of the cooling engine.

Audrey sat stiffly in the passenger seat, her fingers curled into the fabric of her coat. The city lights blurred past her window, smearing into gold and red streaks, but her mind was frozen in that hotel room—Noah's vacant stare, the card resting on his chest like a taunt.

Eddie's grip flexed around the steering wheel, his other hand resting lightly on the console between them. He stole a glance at her. "You need to call Sydney."

Audrey inhaled sharply. "I just found my sister's lover dead with a Tarot card on his chest." Her voice was flat, but the weight behind it crushed the air from the car.

Eddie didn't fill the silence. Instead, he reached over, giving her hand a brief but firm squeeze before pulling his own away.

Audrey exhaled, rolling her shoulders. "She'll know what to say."

Eddie pulled out his phone and handed it over. "FaceTime her. I'll drive." A beat. "Fair warning—she'll probably chew you out first."

Audrey shot him a look. "Sounds about right."

Sydney's face appeared on the screen; her brow furrowed as she adjusted the camera. "Audrey? Eddie? What's going on? It's late there."

Eddie glanced at the phone and gave a sheepish smile. "Hey, Syd. Don't shoot the messenger, but Audrey's had a hell of a night."

Audrey didn't say anything at first, her fingers fidgeting with the phone. Sydney's eyes narrowed as she took in her friend's expression, then darted to Eddie, who was now focused on the road.

"Spill," Sydney said, her voice softer now. "Aud, what happened?"

Eddie cut in. "We found another murder victim in a hotel room. Strangled. Card on his chest. Looks like the Magician struck again."

Sydney's hand flew to her mouth. "Jesus Christ," she murmured. "Audrey…are you okay?"

Audrey's voice cracked as she finally let her guard down. "No, I'm not okay, Syd. I went to Eve's office and there were three Tarot cards. Just like the ones the Magician leaves. She was acting so strangely, as if she were hiding something. I sensed red flags. I think Eve is the Magician. What if…what if I'm no better than her? What if I have that same darkness?"

Sydney's expression softened, her eyes darting to Eddie's for confirmation of how bad it was. He gave her a subtle nod, his lips pressed together. Sydney's demeanor shifted as she leaned closer to the screen.

"Nope. Not happening," Sydney said. "We are not doing this. You're not her. You never will be. And you sure as hell aren't a killer."

Audrey's lips parted, but Sydney cut her off before she could argue. "We're not going down that road. Yeah, so you found your evil twin. But you know what? You don't need her. You've got me, and I promise, if when we hang out and I leave a Tarot card behind, it'll just be to freak you out, not to frame you for murder."

Despite everything, a small, shaky laugh escaped Audrey's lips.

Sydney tossed her hair over her shoulders. "See? There's my girl. Now get your head back in the game. Find her. Stop her. And then we drink a lot of wine while you trauma-dump on me."

Eddie glanced over. "You see why I want to keep her around?"

Sydney rolled her eyes. "Eddie, you're lucky to know me. Now, keep an eye on Audrey and make sure she doesn't do anything stupid."

Audrey smiled faintly, the warmth of her friends' banter tugging her from the dark spiral she'd been falling into. "Thanks, Syd. I needed that."

"That's what I'm here for," Sydney replied, her voice softening. "Aud, I love you. Don't let her win."

Audrey nodded, determination creeping back into her eyes. "I won't."

"Good," Sydney said. "Now hang up before Eddie says something corny."

Eddie gasped. "I am deeply offended."

Sydney laughed, the sound lightening the tension in the car. "Love you both. Now go be heroes."

Audrey ended the call, staring ahead. The weight still sat heavy, but something inside had shifted.

Eddie shot her a glance. "Feel better?"

"A little," Audrey admitted, the fire in her eyes reigniting. "Let's do this."

Eddie gunned the engine.

Chapter 23

Voices in the Attic

Eve sat rigid at her desk, her fingers curled against the edge as she scrolled through the Magician case file. Its pages lay open, stark and damning, heavy with secrets she had never wanted to face. A murder. A Tarot card. The details blurred as a dull ache pressed behind her eyes. A thread of unease coiled in her stomach, winding tighter with every word. But something about it felt…too close.

Her eyes fell on Anthony's name, and the memories surged unbidden—his charming smile, their stolen moments, the ache of her guilt for betraying her marriage. She'd failed him, and now she'd failed herself. How could she have overlooked what should have been glaringly obvious?

Her vision swam. *No. No, no, no. How did I miss this? How did Dr. Larkin?*

But she pushed the thought aside.

It's not Larkin's fault. I gave him his first police profiling assignment. I trusted him to stay objective.

She skimmed the file again, her pulse quickening as the next names leapt out at her: Costa. Ryan. She whispered their names under her breath as the enormity of the connections began to solidify.

"Ryan wasn't even from this life. He was from years ago—from a time I thought I'd buried. How…how could they all connect back to me?"

Her thoughts spiraled, jagged and relentless. *They were all my patients. All my lovers. Someone knows. Someone has been tracking me. But who?*

Her mind darted to her internship days.

Could it have been another doctor? It was too close. Too intimate. No. Impossible. Who else could have pieced this together?

Then, the thought slammed into her with the force of a wrecking ball.

Holy shit. It's Leo.

Her hand shot to her mouth as if to stifle the thought. Her pulse roared in her ears. Leo—the man she had trusted more than anyone, the man she had built her life with—was suddenly a stranger, a shadow she couldn't escape

No, it can't be him. It can't be.

Who else could know? Who else could know me so intimately? My lovers. My patients. My weaknesses.

Her pulse thundered in her ears as the pieces fell into place, each one more damning than the last. The patterns. It was always there, hidden in plain sight.

Audrey would've pieced this together in seconds. She always does. And me? I missed it. I didn't want to see it. I let it happen.

The heat in her chest spread, suffocating her. Her breaths came in shallow, erratic gasps. She could feel the polished mask she wore slipping, the control she prided herself on crumbling.

Eve forced herself to her feet, her legs trembling under her weight. She stumbled toward the window, the cool glass pressing against her palms like an anchor.

"Breathe, Eve," she muttered through clenched teeth, her voice shaking. But the air around her felt thick and unyielding, choking her as she tried to steady herself.

Her vision blurred. Her chest tightened. Her hands gripped the edge of the desk, white-knuckled as though it were the only thing tethering her to reality.

"Get it together. Rory needs you. You have to pull yourself together."

The panic was relentless, but Eve forced herself to rise, her legs trembling beneath her. The woman she was in this moment was a stranger—broken, unraveling.

Where was the woman she once knew—the poised, composed therapist, the wife, the mother? She was a stranger, fractured and unraveling.

Eve's mind whirred, fragments of memory flashing before her eyes. Pieces she had dismissed or ignored, moments that once felt like love now reeking of something darker, more calculated.

His observations.

"How was Anthony's session today?"

At the time, she had thought it was endearing—a husband interested in her work. Now, it felt invasive. Why had he even noticed Anthony?

His organization.

She remembered Leo's insistence on helping her with her patient files. *You're too busy to deal with this admin work, Eve. Let me take it off your plate.* She had trusted him, letting him create order out of chaos. He had access to everything—names, details, vulnerabilities.

His Dedication. *You seem distracted after your sessions with Constantine,* Leo had remarked once, his tone light, almost teasing. *You're too busy, Eve. Let me help with your notes.* She had brushed it off as harmless banter. But now, she saw the way his eyes lingered, the way his questions dug deeper than they should have. She had trusted him. Let him file her patient reports. Her lovers' reports.

Tell me about Constantine, Leo had said one evening, his voice casual as they lingered over a late dinner.

She'd hesitated, unsure how much to reveal about her tumultuous affair with her patient-turned-lover. But Leo had pressed, his interest framed as concern. *I just see what your sessions put you through, Eve. So I can protect you from too much stress.*

The phrasing struck her now. Not *support* you. *Protect you.*

His timing.

How he always seemed to know when her relationships were starting to fray. How he was always there at precisely the right moment.

You deserve better, Eve. You give so much, and they never give back.

Her memory started flooding with these recollections, each one more damning than the last. Eve started to piece together moments from their marriage that now felt disturbingly out of place. Her clinical training sharpened her focus, turning her husband into a subject of analysis. The signs were there—always there—but she had mistaken them for devotion.

His flattery.

You're the most extraordinary person I've ever known, Leo had said one night, his voice thick with awe as he watched her work.

She had believed it. Every word.

But pedestals weren't built for admiration. They were built for control.

Eve's stomach twisted violently, nausea curling up her throat.

How did I miss this?

But now, with the lens of hindsight and professional detachment, she recognized the undertone: a need to own her brilliance, to keep it close.

Her mind connected it to a concept that she had once taught a graduate seminar about. Pathological idealization. *Leo's admiration wasn't about me; it was about his version of me. One he could shape, protect, and keep.*

The isolation.

You don't need them, Eve. They don't understand you like I do, he had said when she'd hesitated to attend a colleague's networking event. At the time, she'd seen it as protective, a partner's desire to shield her from draining relationships.

Now, she recognized the tactic—*classic emotional isolation masked as care.* She'd counseled couples about this dynamic before. "Control through separation," she muttered under her breath, her fingers twitching as the professional diagnosis settled in.

The micromanaging.

Leo had insisted on organizing everything—her schedule, her workspace, even her wardrobe. *You shouldn't have to waste time on these little things, Eve. You're meant for bigger things*, he'd say with a smile that had felt so sincere it disarmed her.

She saw it differently now. *Micromanagement cloaked in chivalry.* Her mind dissected the behavior. *It wasn't about helping me; it was about controlling my world, making me dependent on his systems and methods.*

His fixation.

This color suits you better, he had said as he gently moved her hand away from a form-fitting dress she'd picked out for an office event. *It makes you look more powerful.* He'd always been so specific, so invested in how she presented herself. She'd found it charming, thoughtful.

But now, she saw the pattern. *His choices for me always leaned toward projecting authority, elegance, perfection. He wanted me to be the version of me that reflected his control*, she realized. *Always polished, always untouchable.*

Her professional instincts clicked into place, despite the rising panic threatening to derail her thoughts. "Pathological possessiveness…possibly covert narcissism," she whispered. *His obsession isn't love. It's fixation. I'm his ideal, not his equal.*

Her mind cycled through the traits she'd read in countless journals: *the subtle erosion of autonomy, the fixation on perfection, the quiet manipulation.* Each memory slotted into place like a puzzle forming an image she could no longer unsee.

How did I miss this? How did I not see him for what he is? Leo is the Magician. It was there, always there, hiding in plain sight beneath the façade of the perfect husband.

She closed her eyes, piecing together the moments that now seemed so obvious in hindsight—his carefully placed questions, his subtle control. *He is a predator who has built his world around me—a world I hadn't seen until now.*

Eve began diagnosing Leo with chilling precision, her thoughts clinical even as her emotions threatened to spiral.

"Compensatory narcissistic traits with a focus on relational dominance," she muttered, her voice shaky. "Manifesting as hypervigilance over perceived threats to his control."

Her thoughts snapped to Rory, her daughter—her anchor. Rory was at a sleepover tonight, but even that brought no comfort. Eve's protective instincts surged, momentarily overpowering the suffocating weight of fear.

Is she safe?

Cold terror sliced through her, sharper than anything else.

Leo would never hurt her. Would he?

The thought cracked something inside her.

I have to keep her safe. No matter what. No matter what it takes. I need to run.

Her steps echoed down the hallway, her hand brushing the wall for balance. She yanked open the bathroom cabinet, palms shaking. The Xanax bottle rattled as she fumbled the cap off, dry-swallowing a pill—bitter on her tongue. Her heart pounded.

Just breathe, Eve. Get it together. For Rory. For yourself.

As she turned back toward the hallway, her gaze snagged on the attic door, or rather, the string dangling from it. The door was slightly ajar, the faintest sliver of light spilling into the darkened corridor. She tilted her head, puzzled. She reached for the ladder. It jerked downward with a groan, a sound that clawed at her nerves. Dust filled the air.

Did Leo leave it open? He always warned me not to go up there. Said it wasn't safe…

She stepped back instinctively, her heart skipping a beat. The sharp smell of dust wafted down, stirring a prickle of unease at the base of her spine.

Her eyes lifted to the faint glow above. *Why is the light on?* Her irritation flared, momentarily overriding her unease. He probably left the light on too. Always running up the damn electricity bill.

Eve ascended the creaky ladder, Leo's warnings resurfacing in her mind. *Unsafe due to repairs, Eve. Stay out.*

The light spilling into the dim attic contradicted his words. Unsafe for whom? The thought surfaced, unbidden, her unease mounting with every step.

The dim light filtered through the single bulb, casting eerie shadows across the cluttered space. Boxes, old furniture, and forgotten mementos were scattered haphazardly. The far corner of the attic was meticulously arranged, a stark contrast to the chaos of scattered boxes and forgotten belongings.

Photos of Eve. Her professional headshots hung alongside candid snapshots she hadn't known were taken. Intimate moments. Stolen glimpses she thought were private, now on display like trophies.

Pictures of her lovers. Each man was represented, their faces captured in secret, often with Eve walking beside them, kissing them, eating at a restaurant, etc.

Tarot cards. Her prized deck was splayed out, certain cards pinned to a corkboard.

Patient files. Stacks of files sat neatly, annotated with cryptic notes: *Unworthy. Her judgement. A stain on her purity.*

The pieces clicked into place with terrifying clarity. Every tender gesture from Leo, every supportive comment, now felt like a calculated move. His obsession with her wasn't love—it was control, ownership.

This isn't a shrine. It's a crime scene.

Her breath quickened, her chest tightening as she took in the magnitude of what she was seeing.

Eve's body reacted before her mind could catch up. Her hands trembled violently, and her vision blurred as her breath came in short, shallow gasps. Her polished exterior—the persona she had carefully cultivated—cracked under the weight of the truth.

Audrey will see this. She'll think I knew. She'll think I let it happen.

The thought sent her spiraling further, guilt and paranoia entwining like vines choking her rationality.

She closed her eyes and placed a hand over her heart, applying the same grounding techniques she'd taught her patients.

Four seconds in. Hold. Four seconds out. Breathe.

Gradually, the storm inside her began to settle. Her breaths deepened, though her hands still trembled.

Eve's gaze fell back to the corkboard, the Magician card pinned at the center like a grotesque crown. Her voice broke the silence, trembling but resolute.

"It's you, Leo. You're the Magician."

The words hung in the air, solidifying the nightmare she could no longer deny. With shaking hands, Eve turned and descended the stairs, her mind already racing with the next step: calling Audrey.

How do I tell her?

She rehearsed the words in her head, but nothing sounded right. Nothing would make this truth easier to bear. *Audrey, I didn't know. I swear I didn't know.* Even in her mind, the words sounded hollow.

Her eyes flicked to her cell phone on the coffee table, the screen dark but loaded with consequences. The press of fear bore down on her. Eve felt something sharper pierce through—resolve. She had to protect Rory. She had to stop Leo. Even if Audrey judged her, even if she never believed her—this was the only choice she had left.

Eve reached for her phone.

The ringing felt eternal, each buzz drilling into her already fractured nerves. Eve's grip on the phone tightened, her fingers cold, her breath shallow. She felt like she was on the edge of something—something vast and irreversible.

Then, finally—

"Eve?" Audrey's voice came through, sharp, clipped, carrying a weight that made Eve's stomach twist.

She squeezed her eyes shut, willing herself to steady. "Audrey," she forced out, but her throat felt raw, strangled by panic. "It's Leo." Her voice cracked. "He's the Magician. I'm sure of it."

A pause. Silence thick as concrete.

Eve's heart pounded in her ears, her own breath suddenly too loud, too jagged.

When Audrey spoke again, her voice was unreadable, but there was something dangerous beneath it. "Do you realize what you're saying? Do you know what this sounds like?"

Eve's chest constricted. She knew exactly what it sounded like. The liar. The manipulator. The woman with too many secrets. But this wasn't about her. Not anymore.

"I know," she rasped, swallowing against the rising bile. "But it's the truth. I can prove it. The victims—they're all tied to me. Anthony McCall, Constantine Giannopoulos and Ryan Williams." She inhaled sharply. "They were my patients." Her voice trembled. "My lovers."

The last word barely made it out.

A pause. Then a shift in Audrey's breathing, something sharp-edged creeping into it.

"And why didn't you say anything before?" Audrey asked, her tone suddenly razor-thin. "Why now?"

Eve's pulse roared. "Because I didn't know!" The words tumbled out, too raw, too desperate. She clutched at them, tried to steady herself, but the weight was too much. "I didn't see it until tonight. I went through the case files. I found...things."

A slow inhale from the other end. Controlled. Calculating.

"Things?" Audrey's voice cut through Eve's fraying mind. "What kind of things, Eve?"

Eve pressed a hand to her forehead, forcing herself to breathe, to focus. "In the attic," she whispered. "Leo kept—he kept a shrine. Pictures of me. Of them. Tarot cards. Notes on my patients. It's all there, Audrey. He's been watching me, controlling me, and I didn't see it."

The silence stretched, suffocating.

Eve's heart stuttered. She could feel Audrey's doubt, thick and impenetrable. Audrey didn't believe her.

"I know I've lied," she said, softer now, fighting to keep her voice steady, to make her listen. "I know I've made mistakes. But this isn't about me. It's about him. You have to believe me."

Nothing.

Then, Audrey exhaled—long, slow, measured. Not relief. Calculation.

"That's convenient," she finally said, voice like ice. "After all this time, you suddenly find all this? The same night Noah ends up dead?"

Noah.

The name hit her like a hammer to the ribs.

Eve's breath caught. "Noah..." The phone trembled in her grip.

"Yes, Noah." Audrey's voice sharpened. "We knew he was meeting you tonight. And now he's dead. Strangled with a Tarot card on his body. The Magician's calling card. How do I not think you're trying to deflect, Eve?"

Eve's vision blurred. The room around her tilted. The phone nearly slipped from her fingers.

Noah. Dead.

She swayed, a sound escaping her throat that didn't even feel like her own.

"I didn't know," she choked out, and then it came—the collapse. The sob tore from her, violent, unstoppable, shattering the last of her defenses. "I didn't... Noah... He... We—" The words fractured. Fell apart.

Audrey was quiet.

Too quiet.

"You're one hell of an actress, Eve," she murmured.

Eve flinched. The words landed like a slap, but she didn't care. None of it mattered. Not her reputation. Not her mistakes. Not the tangled web she had woven over the years.

Because Noah was dead.

And Leo had killed him.

Eve pressed her fingers against her lips, trying to steady her breath. But her mind wouldn't stop, the grief wouldn't stop. She thought of Noah's laugh, the way he had looked at her like she was something worth saving—and now he was gone.

Audrey spoke again, but something was different this time. Softer. Hesitant.

"Eve," she said. "Tell me everything. Start from the beginning."

Eve nodded instinctively, even though Audrey couldn't see her. "I went to grab a Xanax after I discovered the shrine—after I saw the victims were all my lovers." The words rushed out, tumbling over themselves. "And then Noah—oh my God— Noah—" She squeezed her eyes shut, inhaled sharply, forced herself to focus. "The attic door was open. The light was on. I went up, and I found it. It's all there, Audrey. I can show you. Just come here."

The silence stretched again.

Then, finally—

"Stay where you are," Audrey ordered. "Don't move. We're already on our way."

Eve barely registered the click of the call ending.

Her entire body was trembling.

Audrey knew about Noah before she did. The thought sent a ripple of unease through her.

That means...they were watching. *Following me.*

The realization landed like a stone in her gut.

Was that why they were coming now? Not because they believed her—but because they suspected her?

A sharp inhale. Her grip on the phone tightened. *Of course they would think it was me.*

She felt it now—how the walls were closing in.

Leo had built the perfect trap, and she had walked right into it.

She sucked in a shaky breath, pressing her hand against her stomach as if that could stop the nausea. Stop the horror of it all.

She thought of Rory, of the innocence she had to protect.

Leo had taken everything from her. He would not take her daughter.

Eve wiped at her damp cheeks, swallowing down the wave of emotion threatening to drown her. She had one chance. One move left.

She looked down at the phone in her lap, the screen dark.

Her lips parted, whispering into the silence.

"Please, Audrey." Her voice broke. "Please believe me."

And then, quieter, darker—

What happens if she doesn't?

As the call ended, Eve slumped onto the couch, her body trembling. The Xanax dulled the sharp edges of her panic, but couldn't touch the dread that lingered. She stared at the phone in her hand, her mind racing as Audrey's words echoed in her ears.

"She knew I was at the hotel with Noah," Eve whispered to herself, her voice barely audible. The pieces began to align in a way that sent a fresh wave of unease through her. *Do they think I 'm the killer?*

She pressed a hand to her chest, trying to steady the thundering rhythm of her heart. *Audrey had mentioned Noah—his death, the calling card. She had known where I was, but why? Had they been there, watching? Following me?*

"Is that why they're coming here now?" she murmured, her stomach knotting with dread. "Not because they believe me, but because they suspect me?"

Of course, they would think it was me. The victims are all tied to me. Audrey's words carried a charge she hadn't fully processed until now. *She thinks I'm the killer. That's why they were at the hotel. That's why they're coming here.*

Her mind spiraled further, replaying every interaction with Audrey and Eddie. *Was every look, every question, drenched in suspicion? Was I blind to it because I was too consumed with my own guilt?*

The thought hit like a punch to the gut, and tears stung her eyes as she remembered Noah. Just hours ago, she had been with him—laughing, kissing, finally allowing herself to feel something real for someone. *And now he's gone.*

Her chest tightened, and a sob broke free, raw and guttural. She pressed a hand to her mouth, trying to contain the sound, but it was useless. Her grief spilled over, her polished composure crumbling as she curled into herself.

Audrey's voice echoed in her mind, sharp and skeptical: *All tied to you, Eve.*

For a fleeting moment, she wondered if she should run— grab Rory from her friend's house and disappear before Audrey arrived. But the thought dissolved almost as quickly as it formed. Running would only confirm their worst suspicions.

Eve exhaled shakily, forcing herself to sit up straighter. If Audrey believed she was the killer, then she had to convince her otherwise. The truth was her only weapon, fragile as it seemed.

She looked at the phone in her hand once more, whispering a silent prayer. "Please, Audrey. Please believe me."

But the question lingered, sharp and unrelenting: *If they think I'm the killer...what happens when they get here?*

Eve pressed the call button, her foot tapping anxiously against the tiled floor. The line barely rang twice before Lilah's signature, breathy voice filled the receiver.

"Darling, is this a booty call? Or are you about to tell me you've met someone who's finally as fabulous as me?" Lilah quipped, her tone dripping with exaggerated amusement.

"Lilah," Eve cut in, her voice tight. "I need you to listen to me. It's important."

There was a pause, then Lilah's tone shifted slightly. "Oh, honey, you sound...stressed. And not the 'I chipped a nail on my way to brunch' kind of stressed. What's going on?"

"I need you to pick up Rory," Eve said, her words rushed but deliberate. "She's at Kenzie's house in Lincoln Park. Just tell her parents I had an emergency, and you're taking her to your place. I'll shoot you over the address now."

"Wait—what?" Lilah's voice climbed an octave. "What kind of emergency? Are you okay? Is Rory okay?"

"Lilah, stop," Eve snapped, pinching the bridge of her nose. "Everything is fine. I just need Rory out of that house and safe with you. Please, can you do this for me?"

There was an audible inhale, followed by the distinct sound of Lilah pacing. "Alright, of course. You don't have to ask twice. Plus, Rory knows I have the good chocolate at home."

Eve exhaled sharply, relief trickling in despite the knot in her chest. "Thank you."

"But, Eve," Lilah continued, her voice softer now, "are you really fine? Because you're not fooling me. You sound...well, like you're about to jump out of a window."

Eve swallowed hard. The concern in Lilah's voice was genuine, cutting through her usual dramatics. "I'll be okay," she said quietly. "I just need to handle a few things first."

Lilah let out a sigh of disapproval. "You better not be trying to do everything on your own, Miss High-and-Mighty Psychiatrist. You might be the brains, but I'm the brawn—and the beauty, obviously."

Despite the tension, Eve's lips twitched into a faint smile. "You're a lot of things, Lilah, but subtle isn't one of them."

"Good," Lilah shot back. "Subtle doesn't save the day. I'll get Rory and keep her safe. You just…do whatever it is you're doing. But for the record, I don't like this. You're giving me bad vibes."

"Just trust me," Eve said, her voice steadying. "I'll explain later."

"You better," Lilah huffed. "And if this turns into one of those true crime documentaries, you'd better make sure they cast someone fabulous to play me."

The call ended before Eve could respond, leaving her with a flicker of gratitude amidst the chaos. Lilah might be dramatic, but she was exactly what Eve needed right now—someone who could handle the situation without falling apart.

Eve set the phone down and exhaled, staring at the counter. For a fleeting moment, she envied Lilah's simplicity, her ability to inject levity even into the gravest situations.

But this isn't a game. And the stakes are far too high.

The phone buzzed on the counter, breaking the stillness. Eve snatched it up, her breath catching at the name on the screen.

"Eve, listen to me," Audrey said firmly. "Stay put. Don't do anything. In case Leo gets there before we do, don't let him suspect you know."

"Rory's already safe," Eve cut in, gripping the counter. "Lilah's getting her. She's out of the house."

A pause. Then Audrey exhaled. "Good. That's the most important thing." Her voice softened, just a fraction. "We're close. Hold on."

The line went dead, leaving Eve in the echoing silence of her own thoughts. She placed the phone down, her hands still trembling.

The urge to run bubbled up again, insistent and primal. Her eyes darted to her car keys on the counter, to the front door. It would be so easy to leave, to grab Rory and disappear into the night.

He'd find us, she thought bitterly.

The realization settled like a weight on her chest. *Running doesn't protect Rory. It doesn't protect anyone. Staying means facing Leo, but it's the only way to stop him.*

Eve straightened, inhaling deeply. She turned to the kitchen window, staring out into the dark yard. Her reflection stared back, faint and shadowed, yet steadier than before.

"You're not running," she whispered to herself. "You're standing your ground. For Rory. For yourself."

The resolve in her voice felt foreign, but it gave her just enough strength to turn away from the window. She grabbed a glass of water from the sink, her hands steadying.

Now, all that was left was to wait.

The front door creaked open, the sound slicing through the silence like a knife. Eve's body stiffened, her fingers hovering over the glass of water she had poured moments earlier. She had planned every detail—the television in the background, the untouched stack of patient notes on the counter, the single glass of water. Normalcy, she reminded herself, was her armor. But the tightness in her chest betrayed her slipping grip on composure.

"Eve?" Leo's voice floated through the house, smooth and familiar, yet carrying an undercurrent she couldn't ignore.

"In the kitchen," she replied evenly, willing her voice not to waver. She picked up the glass and finally took a sip, forcing her fingers to steady.

Footsteps. Slow, deliberate. She kept her eyes on the wine glass as his presence filled the doorway. The burden of his gaze pressed against her, assessing, scrutinizing. A chill worked its way up her spine, but she willed herself not to react.

"Hey, sweetheart," he greeted, his voice as calm as ever, affectionate even. "Still up? You've been working too hard."

Eve lifted her head, forcing a smile, making sure it didn't seem too eager, too forced. Keep it natural. Keep him from suspecting.

Her expression was just shy of natural. "Couldn't sleep. I've been buried in paperwork all day."

Leo crossed the room with a practiced ease, his gaze landing on her. His movements were deliberate, calculated, as if he were observing a specimen under a microscope. He leaned down, brushing a kiss against her cheek. The gesture should've been comforting. Instead, it made her skin crawl.

"You look tired," he murmured, his hand reaching up to tuck a strand of hair behind her ear. "Have you even eaten today?"

Eve swallowed hard, her heart hammering in her chest. "I snacked here and there," she replied lightly. "You know how it is."

As he pulled back, his eyes flicked to her shoulder. With the precision of a surgeon, he plucked a stray hair from her sweater and held it between his fingers like it might hold the answers he sought.

"This isn't yours," he said softly, his tone devoid of accusation but steeped in meaning.

Eve's stomach lurched, but she held her ground. "Probably Rory's," she said with a shrug, her voice steady.

Leo chuckled, a low sound that sent a shiver down her spine. "That girl. Always leaving traces of herself everywhere."

He moved to the refrigerator, opening it with a casual air, but Eve knew better. His every movement was purposeful, probing. "So, how was your evening?" he asked, his tone light as he pulled out a bottle of water.

"Quiet," Eve replied, keeping her voice measured. "I barely moved from my desk."

He glanced toward the hallway. "The attic door is open. I told you not to go up there. It's not safe."

The blood drained from Eve's face, but she schooled her expression into careful neutrality. "I saw it earlier," she said lightly, as though it were an afterthought. "But I didn't go up. It was probably the wind."

Leo's eyes flickered. But, it was enough. She could see the calculation, the reevaluation. "The wind?" he repeated, his voice dripping with skepticism.

Eve's hand tightened around the edge of the counter. His scrutiny pressed down on her like a physical force. "It gets drafty up there, doesn't it?" she offered, injecting just the right amount of indifference into her tone.

For a second, Leo froze, his body going rigid. Then he laughed, the sound low and humorless. "I suppose it does," he said, his gaze never leaving hers.

He moved toward her, his proximity suffocating. Eve's instincts screamed at her to run, but she stood her ground, forcing herself to remain calm. She could feel the tension radiating off him, an almost tangible energy that made the air thick with unease.

A flicker of something passed over Leo's face—disappointment, suspicion, something darker. He crossed the kitchen, circling her slowly; a predator assessing its prey.

"You know," he began, his voice still smooth, "I was thinking about how perfect our life is. How much effort we put into keeping it that way."

Eve's forced herself to nod. "We've worked hard for what we have."

His smile didn't reach his eyes. "We have. And I'd hate for anything—or anyone—to disrupt that."

Eve's pulse pounded in her ears. He knows. He has to know. But she couldn't give him the satisfaction of seeing her crack. "Why would you say that?" she asked, her tone even. "Nothing's disrupting anything."

Leo leaned in slightly, his voice dropping to a near whisper. "Isn't it?"

The air between them felt electric, crackling with unspoken accusations. Eve met his gaze, her mind racing through every psychological tool at her disposal. Stay calm. Don't escalate. Use his need for control against him.

"Leo," she said softly, injecting warmth into her tone, "is something bothering you?"

He tilted his head, studying her like he might dissect her. "Not at all," he replied smoothly. "Just...wondering if we're still on the same page."

Eve tilted her head, mirroring his gesture. "Of course we are. Why wouldn't we be?"

Leo stepped back, his expression unreadable. "Just making sure. Change is in the air, don't you think?"

Eve's pulse quickened, but she kept her smile intact. "Change can be unsettling," she said softly, her words a veiled challenge.

He nodded, his eyes narrowing slightly. "Unsettling, yes. But necessary."

He placed the bottle of water on the counter, then turned toward the hallway. "I'll be upstairs if you need me."

Eve watched him retreat into the hallway, the sound of his footsteps fading until only silence remained. She stood frozen, sweat dampening the back of her neck, her pulse thudding in her ears. One chilling truth settled in her chest: *Leo knew she'd been in the attic.*

Then—another sound.

Footsteps. Faint. Approaching.

Leo's head snapped toward the window, his jaw tightening. He hadn't gone far after all.

She took a small step back, her heel barely grazing the floor.

Leo turned sharply, already moving toward her. His eyes dark and unreadable. "What did you do, Eve?" His voice was quiet, but the words were venomous.

She didn't move. Didn't blink. For a breathless moment, silence flooded the space between them. "Nothing," she replied quickly, her tone calm but firm. "I didn't do anything."

He advanced a step, the space between them shrinking. "You called her, didn't you?"

Eve didn't answer, her mind racing. She had no way out, no way to stall him further. All she could do was hold her ground.

"You've always been so meticulous," Leo murmured, his tone soft but laced with an undercurrent of menace.

Eve forced a laugh, her voice tight. "Well, you know me. Can't stand a mess."

Leo's chuckle followed him as he strode to the garage door. "This isn't over," he said quietly. Then, like a shadow, he slipped past her and into the hallway toward the garage.

"Leo!" Eve called out, her voice sharp with desperation. But he didn't stop, didn't even glance back.

Audrey's voice rang out from the front door. "Eve! Are you okay?"

Eve bolted toward the hallway, but Leo's footsteps echoed loudly in the garage. The danger wasn't over, but for the first time, Eve didn't feel alone. She yanked the door open just as she heard the screech of his car tires, his taillights blazing as he tore down the driveway.

Audrey and Eddie rushed inside, guns drawn, their faces taut with determination.

The two sisters shared a look—one of fear, trust, and unspoken understanding. "Which way?" Eddie barked.

Eve's mouth felt dry, her body unsteady. She lifted a trembling hand and pointed. "He's heading west. He—he saw you. He knew."

Audrey stepped closer, scanning her face. There was something different in her sister's eyes—not just skepticism, but something softer. Something almost like trust.

"You okay?" Audrey's voice was lower now, quieter. "I thought you were him, Eve," Audrey admitted, her voice low but steady. "I thought I was walking into a trap."

Eve wiped her face with trembling hands, her sobs subsiding into uneven breaths. "I let him into my life," she said, her voice raw. She let out a shaky breath. "I let him in, and I didn't see what he was."

Audrey's jaw tightened. "We'll find him," she said, not a promise, but a certainty.

Eve met Audrey's gaze, searching for the doubt she had come to expect. But this time, something was different. The skepticism was still there, but beneath it—just for a flicker—Eve saw something else. Something she hadn't dared to hope for. Audrey believed her.

She watched as Audrey and Eddie raced back to their car, their pursuit already in motion. The sound of Leo's engine faded into the distance, but its menace lingered. Eve sank into the nearest chair, her body trembling as the adrenaline began to wane.

The realization hit Eve like a sledgehammer, an almost physical sensation that took her breath away. The life she had built, the home she had so carefully crafted, the family she thought she knew—was all a lie. Leo, her husband, the man she trusted with everything, had been hiding in plain sight, wearing the mask of a perfect husband and father. But now, standing alone in their pristine entryway, Eve felt the sharp sting of betrayal. The walls that once felt so secure, the very foundation of her life, were crumbling, leaving her exposed and vulnerable. Everything she thought was solid now felt flimsy, and the world she had been living in seemed to twist and stretch as if it might snap at any moment.

Her gaze darted around the foyer, and she saw only the faint remnants of the life she'd once believed in. The gleaming surfaces, the smell of fresh-cut flowers, the framed family photos—every detail that once felt like warmth and safety now felt like a cruel mirage. The echoes of her own thoughts reverberated through the space: *How did I not see it? How did I not see him?*

She could still feel the traces of him—his calm, collected demeanor, the way he'd held it all together when everything inside her was falling apart. But those pieces of him, the ones she had clung to for so long, were merely another layer of the mask. A mask he wore to hide the obsessive control, the manipulation, the jealousy that now seemed so glaringly obvious. It wasn't just that Leo had lied to her. It was that she had allowed herself to believe in a version of him that was never real. It was as if she had built a castle on sand, and now the tide had come in, washing it all away.

Eve wrapped her arms around herself, a shiver running through her. *Had I been that naive?* The guilt gnawed at her, a quiet voice that whispered in the back of her mind, accusing her of being complicit in this facade. She had been so consumed with keeping up appearances—balancing her career, her family, the expectations of being the perfect wife—that she had ignored the cracks. She had ignored the signs, the moments when something felt off but she was too afraid to acknowledge it.

And then there was the guilt over her own choices. The affairs. The moments of weakness when she had been unfaithful, seeking solace in someone else's arms. In her mind, the connection with those men had been more than physical; it had been an escape, a way to feel something real when she felt increasingly disconnected from the man who should have been her rock. She had rationalized it. She had told herself it was a mistake, a lapse in judgement. But now, with everything falling apart around her, she wondered: *Did I break him? Was this my fault? Did my actions push him to this point?*

Eve understood the psychological complexities of human behavior. She had spent years studying people, dissecting their motivations, unraveling their emotional landscapes. And yet, as she stood in the midst of her shattered world, she couldn't help but wrestle with the notion that perhaps her actions had contributed to Leo's unraveling.

But deep down, Eve knew better. She knew that Leo's obsessive traits, his need for control, his manipulations, didn't come from her mistakes. She had seen these tendencies long before their marriage began to fray. Leo had always been deeply insecure—his need to dominate, to be the center of attention, his obsessive jealousy, were all innate traits. Eve knew this. She knew that the cracks had been there from the beginning, buried beneath the polished surface of his charm. She had seen the signs but had chosen to overlook them, to justify them as quirks or stress. She had bought into the illusion he so carefully crafted, never suspecting the true depths of his darkness.

But could I have stopped it? Could I have prevented this? The thought gnawed at her again. Leo's obsession with control had festered beneath the surface for years, but now, with the truth exposed, Eve wondered just how far it had gone. How many others had been hurt in Leo's wake? How many had suffered because of his need to possess, to control, to dominate?

Eve felt her stomach twist as the thought passed through her mind. The reality of Leo's true nature made her wonder just how many lives he had destroyed before hers. Had he been responsible for other deaths, beyond the lovers she had betrayed him with? She knew how patterns of behavior often revealed darker truths—how deep-seated obsessions could lead to extreme actions. Leo had always been meticulous, calculating, controlling. Now, with the terrifying revelation that he had a taste for blood, Eve wondered how much of it was buried beneath the surface.

Her mind flashed back to the stories she had heard over the years—the subtle hints, the cryptic conversations with his colleagues, the odd way people seemed to disappear from his life. She had always chalked it up to coincidence or bad luck. But now, standing in the wreckage of everything she thought she knew, the pieces started to fall into place. The man she had once loved was something far more dangerous. And Eve was left to grapple with the horrifying possibility that he had been hiding his true nature all along.

The thought made her stomach churn. What if she had ignored more than just the small signs? What if there were other victims—other lives lost to his obsession?

Eve closed her eyes and took a shaky breath, forcing herself to focus. She couldn't let herself be consumed by guilt. She couldn't let Leo's madness control her. As much as she regretted the parts of herself that had allowed this nightmare to unfold, she had to stay strong. She had to protect Rory. And as much as she hated to admit it, she had to protect herself too.

Without thinking twice, Eve grabbed her keys and rushed out the door. She needed to get Rory to safety, and there was only one person she could turn to.

Eve drove through the streets in a daze, each passing car seeming like a threat. The headlights felt like spotlights aimed directly at her, and every shadow cast by the streetlights felt like someone watching her, waiting to pounce. Her mind was a blur—no clear direction, no clear thought.

When she reached Lilah's house, she didn't hesitate. She didn't knock—she just let herself in, her hands shaking as she fumbled with the door handle. Her chest was rising and falling with quick, shallow breaths, her body almost vibrating from the fear of what she had just learned about Leo. Her perfectly styled hair and bright red lipstick felt like a distant memory, the image of a woman who no longer existed. The reality was staring back at her: disheveled, frightened, broken.

Eve sat there beside Lilah, her chest heaving with panic, as her mind raced with everything she could no longer keep inside. Lilah's usually flamboyant persona softened for just a moment, her hand gently resting on Eve's arm. "Okay, breathe. Just breathe," she said, her voice calm yet strained. Eve tried to follow her advice, but the floodgates had opened, and she couldn't stop herself.

"I don't know how this happened. Leo... He's not who I thought he was. He's a killer, Lilah," Eve blurted, her voice raw. "I've been living with a man who's been hiding a monster all along. He's been hiding everything from me—from all of us. And I—I didn't see it. I didn't want to see it." She squeezed her eyes shut, but the images flashed in her mind regardless.

She took a shaky breath before continuing, barely able to keep her composure. "It's worse than I ever imagined. The worst part is—he's been killing my lovers. All of them. They were my lovers, Lilah. I was the one who let it happen. I was the one who—" Eve choked on her words, her voice trembling as the guilt surged.

Lilah stiffened, but Eve was already spilling everything, the truth coming out in a frantic torrent. "And...and then there's this shrine—this...shrine in our attic, Lilah. A shrine to the people he's killed. I saw it. I found it by accident, hidden in the attic. His obsession with control, with power, it's been right in front of me the whole time." Eve's voice faltered as she closed her eyes, trying to block out the memories that threatened to drown her.

The wave crashed down on her. How had she not known?

"And you know what? My sister...she thought I was the killer. She thought I was the one doing this. I can't believe it. It's all so wrong." The words tumbled out, raw and unfiltered. Eve's chest tightened, the shame and fear building with every confession.

Lilah sat motionless taking in Eve's words. Her sharp, confident demeanor had slipped away, leaving her silent and stunned. Eve could feel her friend's uncertainty, could sense the unease that had crept into the air between them. Lilah was used to navigating any drama with flair, but this was different. This wasn't a situation she could charm her way through. It was too dark, too real.

Eve forced herself to calm down, wiping the tears that had begun to fall without her consent. Her chest felt tight, as if the very air had thickened, making it harder to breathe.

"I need to get Rory out of here," Eve said, her voice cracking. She had known the words were coming, but dreaded saying them. "I can't keep her in the dark anymore. I don't know what he's capable of, but I can't risk her getting hurt. I—I don't know how to protect her from him." Her hand trembled as she wiped her eyes again, the gravity of the situation weighing down on her every word.

Lilah nodded slowly, her fingers tapping nervously against the armrest. "I get it. I'll help. But, Eve…you've got to tell her something. She's not stupid. She's going to want answers. And right now, you're not giving her any."

Eve's heart broke at the thought. She couldn't imagine sitting down with Rory, telling her the truth about Leo, about everything. The burden of it all threatened to crush her, and her fear for Rory's future was suffocating. Rory was already so perceptive—how would she cope with this new reality? How could Eve possibly shield her from the truth, when the truth was so dark, so terrifying?

Before Eve could respond, Rory's voice cut through the silence.

"Mom?" Rory's small voice carried into the room from the doorway, tentative, uncertain, and full of questions. She stood there, arms crossed, her dark eyes narrowed as she took in the tension in the room. It was as though she had been waiting for this moment, sensing it, reading the unspoken words between the adults.

She stepped closer, her feet barely making a sound on the hardwood floor. Her voice barely above a whisper, she asked, "Why do you look so scared?"

Eve swallowed hard, wishing she could protect her from the truth. "I—I'm just tired, sweetie," she said, her voice trembling despite her best efforts to hold it together. She wanted to protect Rory from this, but deep down, she knew she couldn't. Rory wasn't a child anymore. She wasn't naive.

"Where's Dad?" Rory's question was simple, but it made Eve's stomach turn. Rory wasn't just asking about where Leo was. She was asking about the man Eve had spent years loving, the man Rory had trusted. But Eve couldn't lie anymore. She couldn't shield her from this. Not anymore.

Eve's voice caught in her throat as she stood, struggling to find the words. "I...I don't know where he is right now, sweetie," she managed, her voice coming out tight, strained. She forced a smile, but it didn't reach her eyes. "He's...he's not here."

The room grew heavier, thick with tension. Eve didn't know how to start the conversation. She didn't know how to explain to her daughter that the man they had both trusted, the father Rory adored, was a monster.

And as the silence stretched on, Eve realized that no matter how much she tried to hide, Rory would always see through her. She had always known more than Eve was willing to admit. Rory's quiet, knowing gaze was truth Eve could no longer escape. And in that moment, Eve knew that her daughter would have to face a darkness that had consumed their family, whether she was ready or not.

Chapter 24

The Weight of What Was Ours

6:46 p.m. Leaving Home

Leo's foot slammed against the gas pedal before he had even fully cleared the driveway. The tires screeched against the brick pavement, a sharp protest against the silence of the affluent neighborhood. A woman walking her golden retriever froze on the sidewalk, her head snapping toward the sudden roar of his engine. The dog barked, pulling against its leash, its instincts sharper than its owner's. Leo barely registered the sight of her wide eyes before jerking the wheel, narrowly avoiding the curb as he barreled onto the main road.

His mind was a cacophony of sound—Eve's voice, sharp and trembling, repeating the words. *He's the Magician.*

The thought sent an electric jolt through his body, like a live wire pressed against his spine. She knew. She knew. His perfect, carefully controlled world had shattered in an instant, and now there was nothing but wreckage left in its wake. His breath came in short bursts, his hands slick with sweat against the leather steering wheel.

The smooth streets of their quiet enclave gave way to the on-ramp for I-294. The moment his tires hit the highway, he pushed the speedometer past eighty, weaving between sedans and SUVs with reckless urgency. The city was miles ahead, the distant skyline just beginning to glint under the last rays of daylight. He needed distance. He needed time to think.

But the thoughts wouldn't stop. Eve's face burned into his mind. His jaw clenched so hard his molars ached.

And now? Now she looked at him as if he was the monster.

A horn blared beside him as he nearly clipped the side of a black Mercedes. Leo barely flinched, gripping the wheel with white-knuckled force. He was coming undone. His carefully measured control—the control that had kept him safe for years—was slipping away, crumbling like wet paper in his hands.

His vision blurred for a moment, his temples throbbing with the force of his own heartbeat. His fingers flexed and unflexed around the wheel, as if testing whether his hands were still his own.

Did I go too far?

The question snaked through his mind, insidious and taunting. His kills had always been precise, necessary. But had it been too much? She hadn't understood what he was doing for her?

His stomach churned, nausea rising like bile in his throat. He couldn't think like that. Not now. Not when the walls were closing in. He needed a plan.

Downtown. He had to get downtown. The city would swallow him, give him cover, keep him from being caged like a rabid animal.

Leo pushed the car faster, cutting across lanes as he veered toward the exit for I-90 East.

7:05 p.m. Speeding Down I-90 East, Heading into Chicago

The city loomed ahead, a jagged silhouette against the bruised dusk. The headlights of passing cars streaked through Leo's rearview mirror, refracted into halos of red and white as his vision blurred. His grip tightened on the wheel, his knuckles bloodless.

He couldn't go home. He couldn't fix this. He had lost everything.

Eve's eyes, wide with revulsion, had said it all.

His jaw clenched and his muscles coiled. The perfect life he had built—curated, controlled—had shattered in a matter of minutes. Eve had recoiled from him, her expression not of fear, but of disgust.

The speedometer pushed past ninety.

His pulse pounded against his skull as flashes of their faces surfaced—Eve's lovers.

Their confusion. Their realization. Their terror. Their gurgled last breaths.

The delicious pause before they begged.

The moment he decided how much suffering they deserved before he ended them.

Had he been a fool all along? A placeholder she tolerated while giving herself to lesser men?

His stomach twisted. The shrine. The altar of his devotion— curated, sacred. Personal belongings. Photos—some she knew about, some she didn't. Every piece was a testament to his love.

She saw it.

Had she understood? Or had she dismissed it as sickness? Madness?

A sharp blare of a horn snapped him back as taillights flared red in front of him. He yanked the wheel, the car fishtailing before finding traction. The driver behind him laid on their horn, furious. Leo barely heard it. Let them crash. Let them all burn. Nothing mattered now.

Rory.

His daughter's name lodged like glass in his throat.

The moment she knew—if she didn't already—she would hate him.

She would look at him like Eve had.

Like he was something to be erased.

There was no way out.

He couldn't go home.

The police were coming.

By morning, his face would be on every screen in Chicago.

Do I run?

He had money. Connections. He could disappear before they locked the city down.

Do I turn myself in?

The thought was crushed before it fully formed.

He wouldn't rot in a cell.

He was better than that. Smarter than that.

But the darkest thought yet slithered into his mind.

Or do I end it here?

His foot hesitated on the gas. The thought rooted itself, insidious and tempting.

It would be easy.

Just let go.

Let the car rip through the guardrail, plunge into the abyss.

End it before they could strip him of everything. Before they could reduce him to a monster in a cage.

But—

No. Not yet.

A sliver of control remained.

Leo gritted his teeth, exhaling sharply as he pushed the car forward. He wasn't done. Not yet.

The city swallowed him as he passed the first green exit sign for downtown.

7:28 p.m. Entering Downtown Chicago

The golden glow of streetlights flickered on as the sun finally disappeared, plunging the city into artificial twilight. The illuminated skyline loomed ahead, indifferent to his descent.

Downtown Chicago – Exit 51C.

Leo shot past the old water tower on Michigan Avenue, its Gothic frame a fleeting specter against the darkening sky. The black steel skeleton of the John Hancock Center towered in the distance, as unyielding as fate. To his left, the neon glow of The Drake barely registered—an icon of wealth and luxury, the world he had once commanded, now slipping through his fingers.

He was running out of road.

His mind spiraled, replaying the moment Eve had truly seen him.

Revulsion. Horror. Disgust.

She had seen the real him.

The faces came next. The men he had erased from existence.

Their final gasps. Their useless pleas. The moment of release as their bodies stilled, no longer a threat to what was his.

The blare of a horn snapped him back just in time to slam the brakes. He barely avoided ramming into a taxi. The L train rattled overhead, flashing silver in the dark.

State Street was alive.

Tourists snapped photos near Tribune Tower. A street performer hammered out a beat on an overturned bucket. Couples strolled past Millennium Park, laughing, oblivious.

Normalcy hummed around him. Leo clenched his fists. He was already gone.

The gut-punch of it nearly took his breath away.

There was nowhere left to go.

He couldn't go home.

He couldn't disappear—not when every news station would soon be plastered with his face.

And he sure as hell wouldn't rot in prison.

The air in the car thickened, suffocating.

Leo's fingers flexed on the wheel as a final question settled, heavy as stone.

Do I run?

Or do I end it?

His foot eased off the gas.

A decision was coming.

And for the first time, he wasn't sure he was the one making it.

7:55 p.m. Wabash Avenue Bridge

The brakes screamed as Leo wrenched the wheel, his car skidding onto the shoulder of the bridge. The Wabash Avenue Bridge loomed above the black, glassy expanse of the Chicago River, its steel framework stretching out in crisscrossed lines, massive and unmoving against the fog creeping in from the water.

Leo shoved the door open, the icy night air slicing through him as he stepped out, his breath immediately visible in the cold. He barely felt it. He was numb.

The click of his shoes on the pavement felt surreal as he took slow, measured steps toward the edge, the rhythm of his movement echoing against the steel girders above. His coat flapped against his legs, caught in the wind rolling in from the river. He barely noticed.

The water was waiting.

Black. Silent. Depthless.

It stretched below him, fractured by the neon reflection of the city skyline—broken colors, distorted shapes, as fragmented as the pieces of his life.

Leo's hands clenched into fists. His pulse pounded in his ears.

This is it.

He had played every move. Controlled every moment. He had built something—his life, his marriage, his family. He had held Eve in his hands.

And now?

Gone.

A bitter laugh escaped him, lost immediately to the wind. He tilted his head back, staring up at the towering silhouette of the Trump Tower, its mirrored glass reflecting the clouds as they rolled in from the lake. The spire blinked red at the very top, a warning light for planes—or maybe for men like him.

The weight settled deep in his chest, pressing down like hands forcing him to his knees.

I can still disappear. I can still make it.

The thought flickered—*Escape, vanish, start over*—but it was weak, hollow. There was nowhere to go.

Leo stood at the edge, his fingers curled tightly over the frozen railing.

The headlights of passing cars flickered like dying embers. Shadows stretched long, twisting under the streetlamps—like ghosts waiting to claim him.

And then—footsteps.

A voice—distant, indistinct—carried on the wind.

He didn't need to turn to know.

Audrey.

But it didn't matter.

The moment had already arrived.

He inhaled, slow and deep. The wind howled. And then—nothing. He was falling.

7:58 p.m. The Jump

The water wasn't water.

It was a knife. A thousand knives, stabbing into his skin all at once.

The second he hit, his body revolted. Every nerve, every muscle seized violently, locking him into a rigid, frozen state. He couldn't breathe. His lungs screamed, but the icy water clamped down on his chest like a vise.

This is what drowning feels like.

The cold was beyond pain—it was annihilation.

He sank fast, his heavy coat dragging him down, down, down. The black water wrapped around him, swallowing him whole, devouring him like an abyss.

His fingers burned, then went numb. His legs were dead weight.

Panic flared. His brain screamed at his limbs to move, to fight, but the cold had already stolen his body from him. He tried to kick, but his legs wouldn't respond. His arms flailed uselessly, sluggish, the water pressing in from all sides.

The world above him blurred into warped streaks of gold and white. The streetlights on the bridge—so far away now. The distorted hum of the city faded. The rush of his heartbeat in his ears slowed, muffled by the crushing silence of the river.

His chest convulsed.

He needed air.

His mouth opened instinctively—a fatal mistake.

Freezing water rushed in, filled his throat, his lungs.

It felt like fire.

He choked, body convulsing violently, but there was nothing to expel—only more water. More cold. More death.

His vision blurred. Darkened.

No. Not like this.

His body screamed, but his mind—his mind had never felt so clear.

You jumped, didn't you? You wanted this. You knew there was no way out.

Maybe it was the oxygen deprivation. Maybe it was the shock. But suddenly, a strange sense of calm settled over him.

The secrets. The lies. The killings.

Eve.

Rory.

Audrey.

Everything faded into the black depths around him.

Leo stopped fighting.

His limbs went slack.

The current dragged him deeper.

And then—

Darkness.

8:09 p.m. Chicago Riverbank

The world was blurred shadows and frozen silence.

Leo's body lurched forward, gasping. His chest burned, his throat raw from the water he had inhaled. His limbs didn't work right. His fingers clawed at the frozen concrete, slipping, scraping. His body refused to obey, numb, dead weight. He dragged himself forward—an inch at a time.

His drenched clothes clung to his body, the weight of them unbearable. His muscles spasmed violently, his teeth clattering so hard he thought they might break.

The air hit his skin like broken glass, even colder than the water.

Move. Move.

He staggered forward, legs barely responding, leaving a trail of slick, wet footprints on the pavement. The Chicago skyline loomed above him, its lights too bright, too real. It felt like he had stepped into another world—one where he didn't exist anymore.

A shadow shifted under the bridge.

Leo's eyes snapped toward the movement, breath hitching in his throat. A homeless man sat hunched against the concrete wall, wrapped in a ratty, dirt-streaked blanket, rocking slightly to keep warm.

Warm.

Leo didn't think. He couldn't.

His body moved on instinct, pure survival.

The man barely stirred as Leo snatched the blanket from his frail shoulders. A faint mumble of protest—nothing more. The man barely had the strength to lift his head.

Leo wrapped the damp, filthy fabric around himself, clutching it tight. The wool stank of sweat, piss, and old cigarettes, but it didn't matter.

It was a barrier.

Between him and the cold.

Between him and the world.

Keep moving.

His feet dragged, half-frozen, as he slipped into the nearest alleyway. The river behind him, the city ahead—a labyrinth of light and shadow. His body screamed for warmth, for rest, but he couldn't stop.

Not yet.

He kept his head down, shoulders hunched, disappearing into the night.

A businessman wrinkled his nose as he brushed past. A woman slid a few seats away. But no one stopped him. No one saw him. No sirens chased him.

8:32 p.m. Washington/Wabash L Station, Chicago

Leo's body trembled uncontrollably, each step a battle against the bitter wind slicing through the Loop's steel and stone canyons. His soaked clothes clung to his skin, heavy as lead, leeching what little warmth remained in his body. The stolen blanket barely helped—it was damp, filthy, and useless against the relentless Chicago winter.

The city pulsed around him, indifferent to his suffering. Car horns blared, neon signs flickered, and pedestrians brushed past without a second glance. He moved forward in a daze, his breath coming in ragged gasps, each inhalation a sharp knife against his frozen lungs.

Then he heard it—the unmistakable screech of an arriving train. His head snapped up, vision still blurred, but his survival instincts locked onto the glowing Washington/Wabash Station sign ahead. The elevated platform loomed above, a golden-lit refuge against the darkness swallowing him whole.

He staggered toward the station, his limbs sluggish, his joints locking up from the cold. The stairs leading up felt impossibly steep, each step a test of sheer willpower. But he climbed, gripping the rail with hands that no longer felt like his own.

Reaching the top, he lurched toward the turnstiles, but his pockets were empty—no wallet, no transit card, no proof of the man he had once been.

No time to think. No time to hesitate.

Leo inhaled sharply, gathered what little strength remained, and vaulted over the turnstile, landing hard on the other side. The impact sent a searing pain through his knees, but he barely registered it. A few people turned, startled, but no one stopped him. No security guard chased after him.

Shuffling toward the platform, he caught sight of himself in the reflection of a glass panel—soaked to the bone, shaking, his skin pale and lips cracked. He barely looked human.

The train arrived in a rush of hot air from the tunnels below, its doors hissing open. Leo stepped inside, forcing his numbed fingers to grip the overhead bar. The doors slid shut behind him.

The warmth of the car hit him like a drug. It wasn't much—still chilled by the drafts sneaking in—but compared to the brutal wind outside, it felt like salvation. His muscles spasmed violently as his body struggled to adjust. He clutched the stolen blanket tighter, curling inward as he collapsed onto a seat near the door.

Commuters filled the car, but they barely acknowledged him. A businessman typed on his phone. A young woman stared blankly out the window. A pair of college students whispered about an upcoming exam.

No one saw him. No one knew who he was.

As the train lurched forward, Leo closed his eyes, his body still convulsing from the cold. He had no plan, no destination.

But he had escaped.

For now.

Chapter 25

Beneath the River, Above the Flame

7:05 p.m. – Speeding Down I-90 East, heading into Chicago

The city blurred past in streaks of neon and steel, a distorted mirage in the rearview mirror. Chicago's skyline loomed ahead, jagged against the twilight—a city built on shadows, watching from the distance. Audrey's pulse pounded in her ears, drowning out the wail of sirens behind her.

Leo was running.

Her hands gripped the wheel so tightly that the tendons in her wrists ached, her breath shallow and tight. The leather felt damp beneath her fingertips, slick with sweat. The car responded to every flick of her wrists, every shift of her weight, a silent partner in the chase.

Ahead, Leo's taillights flickered like dying embers, swallowed and spat out again by the dense web of traffic. He was fast—too fast, too reckless. Audrey's foot pressed harder against the gas, the needle climbing past seventy, past eighty. The engine snarled in response, surging forward.

"He's gonna kill someone," Eddie muttered beside her, knuckles white where they gripped the dash.

Audrey didn't blink. "Not if I get to him first."

She could feel it now—the shift in the chase. This wasn't just about escape. Leo wasn't thinking straight. His movements were jagged, unpredictable. He swerved between lanes, barely missing a semi that let out an enraged blast of its horn. The scent of burning rubber clung to the air, acrid and thick.

Audrey followed, weaving through the congestion, her heart hammering in her throat.

The city was alive around them, a breathing, pulsing thing. The cold air slipped through the cracked window, sharp against her skin. The thunder of an L train rattled overhead, drowning out the chorus of honking horns.

She barely registered it. Her world had narrowed to Leo's car and the widening gap between them.

She had to close it.

Leo barreled through a red light. A cab skidded sideways, tires shrieking against the pavement. The driver's silhouette threw up a frantic hand, his curses lost to the roar of engines. Audrey sucked in a breath and took the intersection a split-second after him, her stomach lurching as she narrowly missed the rear bumper of a sedan.

Eddie swore. "Jesus, Holliday."

She ignored him.

The pavement gleamed wet beneath the glow of streetlamps, reflecting the distorted streaks of brake lights. Leo swerved violently left onto Lower Wacker Drive. Audrey followed—a heartbeat too late.

Her back tires caught the edge of an oil slick.

For a breathless moment, the car fishtailed. The world tilted. A flash of headlights, a glimpse of steel railings—

Audrey yanked the wheel hard, the tires screeching as they found traction again. Her breath came fast, sharp. She had nearly lost it.

But so had he.

Leo was running on instinct now, not strategy. His car jolted dangerously close to the median before correcting. He was out of control—and he knew it.

This wasn't just escape. This was desperation.

Audrey's stomach twisted as realization settled, cold and heavy.

Leo wasn't trying to get away. He was spiraling.

And spiraling men did stupid, irreversible things.

She gritted her teeth. She had to stop him before he ran out of road.

7:54 p.m. Wabash Avenue Bridge

The car skidded to a stop so violently that Audrey's teeth clacked together. The tires shrieked against the frozen pavement, the steering wheel jerked in her grip, and for a split second, she thought she'd lost control. Her breath tore from her lungs as she slammed the car into park, yanking the door open before the engine had fully cut off.

The cold hit her like a blade, slicing through her coat, through her skin, through her bones. Her breath crystallized in the air, vanishing as quickly as Leo had. Eddie shouted behind her, but the words were muffled, distant. The city was loud, but inside her head, there was only silence. A thick, drowning silence.

Then—a shadow.

A flicker of movement beneath the bridge lights.

Her breath caught—sharp, like a knife between her ribs. She saw him.

Leo stood near the railing, body rigid. His coat whipped violently in the wind, his face unreadable from this distance—

but his posture told her everything. His breath came sharp and shallow, misting the air in front of him. He turned his head slightly. Maybe he saw her. Maybe he didn't. But Audrey saw him.

His body went still, then—he jumped.

A shift.

A breath.

A blur.

"Leo!" she screamed, but the wind ripped the name from her throat, scattering it across the bridge.

She scanned the water desperately, frantically. He had to come up. He had to.

But the river gave her nothing.

No movement. No shadow breaking the surface. No second chances.

Just silence.

8:00 p.m. The Aftermath

The wind howled like a wounded thing, shrieking through the steel beams of the bridge. Her body moved before her brain did, instinct overriding reason, her pulse hammering against her ribs as if it were trying to break free of her chest.

The river was black ice, a merciless void that had already swallowed him whole. She moved, but the ice caught her boot. A sharp skid, a near fall—her fingers grasped at the cold steel railing, steadying herself just as Eddie's voice cut through the wind behind her.

"No!" Eddie's voice was a growl, low and commanding, the kind of voice that didn't take no for an answer. His grip was iron, locking around her midsection, holding her against his chest as she struggled.

Audrey thrashed, twisting, shoving, her boots scraping against the frozen pavement. The bridge tilted, the city lights blurred—she couldn't breathe, couldn't think, couldn't do anything except fight.

"Let me go!" she shrieked, her voice raw, wild. She kicked at his shins, elbowed his ribs, but Eddie didn't budge.

His voice was a growl, low and commanding. "Goddammit, Audrey! You jump in there, you're dead too!"

She struggled, breath heaving, body thrashing against him.

"He ruined everything, Eddie!" Her voice cracked. "He—he took everything, and now—now he just—"

A sob ripped from her throat before she could stop it.

She went limp.

The fight drained from her body, leaving her sagging against Eddie's chest, her fingers still curled around his arms. Her breaths came in short, broken gasps, her ribs aching from the force of them.

Eddie held her tighter—not just to restrain her now, but to keep her together.

"We'll find him, Audrey," he murmured, his voice rough but steady. His chin rested lightly against the side of her head, his arms a cage around her. "This isn't over."

She squeezed her eyes shut, her forehead pressing into his shoulder, but the guilt kept coming, thick and suffocating.

Her father would have caught him.

Her father wouldn't have let Leo slip through his fingers.

Her father wouldn't have failed.

But she had.

Eddie's voice softened, cutting through the storm inside her head. "This isn't on you."

Audrey let out a sharp, bitter laugh, her body still shaking. "Doesn't feel that way."

Eddie exhaled, long and slow. Neither of them moved. The world shrank to just this—his arms around her, the wind biting at their skin, the cold, gaping void where Leo had been.

Then—sirens.

Distant at first, then closer.

Red and blue lights flickered against the steel beams of the bridge, casting ghostly shadows across the pavement. Backup was here.

Eddie finally loosened his grip, but his hands didn't leave her arms. He waited—waited for her to breathe, to blink, to come back to herself.

Her jaw clenched. She wasn't okay.

But she had to move.

Had to keep going.

Her body felt weightless as she stepped away from Eddie, as if the moment had hollowed her out from the inside. She turned toward the river one last time, searching, pleading for any sign of him.

Nothing.

She swallowed it down.

Then, without looking back, Audrey squared her shoulders and walked toward the flashing lights.

Because this wasn't over.

And she wasn't done.

Not yet.

The Next Day

Audrey found herself sitting across from Chief Reynolds in the precinct, the air thick with frustration and guilt. She had barely slept, the weight of the unresolved case pressing down on her like a physical burden. Her eyes were tired, her mind racing with thoughts of Leo—the elusive killer who had escaped her grasp. It all felt too real now—he was still out there, somewhere, and she had failed to stop him.

"Audrey, talk to me. What happened last night?" Chief Reynolds' voice was rough, a mix of exhaustion and concern.

Audrey inhaled deeply, trying to steady herself, but the words stuck in her throat. This was the moment—the moment she had to face the truth of her failure. She swallowed hard before speaking, her voice betraying the rawness she had been holding back for hours.

"He jumped into the river. The Magician. Leo. I couldn't stop him in time," she said, her voice cracked. It was still so fresh—the feeling of failure. She had been so close, and yet, he had slipped away.

Chief Reynolds looked up from his desk, his expression a mixture of disbelief and concern. He pushed his chair back, standing up as he crossed his arms.

"What do you mean, jumped?" His brow furrowed as he processed what she was saying. "The water's freezing this time of year. He couldn't have gotten far."

Audrey's hand tightened into a fist, the frustration and helplessness surging. She knew what she had to say next wasn't easy.

"We sent the dive team in right away," Audrey continued, her voice steadying, though the exhaustion still rang through her words. "They searched for hours, but they didn't find him. He vanished."

The silence between them felt heavy. Chief Reynolds turned away from her and paced behind his desk. He gripped the back of his chair tightly, his mind racing. Audrey could feel his frustration, but also his understanding. This wasn't just on her —it was on all of them.

"Damn it, Audrey," he muttered under his breath, his voice low. He was visibly agitated, his hands balled into fists at his sides. "He got away."

He stopped pacing and turned to face her, his eyes searching her face for something—anything—that might help him understand this.

"Where are we now?" Chief Reynolds asked, his voice hard but tinged with concern.

Before Audrey could answer, the door opened and Eddie stepped in. He had been waiting outside, sensing the tension in the room. He had heard her voice crack when she spoke about Leo's escape, and he knew she needed support. It was evident in the way she carried herself—like a woman drowning under a burden too heavy to bear.

"She was about to jump in after him, but I wouldn't let her." Eddie's voice was calm but firm as he stepped forward, his eyes shifting to Audrey before focusing on the Chief. "The water's icy, and there's no way I was going to let Audrey get hurt."

Chief Reynolds eyed Eddie, his expression a mixture of respect and gratitude.

"You stopped her?" The Chief's tone was sharp, but there was no malice in it. "Good call. We need her in one piece to help solve this, not to drown in some fool's errand."

Eddie nodded, but his gaze softened when he turned to Audrey. "Exactly." His voice lowered, more empathetic now. "We did everything we could. We sent in the dive team, the Marine unit. We combed the area for hours. Leo's gone, Chief. We have to face that."

Chief Reynolds rubbed his temples, his frustration mounting as he struggled to accept the reality. "Damn it," he muttered, before lifting his head. His eyes were steely, responsibility weighing heavily on him as well. "This isn't over. Get them back in the water. Full team, full search. We have to find him."

Audrey's chest tightened at the chief's words. She had wanted to give up. She had wanted to walk away, to say that she couldn't do this anymore. But she knew he was right. They couldn't stop. Not now.

"We're not giving up, Chief," Audrey said, her voice now steadier, more resolute. "But he's not going to be easy to find."

Chief Reynolds nodded, his expression softening slightly. "I know. But we keep pushing. You did everything right."

Audrey's eyes flickered for a moment. She couldn't shake the guilt that pressed down on her chest, but the chief's words—

however simple—offered a small bit of relief. Maybe she hadn't failed. Not entirely.

"I don't know anymore." Audrey's voice cracked slightly, betraying the emotions she was desperately trying to keep hidden. "I failed. I couldn't stop him. I couldn't catch the bastard. My dad probably would have and now I'll be an embarrassment."

"Your father would be proud of how you've handled this, Audrey," Chief Reynolds said, his voice steady. "Hell—he *is* proud. I know the kind of man he is. I've worked beside him. I've butted heads with him." A small, knowing smile pulled at the corner of his mouth. "And I've seen how he talks about you when he thinks no one's listening."

That landed harder than any praise could have.

"He always said the toughest part of this job isn't solving the case, it's carrying the ones that don't end the way you want them to."

Reynolds stepped closer, his tone gentler now. "You've done the work. You've got his grit—and your own way of seeing the world. But you've done everything you can. That's all anyone can ask."

Audrey's chest tightened. She wanted to believe him. She wanted to believe she had done enough. But the guilt still gnawed at her.

Eddie gave Audrey a soft, supportive smile, but the tension in his body was still palpable. He wasn't going to let her fall into the trap of self-blame.

"By the way," Eddie began, his voice cutting through the heavy silence, "When we got to her house, Eve filled us in on everything, including the creepy shrine Leo set up. You know, typical stalker behavior. It's…unsettling. Pictures, Tarot cards, news clippings—sounds like something we should check out."

Audrey shook her head, incredulous. "Leo's a real piece of work."

"Yeah, I mean, could've been worse. You could have been the one married to him."

Audrey nodded. "I'm starting to think I dodged a bullet."

"Exactly." Eddie let out a theatrical sigh. "You get all the perks of being the lucky twin—no creepy shrine, no dead husband, and no murderous ex-lover haunting you. You're winning."

Audrey let out a laugh, the tension easing a little. "Yeah, I guess so. I'll take my chances with the shrine. But seriously, we need to get there and see what else Leo left behind. He might've slipped away for now, but I'm not letting him get away with it."

The chief, having listened quietly to their banter, nodded. "I'll get a team out there. You two head over and check it out."

Audrey nodded, her mind now focused on the next step. "Got it. We'll head over now." As she and Eddie walked out of the chief's office, a renewed sense of purpose settled over her.

The air in the attic was thick with dust, every breath sending tiny particles into the air. The flickering beams from Audrey and Eddie's flashlights cast long, uneven shadows across the cluttered space. Boxes, old furniture, and forgotten mementos littered the room, but it was the far corner that immediately drew their attention.

In the corner, behind stacks of old furniture, was the shrine. It was as if it had been set up intentionally, hidden in plain sight. The meticulous arrangement of items in that small area sent a chill down Audrey's spine. The space was starkly different from the rest of the room, carefully curated—like a twisted art installation. A cold, eerie sense of ownership seemed to hang in the air.

Audrey's breath caught as she scanned the space. "Jesus," she muttered under her breath, her flashlight landing on the objects one by one.

The walls were covered with photos of Eve. Professional headshots that Eve had probably never approved to be framed, alongside candid snapshots she hadn't known were taken. A photo of Eve sitting at a café with one of her lovers, the intimacy of the moment now exposed. Her lovers were represented too—men captured in secret, their faces frozen in time, all part of Leo's warped trophy collection.

The sound of Eddie's breath behind her broke the silence. "What the hell is all this?"

Audrey felt a lump form in her throat as she stepped closer. "This…this is insane."

Her flashlight flickered across the Tarot cards pinned to the wall. There were several of them—carefully placed, some with the edges curled slightly as though they had been there for a long time. The Devil card and the Hanged Man. Their dark, disturbing imagery amplified the twisted energy. Audrey's hand hovered over them, feeling an odd, almost magnetic pull. Leo's descent into the occult was clear now. He had manipulated more than just fate; he had sought to control something much darker.

"Leo must have done this to try to bind her…to possess her, mentally and spiritually," Eddie said quietly, almost to himself, as he took in the sight.

Audrey nodded but felt a sickness in the pit of her stomach. "Yeah, I don't think it's just the love he was after. He was controlling her, all of it… The men, her body, everything. She was his…possession."

They both turned when a floorboard creaked underfoot. Eddie stepped back, and as he shifted, his foot hit something. The floorboard gave way slightly, revealing a hidden compartment beneath the clutter. He cursed softly under his breath as the floorboard shifted farther, revealing a small hidden altar.

Audrey leaned down, her flashlight illuminating the compartment as it opened wider. It was a crude stone slab, stained dark from years of neglect and use, surrounded by black candles—some still partially melted, others long since extinguished. Occult symbols were scratched into the stone with reckless abandon, as if Leo had been desperate to mark something sacred, something powerful.

"This wasn't just a shrine," Eddie said, his voice low and steady. "This was a ritual site. A twisted altar." He stepped closer, his gaze locked on the eerie setup. "I feel like I'm in *Indiana Jones* or something. This place is straight out of a secret tomb, waiting to be unlocked."

Audrey's eyes darted to him, half-amused, half-stunned. "Yeah, minus the traps...I hope."

Eddie chuckled darkly, though it didn't quite reach his eyes. "Let's hope so. But I think we've got something way worse than booby traps in here."

At the center of the altar were four jars, each filled with something that made Audrey's stomach churn. The liquid inside was thick and dark, with a viscous amber hue. As her flashlight shifted across the jars, a metallic gleam caught the light. Audrey's breath caught in her throat, her pulse quickening as she focused on the disturbing sight. The thin, membranous objects floated in the jars, their delicate striations faintly visible in the dim light, giving off an eerie, ghostly sheen.

The surrounding area was a cluttered mess of candles. Symbols were etched onto the walls—runes and marks she couldn't make sense of in the dim glow of her flashlight. A picture of Beelzebub, painted in dark, twisted hues, loomed above them, his eyes hollow, a figure from the dark corners of a nightmare. Audrey knew enough from movies to recognize the demon's influence in the atmosphere of the shrine, but seeing it up close sent a shiver down her spine.

Her eyes drifted across the altar until they landed on a small vial tucked away in the corner. She froze.

Inside the vial was a substance—red, dark, thick, unmistakable.

"Looks like blood..." she whispered, her voice almost too quiet for Eddie to hear.

Eddie's gaze followed her line of sight, his expression unreadable. "Jesus, Audrey... This...this is next-level sick."

Audrey reached for the vial with trembling hands, inspecting it carefully, her fingers brushing the cold glass. "We'll need to get these jars and this vial analyzed, collected," she said, her voice steady despite the queasy feeling rising in her gut. This wasn't just evidence—it was a personal violation.

Eddie's attention shifted as his eyes scanned the photographs surrounding the altar. His gaze hardened as he came to a picture of Eve—her eyes closed, her body distorted into unsettling positions. One picture showed Eve holding Leo as if he were an infant, suckling on her breast, and another with her naked, candles arranged around her like some twisted ritual.

The air in the attic seemed to grow thick with unease as Eddie shifted uncomfortably. Seeing Eve in these photos, naked and vulnerable, made him feel like an intruder—like he was seeing Audrey naked too. The discomfort settled like a weight on his chest.

Audrey turned to Eddie, her face pale. "We need to get Eve up here," she said, her voice shaky. "I can't process all of this alone. These images, these...positions. They're replicas of her—of us. I feel violated...like I'm seeing something I wasn't meant to."

Eddie nodded, unable to meet her eyes. The reality of what they were looking at was hard to digest, but he knew Audrey was right.

Audrey's voice cut through the silence, ringing in the attic as she called out, "Eve, you need to come to the attic. There's more...more than you know. And I'm warning you, it's not going to be pretty."

Eve's voice floated back, a mixture of hesitation and dread in her tone. "I'll be right there."

As the echoes of Eve's words hung in the air, Audrey couldn't shake the feeling that the worst was still to come.

When Eve finally stepped into the attic, her body was stiff with reluctance, her eyes darting around the room as if she couldn't bear to see the twisted shrine again. She had been up here before, but what she saw now was far worse than anything her mind had prepared her for. The shrine, once a shocking discovery, now seemed almost secondary to the altar that stood before her—a grotesque symbol of Leo's obsession.

Her eyes flicked from the altar to the photographs, to the Tarot cards pinned to the corkboard, and then to the vial of blood. The sight of it made her stomach twist. Her breath caught in her throat, her skin flushed with a cold sweat. "What the…" she whispered, her voice barely audible. Her hand instinctively reached for the corner of the room as she stumbled slightly, trying to steady herself.

Her eyes were wide, searching the room for anything that might make sense of this nightmare. But nothing did. "I never…I never saw this," she murmured, her voice trembling with disbelief. "This—this wasn't even in my head. He made this…for me?"

Audrey could see the shock on Eve's face, the horror of realization dawning on her like a veil being lifted. This man built an entire world around her, a world that now seemed suffocating, suffused with darkness.

"He was obsessed with controlling everything, Eve," Audrey said softly, stepping closer, her hand resting gently on Eve's shoulder. "Your life, your relationships, your body…all of it."

Eve looked around the room, taking in the disturbing altar with its melted black candles and strange symbols. Her eyes were drawn back to the jars in the center, filled with an oily, viscous substance. She stared at them for a long moment, her face paling even further, as if the world itself was tilting beneath her feet.

"What…what are these?" Eve whispered, her voice catching in her throat. Her eyes never left the jars, unable to tear herself away. The sickening realization settled deeper within her. "What is this?"

Audrey took a steadying breath, knowing the pain Eve was feeling—this wasn't just the discovery of Leo's obsession. This was something far worse. "I don't know, Eve. But we'll get it analyzed. We'll figure it out."

Eve's gaze shifted from the jars to the vial of blood—its dark crimson color unmistakable. She recoiled slightly, but didn't look away. The vial seemed to pulse with a life of its own, a stark reminder of how far Leo had taken his delusions. "Is this—?" Eve began, her voice a raw whisper.

Audrey's jaw clenched as she stepped closer to the vial. "Yes, it looks like blood, Eve. But I don't know whose it is. We'll get it tested. We have to."

Eve stood frozen, her mind reeling. She wanted to scream, to run, but her body refused to move. The sight of herself—her distorted self—staring back at her from the photographs made her feel nauseous. Pictures of her, yes, but in positions that were far from intimate. Leo had created…a puppet.

Some of the images depicted Eve in explicit poses. One picture showed her with her legs spread wide, a candle placed between them, the flame casting eerie shadows on the surrounding skin. Another showed her with Leo's hands grasping her breasts, his fingers digging deep into her flesh.

The most disturbing image of all showed Leo's hands wrapped around her throat. The pose was one of complete submission, as if Eve had been reduced to nothing more than an object for Leo's twisted desires. The pictures seemed to scream with a sense of ownership and control, as if Leo had seen her as nothing more than a possession to be used and manipulated at his whim.

Audrey bit her lip, the anger rising in her chest at the sight of what Leo had done to Eve's body, her image. "It looks like he might have drugged you, Eve. He made you pose. You were his object."

Eve staggered back slightly, her hand reaching for the wall to support herself. The room felt like it was closing in around her.

Her voice broke. "I didn't know how deep this went. How could I have been so blind?"

Audrey nodded, standing up and offering her hand to Eve. "Right now, we need to get all this documented. This is what we're going to use to bring Leo down."

As Eve stood with Audrey's help, she couldn't shake the sense of violation that hung in the air. Leo had made her part of his twisted world, and now she was left to pick up the pieces.

The forensics team came up and started cataloging each photo, Tarot card, and object, the sound of their footsteps echoing eerily in the attic. Their once safe home now felt like a mausoleum to Leo's twisted love, his obsession now fully on display for all to see.

The realization came to Eve that Leo had built this world with every moment of her life, her love, and her betrayal woven into it. She felt exposed, vulnerable, as though he had stripped her bare and left her with nothing but the remnants of his madness.

As the sound of their voices and the crinkle of paper filled the room, one thing was certain—the past wasn't just behind them. It was right here, and Leo's obsession would continue to haunt them all.

Chapter 26

To Carry a Ghost

The soft click of Eve's office door closing echoed in the quiet room as Caroline continued her tirade about her mother's behavior. Caroline was a regular patient, and over the years Eve had grown accustomed to her complicated relationship with her overbearing mom. Normally, Eve could focus and offer helpful advice, but today, her mind kept drifting. It wasn't Caroline's words; it was her own body betraying her. The nausea that had plagued her over the past few days was back again, more intense this time. It twisted in her stomach, sending sharp pangs through her abdomen.

Eve blinked, trying to focus on Caroline, but her vision swam slightly. She grabbed onto the edge of her desk to steady herself. Caroline's voice became muffled, the words merging together like a dull hum.

"…and when she said that I should just be grateful for what I have, I wanted to scream. But I held it in. I don't know why I can't just tell her how I feel. I mean, it's just so frustrating, Eve. I don't know how much more of this I can take. You know?"

Eve nodded absently, forcing herself to keep her attention on the patient. But Caroline's voice sounded farther away now, like she was underwater. It wasn't just the dizziness—Eve felt utterly exhausted. Her eyes glanced around the room. The walls of her office felt suffocating, the weight of her own emotions bearing down on her.

"Eve?" Caroline's voice broke through the fog, sharp with concern. "Are you okay? You've gone completely quiet. You've been staring into space for the last minute. You look…off."

Eve blinked and quickly tried to focus on Caroline. Her words were well-meaning, but Eve could feel the tension building in her gut. Off? She wasn't just off—she was sick. The dizziness swelled again, and this time, she couldn't ignore it.

"I'm just…" Eve paused, trying to find a reasonable excuse. "I'm just listening, Caroline. You're making good points."

But Caroline wasn't convinced. Her eyes narrowed, scanning Eve's face with a mixture of worry and confusion. "Are you sure? You don't look so good. You're not…sick, are you?"

Eve looked at her, catching the genuine concern in Caroline's eyes. She forced herself to sit up straighter, the effort exhausting. No, not now. She couldn't afford to fall apart in front of Caroline. Not in a session. Not when she had a job to do.

She forced a smile. "I'm fine, Caroline."

Suddenly, Eve's legs got shaky beneath her. She wasn't sure if it was exhaustion or something else, but her body was rebelling. Her stomach lurched again, and she barely made it to the bathroom before it happened. The vomit came in violent spurts, leaving her shaking on the cool bathroom floor. The cold tiles against her cheek brought a semblance of clarity, and she struggled to stand, her breath ragged in the silence.

She stared at herself in the mirror. Her face was pale, drawn. What the hell was going on? She hadn't felt this way since...since everything had started spiraling out of control.

Her cell phone buzzed, and she looked at the screen. It was Lydia, her receptionist. Eve pressed answer before the phone had a chance to ring again.

"Eve, are you okay?" Lydia asked, the concern thick in her voice. "Caroline's really worried about you. You don't look well."

"I need to reschedule the rest of the appointments for today," Eve said, her voice steady but distant. "Please, tell my patients I'm not feeling well."

"Will do."

"Thanks, Lydia," Eve said, her throat tight. She ended the call quickly, her mind spinning faster than she could control.

She walked over to Dr. Larkin's office. "Jordan?" Eve's voice shook as she spoke. "I can't see my clients today. I need you to manage things while I'm away. Please."

"I've got it, Eve," Jordan replied immediately. "Don't worry about anything here. Go take care of yourself."

The bile rose so fast Eve didn't have time to close the door of her house. She barely made it across the tile before she was on her knees, retching into the toilet bowl, the cold porcelain echoing her heaves in a hollow, almost accusatory way. The bathroom light above buzzed faintly, flickering as if unsure whether to stay on— offering no mercy, no reprieve.

Her stomach convulsed in waves, long after there was anything left inside her. By the third round, all that came up was acid and air, a violent emptiness that left her body trembling and her vision star-speckled. Her palms pressed flat to the floor, slick with sweat and shaking. The tiles were freezing beneath her skin, and for a second, she let her cheek rest against them, as if the cold might draw the fever out of her.

The silence afterward felt like a punishment.

She inhaled slowly, eyes fluttering closed, but even behind her lids the world pulsed. Red. Then black. Then a flickering memory:

Leo standing in the doorway of their bedroom, once upon a time, smiling—shirt unbuttoned, his face boyish in that rare, unguarded way. He'd held a glass of wine in one hand, a book in the other. *You need to take a break,* he'd said. *Come to bed.*

The same hands that once held her now curled around the necks of men. The same voice that whispered *I love you* had ordered someone to beg for their life.

She blinked hard, the image vanishing. In its place: the rust-tinged scent of blood. Her memory conjured it from nowhere, sharp and coppery, twisting her already raw stomach.

She crawled back against the wall, her breath ragged. Her shirt clung to her back, damp with sweat. The air was thin. It felt like she was breathing through gauze.

Was this stress? Trauma? Something else entirely?

A sharp pulse rippled through her abdomen, low and strange. Foreign.

She gasped and grabbed her middle instinctively, as though expecting something to move beneath her skin. But there was nothing. Just the hollow ache, the nausea, the mounting certainty.

This wasn't just psychological.

Her body was speaking to her in a language of revolt—rejection—rebirth.

Eve closed her eyes and tilted her head back against the wall, allowing the porcelain to cool her fevered skin. Outside, a car passed on the street, headlights casting brief ribbons of light through the slats in the blinds. For a second, she imagined they were searchlights. That someone was looking for her. That someone *knew.*

She dragged herself to her feet, one shaky hand on the counter for support. She stared at the face before her—not in that fleeting, unconscious way most people did, but with the wide-eyed, hollow stillness of someone trying to recognize a stranger. She looked like a ghost wearing her skin—translucent, rimmed in red, haunted with something older than exhaustion.

Not Eve the therapist.

Not Eve the wife.

Not even Eve the woman.

Just...*being reduced to splinters.* That woman didn't throw up into toilets. That woman didn't keep secrets coiled like vipers beneath her ribs.

This woman—the one in the mirror—was cracked down the middle. Split between past and future, shame and survival.

"You're the published psychiatrist," she whispered, but her voice was hoarse, brittle. "You're supposed to have answers."

The mirror offered none.

She turned the faucet on and splashed her face with cold water, her fingers trembling. The droplets hit the sink like tiny bullets. She gripped the counter with both hands, her head hung low, the mirror above now fogging with steam from the hot water she hadn't meant to turn on.

Her mind whispered a single, terrifying possibility.

You're pregnant.

She didn't say it aloud. Saying it would make it real. Instead, she closed her eyes—and listened. To the drip of the faucet. To her heartbeat, fast and hollow in her ears. To the breath she held in her lungs like a prisoner.

The fear didn't pass.

It thickened.

It settled into her bones.

The mirror had stopped fogging, but Eve hadn't moved.

Another memory: Noah had looked at her like she was gravity itself. Like she anchored him to the world.

He trusted you.

She blinked. Her throat tightened.

Another flash: Leo's shrine. The rows of stolen artifacts. The photos. The carefully preserved traces of every man she had touched, desired, loved.

He worshipped you.

A chill rolled through her.

The two men had mirrored each other in opposite ways—Noah in vulnerability, Leo in violence. And in the middle of that reflection stood Eve.

The woman who let herself be loved by both.

She pressed a palm flat against her stomach, the nausea returning not as sickness now—but as fear. Heavy and blooming.

She didn't need a test. Not yet. Not officially.

Her body already knew.

The symbolism wasn't lost on her. Of course it would come now. Of course her body would betray her with the ultimate secret: creation in the midst of destruction. New life inside a woman grieving a death she couldn't explain to anyone.

It felt like irony.

Or maybe it felt like punishment.

For a second, she imagined her reflection stepping out of the glass and answering her. The version of herself that wasn't scared. The one who hadn't slept with a patient. The one who hadn't married a monster. The one who didn't flinch at the thought of being a mother again.

The phone was cool in her palm, but her fingers felt too hot, twitchy with indecision. Eve stared at the screen for a full minute before pressing Lilah's contact. It was almost muscle memory—second nature to reach for the only person who had seen her through the worst, even before the façade was this fractured.

It rang once.

Twice.

By the third ring, she nearly hung up.

"Hey, honey," Lilah's voice poured through the speaker like a warm blanket—half-concerned, half-casual, the way only someone who knew your entire origin story could be. "Been thinking about you all day. What's going on?"

Eve leaned against the kitchen counter, her eyes drifting to a crooked magnet on the fridge. Rory had made it in kindergarten—a pink paper heart with glitter that never fully stuck. It sparkled under the morning light sometimes. It looked dull now.

"I'm not okay," Eve said, no preamble.

Silence crackled for a beat.

"Okay," Lilah said slowly, her tone sobering. "Is it Leo? Audrey? Something new?"

"I've been sick," Eve replied, and even that small confession felt like exhaling glass. "Not like a cold. It's deeper. A fatigue in my bones. My stomach is—" She cut herself off, pressing a hand to it as if to quiet the rebellion inside.

Lilah's voice softened immediately, stepping into that space the way she always did. "How long?"

"A few days. A week, maybe longer. At first I thought it was stress. But it's not going away. I'm dizzy all the time. And this morning...I threw up in my office bathroom."

Another beat of quiet.

"Eve..." Lilah's tone shifted. "That doesn't sound like stress. That sounds like pregnancy."

Eve's breath caught. Even though she'd considered it, even though her own body had practically announced it in red flashing lights, hearing it aloud twisted something sharp inside her.

"No," Eve said too quickly, almost reflexive. "No, I mean— Leo and I haven't...not in a long time. There's no way it's his."

She swallowed, the words tasting bitter as they escaped. "But Noah...before everything fell apart. Before Leo...before the shrine. There was Noah."

Lilah didn't gasp. She didn't flinch. She didn't even pause long enough for judgement to sneak in.

Instead, she said, "Then it's probably his."

The certainty in her voice felt like a hand steadying a swaying boat.

"I haven't taken a test," Eve admitted. "I was scared to. I think I still am."

"That's okay," Lilah said gently. "You don't have to rush anything. But, Eve…your body already knows. And deep down, you probably do too."

Eve's vision blurred. Her pulse was suddenly loud in her ears. "How can I have a baby now? With everything that's happened? With Leo out there somewhere—watching, waiting, punishing? And Noah…he's gone. He's gone because of me."

Lilah's voice was quiet, but unwavering. "No, Eve. He's gone because of Leo. That's not on you."

"But this is," Eve whispered, hand pressed flat against her abdomen. "This…this might be all I have left of him. Or it might destroy everything I've tried to keep together."

"You don't have to decide everything tonight," Lilah said. "But you do have to know the truth. For yourself."

Eve nodded, even though Lilah couldn't see her. Her chest ached with too many emotions layered too close together.

"I'll get a test," she said finally. "I just… I don't know what I'll do if it's positive."

"I do," Lilah replied, her voice warm but firm. "You'll figure it out. Like you always do. And you won't do it alone."

The sky had darkened by the time Eve left the house, but she barely noticed. Streetlights flickered to life overhead, casting cold halos across the sidewalk as she moved on autopilot—coat buttoned wrong, keys clenched in one hand like brass knuckles. She didn't even remember grabbing them.

The drive to the drugstore felt like slipping into a dream. Traffic lights passed in muted reds and greens. The heater blew stale warmth into the car, but it did nothing to thaw the chill burrowed beneath her skin.

By the time she parked, her stomach was already knotting again. Whether it was anxiety or nausea, she couldn't tell anymore. Her body had become a stranger—familiar only in betrayal.

The pharmacy's fluorescent lights buzzed overhead like an accusation. The smell of floor cleaner hit her. She hesitated by the automatic doors, one boot scuffing the mat as if her brain was still deciding whether to walk in or walk away.

Inside, the world felt too bright, too loud.

She wandered toward the family planning section, her heart drumming louder with each step. Pregnancy tests were nestled between boxes of condoms and fertility supplements, unassuming in their pastel packaging. Like none of them realized what they were holding.

She reached for the shelf with a shaking hand, bypassing the bargain brand without thinking. The digital one. She needed clarity. No lines. No guessing. Just truth.

As her fingers curled around the box, her eyes snagged on something just beside it—a tiny display of baby pacifiers. Rubber and plastic, in soft pinks and blues. Smiling animals on the packaging.

Her chest tightened.

She blinked and turned away too fast, nearly knocking over a bottle of prenatal vitamins. Her throat felt too tight to swallow.

At the checkout, she kept her eyes low, offering no small talk. The clerk, mercifully, didn't say a word. Just scanned, bagged, and handed it over like it was any other errand. A box of cereal. A pack of gum.

But Eve could barely breathe as she walked out. Her hands shook as she put the test in her purse. Heavier than it should be for something that small.

She climbed into her car and shut the door. For a moment, she didn't start the engine. Just sat there, clutching the steering wheel like a lifeline, staring straight ahead as the condensation from her breath fogged the windshield.

There was no turning back now.

Eve opened the front door just as Lilah's car pulled into the driveway—loud, silver, unapologetically messy, like the woman herself. The driver's side door slammed, followed by the familiar staccato of boots against pavement.

"I brought ginger tea, peanut butter crackers, and three different kinds of prenatal vitamins because I'm an optimist-slash-emotional prepper," Lilah called as she bounded up the porch steps. "And yes, I know it's probably a stomach bug, but on the off-chance it's divine intervention—surprise, bitch—I came armed."

Eve didn't even smile. She just opened the door wider and let her in.

Lilah stepped inside like she owned the place, brushing a scarf off her shoulder with the flair of a cabaret emcee. She took one look at Eve's face and dropped the act—mostly.

"Oh, honey," she said, voice softening. "You already bought the test."

Eve nodded mutely, her fingers tightening around the pharmacy bag like it might dissolve if she let go.

"I don't think I can do it alone," she whispered, voice barely above the hum of the heater kicking on.

Lilah didn't answer right away. She stepped forward, placed one hand on Eve's cheek and the other over her hand, where she clutched the bag like it was evidence in a murder trial.

"Then I'll sit with you," she said. "And when the world starts spinning, I'll be the one holding your damn hair back."

Eve managed a weak laugh—just enough breath behind it to keep from collapsing.

The bathroom light was too bright. The silence too sharp. Eve handed Lilah the box like it might bite her.

Lilah raised an eyebrow. "This is the one you picked? The fancy digital one with the words instead of the lines? Oh, you *really* wanted to suffer."

Eve said nothing. Her fingers moved with robotic precision—tearing the wrapper, fumbling with the test. Her body felt distant, like she was performing for an invisible audience behind glass.

"I'll just…turn around," Lilah offered, spinning toward the door. "Not that we haven't already shared some questionable moments. Hello, that tequila night in Vegas? But dignity, darling. Always leave room for dignity."

Eve rolled her eyes, barely. "You're the reason I blacked out and woke up with a napkin stapled to my bra."

"And you're welcome. That napkin had your future therapist license scribbled on it. Very prophetic."

When Eve returned to the counter and set the test down, the air changed. The jokes dried up. The seconds stretched long.

Lilah sat on the edge of the tub, legs crossed, one elbow on her knee like she was waiting for a jury verdict.

Eve paced. Once. Twice. Her heart thundered.

"I'm not ready for this," she whispered.

Lilah didn't move. "You already are."

They didn't look at each other as the test blinked to life on the counter.

Pregnant.

The word landed like a stone in Eve's chest. Her breath caught, her knees buckled. She sank to the tile floor before she realized she was falling.

Lilah was there in a second—arms around her, grounding her, warm and solid and completely unbothered by mascara streaks or the soft sound of Eve breaking.

"I can't do this," Eve choked out, the words raw. "Not again. Not after everything."

"Yes, you can," Lilah whispered. "You already are. You just did the hardest part—you found out. The rest? We'll face it together."

Eve pressed her forehead into Lilah's shoulder, trembling. "It's Noah's. It has to be."

Lilah exhaled. "Then it's a part of someone you loved. Not a curse, Eve. Maybe…just maybe, it's something else. Something that gets to grow up free of all this pain. You get to decide that."

The silence stretched between them—thick, heavy, but not hopeless.

They moved into the living room, and the mug of tea Lilah made had gone cold in Eve's hands. She sat curled up on the couch beneath an oversized knit blanket, knees drawn to her chest, the pregnancy test tucked somewhere out of sight but not out of mind. The weight of it still lingered, coiled low in her abdomen like something alive.

Lilah sat beside her, perched like a queen on the edge of a crumbling throne—one leg crossed over the other, hair twisted into a messy knot that looked far more expensive than it was. She'd brought a candle in from the hallway and lit it without asking—cinnamon and clove. It gave the air a warmth the room couldn't seem to muster on its own.

"I feel like a fraud," Eve said quietly, her voice hoarse from crying. "I spend my days helping people sort through their trauma. I give them steps. Mantras. *You're not defined by what's happened to you.* But here I am, sitting in my own disaster, and I can't even decide if I want to keep a baby that feels like a reminder of everything I did wrong."

Lilah didn't answer immediately. She reached down and adjusted the blanket over Eve's feet, her movements uncharacteristically gentle.

"You're not a fraud," she said. "You're human. Tragic, poetic, painfully self-aware human."

Eve blinked hard. "I was falling for Noah. I think I loved him…not in the traditional sense, maybe. But it was real. And now—he's gone. Murdered. By my husband. And I'm pregnant with his child. Lilah…what the fuck do I do with that?"

Lilah leaned back, arms crossed loosely. "You do the one thing you've always done—even when you were barely holding it together: survive. You get up. You decide, day by day, if this child represents love or loss. Or maybe both."

Eve shook her head, her voice cracking. "I feel like I destroyed everything. Rory's life. My marriage. My career. My integrity."

"You didn't destroy anything," Lilah snapped. "Leo did. Don't you dare take the blame for a man who killed people to control you. He ruined *his* life. Not yours."

"But I let him in," Eve whispered. "I let him get so close, for so long. I kept secrets. I lied. And I still don't know if I can love this baby the way it deserves to be loved."

Lilah studied her for a long moment. "Let me tell you something about love," she said, her tone suddenly sharp. "It doesn't show up perfect. It doesn't ask if you're ready. It just kicks in the goddamn door and demands to be seen. If this baby is part of Noah and part of you, then maybe—just maybe—it's a second chance. Not a punishment."

Eve's eyes brimmed again, but this time the tears didn't fall. "I thought I could have it all. Family. Career. A picture-perfect life. But maybe I was just pretending. Pretending to be a mother. A wife. A therapist. Now I don't even know who I am."

"You're Eve," Lilah said. "The woman who built a life from ashes and still gave her clients hope when she had none left for herself. The woman who got up off a bathroom floor today when her world cracked wide open. The woman who chose to *know* the truth instead of hiding from it. That's who you are."

Eve let the silence stretch between them.

"I don't know what comes next," she admitted.

"You don't have to," Lilah said. "Tonight's not for answers. It's for survival. You're allowed to not be okay."

Eve leaned into her friend, her head resting lightly against Lilah's shoulder. The fear didn't win.

Not yet.

"I have to call Noah's mom," Eve whispered.

Lilah's brows lifted. "Oof. That's…yeah. That's a *scene*." She took a sip, then lowered the mug and softened. "You sure you want to do this right now?"

"No." Eve's voice cracked. "But I have to."

Lilah nodded, then gestured with a dramatic flourish. "Alright then. Do the rehearsal take. Get all the messy versions out first so we don't accidentally traumatize the woman further."

Eve blinked, then gave a breathy laugh despite herself. "Okay."

She swallowed, tightened her grip on the phone, and stared down at the screen.

"Hi, Mrs. Watson. I'm Dr. De la Gardie, your son's therapist…and also someone who…slept with him. And now I might be pregnant with his child. Oh, and my husband murdered him."

Lilah held up a finger. "Okay. Solid plot twist. But maybe lose the word *might*—and maybe don't lead with the murder."

Eve exhaled shakily. "Let me try again."

Her second attempt was quieter. "Mrs. Watson… I'm so sorry to bring this to you. But I was very close to your son. We were involved. And now…I believe I'm pregnant. I wanted you to know."

Lilah gave a slow nod. "Better. Still brutal. But better."

Eve stared at the emergency contact number in Noah's file, heart pounding in her chest like a fist against glass. "Okay. No more rehearsing."

Lilah shifted closer, placed a hand on her knee. "I'm right here."

Eve pressed call.

Each ring stretched like elastic—thin, taut, ready to snap.

Then—*click.*

"Hello?" A woman's voice. Dry. Guarded.

"Mrs. Watson?" Eve said gently, her voice tight. "This is Dr. Eve De la Gardie. I was… I am…Noah's therapist."

A pause. "Yes. I remember." Her voice was clipped. "Why are you calling me?"

Eve swallowed. "There's something I need to tell you. It's not easy. But I believe it's important."

Another silence.

"I was close to your son. Professionally. And also…personally."

The silence didn't stretch this time. It shattered.

"What the hell does that mean?"

Eve flinched. Lilah reached over and slid her wine glass away.

"I'm saying we were involved," Eve continued. "Outside of therapy. It wasn't planned. It just…happened. And I believe I'm pregnant. With his child."

Mrs. Watson's voice froze—just once. And then: "What kind of goddamn sick joke is this?"

Eve's throat tightened. "It's not a joke. I know how this sounds—"

"No, you don't!" the woman snapped, grief lacing every word. "My son is dead. You think I'm just going to sit here and listen to some woman tell me he left behind a baby? After what that monster did to him?"

"My husband," Eve whispered, hating the word. "Leo. He…he killed Noah. I didn't know what he was capable of. If I had—"

"You don't get to say that," Mrs. Watson said, her voice shaking. "You don't get to call me and act like you're the one hurting. My son was all I had. And now you're telling me you're carrying a part of him?"

Lilah's hand tightened around Eve's.

"I just needed you to know the truth," Eve whispered. "I don't know what I'm going to do yet. I'm…I'm still trying to process it."

On the other end of the line, Mrs. Watson's breath trembled. "I can't take any more of this. I can't have more pain dropped on my doorstep without warning. If it's true—if it's *really* his child—then you get the proof. DNA. And then you decide what you're doing with it. Until then? Don't call me again."

Click.

The call ended.

The silence afterward was worse than the storm outside.

Eve lowered the phone slowly. Her hands trembled.

Lilah was the first to speak. "That went well," she said softly. "If we're grading on a curve from hell."

Eve's laugh came out jagged and broken. "She hates me."

"She's grieving," Lilah said gently. "She doesn't know what to feel, so she feels everything."

Tears welled in Eve's eyes, and Lilah opened her arms. Eve collapsed into them.

"I didn't mean to fall for him," she murmured. "I didn't mean for any of this to happen."

Lilah stroked her hair. "No one means to fall into a fucking Greek tragedy, babe. It just happens."

The wind howled outside Eve's bedroom window, dragging long streaks of snow against the glass like claws. She stirred beneath the blanket, her body heavy, her eyes gritty from a night without real rest. For one disoriented moment, she forgot everything— then her stomach lurched, and it all came rushing back.

The test.

The call.

The impossible truth growing inside her.

The house felt hollow. Too quiet. Lilah had slipped out just before sunrise, muttering something sarcastic about outrunning the traffic before Chicago became a snow globe of existential dread. Eve had hugged her longer than usual, and Lilah hadn't said anything about it—just gave her a look. The kind that meant *I know you're not okay, but I'm here when it shatters.*

Eve pulled herself upright. Her body ached, the nausea returning in slow, merciless waves. She swung her legs over the edge of the bed, her toes brushing against the cold floor. A shiver rippled through her spine.

The entire world outside had vanished beneath a sheet of white. The snowstorm had come in hard and fast overnight, frosting every surface, blanketing the trees, cars, and sidewalks in silence. There was something unreal about it—like waking up inside a dream where time had stopped, or worse, refused to move forward.

She padded down the hallway, each step soft, the creak of the old hardwood echoing louder than it should. As she passed the front door, a strange stillness pulled her attention sideways.

An envelope sat on the doormat. Just barely slipped through the mail slot.

Cream-colored. Unmarked.

Her heartbeat stuttered.

Eve stared at it for a full ten seconds before moving.

She bent slowly, her breath catching in her throat as she picked it up. The paper was cold in her hand—too cold, as if it had been left outside longer than it should've. Her name wasn't on it. No address. No stamp. No sender.

Just a perfectly folded envelope, thin but weighted.

Her fingers hovered at the flap—then peeled it open.

Something slid into her palm, delicate and cold.

A Tarot card.

The Queen of Pentacles.

The card was pristine. The colors vibrant, the image familiar—too familiar. The Queen sat on her carved stone throne, surrounded by ivy and roses, a golden pentacle held in her lap like an offering. Her face serene. Her eyes watchful.

Eve's hands went clammy. Her stomach twisted.

Not fear. Not now.

Resolve.

She remembered showing Leo her Tarot deck once. It had been early in their marriage, when she still thought she could reveal pieces of herself, and he would cherish them. He'd barely looked at the cards, dismissing them with that patronizing smile she had grown to hate. But he had seen the Queens.

And now this.

The Queen of Pentacles—fertility, domesticity, motherhood, abundance.

And in this context?

A threat.

A message.

A warning.

I know.

I still see you.

You're mine.

Eve's jaw clenched as she stared down at the card. A tremor passed through her—but not from fear.

From fury.

She was done playing his game.

The air outside screamed against the windowpane, wind slamming like fists against the glass. But inside, Eve stood still as stone, the card clutched in her hand, her pulse steadying with a strange, quiet clarity.

She wasn't going to run.

Not anymore.

Chapter 27

The Queens are Watching

Audrey watched Eve from across the kitchen table, nursing a mug of something herbal that neither of them had bothered to identify. The candle between them flickered low, casting shadows on Eve's face that made her look even more hollowed out than usual. She was pale, silent, barely blinking. A woman cracked open.

"I don't know what to say," Audrey admitted.

"Then don't," Eve murmured. Her voice was threadbare. "Just sit with me."

So she did. No cop instincts. No big sister energy. No sharp edges. Just presence. Just breath.

They sat like that for a while, wrapped in the kind of silence only sisters could share—dense, but not uncomfortable. Shared oxygen. Shared blood. Shared fracture.

Eve finally broke it. "I'm not sure I can do this."

Audrey didn't ask what "this" meant. She didn't need to.

"I think you already are," she said gently.

Eve gave a small, humorless smile. "You sound like Lilah."

"You told her?" Audrey asked softly.

"She was with me when I took the test."

Audrey nodded, her fingers drumming lightly on her mug. "And the card?"

Eve's gaze darkened. She tilted her chin toward the side table. Audrey followed it.

The Queen of Pentacles sat alone beside a coaster. Pristine. Centered.

"I found it this morning."

Audrey stared. A chill tiptoed down her spine.

"He knows," Eve whispered.

Audrey had asked if Leo ever used Tarot when they were together. Eve had said no. He'd dismissed it back then—mocked her for being "mystical." But the shrine had told a different story. Rows of preserved cards sorted like trophies. Pages of notes.

He'd used it. Obsessively.

He hadn't just killed. He'd curated his violence like an exhibit. And now, the Queen of Pentacles showing up at Eve's door wasn't random—it was personal.

"You're not safe here," Audrey said, before she could stop herself.

Eve's eyes flicked to hers. "I'm not safe anywhere."

That was probably true.

Audrey sat back, letting the thought take root. "Do you want me to stay the night?"

"I think I just want to sleep."

"Okay."

She stood but something gnawed at her gut. Not just the card. Not just Eve's exhaustion. It was the feeling she got before walking into a crime scene. The moment before a door swings open and nothing is the same after.

Eve didn't walk her to the door. Didn't hug her goodbye. Just said thank you, in that tiny voice that sounded like she was trying not to disappear.

Audrey stepped out into the cold.

And her gut twisted tighter.

When she got home, she slumped onto the couch in her apartment, arms folded, the build-up from her conversation with Eve pressing heavy on her shoulders. She made herself a cup of coffee with Bailey's Irish Cream and left it untouched on the table beside her, the condensation bleeding slowly down its side.

The Tarot card Eve received haunted her. She hadn't said much after Eve showed it to her. Couldn't. There were too many thoughts pulling at her focus—Leo, the shrine, Rory, Eve's pregnancy. The card was the final thread—and it had snapped something loose in her.

Her phone buzzed. Sydney. Audrey exhaled and answered. "Hey."

"Hey, Aud." Sydney's voice was always brisk, always cool, but there was a crack in it now—just faint enough to raise red flags. "So…weird thing. I got something in the mail today. Like…*really* weird."

Audrey sat up straighter. "What do you mean?"

"A Tarot card," Sydney said, and Audrey's blood ran cold. "No return address. No note. Just…a card in a blank envelope. Queen of Cups."

Audrey stared at the wall, trying to process the words. "Wait. Are you serious? Eve got one too. The Queen of Pentacles. Today."

A long silence. Then: "What in the actual fuck, Audrey?"

"Yeah." Audrey rubbed her forehead, pacing. "We think it's Leo. But if you're getting one too…"

"He doesn't even know me," Sydney cut in. "I've never met him. I've barely talked about all this outside of you."

"That's what I don't get," Audrey murmured. "Why you? Why now?"

Sydney's voice dropped lower. "Audrey... What if it's not just about Eve anymore? What if he's watching *all* of us?"

Audrey's heart pounded. "I need to check my mail."

"Do that," Sydney said. "Call me back if you get one. Please."

Audrey ended the call and grabbed her coat, her pulse hammering in her ears. Her mailbox was down the hallway, tucked behind the stairwell like a forgotten relic. She hadn't checked it in days.

Her fingers trembled as she unlocked the metal door. Inside, sitting on top of a flyer for discount dry cleaning, was a single cream envelope.

Unmarked.

She didn't open it right away. She stared at it like it might hiss or bite. Finally, with slow precision, she peeled it open.

The Queen of Swords slid out into her palm.

Her stomach dropped.

Cold, resolute, intelligent. The card stared back at her, sword raised, crown high. The irony wasn't lost on her—Audrey, the cop. The rational one. The sharp one. And now she was part of someone else's twisted deck.

She clutched the card and jogged back to her apartment, breath fogging in the cold. Her mind was already racing.

Sydney.

Eve.

Her.

Who else?

She grabbed her phone. "Eve," she said the moment her sister answered. "We were wrong. It's not just you."

Audrey hadn't even finished relaying everything to Eve when her sister's screen lit up again—Lilah. Audrey gestured toward the call.

"Answer it on speaker," she said.

She swiped to answer. "Lilah?"

There was no hello. Just the familiar, frantic rhythm of Lilah mid-rant: "Please, for the love of all things holy and chaotic, tell me I'm not the only one who just received a Queen of Wands in the goddamn mail."

Audrey sat up straighter. "Wait, what?"

Eve closed her eyes. "You got a card too."

"Yes! A Tarot card! No note. No return address. Just this smug-ass queen holding a sunflower and staring into my soul like she knows I haven't done laundry in a week."

Audrey pulled her phone closer. "Lilah, this is serious. That makes four of us."

"Wait—*four?*" Lilah's voice sharpened. "Who else got one?"

"Sydney," Audrey said. "Queen of Cups. Eve got Pentacles. I just pulled Swords. And now Wands. That's every Queen in the deck."

There was a pause—unusual for Lilah. When she spoke again, her voice was quieter. "What the hell does that mean?"

Eve stepped in, her tone tight. "It means he's watching us. Again. And he's not just targeting me now—he's extending this. Building a pattern."

"Leo?" Lilah asked, and even she couldn't keep the dread from leaking through. "You think he's alive?"

Eve's voice hardened. "Yes. I do."

"And he's sending Tarot cards now? Like some sadistic Hallmark Channel villain?"

Audrey let out a dry exhale. "We found the shrine, remember? The kings. The rituals. He's been obsessed with this symbolism from the beginning. This is his language. And now it's evolved."

Lilah groaned. "Great. So I'm not just someone's fabulous, emotionally unhinged best friend—I'm officially part of a psycho's queen collection?"

"I think we all are," Eve murmured.

For a beat, the only sound was breathing—sharp, uneven, real. Then Lilah spoke again, this time raw:

"I don't like this. I'm staying with Rory right now, and if Leo's trying to scare me, it's working. What if I'm a target because I'm close to her? Because he knows I'll protect her?"

"You're not alone," Audrey said firmly. "That's why we're doing this together. No one's going off the grid. No one's handling this in isolation. We build a plan. We stay connected. We don't let him divide us."

There was a pause. Then, Sydney's name popped up in Eve's call queue. Audrey and Eve exchanged a look.

"Let's conference them all in," Audrey said. "If this is a war, it just became a council."

The screen split into four.

Sydney appeared first—eyes wide, hair pulled into a messy ponytail, her hoodie twisted sideways like she'd either just woken up or just finished fighting off a demon. "Okay," she said. "We're all here. Now somebody explain why my mail has turned into a horror movie prop."

Lilah was already mid-sip of a giant iced coffee. "Welcome to Queen Club, darling. It's like Fight Club, but with better cheekbones and a lot more trauma."

Audrey cut through them. "Let's stay focused. We each got a card. All four Queens. No postmark. No handwriting. Leo's trying to tell us something."

Eve held hers up. "Queen of Pentacles."

Sydney raised hers like it might bite. "Queen of Cups."

"Queen of Wands," Lilah said, flipping it onto the kitchen table. "Not to brag, but she's hot."

Audrey held up her own. "Queen of Swords. He knew which ones to send. He didn't just pick randomly."

Lilah's eyes narrowed. "You're saying he's assigning us roles? Like some twisted royal court cosplay?"

Eve nodded slowly. "I think he's been studying us for longer than we realized. These cards...they're deliberate. Psychological profiles disguised as gifts."

Sydney leaned closer to the screen. "Okay, look—I know this probably sounds insane, but I actually *do* know a thing or two about Tarot. Creepy symbolism is basically my side hustle." She held up her card. "Queen of Cups. Emotional depth, intuition, empathy. The therapist of the deck—which is ironic, considering Eve's the psychiatrist."

Eve furrowed her brow, intrigued. "So what about the rest of us?"

Sydney nodded toward Lilah. "Queen of Wands is fire. Confidence, charisma, sexuality, power. Big Leo energy—no pun intended."

Lilah raised an eyebrow. "I mean...not wrong."

Sydney turned to Audrey. "Queen of Swords—intellect, strategy, truth, boundaries. You don't lead with your heart, you lead with your head. Total badass, but also the one who cuts through everyone's crap."

Then her eyes landed on Eve. Her voice softened. "Queen of Pentacles is the nurturer. Fertility, grounding, security. She's the one who builds the home—even if she doesn't know where hers is yet."

A silence followed.

Lilah broke it. "So I'm the flame, Sydney's the feeler, Audrey's the blade, and Eve's...the womb?"

Sydney sipped her tea without flinching. "Basically. We're a full court. And I hate to say it, but I don't think Leo's just playing games. I think he's telling a story—through us."

"Cool, cool," Lilah said, folding her arms. "So we just die in dramatic order now, or is there, like, a twist ending where the queens rise and murder the king?"

Audrey's voice cut in, firm. "No. We figure this out. We flip the narrative before he writes it for us."

Lilah sighed, eyes flicking to her card. "Let's be honest. If he's sending these, he knows where we are. He's not hiding. He's circling."

The pause was longer this time. Heavy.

Sydney broke it with a dry laugh. "I've handled more fake corpses than I can count. But this? This feels worse. Because it's real. Because no one yelled 'cut.'"

Eve's voice was barely above a whisper. "None of us auditioned for this role."

Lilah chimed in from the background, her voice still shaky but with a touch of her usual humor. "So, should I start preparing my escape plan? I'm thinking I'll get a head start before the crazy psycho shows up at my door."

Sydney pinched the bridge of her nose. "Yeah, you do that, Lilah. But in all seriousness, we need to figure out how and where Leo's sending these cards from? There wasn't any kind of postmark on my envelope."

Audrey glanced at Eve, her mind already racing through possible scenarios. "I don't know. But Leo's obsession with Eve has always been the driving force. Now he's escalating. He wants us paying attention. And it looks like he wants to push us to our breaking points."

The FaceTime call ended; Eve, Audrey, Lilah, and Sydney now understood the severity of the situation. They were going to have to be ready for whatever came next.

Chapter 28

The Hermit's Whispers

Leo had always been driven by one singular force: control. From his earliest years, marked by instability and neglect, he had sought mastery over everything around him. His childhood was a blur of cold, indifferent parenting—his father distant and preoccupied, and his mother emotionally absent, consumed by her own manic depression. Affection from her was rare, given only when it suited her, and even then, it was distant, conditional.

This lack of warmth planted the seeds of Leo's insatiable hunger for power. The absence of love was a wound he would never heal from, and it shaped him in ways no one could fully understand. For Leo, love wasn't something you earned—it was something you took, and you held it tightly, never letting it go. It wasn't just about admiration or respect—it was about possessing and dominating, ensuring that those around him had no choice but to need him.

Ironically, Leo found a reflection of himself in Eve. Both had been shaped by families where love was scarce, where achievement became the substitute for affection. Eve's distant relationship with her mother mirrored Leo's own emotional isolation. She had learned to thrive in an environment where nothing came easy, where validation came only through success. In Eve, Leo saw not just a woman of beauty and strength, but a mirror to his own ambitions. She had survived her own version of neglect, and in her, he saw the same drive to overcome the odds. She was the perfect partner, someone who had overcome her own struggles to build something great—someone who, just like him, knew the value of control.

When Leo first laid eyes on Eve, he saw everything he had ever wanted. Strong, independent, and beautiful, she seemed perfect. But to Leo, perfection wasn't something to admire—it was something to conquer. Her independence unnerved him. A woman like her was too perfect, too free. And Leo couldn't let that kind of perfection exist independently of him. He had to have her, not just as his partner, but as his possession.

At first, Leo's charm had seemed sincere. He was attentive, protective—everything Eve thought she had been missing. He had offered emotional support, a sense of being cherished, something she had longed for. But beneath this mask of affection, something darker was taking root. What had started as admiration quickly morphed into possessiveness. His infatuation transformed into an all-consuming obsession. Leo didn't just want to win her heart—he wanted to possess her entirely. She wasn't his equal, she was a prize to be claimed.

As the relationship progressed, Leo began to realize that his usual methods—charm, manipulation—weren't enough to keep her. There was always a part of her that remained untouchable, a piece of her that resisted his control. And that gnawed at him. The more he sought to control her, the more he realized that mere psychological manipulation wasn't enough. He needed something more, something deeper, something that could transcend their relationship and bind them together in a way that he couldn't be denied.

That's when Leo turned to the occult.

It wasn't an immediate obsession; at first, it was just a curiosity. A fleeting interest. Leo didn't dive in recklessly. He wasn't yet consumed by the need to control every inch of Eve's existence. But it was an itch—a need to tap into something greater, something beyond his own limitations. Something that could give him power over fate itself.

The Tarot deck came into play one evening, unexpectedly. Eve had always kept the deck tucked away, hidden in a drawer. It had been part of her past, something she no longer actively used but had kept for its sentimental value. It wasn't an active part of her life anymore, but Leo had never seen it before—at least, not up close. As they relaxed together, Eve casually brought it out. They joked about it at first, with Leo teasing her about how it seemed so far removed from the sharp, grounded, no-nonsense woman he thought he knew. Eve, with a smile, told him that it was just something she'd kept around for years, the artwork and hidden meanings of the cards appealing to her intuitive side. It wasn't anything serious, but it had always fascinated her.

And that was the opening Leo had been waiting for.

What was a trivial joke for Eve became something much more for him. He saw something in the deck—something that had always been there but had gone unnoticed by her. The Tarot was no longer a simple tool for Eve's introspection; it was a vessel for Leo's madness. It became a way for him to manipulate and bend fate to his will, a way to solidify his control over her. Each card in the deck had its own set of symbols, its own meanings.

Leo had heard the whispers about the killer in the news. The media had dubbed him "The Magician." It was a name that resonated deeply with Leo, sending chills down his spine. It was as if the universe itself had handed him a title that matched his desires—his need to control, manipulate, and reshape reality.

The Magician card in the Tarot was the card of power, mastery over the elements, and bending the world to one's will. It felt as though the card had been made for him. Leo saw a symbol that encapsulated his delusion—his ambition to dominate, to shape everything around him with his sheer will.

He began pulling cards with purpose—each a deliberate step in his twisted game, a calculated move in a chess match only he understood. His ultimate goal was clear: absolute control over Eve, a control so profound that it would bind her to him in a way no one else could ever disrupt. He saw every relationship in Eve's life as a threat—anyone who could take her from him was an obstacle to be removed. The first victim, Ryan, was not just a casualty of Leo's jealousy—his death had been a critical step in Leo's ritual. With Ryan's murder, Leo believed he was clearing the path to a perfect union with Eve, one that transcended fate, time, and even death itself. In his mind, he wasn't just obsessing—he was playing God.

This obsession with control led Leo to create a shrine—a dark manifestation of his deepest desires. The altar in the attic, surrounded by the eerie remnants of his victims, was his ultimate act of possession. The jars containing retinas were not just trophies; they were pieces of his victims' souls.

As a coroner, Leo's anatomical knowledge of the body was unparalleled. He knew that the retinas, being a part of the eye, were not typically examined during an autopsy unless there was suspicion of foul play or specific circumstances that warranted it. This made them the perfect target for his twisted obsession. As Leo worked on preserving the retinas, he would carefully make a small incision in the sclera, the white part of the eye, to access the retina. He would then use a specialized tool to gently pry the retina loose from its attachment to the choroid, taking care not to damage it in any way. The retina would be removed in its entirety, the eyes themselves left pristine, with no visible injuries or trauma. The process was meticulous and required great care, as Leo needed to avoid damaging the delicate tissue. The retinas would be stored in a special solution that would prevent decay or degradation. And with each new addition to his collection, he felt himself becoming more invincible, more omnipotent.

The Tarot cards that Leo had sent were far more than cryptic messages—they were the final act in his play, each card a calculated step in his scheme to reassert control. Every woman who received a card was a reminder: they were all extensions of Eve, and through Eve, Leo's ownership over her world was absolute. Each Queen card was not just a symbol; it was a stake in the ground, marking his claim on their destinies.

The Queen of Pentacles to Eve was a mark of her perceived role in his twisted vision of their perfect future. She was the anchor, the one who could nurture, ground him, and provide stability—a role he intended to dominate. He saw Eve as the mother, the caretaker, the one who could give him everything he believed he deserved, and yet he felt her slipping away. The Queen of Pentacles reminded him of everything he could never truly control—everything he needed to own.

Audrey, the mirror to Eve, received the Queen of Swords, a symbol of intellect, independence, and autonomy—qualities Leo could never stand to see unshackled. Audrey's existence, being Eve's identical twin, was something he could not ignore. He saw her as another layer of Eve—a direct reflection of her. Because they shared identical DNA, Leo now viewed Audrey as no different from Eve. In his twisted logic, she was an extension of Eve, just as much a part of his world to control. Her intellect and strength only fueled Leo's need to possess her, just as he sought to control Eve. The Queen of Swords card was a taunt— a reminder that despite his manipulation, Audrey, like Eve, could not be fully controlled. But Leo was determined to make her his own, regardless of the challenge.

Lilah, wild and free, was marked with the Queen of Wands. In her, Leo saw the joy and spontaneity that drew Eve away from him, that created a bridge between Eve's world and a life that didn't belong to him. He couldn't stand the light Lilah brought; the energy that threatened to break the carefully constructed dark world Leo had built. The Queen of Wands symbolized everything Leo sought to break—the spirit, the confidence, the ability to live outside his reach. The card sent a chilling message: even Lilah, who had always been an outsider in his eyes, was now a part of his plan.

Finally, Sydney, who had always been Audrey's support, the one who brought calm and clarity, received the Queen of Cups. To Leo, Sydney's nurturing nature was a threat to his perfect vision for Audrey. Her ability to anchor Audrey emotionally, to offer empathy and understanding, was something Leo wanted to strip away. The Queen of Cups symbolized intuition and emotional intelligence, qualities Leo saw as weapons that could disrupt his control. He sent it to remind Sydney—and Audrey—that no bond would be left untouched by his need to dominate.

Each card wasn't just a playful gesture. It was a clear declaration of control, a reminder that Leo wasn't just a man obsessed—he was a god, manipulating their fates, twisting the world around them, creating a web from which they could never escape.

But Leo's descent into the occult had not been a solitary one. There was another—a presence who had quietly guided him deeper into the dark arts. This figure, known only as "the Hermit," had helped Leo understand the deeper mysteries of control and fate, teaching him how to bend the world to his will. The Hermit's lessons had been subtle, indirect, but profound—Leo's knowledge of the occult deepened, and with it, his belief that he could manipulate not only people, but destiny itself.

But even as Leo felt the power surge within him, he knew he wasn't the sole architect of his twisted path. The Hermit's influence lingered in the shadows, a reminder that Leo's obsession with control wasn't purely his own. The figure remained elusive—impossible to pin down—but his teachings had ignited something dark and powerful in Leo.

What Leo didn't realize, though, was that the Hermit's guidance had come with its own set of consequences. He had unknowingly become a pawn in a larger game—one that had been set in motion long before Leo ever laid eyes on Eve. But that would come later.

As the moonlight filtered through the window in Prague, Leo watched, listened, and planned, and now the final stage of his ritual had begun. The women, each marked by their card, were just pawns in his greater design—a design that had only just begun to unfold.

The city, steeped in its dark history, became the perfect backdrop for his continued descent into madness. Surrounded by the whispers of occult practices and alchemical rituals, Leo was free to manipulate fate in the shadows, as if the very city itself was a reflection of his intentions.

The women, unaware of his location, felt the growing grip of his influence even from across the world. He had orchestrated every move, every step of the game, and now, they were all caught in the reflection of his twisted game.

www.ingramcontent.com/pod-product-compliance
Lightning Source LLC
Chambersburg PA
CBHW030331120726
47901CB00007B/1755